Losing It

David Allan

1

'Who are you with?' Danny asked, competing with the music.

'Just a couple of friends,' Joanne replied. She pointed to her friends dancing obliviously.

Danny tilted his head back, causing his chin to jut out in a rather arrogant manner. 'Fancy a chat?'

'Where?' she inquired.

Danny nodded, his eyes aimed towards a door to the side of the bar.

Thirty seconds later they were in a cubicle in the girls' toilets. The toilet was empty and the deep bass of the music could be just made out in the distance. Danny pushed Joanne back until she was sprawled over the cistern and slid her knickers off from under her dress. She gave in to his dominance, impressed by his lean but heavily muscular frame. He entered her without protection.

Thrusting deeply, the passion started to rise. Danny asked her why she had ignored his text – completely out of context. This threw her a bit but a swift right hook to the side of the head brought her round. It was followed by a left palm to the face and a vicious grip of the hair with his right hand. Joanne yelped in pain. Fuck me! she thought. I like it rough but not that rough!

She took it at first, deciding to go along with the unusual sex play but it began to spiral out of control. The more she panicked, however, the more Danny plugged away and excited himself. The punches assailed themselves upon her visage and Joanne didn't know whether to scream, cry or plead for mercy. A crescendo came as Danny exploded inside her. Simultaneous to this was his repulsive act of violence. He smashed the bottom of his fist down upon her nose, breaking the cartilage, causing bleeding, and sent her into a state of unconsciousness. Her pain had been his arousal material.

'Let's go!' Danny said to Steve as he ran back to the bar.

'What?' Steve looked on in confusion

'Leave that!' Danny continued, indicating to the drink. 'We've gotta go. Now!'

They ran through Collet Square and down a side alley by The Wanderer, a popular Australian bar.

'What's going on?' Steve sputtered. He eyed Danny with caution.

'Fuck! Fuck! Fuck!' Danny was winding himself up. 'What the fuck have I done?' He wiped the sweat from his forehead with his sleeve and spat out the tangy taste in his mouth.

Steve looked on, incredulous. 'What? What is it?'

Danny stopped dead in his tracks and stared intently at the wall in front of him. He wondered what it was - some sort of dilapidated building, perhaps, unused for years. A thousand images seemed to flicker through his mind at once. He thought of his mum then his ex-girlfriend, then back to his mum. He pictured himself inside the dilapidated building although he was unsure what he doing there. He imagined he was alone although he could feel a presence. His mind flitted back to the image of the girl he had just left in the toilets.

Steve looked on for what seemed like an eternity, but said nothing. He had Danny down as quite odd due to his strange sense of humour and acute observations of life, but even this was unusual behaviour for him.

'Have you ever noticed,' said Danny, 'that Mars Bars are getting smaller, yet the price keeps rising. It's all part of the huge government conspiracy to oppress the nation. You don't realise,' he continued, 'how controlled our lives are.'

Steve was speechless. All he could do was to raise an eyebrow and give a very slow, deliberate nod as if he was taking it all in and mulling it over, his bright, green eyes widening to their full capacity. He always appeared to be ready to burst forth with a profoundly intellectual retort that would open Danny's whole philosophy right out and stretch it to its limit. He never did though. Danny was his best friend and Steve felt he knew him well. Times like this, however, frightened him.

He tilted his head to catch Danny's attention and he saw that look again: the one Danny held after beating those three blokes to within an inch of their lives.

It was two years ago and they were on a night out in Chessborough. Danny had been his usual Casanova and managed to get some girl's number. Not just any, though. He'd gone for Peter Murphy's girlfriend. Peter was one of the "heads" in Chessborough and the unofficial message on the street was that 'very few fucked with him.' Years of bare-fist fighting and gun feuds over drugs had toughened

4

Murphy up no end. He was nicknamed Morph due to his surname and his natural ability to seemingly go through walls - usually front doors to be precise.

Very often he would carry a dispute to a person's house, burst his way in mob-handed and start carving the residents up with his machete. And here was Danny walking out of one of the bars that Morph owned with his girlfriend's phone number written on the inside of a cigarette box. He couldn't put it straight into his mobile as he had lied about having one. He liked to remain in control.

'What the fuck d'ye think you're doing, ye cheeky bastard?' came the raspy voice of Morph from over Danny's shoulder. As he turned, Morph's fist was speeding towards Danny's jawline. Danny dropped his head as he recoiled to absorb the blow and it worked. Morph's fist came crashing into the front of Danny's head.

Fantastic! he thought. *Hurt like fuck but Morph came off worse.*

Danny literally felt the crunch as two of Morph's knuckles pushed their way up through his hand leaving permanent damage. This one incident had cost Morph his reputation as a fighter. He couldn't risk fighting with only one hand? He would still go on hitting people but he would use his elbows a lot more - or a baseball bat. If his punch had connected on Danny's chin the chances are he would have had severe brain damage. The sheer force of the fist of this nineteen-stone bodybuilder, and ex-professional boxer, was reputed to be like a bus coming towards you.

Fortunately, however, Danny had used his head; he always did. In fact, he even used it again. After Morph winced with the pain Danny flew at him like a torpedo striking a ship. His head smashed its way onto Morph's nose and this knocked him clean out. The two bruisers with Morph tried their hands but only half-heartedly. They were known as the McCormack Brothers and their reputation preceded them. The fight was taken out of them, however, as they had never seen anyone knock Morph out. Now they were worried. Danny swept the first one to the floor and he cracked his head. He fell like a child and made no attempt whatsoever to support himself.

It's normally drunks, he thought, who fall straight like that and crack their heads.

It didn't make sense to the onlookers. These guys were animals usually – they had fought the best, which was why Morph paid them so highly, and their "back up" from Morph was enough for the toughest of men to give them a wide berth. Even some of the other "heads" would praise them and pass on the statement that, incidentally, the McCormack Brothers started themselves: they 'would have it with anyone'.

The second brother was quickly put unconscious with a choke-hold. To the people watching it seemed easy. What was all the fuss over the McCormack Brothers? Unbeknown to the witnesses, though, they just weren't fighting at all.

After stamping on both their heads Danny held his intense, soulless stare for a second. It was more than creepy, it was disturbing. His eyes seemed to burn into their target and right through the other side. It reminded Steve of a famous painting. He couldn't remember the artist's name but he knew it was the one where the painter paints himself painting a picture. This was the look on Danny's face – endless and cold but almost cyclical. As if there was someone else looking out or Danny himself was having an out-of-body experience. It made Norman Bates look about as threatening as his dead mother, thought Steve. His eyes changed too, as if he had just regained entry into his body. Something evil was still there but it seemed latent, suppressed.

Danny stepped over the almost corpse of Morph and kneeled down aiming his mouth towards his ear.

What the fuck are you going to say to him? Steve questioned in his head. Let's just get out of here. But Danny was in no mood for chatting. He snatched his mouth away from Morph's head and turned to Steve. Steve couldn't believe what he was seeing. Danny, with blood dripping down his chin, was smiling as he spat out half an ear on the floor.

'He won't forget me in a hurry!' he said.

Steve wanted to run and keep running until he dropped. He couldn't though. All his organs wanted to go their own way and each part of his body had different ideas. His hands dropped limp so he couldn't cover his face. His feet glued themselves to the floor and refused to move. His brain said 'Don't look' but his eyes were stubborn. And as for his stomach – it insisted on emptying its contents there and then.

That was two years ago and how Morph had never caught up with Danny was a mystery. The biggest problem he had was that nobody knew who Danny was. He never went back to Chessborough after that, nor Steve for that matter. He also decided that it probably wasn't wise to call that girl.

The intense stare that Danny held that night over two years ago was back. Danny had either done some damage, Steve felt, or was about to. And the chances are – after rushing out of Edgar's – he had already done it.

Two girls were walking into the ladies' toilets, chatting. 'I don't sleep with them on the first date,' said the first. The second agreed, although she wasn't so sure. A trail of blood was running under the door and was starting to coagulate.

'Ugh! Someone's been sick.' Just then she realised what she had said. This wasn't a trail of red liquid that you usually saw on a Friday night as office workers all over the city congregated in bars knocking back shot after shot with no food inside them since lunch. They usually got to about 9pm and then vomited some red, blue, or green substance all over the floor.

Both girls were disgusted as they realised that it was blood trickling out from under the door. One of them was bold enough to push open the cubicle door yet this was something that she would regret for weeks.

If only she knew what nightmares would ensue – the girl had been brought up in a small town and hadn't even seen a nose bleed.

'She's dead, she's dead!' she screamed. 'Oh my god! She's dead!' and proceeded to vomit some of that green stuff.

2

Seconds later, three doormen were standing over Joanne.

Paul, the head doorman turned to one of the girls who had only that minute stopped vomiting, but was still visibly upset. 'Get her out of here would you, love?'

Joel, the heaviest of the three doormen, looked on anxiously. 'Is she okay?' He considered himself streetwise, but he was only eighteen and the world was becoming scarier every day. As he focused on Joanne's cold, grey complexion, his own face drained of its natural colour-Jesus, what a mess, he thought.

It was his older brother, Eric, who had first suggested he work the doors, but Joel didn't have the stomach for this, despite years of martial arts training. It was supposed to be his job to control violence and, in this line of work, you had no choice- but he hated it. Only a fortnight ago he was confronted by an eighteen-stone monster smashing bottles over people's heads. How do you control that? He'd tried to reason with him but ended up with a dozen stitches and a night in casualty. 'A cokehead,' Eric had called him. A nutcase more like. It took six police officers with CS gas and batons to restrain him.

'In this job,' Eric Had tried to explain, 'you have to fight fire with fire.' He'd seen Joel panic and knew he hadn't handled the situation well. 'Start off nice and easy but be ready- you have to be one step ahead all the time.'

Joel thought that might be okay for fellas like him and Eric, but what about this poor kid? What the fuck did she do to deserve this? 'It's a fuckin' sick world,' he said.

Paul ignored him. 'She's comin' round,' he said.

Danny's intense stare dissolved and the faint impression of a smile came over his face. Steve recognised it immediately – when he stood menacingly with half of Morph's ear between his teeth. The thought itself made him nauseous, but fear took over. Too frightened to take his eyes off him, he wondered, what the fuck goes on inside his head?

On the surface Danny seemed mellow but clearly his mind never stopped. He let nothing pass, analysed everything, scrutinised every detail of behaviour, and looked for reasons for all things. Steve knew that Danny's mind was racing. He could see it in his eyes.

Danny replayed an event in his mind. He recalled a conversation with a tax inspector in a wine bar on Anderton Road. They had met accidentally over a mix up with drinks yet they got on well. That is, until the point where the subject of tax came up. Whether this guy was playing devil's advocate or not was irrelevant to Danny. His face flooded with blood and a fire rose within his stomach. Up to now this guy had seemed extremely intelligent, he thought, yet he was to learn more. Danny found him irritating and it totally frustrated him. *He hasn't got a clue. How can such an intelligent guy be such a nerd, so brainwashed?* So frustrated was Danny that the conclusion of the conversation came when he finished his lager and smacked the inspector over the head with the empty bottle. It smashed in his hand and the guy dropped to the floor groaning; his head bleeding.

'Wise up!' screamed Danny, and stormed out of the bar.

The anger he portrayed that night was always at the back of his mind and whenever something violent happened he would recall it. It was an act of impulse and at the time he felt that he had no control over it. It didn't seem to faze him, however. In fact, it brought an excitable feeling inside him.

The reason for Danny's smile was that the thought of Joanne lying there, bleeding, had excited him. He wasn't thinking of the consequences of her beating. He seemed to get off on it. That is, until the guilt took over. Danny's moral conscience told him it was wrong but he ignored it. This was exactly the societal message he had heard all of his life. Echoes of phrases from his old form tutor at school played out in his head: 'Violence is wrong! Fighting is bad! Make love not war!'

These were the messages that he had been subjected to as a child and the philosophy that, in his eyes, he had followed. There were, though, if one was to add them up, several incidents at school where Danny was involved in violence. Some he was reprimanded for but in general he had gotten off lightly. Nobody ever saw him as violent; the majority of people liked him, and the time when he put John Edmunds into hospital for two days by breaking a chair over his head was one of the luckiest escapes he had ever had.

'The chair must have been broken,' he said to the headmaster, "'cos when John sat down he fell right through it and cracked his head on the floor. I hope he'll be okay.' This would account for the mild brain damage John sustained from this. He was to have learning difficulties for the rest of his life and yet he had been, by far, the smartest kid in the class. Fortunately for Danny, John remembered nothing of the incident and as for the witnesses... well...there were only two: Jack and Edgar and they swore a vow of secrecy when confronted with Danny's emotionless stare.

'You two weren't here, all right? Now fuck off!' he suggested.

They both put their heads down, left the room and never mentioned it to anyone, not even each other, again.

'Danny, Danny...DANNY!' Danny snapped out of his thoughts. Steve was desperate to get his attention. 'What's happening, Danny? You've gone all weird on me.'

'I'm okay,' he sighed. 'Let's go and get a drink.'

Steve, frustrated with Danny's behaviour, yearned to climb inside his head for a mere five minutes but he saw fit to put off asking questions for another time.

Most incidents in the city centre did not make front page headlines as there was violence and fighting every week and the tabloids liked to retain the shock value for the more severe incidents. However, the local paper jumped at the chance of this story. The story told of a woman beaten to near death in the toilets of a city centre bar. That bit was right but what they got wrong, however, was that they mentioned a small group of girls ganging up and bullying her. The fact that the bar was quiet seemed irrelevant. There had been five girls thrown out of a nearby bar for fighting and someone had made the suggestion that there was a connection, so it stuck.

The angle the press were working on was the rise of "women drinkers" and their "alcohol-related escapades". It was a current issue they were exploiting. Even the police were searching nearby CCTV for these girls. They saw Danny and Steve running across Cheen Square but disregarded it as they had the time wrong. And the CCTV in Edgar's wasn't even recording.

A deputy manager who was only standing in for the weekend had forgotten to programme it to record onto a disc and the old recording had finished and had stopped itself. It seemed that Danny had a lot of luck on his side.

After two weeks the police had pretty much washed their hands of the case and Joanne remembered nothing at all of the night. She didn't even remember going out that evening. Her last recollection was her second-to-last client on Friday afternoon. She was a self-employed hairdresser. After leaving Mrs Jacobs' at 2.30pm she took on her last client of the day: Mrs Eastham, an old neighbour from when she had lived with her parents. Mrs Eastham's thick mop of curly, red hair always proved a challenge for Joanne so it was one client who held out particular in her mind. Her memory after this was mainly blank, interspersed with the odd snippet of a face or two; nothing she could add any meaning to.

Her friends were questioned as witnesses but none of them had seen Danny. They had, however, seen the small group of girls and, much to corroborate the wrong story, remember that they had a brief, visual stand-off with them in another bar.

'That's why we came to Edgar's,' said one of them. If we'd have stayed in the Metro it would've kicked off.

'Hmm,' said the officer in charge, 'it all fits.'

'It's called speed dating,' said Steve. 'All the lads sit on one side of the room and all the girls sit on the other. Then the guys move around and you have three minutes to talk to each girl. At the end, you go away with the information for the website and you send in votes for the ones you like. They then make a small charge and pass on your details to the interested parties.'

'I'll give it a go, I suppose,' Danny said, sounding almost disinterested. 'Could be a laugh!' And it was, for him.

Deep down he never treated dating seriously, although he did seem to come across in earnest and his gift for conversation convinced most girls that he was a good catch. Even the ones who thought he was not their type were interested. There was something about him that was intriguing. His character was strong and his personality was pleasant. Moreover, being a natural quick thinker and quick with the wit he didn't even need to access his abundant charm, unless he felt the girl was particularly stubborn. Conversing with women came natural to him yet it also proved to be a battle at times. He would usually win in the end but then he would hate them for it. The majority of the time he loved women and enjoyed their company immensely yet there were also times when he despised them and found them utterly repulsive,

12

especially if one crossed him and his outbursts of loathing were growing.

After a relationship he used to think: *I'm just bitter, I'll get over it,* but as the years rolled on long relationships became few and far between and he regularly resorted these days to crazy nights of wild sex. Sex would last for hours and to a large extent the girls were abused. They enjoyed the lovemaking but found the violence and rough handling a bit too excessive at times and he always seemed to push it that one step further.

It was a Thursday night and Danny had been having sex with Julie, a lap dancer, for about two hours, on and off. They were in the throes of passion and both were enjoying it but Danny felt that he needed more. He was taking her from behind and decided to hold her in a choke. His left arm rested along the back of her neck whilst his right came around it gripping his own arm. This dominant position for Danny gave her a thrill. The power she held from lap dancing was incredible and she loved it. Men would do almost anything and she was in total control.

Contrary to this, though, was her lovemaking. She loved to be subservient and allow the man full control. She had no respect for weak men which was probably why her job seemed so far away from her own life. Passions rose, however, and Julie insisted on a bit of pain. Danny began to choke her but was hesitant. He remembered a girl whom he had gone out with for six months and had choked to a state of unconsciousness in exactly the same position. He had managed to convince her that her orgasm was so powerful that it had knocked her out and she bought it. After all, she was delirious and she worshipped the ground he walked on. She would have believed anything that came from his mouth.

He released his grip as the thought of his ex-girlfriend lying there, dazed, softened him.

'Grab me!' said Julie, so the hold was on again. He was pumping away faster now and she was getting more and more excited.

'Harder!' she demanded, so he drove it into her. 'No! The hold.' He tightened his grip but felt uneasy. 'Harder!' He tightened again but then released. Julie was nearing a climax and far from satisfied with his release. 'Put the fucking choke on, you faggot!'

Where the fuck did that come from? He decided to grip her.

'Bang it on.' She needn't have worried...he was about to. The thought of her questioning his heterosexuality sent him over the edge.

He squeezed the choke on and the very life seemed to drain from her. She gasped for breath but he held hard. Did she want him to release or was she enjoying it? he wondered He didn't care; she was getting it anyway. He held the choke for about eight seconds and the blood drained from her face. The gasping stopped and she went limp. He was still thrusting into her and seemed excited at the fact that she was out cold. He couldn't hold the dead weight for long, though, and threw the body to the floor. Her face smashed into the carpet and the blood from her nose began to trickle out like a small brook at the bottom of a mountain.

How pretty! he thought, and spat on her.

When she came to she was groggy and Danny was gone. He was glad he was in her flat because if she had bled like that in his flat he would have really lost it. He loved the sex but hated her for what he felt she had turned him into.

Danny sat down in the speed dating and in front of him was a young blonde girl of about twenty two. Her hair stopped short at her shoulders and cascaded over one eye at the front which appealed to him. Sensing a pleasant aroma exuding from her, a smile slowly formed on his face, widening progressively as he took in her beautiful features.

'Hiya!' she said. 'I'm Nicky.'

'Hi! I'm Danny. Don't tell me, you work every day of the week and you're teetotal. You never get to meet anyone in your workplace and you hardly ever go out. When you go out the guys are all morons that come up to you with the worst lines in history. All you want to do is to talk to them and get to know them; all they want to do is to get into your knickers.'

Her eyes widened and a smile shot across her face like a bolt of lightning. She was speechless. He was almost exact in his prognosis. She didn't have to work weekends but after splitting up with her boyfriend last month she decided to keep occupied and save up for a holiday with her friends. She wasn't teetotal but she did have a take-it-or-leave-it attitude towards alcohol.

'You see, you're too pretty for speed dating,' he continued. 'If you were in a position of meeting people on a regular basis you would have hundreds of blokes after you.' She blushed. She was buying all this. It wasn't that Danny said the most profound things all the time it was just the way he put them across. Sometimes his comments were as corny as anybody's yet the sincerity with which he portrayed his emotions carried them through.

She mopped up his words for the full three minutes, blushing a little here and there, then confirmed in her head that he was a 'yes'. It was lucky that none of the girls knew each other as he spouted the same speech to two more of them. He would have carried on for a fourth but the fact that it was starting to bore himself meant he would change the conversation.

Steve did okay, too. He got himself two votes and went out with both of them. The first was not really his cup of tea. She was somehow different on their date than she had been on the day. *She never seemed this boring,* he thought.

His second date was ideal. Her name was Lisa and she was 25, a year younger than Steve. He couldn't help noticing her long flowing brown hair, impressively straight and complimenting her immaculate appearance. Lisa had split up from her boyfriend about three months previously and had not dated anyone since. She was still not really interested in dating- having only come to keep her friend company- but she found herself drawn to Steve. Steve came across well when it came to women. Not gifted with the art of conversation as much as Danny yet he could hold his own. He was also not as successful as Danny when it came to women although his wit and personality meant that he was a 'catch' in his own right. He treated women well and whoever dated him was in for a treat. He believed in spoiling a girl and- as he saw it- 'dating her properly'.

Steve and Lisa clicked from the start. Steve was committed to his beliefs and faithful to his relationships. He respected Danny for what he stood for- although he wasn't sure exactly what that was- and he sometimes wished he could do the same, yet it wasn't in his nature to abuse people.

Danny, however, was slowly, but surely, beginning to despise relationships. He was out for what he could get, these days, as was illustrated by his first date from the agency. Her name was Catherine and she worked in a bank. She was young for an assistant manager- only 22- but extremely intelligent and mature for her age. She treated everybody fairly and respected all, never speaking down to anyone. The older staff in the bank admired her for her manner as well as her looks and used to forget that she was only 22. Even outside the bank people held admiration for her, with her long blonde hair and glowing blue eyes she was the epitome of innocence.

They had arranged to meet in Ronnie's Bar in the city centre-Danny's idea- at 8.30 on Thursday evening. Catherine arrived at 8.20, prompt as ever from her training in the bank. She was not shy but not overconfident either so she decided that getting a drink on her own was no big deal. She would just sit at the bar and wait. After all, she could look over her diary and see what clients were booked in for the next day. She usually dealt with small businesses yet her other skills lay in mortgage advice and the bank exploited this.

'A single vodka and diet coke, please,' she said in reply to the barman's offer of: 'What can I get you, babe?'

The barman was about twenty two, tall and quite good looking but he knew it. His dark-brown hair was pushed back in what looked to be one smooth run that finished at his rear neckline. It was oily in appearance and reflected the light from the optics occasionally, Catherine noticed. Apparently that was the fashion although it was not to Catherine's taste. He spun a glass round in his right hand and placed it under the vodka optic; his left hand suspended in the air as if for balance. Catherine looked at his feet and was quite disturbed by his stance. *This guy's only putting vodka in a glass,* she thought, *yet he looks like he's about to go Fencing.*

As he spun himself over to the fridge to lift out the lemons he seemed to be doing- what could only be seen in Catherine's mind as- 'handbrake turns' on his feet. That was her only possible explanation for it. Her mind cast itself back to her time at college when she did her A-levels. The boy racers used to spin their cars on the gravel car park. They would do 360 degree turns using only the handbrake to grind to a halt. Here was this guy doing it with his feet.

The barman flicked a slice of lemon into the air and caught it in the vodka glass. *A neat trick but he obviously doesn't get out much outside of work.* And then came the crescendo- he held the glass out in front of him, away from his body, whilst the coke pump was raised above his head as if he was about to perform a major operation.

'Excuse me, erm...' Catherine interrupted. And interrupt she did for he scowled at her as his 'major operation' had been held up and his concentration broken. Snapping out of it he smiled and said: 'Pablo! My name is Pablo.'

'Err...Pablo,' she struggled, 'DIET coke, yeah?'

'Of course, babe!' He winked at her.

Oh god! Is this guy for real? She didn't mind being called 'babe', in fact she found it rather sweet when it came out naturally in

16

conversation, but this Pablo was sleazy and had the ability to make 'babe' sound like 'piece of meat'. He could have called her by her name and she'd have still cringed.

He delivered the drink and smiled at her.

'The first drink is on the 'ouse, madam, for such a beau-ti-ful lady.' *Where did this foreign accent come from all of a sudden?*

'Thank you,' she replied. Catherine was always polite. Pablo slid off down the bar but Catherine could no longer see him for who he really was. She drifted off into a daydream and imagined Pablo as the cartoon character Johnny Bravo, zooming up and down the bar serving drinks at super high speed. He threw two bottles of lager in the air then performed three somersaults and one half-turn before landing perfectly on the bar and catching them, their tops dropping to the floor. Pushing his hair back with his greasy palm, he swished across the floor and skidded to a stop at the till before shouting: 'Whoa, momma!'

The return to normality came as Catherine focused on a bottle of French lager in the fridge. Staring intently, her eyes zoomed out until Pablo broke her gaze. 'You are alone, madam? You have no boyfriend?'

Her head remained static whilst her eyes rotated upwards to catch his. 'Yes... err, no. I'm on a date. Just waiting!'

'Perhaps 'e 'as, 'ow you say it, stood you down.'

'UP!' she corrected, but then wondered why she'd bothered. *This guy's no more foreign than I am. I'll put it on his toes.* 'Where are you from?'

'Oh, sorry madam. I am not allowed to say,' he bullshitted. 'Perhaps if I was to get to know you a little better...maybe we could chat over dinner?'

This guy is really forward, she thought. 'Well, I'll have to see how my date goes. It's only fair. You're absolutely gorgeous and charming,' she bullshitted back, 'but I have to do the decent thing. After tonight...well...who knows!'

Pablo's eyes lit up and he swirled himself over to the till where he took up a pen and ripped a piece of receipt out. He scrawled his number on it then swirled back to her in one amazing pirouette. The whole movement was like a theatrical act and had there been music to accompany him she would have applauded. 'There, madam! You call me and I will reveal to you the intriguing story of my entry into your beautiful country.' She blushed, more out of embarrassment for him than anything, as he slid away smugly to serve another customer.

Catherine looked at her watch- 8.38- and as she did so a hand rested itself on her shoulder.

'Hiya, babe.'

It was Danny. 'Sorry I'm late. What you having?'

'Erm…vodka, diet coke please.'

Danny glanced over to Pablo who caught his eye and raised his thumb in acknowledgement. 'I hope you haven't been bored,' he said.

'Oh no,' she smiled, 'I've had Pedro to entertain me.'

She showed him the till receipt. Danny took it and his blood started to boil inside. On the outside, however, nothing showed and he managed to contain his rage. He took a piece of chewing gum from his mouth that he had been chewing for the last half hour and pushed it into the receipt before wrapping it strategically. He then placed it into an ashtray on the bar before looking at Catherine and smiling. Inside his head were thoughts of strangling her.

Fucking slag! All the fucking same.

Pablo arrived to break his concentration. 'Yes sir?'

'A lager and a vodka and diet coke, please.' He stared intently at Pablo, his thoughts drifted…

…stepping onto the bar and jumping down the other side, Danny headed towards Pablo. A faceless crowd observed, distorted voices in the distance. Pablo was punching prices into the till as Danny's right hand cupped his chin and his left held the back of his head. Pablo's eyes rotated to fix on Danny and he glared at him, speechless. Danny lifted Pablo's head off its pivot- twisting it violently and sharply- and snapped his neck. It clicked repeatedly, mimicking the sound of a turnstile…

'You all right, Danny?' asked Catherine.

'Hmm!' he mumbled as he drifted back to reality.

'Sixa-poundsa-ten please,' said Pablo in his slipping foreign accent. Danny looked at the bar; the drinks sat in front of him. He looked up at Pablo and said: 'And one for yourself,' as he handed him a ten-pound note.

After about twenty minutes they were nearing the end of their drinks and had decided to move on. They had both gelled instantly and Catherine thought that Danny was fantastic. *He's good looking,* she thought, *funny, intelligent. I can't fault him.*

Thoughts were streaming through Danny's head at the same time as he tried to weigh her up. *She's pretty, intelligent, likes my jokes. Nice girl! Fucking slag, though! Am I supposed to be jealous just because other men allegedly want her number?*

They put their empties on the bar and Danny waved to thank the barman. Catherine smiled.

'Bye Pedro.'

Pablo placed his thumb to his ear and his little finger to his mouth in the shape of a phone. Catherine winked. As they were walking out she overheard Pablo serving someone else. 'Give us a pint, please Paul,' requested the customer.

'Okay mate,' came Pablo's reply. For some reason his accent had changed.

'My round,' said Catherine in the next bar. 'Lager?'

'Please.'

'So what is it you do for a living?'

'I'm an electrician.' Danny told the truth about his work. He felt he never had to lie about his job as girls either liked him or they didn't and they had usually made up their minds about him before the subject of careers came up.

'That's great,' Catherine said. That explains the spark between us.' She winked but Danny was unsure how to react.

At the end of the night they went their separate ways. They snogged briefly but that was the extent of their physical contact. It was only briefly because sometimes Danny hated kissing. He always felt that he was no good at it or feared that the girl would be no good. After a short time with one girl he would develop a system in his head, yet when he moved on to another it would be all wrong. Some girls sucked his lips off- he enjoyed this- whilst others stuck their tongues in- he didn't like that. There was one girl, once, whom he used to enjoy swirling tongues around with but since then nobody ever seemed to get it right. Some girls just pecked but he didn't mind that. Others seemed to envelop his whole head with their mouths and hermetically seal off his features. 'For fuck's sake!' he would say, 'Let me come up for air.'

We will probably develop our own system for kissing and I may even find that I really like it. In the meantime, though, it was cut short and this made Catherine feel insecure.

Lying in her bed that night her thoughts went out to Danny. *I really like him...and I think he likes me...but he didn't really want to kiss me.* She put it down to shyness and smiled as she drifted off to sleep, without a care, content in her own little world.

Danny's second date was more successful, he felt, even if he had forgotten her name when he stored her number, storing her as 'bird'.

The girl bored him from beginning to end and the only reason that he tolerated it was because he found her to be absolutely gorgeous. 'I'm tired,' he said. 'Sorry, I know it's only early.' It wasn't even ten o'clock and they had only been out for an hour. Danny thought he would try his hand: 'Do you fancy picking up a bottle of wine and a DVD? It's only Tuesday, there's not gonna be anywhere busy tonight.'

This was the clincher. What she would say next would make all the difference as to whether Danny was to tell her to fuck off, leave her politely or stay for the duration.

'I don't know,' she sighed. 'I don't think I should. I hardly know you.'

Not the best answer, he thought. It wasn't positive but then it wasn't negative; it was neutral. There was definitely potential. He could sense a weakness. If she had said 'no' outright then he would have made his excuses and left. 'Always best to cut your losses,' he would say to Steve. As it was though, he felt that she just needed a little persuasion. *A few more drinks will open her up.* This accompanied with a lecture on putting the world to rights- revealing his moralistic outlook- and a few jokes thrown in to relieve the boredom and illustrate his sense of humour. Moreover, his strategic machination of talking about his ex-girlfriend, to reveal utter honesty and commitment, he always found to be the perfect ingredient for her to feel that she really knew him.

Around 12 o'clock they were in a taxi heading back to Danny's. There was wine in the fridge and he had over 200 DVDs. These weren't needed though.

They pulled up outside his flat and Danny threw the driver a ten pound note. 'Keep the change,' he said. As they staggered up the path to the huge front door, Danny's date inquired: 'Where are we?'

'Just off Lank Lane,' informed Danny. 'My flat. Sssh!!!'
As they entered the living room Danny asked her if she would like a glass of wine.

'Please.' she answered.

'I've lost all the numbers on my phone,' Danny moaned. 'I think it's faulty. Can you put your number back in for me?' He was lying of course. There was nothing wrong with his phone he just had an ulterior motive.

'Of course,' she replied and began to punch her details in to the phone. Danny watched over her shoulder: M-I-C-H-E-L-L-E. *Michelle,* he thought, *so that's your name.*

He impressed himself at how he had gotten this far without remembering her name. He didn't care much for her and most of the night was spent staring at her tits, anyway, as he thought of Catherine.

Michelle could certainly talk and before Danny realised it he knew almost everything there was to know about this girl. She worked in a clothes shop; she had been there for nearly two years, and loved it. She enjoyed horse riding and playing tennis at the weekends, and every film currently on the cinema she had seen and so on and so on...*Big Deal!*

She only had two mouthfuls of wine before they were snogging on the couch. To be precise, she was snogging him whilst he played with her tits and ran his hand up her thighs. Her legs were soft and obviously hair-free. He had a clear ride to the top but the entrance was closed. His hand became trapped between her thighs and he fought hard to prise them apart. They weren't budging, unfortunately, and he could sense the profound pressure of them clamping together as they stopped the blood supply to his fingers. Danny wondered what the next step would be; how he was going to tackle the impregnable thighs. *A bit of heavy breathing*, he thought, *and some passionate snogging.*

Even though he was not a big fan of kissing he was aware of the effect of it. After a few seconds of this Michelle began to get excited. She grew wet and felt a tingling sensation all over. The two pillars that guarded the entrance slowly started to give way to allow entry. A few seconds play on the outside and then 'boom!'- he was in. Michelle responded in the most perfect manner for Danny: she was loving it. In the space of a few minutes her skirt was up, her knickers were off, and Danny's fingers were inside her. This went on for quite a while before he sought to enter her more intimately.

Once inside her, he thrust slowly as if to break her in. 'I don't do this with everyone you know?' pleaded Michelle.

Like fuck you don't! were the exact words in his head. *Why do girls always say that? Do they think I'm stupid? A first date, I'm banging her like crazy- with no protection- and she's claiming her chastity. Of course, I'm no angel but then I never suggested that I was.*

Their pace quickened and the moaning grew. 'Do you like it rough?' Danny asked and slapped her arse. She responded badly at first with an 'Ouch!' but then moved on to more promising sounds.

21

Danny, always the adventurous type, decided to push it as usual. He slapped her across the face. This wasn't good as she looked disgusted. He slapped her again, and again, and she complained strongly. Getting excited from this, he punched her.

'Shut the fuck up,' he warned, but Michelle was in pain and starting to fear for her life. He could feel her inner thighs squeezing and her vaginal muscles clenching.

That feels good. He punched her again and the involuntary muscle contractions almost pushed him over the edge. He held back though. Had he finished there and then he probably would have released Michelle and let her go home. As it was, she was to receive more violence.

He seemed to be holding out for a powerful orgasm as he punched her repeatedly about the head. She screamed and struggled to release herself but Danny had pinioned her arms in between punches. When he eventually released her arms they moved to cover her face. He still pounded her about the head, though, until he knocked her unconscious. He then turned her over and held her in a choke, as he had done to Julie, whilst he entered her from behind.

Thrusting away, he held the choke for quite some time, tightening it as he neared orgasm. His grip was held for about two minutes and gradually released as he calmed himself. He had never held on to anything for this length of time before but he was still throbbing inside her.

Perhaps I go a bit too far, he thought. *I do get carried away. Not every girl likes to be punched about the head. It was good though. And I don't suppose I did go too far.*

Unfortunately, he had gone too far. He had starved her brain of oxygen for nearly two minutes. He worried about any potential brain damage. He needn't have, though, for this girl was beyond that- she lay dead beneath him. Realising the consequences of his actions Danny lay on top of her and wept for an hour before falling asleep.

3

When he awoke, only two hours later, the daunting sight in front of him was too much to comprehend. He shook the lifeless corpse.

'Michelle, Michelle... Wake up,' he cried. 'For fuck's sake, wake up!' Fear transformed itself into anger and he rattled her body frantically. 'Wake up you fucking slag!' he screamed and commenced beating her about the head. Her slack cranium flew from side to side but she never woke up. Realising his efforts were futile, and assessing the situation differently, he stopped and tried to calm himself. *This can't be happening*, he thought, as he flew into the kitchen to look for the bottle of whisky that Steve had brought round at Christmas.

He couldn't stand whisky, usually, so it had sat at the back of his food cupboard for six months. He was saving it for either somebody else drinking in his flat or the event that he might give it a second attempt one day. At present, though, it appeared that this was probably the only sedative he could lay his hands on at short notice. It looked like today would be that day he was saving it for. *Great! The bottle is still there.*

He snatched a Short glass from out of a unit on the wall and made his way back into the living room. He then turned a chair away from the dead body so that he had his back to it, and repositioned the TV so as to take his attention away. Pure escapism! That's what he needed. He flicked though every channel on the cable- adverts, adverts, cartoons, adverts, documentary about World War Two-no, he wasn't in the mood to concentrate- more adverts, news, soap operas...

'Aah!' he sighed as he came to his favourite channel, G.O.L.D. They were showing reruns of Open All Hours. He loved this. *Ronnie Barker and David Jason are such good comic actors.* He never moved out of his seat for over an hour and during that time the whisky was going down a treat.

It was about three hours later when he awoke. He wasn't even aware that he had drifted off- the effect of the whisky had knocked him clean out. Unfortunately, it was having other effects too. His bladder was twitching to empty and his head throbbed. He imagined a mini Steve McQueen in there from the film The Great Escape. He had a glove on his left hand and he repeatedly bounced a baseball off the inside of his head and then caught it again. Danny wished he would stop but he was obviously enjoying himself.

After he relieved himself he looked into the mirror but didn't like what he saw, or who for that matter because he certainly didn't recognise himself. Mustering up enough energy to brush his teeth he collapsed on his bed, face down. And he lay like that until morning.

Steve had a great night. Not as interesting as Danny's but nevertheless a success in his eyes. He had been to the cinema with Lisa and then for a drink and things just seemed to get better and better. Steve's opinion of Lisa was high from the start; he knew a decent girl when he saw one. Lisa, too, was impressed that she could pull such a nice bloke who was genuine, caring, and intelligent. They were both mature in their outlook and neither one of them was into mind games. They could talk about anything and not worry about offending each other.

Steve had put Lisa in a taxi about 11.30pm and kissed her goodnight. They were both nervous about going too far with each other as neither one of them wanted to spoil the potential that they had. And besides, Steve had to be up early for work. He usually picked Danny up about 7.30am and as he had made arrangements to see Lisa over the weekend there was no point in going mad on the first night.

The digital clock on Danny's bedside table changed from 07:29 to 07:30 and even though it was silent it appeared that this was what woke him as his eyes raised their heavy lids at precisely that exact moment. He had slept through the alarm at 6.30am.

He looked round the room like a newborn baby, seeing the world for the first time. The surroundings had been familiar to him for the past three years yet for at least a minute they were unrecognisable. He wondered not only *where* he was, but also *who* he was.

As the walls began to take on their familiarity once more his mind flashed back to a horrible dream he had had. Suddenly he sat bolt upright as if a poltergeist had taken over his body. *Was it a dream?* he thought. His brain had decided that the previous night's events were too much to handle and had made several efforts to shut them out. Unfortunately, they were only temporary as it all came flooding back to him. Now, he was awake. Steve McQueen was awake too and he had a lot more energy this morning than last night.

Danny's mind raced ahead. Hundreds of thoughts and images swirled in and out but not one of them hung around to be processed. He ran to the bathroom and threw water over his face to wake him up as he tried to clear his head. Was he ready to enter the living room? Half of him was because only half of him believed that he had done it. He was half expecting to walk into the living room and see it as it always was – and Michelle wouldn't be there. She was, though, and he ran back to the bathroom to be sick.

He splashed water over his face again only this time it seemed to be a subconscious effort to purge his eyes of the sight facing him in the next room. He felt like Lady Macbeth who constantly washed her hands to take away the metaphorical blood stained on them. *Perhaps I should blind myself,* he thought, *like the great Oedipus.* 'What the eye doesn't see...' but this was ludicrous. And anyway, it wasn't *his* eyes that needed to be averted. He had to find a way of disposing of the body so that not another soul in the world would see.

Danny spun around to the toilet to vomit again. It made him feel temporarily better. He stood up after the last trace of liquid left his mouth and felt ready to take on the disposing of Michelle's body. He walked into the living room and the sight no longer disturbed him. Suddenly, the buzzer of his flat alerted to him that there was someone at the door. *Shit!* he thought, *that'll be Steve,* but there was no way he could go to work today. *But if I don't people may get suspicious and talk. Fuck it!* he went on. *I can't leave the place like this. She'll be stinking soon. She didn't smell too good when she was alive. But what about the plant? Steve will be the only electrician there today. Will they cope without me? It's no use, I can't go in.*

The buzzer sounded again but Danny chose to ignore it. He looked at the clock – it was 7.41am. Steve wouldn't be able to hang about much longer. He had already sat in the car for over five minutes and beeped the horn three times, but Danny was oblivious to this.

Outside, Steve looked at his watch. *Once more,* he thought, and gave the buzzer one last long press. After a brief pause, he came to the conclusion that Danny had probably stayed over at some girl's house. *Funny, though! He usually phoned and his mobile is off.*

7.43am. Steve's van was heading off down the road without Danny. Danny had heard him pull off but decided to twitch the curtain back for confirmation. Turning towards the body he considered what would be his best plan of action.

'First things first,' he mumbled to himself. 'Breakfast!'

7.55am and Steve was driving through the factory gates. He was normally inside by now with a cup of coffee, having clocked in. After 8 o'clock he would be late and even clocking in at 8.01 caused his bosses to have a moan. It seemed unjust as there was never any acknowledgement of all the times he had clocked in at 7.48.

He arrived at the machine and placed his card in the slot at the top. A stamping sound ensued and when he pulled the card out there was 7.58 printed clearly on the IN box. He had made it.

The first part of the morning had gone quite quickly. Before he knew it he was on his first break. 10.30am – usual routine: wash hands, go to your locker, take out your sandwich box and a newspaper (usually The Star or The Mirror), make a brew (as they termed it) and sit down for 15 minutes. The breaks were so monotonous and routine for some of the workers that it was beginning to get difficult to differentiate between them and the work at the factory itself.

The majority of the workers would go out at lunchtime as they usually ate most of their lunch on their first break due to the hard work and early starts. Steve's work was a little different. The factory manufactured cable and Steve and Danny were in charge of maintenance on the production line. There was probably the minimum amount of job variety to keep them going but nevertheless, it did. Steve's manager, John, came into the canteen with a quizzical look on his face. 'You seen Danny, Steve?' he asked.

Steve shook his head. 'No. I was round at his house this morning but he wasn't there. I know he was supposed to be seeing some bird last night so he probably stayed over. I can't see why he wouldn't come in though.'

'He's probably still handcuffed to the bed,' joked one of the packers. The packers were responsible for ...well, packing. The cable would be about 25 millimetres in diameter when it began on the line and it was mineral insulated for use in fire alarms. It would then be drawn out and elongated until it was about 6.5 millimetres in diameter, thereby compressing the minerals tightly. The packers would cut the cable to the desired length and coil it up ready for customer use. They didn't always pack it, though. Sometimes it was left on a huge drum like a giant cotton reel.

'He goes with some strange women though, doesn't he?' chirped in another packer. 'He might have been murdered, ha!' Steve smiled but John merely raised his eyebrows in disgust. Steve asked: 'Isn't he answering his mobile?'

'No,' replied John, 'it's off.'

'Strange! It wasn't on this morning when I called either.'

'Well, I'm not happy. He hasn't rung in and he's turned his phone off. He'd better have a good reason. If he's just sleeping a hangover off and can't be arsed coming in then....'

'No!' interrupted Steve. 'You know him. He's never late or off unless he rings. I'll go round after work. It's just not like him.'

'Maybe he *has* been murdered,' said Joey, the technician's apprentice, overly dramatic as usual. John scowled at him.

'Shut up, Joey, you nonce!'

That was one of the better features of working here; the staff all got on well. They were friendly and could all have a joke with each other. The problem was that somebody always had to be the butt of the joke. It wasn't such a problem, though, as they enjoyed the banter and it was a case of survival of the fittest. And most of the time Joey brought it on himself with his vivid imagination. Joey pictured Danny's body lying there in a pool of blood...

Michelle's body lay there in a pool of blood. Danny had managed to haul it into the bath before tucking into his breakfast. He dipped a piece of toast into one of his softly-boiled eggs and the yolk pushed its way to the top and came running down the side. He thought of Michelle's body with the blood running down her neck.

As he was waiting for the eggs to boil he had decided to put the body in the bath, slit her throat and let the blood drain away. Perhaps later the head would have to be removed. It was an idea that he had that would make it easier for him to dispose of it. He felt he might cut it up, although he had no idea whatsoever what he would do with it. The strange thing was that the thought of blood running down the neck of a dead body did not put him off his eggs. Moreover, as he ate he thought of ways for its disposal.

Danny pierced the outer shell of the egg with his spoon and cut clean through the top of it. As he did so his mind shot to images of decapitating Michelle's corpse- her head coming clean away from her body. The effect of this was a tingling sensation throughout his body that provided an unexpected excitement for him. He literally smiled as he took the head off the egg and was not repulsed one bit.

After breakfast he went to check on his *work* – for that was the way he was beginning to see it. He severed the head from the body using a kitchen knife. Not as easy a task as he had imagined. With the top of the headless corpse towards the plug hole, the majority of blood drained from it.

He had no fear, now, that he would to dispose of the body, he just had to be sure that it was done in the most efficient manner. He picked up the head by its hair and the first thought that came to him was the beheaded Macbeth at the end of the Shakespeare play.

Perhaps I should put it on a spike and display it outside the flat, he thought. *Girls could see this as a deterrent for their immoral behaviour. They'd know that being with me was a superlative commitment and this was the consequence of breaking it.*

How to dispose of the body, then? Acid, perhaps? Like the acid bath murderer. Maybe, but if that was infallible we'd never have gotten to hear about him doing it. Bury the body under the floorboards? No! That's silly. They always smell. How could you get away with it? Cut her up into tiny pieces and drop the pieces down a drain? No! That's how Nielsen was caught. His mind was working overtime. *There's got to be a way*, he thought. *Bury the remains in the garden or somewhere else. If it was somewhere else it may be discovered. In my garden? Christie did it – got caught though. Who's to know?*

Murderers always give themselves away, they always make a mistake. Psychologists reckon that subconsciously they want to be caught in order to be acknowledged for their 'art'. But I don't want acknowledgement. I like my life; I like my liberty. His mind flitted back to the disposal methods. *Buried in the garden then? No! Some dog will go digging there like that Hitchcock film Rear Window and give the game away. It would smell a rat. Well, she was a rat!* He was getting bitter now and also getting nowhere. 'I need time to think,' he mumbled to himself. 'Think Danny, think!' He snapped his fingers. 'I've got it!'

Steve had just corrected the fault on one of the computers on the line. It would tell the roller the exact pressure with which to pound the cable so as to elongate it proportionally. It had lessened in pressure and the cable was coming out too thick. This meant that the diameter of the cable would be too large for the next rollers to handle and this is where the jam started.

Had Steve not been walking past the rollers at that precise moment – sheer coincidence – then the production line would have ceased and probably cost that factory thousands of pounds in loss of sales. Alternatively, and what is more likely to have happened, the cable would force its way along and meet with the obstruction. It would then push away from the rollers and bend into all sorts of shapes. This, too, would be detrimental to the factory and have consequences in thousands of pounds costs as the cable would have to be cut up as waste.

Feeling smug with himself, and sensing the need for a quick skive, Steve popped over to see Barry in the warehouse.

'Hi, Barry. You all right?'

'All right Steve! How's it going?'

'Not too bad. Just tired, today.'

'Late one, was it? I've heard Danny didn't make it in this morning. You two been out shagging again?' Barry asked. Steve was repulsed by this. Most of the time he enjoyed going out and 'shagging'- he and Danny were always on the pull- yet sometimes Steve had a soft spot for girls and didn't like seeing them constantly as 'slags'- Danny's word.

To add to this, he had met Lisa and she was great. Such a girl could turn him around, he felt. She could really straighten him out. He did not regard himself, usually, as a family man but definitely had the potential and certainly believed in 'the one' when it came to women.

The last twelve months had seen him using and abusing women as he followed in the footsteps of Danny. He had a soft spot though, one that he didn't share with Danny. Whereas Danny would just get bored of a girl and delete her number, Steve felt they had a right to be put in the picture. He would often ring them to try to explain the situation:

'It's not you...' he would say, '...it's me. I don't know what I want and I don't want you to get hurt. It's not fair,' or 'I just need a little time on my own. I'm not ready for a relationship.'

Sometimes he would even send flowers to apologise. Danny, however, offered no such explanations. He would ignore calls from girls that he no longer wanted anything to do with.

'Just tell her,' Steve would say as Danny would hold out the phone in front of him as it rang and say: 'Take a fucking hint, slag.' They did after a while but sometimes it would take weeks and it used to irritate Steve when it could have been avoided. Contrary to this, though, was the respect that Steve held for Danny. He wished he could be colder, too, because girls always liked Danny more, even though he would ignore them.

'Why is it...' he enquired one day, '...that you ignore them, or you're horrible to them, and they love you? Yet, the odd occasion that I've been nice to them,' somewhat of an understatement, 'they lose interest.'

'Because they're like dogs.' Danny spat these words out bitterly. 'They're only faithful when they respect their master and even then if they see another dog in the park they wanna hump it. You kick them and they come back loving you. If you're nice to them they become spoilt and bite you on the ankle. Take them out when *you* wanna take them out, and only then, and they love it.'

Harsh words, thought Steve, yet deep down he couldn't help feeling he was right.

'I don't know what he's been up to,' said Steve in reply to Barry's question. 'He was supposed to be out with a girl last night but I don't know how he got on. I wasn't with him. I took a young lady out myself.'

'Oh yeah! What happened?'

'Nothing! Just went to the cinema and then had a drink. Gonna meet up again. This one was nice, respectable.'

'So you never nailed her?'

Steve laughed but he really didn't find it funny. He liked this girl and wanted to give it a chance.

'It's early yet,' he winked, lowering his conversation to the appropriate tone, although he didn't like resorting to this level where Lisa was concerned and found it extremely distasteful.

'You must be slipping, boy. I bet you Danny would've nailed her.'

Steve's mind raced to an image of Danny holding Lisa to the floor and screwing her viciously. He felt sick but also curious as to how one girl could have such an effect on him so soon. Coming to the conclusion that they just bonded really quickly, he felt the urge to escape.

'I'd better get back to work,' he moaned, as he wondered what possessed him to go and see Barry.

However, something inside him compelled him to go back again and have that conversation with him: to talk dirtily about Lisa as if she was just some slag. He had to, otherwise he would feel that he was letting Danny down and he admired him so much.

'She's getting it tonight,' he shouted back, 'whether she likes it or not,' then made a fist.

Using a knife from the kitchen drawer Danny opened the letterbox of his front door from the inside. It was a bit tricky as the spring was strong but he had done it many times before. So often it was that a girl would turn up at his front door demanding an explanation for being ignored. There were days when he would pretend to be out and wonder why the hell he had ever brought her back to his flat in the first place. Sometimes though they lived with parents, or shared with friends, and there was nowhere else to go.

They would get bored eventually and Danny's strategic method of pulling the letterbox open from the inside would afford him a quick spy of an angry female storming down his path...and not one of them ever closed the gate- *spiteful bitches*!

Steve would laugh if he was over in the flat with him and watch with admiration as the master at work displayed his skill, or at least that's how he viewed it.

He doesn't give a shit, Steve would say in his head. He just wants to know who it is.

'Precision peering,' Danny would comment and this raised another laugh from Steve.

Some days Danny would display real arrogance and continue with what he was doing, despite the frantic knocking at the door. He wouldn't turn the music or TV volume down and move stealthily into the hall to squat behind the front door as usual. Instead, he would turn the volume up or bang around in the house defiantly, ignoring the very-often, ill-deserved and confused girl on the outside. Today's 'precision peering,' though, had a different aim and Danny was far from arrogant. Nervously, he peeked out of the letterbox to see if anybody was around- it was quiet. He zipped up his jacket and headed out in the direction of the local retail park. Fortunately, it was only a short walk.

Ten minutes later Danny found himself walking around the domestic appliances in one of the electrical goods stores. He was getting pestered by a sales assistant but for once he didn't mind. He welcomed the help. His mood had changed and he was no longer nervous. As confidence filled his veins he decided to mock the sales assistant slightly, perhaps for escapism.

'This fridge,' he inquired, 'at two hundred and nine pounds. What's so good about it?'

'Well sir...' Here came the spiel. 'This super deluxe model is not only available in white but also the prestigious silver that recreates the '60s' all-American theme. It re-establishes the image of the ideal home, the American dream. A place where the average person can live in luxury. And with the "buy-now-pay-September" you can take advantage of designing your whole kitchen in one go and not have to worry about the repayments.'

'Why, who's gonna pay for it?' Danny said, sarcastically. He thought he would listen to what the sales assistant had to say, for a laugh, yet couldn't help stopping him every now and again to point out any absurdities.

'Well,' continued the assistant, 'it's interest-free for the first six months. Notice the way the refrigerator itself is on the top and the freeze box is on the bottom unlike the old models where there was a lot of stooping. You see, several studies have been conducted on this and research shows that the ratio between fridge and freeze box use is directly proportional to our health and low freeze boxes are not conducive to well being. We in the electrical appliances field strive, constantly, to improve people's lives. All our products undergo vast amounts of scientific research in order to enhance their appearance and improve their accessibility.'

'ACCESSIBILITY? It's just a fuckin' fridge. Either the door opens or it doesn't.'

'No sir, if you'll pardon me correcting you, it's not *just* a fridge...ahem!' He paused slightly to think and Danny felt he had him on the ropes. His automaton-like manner was slipping and a human side to him was showing.

'What else does it do then?' Danny questioned.

Being the professional he was he picked himself back up again and returned to robot mode. 'It's a state-of-the-art food storage unit, designed to give ease of use and years of trouble-free cooling, thereby aiding in the brightening up of one's life. Like I was saying, research has shown that the proportion of use between refrigerators and freeze boxes is 89% to 11%. That means that for nearly 90% of the time you use your refrigerator you have to stoop and this can lead to lumbago and arthritis. Now, with the freeze box on the bottom, investigations have revealed that after ten years of use 70% of users of this model suffer less from arthritis compared with users of old models. Moreover...'

'Moreover!' Danny repeated and laughed. *Is this guy for real? He sounds as if he's writing an essay.*

'Moreover,' he continued, 'the constant stooping throughout the day as one...'

'One?'

'...makes use of the storage facilities in coolage...'

"Coolage!" There's a word.

'...has been purported to have increased depression levels in men between the age of 21 and 40.'

I fall into that. How coincidental. 'I can't afford that though,' interrupted Danny, playing with him. 'You see this one over here for one hundred-and-forty-six pounds. What about that?'

'Very economical, sir, and extremely reliable.'

'But it's got the freezer on the top.'

'Yes but sir's a fit and healthy young male. That shouldn't bother him.'

He was using that irritating use of the third person as if he was talking about someone else. Danny's parents used to do it when he was about eight years old and even then he could see right through it.

'Danny ate all his dinner this evening darling,' his mum would say.

'Good,' his stepdad would reply, 'that'll make him big and strong.' Or his mum would say: 'I don't know what the teacher will say tomorrow when she finds out he hasn't done his homework.'

'No, he'll get into serious trouble.'

I'm here you know, Danny would ponder. *Why are you talking about me as if I'm not?* And deep down Danny's stepdad would hope that he did get into trouble, because he hated him and it was a good excuse to beat him.

Back in the electrical goods' store the sales assistant was still going on. Danny stopped him.

'So what about arthritis when I get older?'

'Well, sir. Studies have revealed...'

Does this guy read "Studies Monthly" or something?

'...that arthritis can be brought on by lack of use of the joints, and regular exercise can prevent this by increasing suppleness and encouraging blood supply to the area. So, if you, say, make eight or nine cups of tea a day; that's eight or nine times into the fridge, combined with meals and general snacking, then that's probably about five minutes of exercise a day. If you spend another five minutes a day walking up the stairs to the toilet to discard the useless liquid, then that's your ten-minutes-a-day exercise regime that will keep you fit and healthy and contribute to longevity.'

Danny couldn't take any more. A joke was a joke but this guy must've been on drugs. In the space of ten minutes he had suggested that a fridge with the freezer on the bottom would enhance his life no end. It would relieve depression and help avoid arthritis- as well as being a FRIDGE. But then, contrary to this, regular exercise in stooping to the fridge below the freezer could prevent arthritis and add to his old age. AND, it cools things. *Fan-fucking-tastic!* How had he coped all his life without one of these appliances?

He decided to come to the point- the purpose of his visit. 'Look,' he said, 'I want a chest freezer. Could you show me them?'

'Certainly, sir.' They walked to where they were. 'Now, the freezing capability of this unit is super-fast acting and aids in the reduction of electricity usage throughout...'

Danny raised his finger to the sales assistant's lips and placed it upon them to quieten him. 'Sshh!' he said. 'Just show me them, cut the spiel.' Danny's eyes burned into him and for the first time in his life the assistant was actually frightened by a customer. He swallowed hard.

'Now, this one. How much is it?'

'Three hundred and seventy-nine pounds sir,' he spluttered. Danny moved to look at another one. 'That's only two hundred and eighty-nine,' he piped up, desperate to win favour with his customer. Danny looked at it and span its length with his arms.

'Too small!' he complained.

'Too small? How much food do you have?' He was getting brave again so Danny put a stop to this.

'Get in it,' he said

'What!'

'You heard me. I want to see exactly how big it is.'

After deliberating a moment and then catching Danny's stare for the second time the sales assistant climbed in, reluctantly. His fear of Danny's eyes meant that he would do anything. He squashed up inside and it reminded Danny of when he used to take sandwiches to work when he was an apprentice. His mum went through a phase of giving him Super Toastie bread. It never fitted in his lunch box and she would have to squash it in. He thought of squashing the sales assistant in but then decided against it. 'You see, too small!' Danny commented.

'What are you putting in it, a body?'

'Yeah.'

The sales assistant sniggered but only through nervousness. He didn't find it funny.

'Get in that one, then.' Danny pointed to another.

'But...'

'Just get in it, will you.'

He did so and Danny closed the lid on him. The sales assistant's face was a picture and he was sweating profusely. After a few seconds Danny opened the lid and smiled at him.

'Perfect! I'll take it.'

Fearing for his life the sales assistant scrambled out of the freezer. 'C-c-c-could you follow me to Customer Service please?'

'Certainly,' replied Danny feeling quite composed, but this soon changed. His question of "how soon can you deliver it?" after they had taken all his details, had not met with good news. He was expected to wait about three weeks. How could he?

'Can I have a word?' He smiled again at the sales assistant whose nervousness doubled.

'Y-yes, sir.'

Danny put his arm around him. 'Now listen...Craig,' he said, noticing his name badge. 'I know how this works. You see, I've got a delivery coming today of frozen foods and my own freezer has packed in. Now, I live with my gran and she's severely disabled. She can't get out much and I work loads. It's a strain, it's a strain.' Craig nodded. 'We have to buy all our food frozen 'cos we just can't get out. I'm so busy- this is the first day I've had off in two months- and...like I said, she's severely disabled.

'We need this freezer, mate. You wouldn't wanna see an old woman suffer would you?' Craig shook his head. It was Danny's turn for the spiel. 'She's been through two World Wars, lost her husband and brought up eight children on her own. It was the strain that disabled her. Her body couldn't take any more so it shut down. She's never walked since. Now surely there's a way of putting that freezer- I'll take that one, the display one, I don't care- on today's delivery.'

'Impossible,' he stated. The lorry leaves early in the morning and we don't see it again until four.

Disappointed, Danny changed his approach. 'I don't wanna have to keep coming back in here every day because my food's all defrosted and wasted.' The thought of his ever returning to the store with those burning eyes frightened Craig. *I'd rather have fuckin' Nosferatu come in than you*, he thought.

Danny placed a twenty-pound note in his shirt pocket, too, and this clenched it.

'Well, it could go on tomorrow's delivery. If I say it's for a friend or relative.'

'Good boy!' He winked at him and left.

4

The mobile phone on the table in Danny's flat was vibrating and ringing simultaneously. He ignored it. It was nine o'clock in the evening and *Open All Hours* was on the TV again.

At least another eleven hours, although it could be up to fifteen. The sales assistant had said between eight and twelve the next morning. How could he get through another night with HER in the bath? He couldn't even take a shower as she was in the way. The commercial break came on and the TV suddenly boomed out in volume.

Why the fuck do they do that? he wondered.

'Do they think their programmes are so boring that everybody falls asleep and they have to wake you up with adverts that burst your eardrums?'

Talking to himself was becoming more of a regular thing now.

'Need cheaper car insurance?' the advert boomed.

'Fuck off!'

He muted the sound, walked over to his phone and picked it up. Scrolling through the caller display he saw that Steve had tried several times to reach him. He was about to put the phone back before he thought differently. If he was to ignore Steve then he might come over again. And even though he might pretend to be out, Steve might decide that there was a problem and feel compelled to break in. Worse still, he might call the police who will come and break his door down for fear of him lying there dead, or being too ill to come to the phone.

Perhaps he's committed suicide? Steve might think. And what would they find once they'd burst through the door? Danny sitting comfortably in an armchair watching re-runs of *Open All Hours* and eating Texas Barbecue Pringles whilst a headless corpse lay in the bath. He had better ring him.

'Hello,' said Steve's voice.

'Hi, Steve. You ok?'

'Yeah, fine. Where are you? Where've you been? Why didn't you show into work? I called round.'

That was three questions. Which one did he want him to answer first? 'I've been ill,' spouted Danny. He wasn't lying in a way- he had vomited. 'I'm gonna go and stay with my auntie for a few days. I've been a bit depressed too. Tell them I'm okay and make my excuses for me would you?'

'Of course. We were starting to get worried.'

Perhaps it was just in time. Another day and the front door would almost certainly have been smashed in and the flat raided with police.

'I called several times,' Steve continued.

'I know. I couldn't find my phone. It was on silent, as I needed rest, and then I forgot where I put it. I won't be home for a few days so you needn't call. Two or three days and I'll be back to work. I've gotta go mate, I need a lie down.'

'All right, Danny. If you need anything, just call me.'

'Cheers, mate. Bye!'

'Bye!'

Danny pressed the picture that had a red phone on it and stared at the mobile's display. Was there anyone else he needed to call? He decided that that would be it for now and turned his phone off.

At about 11pm the tension was getting too much for him. Why couldn't he just have his freezer? He'd paid for it. To take his mind off it he decided to get a shower but had forgotten that Michelle's body lay in the bath. Upon seeing it as he opened the door everything came flooding back to him and he ran out of the bathroom and into the kitchen to puke. After a second or two of liquid expulsion, his stomach had changed gear to 'copious retching'. There was nothing left and he remembered why. He had had nothing to eat all day. His mind was elsewhere and he had been too busy to eat since his eggs at breakfast. *Oh, and those Pringles.* He could smell the Texas Barbecue sauce in the vomit and, seemingly, at the back of his nostrils.

After flushing the sick down the sink- most of it was fluid anyway- he washed his face. He was much better but he was torn between these two people and pictured the torment of Dr Jekyll and Mr Hyde. His moral side had been brought up well and was physically repulsed by the idea of killing or handling dead bodies. He tolerated violence, he even executed it, yet he knew it to be wrong. His 'other' side, though- the one that he feared and seemed to lose control of- was capable of anything no matter how vile, disgusting or depraved. At least, that's how he felt. So what was bringing this side of him out?

He self analysed his inner fears. *Dr Jekyll mixed potions and drank them- that was the cause for him. It was a drug that transformed his personality.* But Danny never touched drugs, apart from alcohol, and that had never had this effect on him before. He thought for a moment. The theme of good versus bad was apparent in so many novels and films, especially horrors, and the good was always backed by Christianity, he believed, thereby adding a religious slant.

Dracula may not be a movie that purports to promote religion yet how do the average people ward him off? With a cross. Vampires were usually bitten, that was their cause. So what is mine? Why should this evil streak inside me suddenly emerge? From where does it get its strength? Can I control it? Indeed, would I even want to?

It seemed to have such a strong personality that he admired it in the same way that Steve admired *him* for his odd behaviour towards women.

Returning to the bathroom he lifted the corpse up out of the bath. It seemed to weigh a tonne. Struggling as best he could, he managed to sit it on the toilet, propped up against the cistern. It was starting to stiffen and it looked vulgar in its headless state. He left the head in the bath by the plug hole and turned on the shower. It didn't seem to bother him showering in front of the head, even with those evil, bulging eyes that seemed to be staring at him as if waiting for revenge.

Once he was finished, he dressed and sat back down in front of the TV. It was now after midnight. He needed a drink and saw fit to fetch a bottle of whisky from the kitchen. On his way back from the retail park he had acquired another three bottles of it. He was getting the taste for it now and thought he might need a few bottles in the house for "emergencies." *These should get me through the next few days until I decide what to do about disposing of the body.*

Steve and Lisa were watching a DVD although neither one of them could say what it was about for they had chatted all the way through it. They were on their second bottle of wine in Steve's flat and the television served only as a background medium for establishing a solid relationship between the pair. The chat was endless and never dried up for a minute; both enthralled in the other's company. They were discussing religion at this particular moment in the conversation.

Lisa stated: 'But you must believe in something, even if it's just other life forms that may be out there.'

'Oh I do,' he replied. 'I don't believe we're the only ones in the world or...the universe.' Steve was an intelligent bloke but unfortunately never thought much for himself. He was opinionated and pushy with his views but they weren't *his* views originally; they were Danny's. And his spiel was merely a regurgitation of Danny's- sometimes almost verbatim. He understood the concepts and liked them- in fact he really did believe in them- yet they had been imposed. Had he never met Danny it is unlikely that he would be so strong in his views.

'I believe there is life out there...' he continued, '...as the earth is a relatively new planet and there are many more "worlds", if you like...' He made a gesture with his fingers in the shape of a rabbit's ears to suggest that the word "worlds" should be in inverted commas, '...for creatures to inhabit.

'In one respect, it is arrogant for us to think that there is something better out there for us...guaranteed. Like a god, for instance, yet it is also arrogant to believe that we are the superlative life form. We're hardly superior to any other animal.'

'...As we're all warring with one another,' Lisa interjected. 'Still, there is killing daily. We still have poverty and people are destroying themselves to earn an honest buck.'

'So you'd say there was no God then, or gods? Because a god who is omnipotent would not allow things like that to happen?'

She agreed but it didn't sound like she did from the tone of her voice: 'But the religious people argue that their god, or whoever they believe in, has left us to our own devices. We need to be strong and stand up on our own two feet.'

'That's a cop out,' he sniped. 'What an excuse to avoid justifying the existence of god.'

'But religions are based on faith, Lisa added. You have to believe, you have to have faith in the omnipotent ruler and not question.'

'Like sheep!' he scorned. 'Aah! It's a mockery. When I was a kid the priest used to say "my flock." How degrading! Even the religious powers treat you like sheep and take the piss out of you.'

'No pun intended but I was playing devil's advocate.'

'Ha ha! But think about it. What do sheep do? They stick close to their shepherd- here a metaphor for God- and they graze the ground around them. They're not even left to wander too far before they're brought back in line. The shepherd's dog- in this case the pope- keeps them all in line. He keeps them ignorant, like the masses in the Dark

Ages. "Why is that tree there?" "Because God put it there. That's all you need to know." I mean, the *Dark* Ages. A period we don't know much about because of the power of the church exercising its right of control. Total oppression!' Steve sounded so much like Danny but he never acknowledged it, not even with himself.

'The victors wrote the history,' he continued, 'and that is how we interpret the past- through biased eyes. And back to these sheep. What do *we* do? We fucking eat the fuckers in return for their loyalty.'

He shut up then realising that he had built to a crescendo and had sworn in front of Lisa. A no-no in his eyes. He disliked this. *She is decent and I haven't heard her swear. So why should I?* he mulled. *After all, I don't even like it myself.* Fortunately, she just laughed. She never swore unless she was angry but this didn't bother her. She just wasn't too keen on anybody whose entire vocabulary consisted of fifty percent swearing.

People who use the 'F' word, she thought, *about three times in one sentence, doubling and tripling it up for use as nouns, verbs (transitive, intransitive), adjectives and even fucking adverbs.*

'So on Judgement day,' she pressed, 'when God says to you "It's Perdition for you my boy. The great fires of Hell await." What will you say?'

Steve was ready with his answer. Fortunately, Danny had told him this one too. 'I'd say: "Well yes. I have questioned you. I didn't believe because I'd never seen any proof." Faith can lead to death. If I believed I could fly, I could jump off a building and kill myself. I could be a martyr, perhaps, like a suicide bomber, with my reasons. Everyone would say I was stupid but my argument would be that it was faith. I believed, therefore I acted.

'Even though nobody has ever flown in that manner, if you believe you can then that's all that matters. I would also say: "You're the god. You made me- I am a creation of thine own hands therefore you control me. If I get too big for my boots and question you then only you can be to blame. If you didn't want me to question your existence and your methods then you shouldn't have given me this much intelligence but instead created me ignorant.

'If you didn't want me this intelligent with the capacity for free thought- and you've shown me no evidence of your existence, apart from hearsay and controversial documents, thousands of years old- then how can you expect me to believe unconditionally?" It's the duration of my life that counts, and what I see. These are the things

41

that I can comment upon. Anything previous to this and I'm expected to take people's word for it. And it's not even universal thinking-everyone believes different things and the evidence seems all hearsay. Other than arrogance, who's to say which particular religion is good, or more to the point true?'

Lisa pushed up her bottom lip as if to make a sad face- it meant that he had a point and she was thinking. Simultaneously, she had also raised her left eyebrow and tilted her head to the left. She was impressed by his views. Not because she felt particularly the same way. She was just happy to talk to somebody whom she considered intelligent and had a decent opinion on things, regardless of whether he was right or wrong. Thank goodness for Danny!

2am and Danny was starting to feel a bit drunk from the whisky. This time he hadn't bolted his drinks down to get pissed quickly but merely sipped slowly and enjoyed the evening. It was kicking in now though, and motivating him to do something. He stepped into the kitchen and reeled off seven heavy-duty bin bags from the roll. He then proceeded to cut the insides of each one in order to open them out. He also found a strong carrier bag that he had purchased in the local supermarket for ten pence. "Bag for life" it was called, strong with sturdy handles. *That'll do. Now, sellotape. Where is it? In the drawer.*

The bathroom seemed to hold a morbid and icy atmosphere, unlike any other room in his three-bedroom, ground floor flat. Was it always like this? Perhaps he had left a window open. No! No windows open and yet the air inside here bit into him and gave him a chill.

Perhaps it's my imagination. Just get on with it. This was a phrase he always used when he had a difficult task ahead of him or if he couldn't get motivated. He would always plod along and then be glad that he had done so afterwards.

He hauled the body over the bath and commenced wrapping the feet with the open refuse sacks. Coming to the end, he sellotaped it to seal it shut. His brain drifted as his hands functioned...

...It was Christmas, four years previous. Danny's girlfriend at the time, Jessica, was living with him. They had a house, a huge four-bedroom semi. Jessica has remained in the house to this day whilst Danny was forced to move out. He always saw the situation as unfair and would often remark to Steve that he had been 'taken for a ride'. They bought the house together; they got it for a low price when the previous tenant, an old lady, passed away. She had no next of kin so it was auctioned off cheaply. It also needed thousands of pounds of renovation work doing on it and a complete rewiring.

Danny did the rewiring himself and Steve helped. One day he would return the favour, perhaps when Steve bought his own house.

It was the ideal home for Danny and he had put all his life savings into it. Jessica, too, but then- she was still there to reap the benefits. Danny didn't do too well out of the deal. Jessica raised the mortgage and paid him off- only thirty thousand pounds. Having bought it for seventy-five thousand and refurbished it entirely, combined with a boom in property prices, it was now estimated to be worth around three-hundred thousand; and to add insult to injury Jessica had a new man in there with her. He was a solicitor who already owned many properties.

That is just greedy, he thought and vowed to burn the house down one day, whether she was in it or not.

That was at the nadir of his bitterness, though, as he didn't always feel like that. Unless this solicitor came into his head he would usually imagine Jessica in a positive manner. They had had good times and Danny liked to re-live these.

The festive season upon them they were busy wrapping presents. They had a lot of friends and, seemingly, a lot more family members. Perhaps they all belonged to her as the most recent Christmas had consisted of a maximum of five presents to wrap. The only way he could compete with back then would be to buy presents for all his ex-girlfriends in the last six months.

Wrapping the refuse sack around the corpse's mid-section, Danny envisioned Jessica coming up behind him and massaging his shoulders; the way she used to. He was on his knees wrapping her mum's present. What it was he couldn't recall he just remembered that she had really loved it and that meant a lot to him at the time. Over the period that he had known Jessica, he had gained the approval of her mum who now saw Danny as her own son. This was the first time ever that a girl's mother had opened up entirely to him and he loved it. He usually had to work hard to gain the mother's respect whilst the fathers, more often than not, just grunted. It was difficult to ever know what they thought.

Jessica's mother had a soft spot for Danny and he loved her more than his own mother. For him, she had done more.

It was only now that something in Danny's mind began to come to light. He had loved Jessica more than any other girl in the world and

43

had never cheated on her. After the first year of their split-up he felt he had moved on; he was sleeping with several different women a week at one stage. Now he was realising that he was still VERY much in love with her. Four years had done nothing in the way of decreasing his feelings. If anything, they had increased them as he had many more women in which to compare her with.

As the memories came flooding back and the effects of the whisky were kicking in, he wept bitterly for about ten minutes before falling asleep- hugging the corpse's lower legs.

Steve and Lisa had had a fantastic time and it got even better by the end. They finished up in bed together but were both nervous. Fortunately they had plied themselves with enough wine to overcome this in order to allow their intimacy to embed itself and let nature take its course.

Their bodies met, naked for the first time. Even though neither of them were virgins, this encounter was particularly special for both of them. They had waited patiently and had fought back urges until they felt they were ready. The time was right; tonight was the night. Curling up in each other's arms they kissed and hugged for what seemed like ages. The fiery passions within them rose to the surface and, for them, the most beautiful action in the world went into progress.

They made love for over an hour; it seemed as natural to them as waves smashing onto rocks. For them, words could not describe the experience. Embraced in each other's arms they drifted off to sleep- at unity with one another and without a care in the world.

3.48 am. Danny's nostrils were ablaze with the smell of decaying human flesh. His imagination may have contributed to the stench but he was quite sure that Michelle's body was in need of preservation. He finished wrapping the body whilst desperately trying to shut out any memories of his past life with Jessica. The corpse was wrapped and more suitable now for manoeuvre. Danny picked the head up by its hair and dropped it into the strong carrier bag.

Bag for life! he thought. *How ironic! If anyone ever finds this, I'll get life.* He looked inside the bag at the head with its bulging eyes staring up at him. *She is a bag but I don't want her for life.* After tying the handles together he placed the bag back in the bath with the corpse.

The next day the chest freezer was delivered quite early and after setting it up and cleaning it Danny decided to test it out. The body fitted well and the head rested on the top.

I need food, now, he thought, *to cover the body up,* and later that day he would buy sixteen packets of frozen sprouts, twelve packets of frozen peas, pies, pizzas, ice-cream and lots of frozen microwave meals. He felt that shuffling the food around, as and when he ate it, may give cause for alarm so came to the conclusion that some sort of base was needed. This base was to consist of ice cubes on top of Michelle's corpse on which the food could lie. He purchased several bags from the supermarket but realised that this was not going to be enough.

I know. I'll call my friend up who runs a bar- he's a manager. He'll give me two full bin bags of ice. That should be enough. Not so long ago Danny had had a barbecue and had used this friend for enough ice to fill the plastic bins that he used for cooling the bottles of beer. He would just have to make a similar excuse up.

'Thanks John,' he said, when he went to pick them up in a taxi. He would have used the company van but he was off ill so he would have to make do with public transport. And anyway, it was only two bin bags of ice and not such a strange action that he would have to cover up to anyone.

'It's my neighbour,' he lied to John. 'He's having a barbecue and he's invited me round. I don't know if I'll go yet but I did promise him some ice. And it's worth keeping in with your neighbours isn't it? You know, for when you want to have a party yourself and blare the music out.' He winked as if to say "next party I have and you're invited." John smiled and put his thumb up to him as he struggled into the taxi with the bags of ice.

Back at the flat, when he had just finished levelling the ice cubes over in the freezer, the doorbell rang. Apprehensively, he reached into the kitchen drawer and took out a knife. He made his way to the front door and carefully attempted to open the letterbox from the inside.

'Hello! We've got your delivery,' shouted the driver of the van parked outside his flat. He sensed that the occupier was nervous and hesitant about opening the door- probably an old lady reluctant to open the door to strangers- and therefore reassured him that he could easily unload the shopping outside his door and be on his way.

Danny opened the door immediately, much to the delivery man's surprise. Expecting to see a little old lady, he was irritated that this young man should have his shopping delivered.

How lazy! he thought, but never dwelt on the matter.

'Just inside the hallway, please,' he informed the driver, fearing he might carry the stuff into the kitchen and start poking around in the freezer. 'I've just painted in the kitchen and I wouldn't like you to get it on your uniform.'

He need not have bothered as the driver had no intention of stepping in any further than the hallway and extending a helping hand any more than he should for this "lazy little toe-rag" as he said in his head. He might have even used these words out loud, too, if he hadn't have been crawling for a tip. Danny slipped him two pound-coins and closed the door quite abruptly without even giving him time to say "thank you." It was just as well as the words "thank you" never even entered his head.

'Bloody good timing, that,'' mumbled Danny to himself. 'Hope you're not too cold dear!' He spoke into the freezer as he threw in the packets of frozen food on top of the ice cubes. 'You just have a long nap, babe, until we decide where to go on our honeymoon.'

5

The following three weeks went by so quickly that they were like a dream for Danny. He had returned to work and made his excuses. All was back to normal. Nobody had even inquired about the missing girl. If Michelle had any family then they were either uninterested in her disappearance or never spoke to her to even know that she was missing.

Danny contemplated the whole scenario in his head. *Somebody must have noticed her absence. If not family, then friends; people she lived with, people she lived next door to. Even if she lived on her own, the correspondence would pile up, bills would not be paid. Did she work? What had her work said about her non-attendance?* Nothing! No inquiries, seemingly, and no talk raised in the neighbourhood. Danny stopped thinking about her – out of sight out of mind.

However, she may have been out of sight but she was not out of site for she remained at the bottom of his chest freezer, preserved well.

'What time are we out tonight, then?' Danny was addressing Steve as they had planned a big night out and he was really looking forward to it. He hadn't seen much of Steve as he spent most of his nights with Lisa.

'About 9 o'clock suits me,' replied Steve. And 9 o'clock it was. They stood in Cheen Square dressed up in their best shirts and trousers and ready for action. Well at least Danny was because Steve had a girlfriend now and even though that meant nothing to Danny it meant a lot to Steve. There was no way he was going to spoil their relationship. If only Danny knew, he had plans for a "wild night with a couple of slappers on the go" as he'd informed Barry in the stores earlier that day.

'What about these two?' asked Danny, pointing to two girls sat outside at a steel table.

'Yeah, whatever!' came the reply. Not as eager as usual, but that wouldn't stop Danny.

Danny tried his hand: 'I know you, don't I?' The girls looked up towards him and the brunette to whom he had addressed the question looked puzzled. She would have said "no!" sarcastically to this corny line yet he was good looking, she thought, so she waived the sarcasm.

'Did you go to my school? Or have I worked with you somewhere?' Danny persisted and Steve felt he must have something up his sleeve. He wouldn't normally come out with lines like this. 'It's Stephanie, isn't it?'

The girls eyes widened in amazement and suddenly all thoughts of cheesy lines vacated her head. And Steve's too, for that matter. *Fuck me*, he thought, *he does know her.*

'I can't think where I know you from,' she stated. 'St. Edmond's school?' That was it. He was in without the slightest appearance of trying.

They chatted for a few minutes but neither one came to the conclusion about where they had previously met. Things were going well but there was always a snag – her mate.

What's wrong with Steve? She's gorgeous. Why isn't he doing the business? But Steve had Lisa now, and he was smitten. He spoke to the other girl, but only briefly, and for the most part the conversation lay heavily on Danny and Stephanie who was stretching her brain to recall where she may know him. Sensing her friend's boredom, though, she sought to make excuses and leave but not before she had got Danny's number. She wasn't going to pass an opportunity like this up. He appeared to be being just polite but she liked him and would have to be bold.

'Well give me your number and I'll give you a call,' she said, desperate to make it sound innocent. Danny leapt at this but he remained composed.

'Sure! We can meet up, have a coffee and catch up on old times.'

They exchanged numbers and also a polite peck on the cheek before the girls moved on. *Fantastic!* Danny thought, and he had not even needed to make a move. He had his plan in reserve but it was not needed. He was to tell her about him previously having a crush on her and how he was too shy to ask her out but she didn't even need to buy that as she was sold on his looks. He turned to Steve: 'Why didn't you get into her mate? She was gorgeous.'

Steve just shrugged and tried to change the subject: 'Where do you know her from then?'

'I don't, I've never seen them before in my life.'

'Then how did you know her name? And how did you know all that stuff about her school and that place she worked in?'

48

'The school stuff I made up, and she bought it. She told me the name and I just added the rest. The stuff about her previous workplace, I exaggerated slightly but I knew a bloke who used to work there and he told me about his boss, and as for her name... I heard her on the phone when her mate was at the bar. When we first got here she was dialling someone and I heard her say: "Hi Maxine, it's Steph, Angela's mate..." so I swooped in there.'

Steve shook his head disapprovingly but was smiling. He rolled his eyes back and exhaled air through his nostrils in one sharp and rapid outburst as if something funny had just occurred to him. 'Sly old dog, you!' he laughed.

They had to visit three more bars before they spoke to any other girls. This might sound good to the average person but for Danny it was a slow evening. Steve sat in the corner whilst Danny chatted to two girls at the bar. A little out of character for Danny he unfortunately moved in on the wrong one; the one that wasn't interested. She had been a bit off with him whilst her mate was all over him so Danny must have felt the urge for a challenge.

'Why don't we talk about it another night?' he said to her. 'I'll call you and we can go for a drink.'

'I don't think so' she replied, cold and smug. She looked him up and down, condescendingly.

Does she think I'm a piece of shit, he wondered, *looking me up and down like that? Arrogant bitch!*

He walked off. The other girl, with the red hair, had obviously been interested so why didn't he pursue her? No! He had to go for the *...arrogant, sunbed-obsessed blonde, bimbo-of-a-mate.* 'Slag! Who the fuck does she think she is?' he said, returning to Steve. I'll smash her fucking head in.'

'Calm down!' pleaded Steve. 'She's not worth it.'

'Fucking right she's not worth it. Fucking slut! Let's go.'

They left their drinks and just walked out, Steve following Danny. Steve would have liked to have finished his drink but he could see Danny was in a mood and didn't want to aggravate him anymore, so he complied. He was pissed off and needed a mate and Steve was always supportive. It was unusual of Danny to show his emotions in this way. He hated rejection, and Steve knew he did, but he had never before displayed this hatred in such a powerful manner. Prior to this, if Steve was asked about Danny's views on rejection he would have said: 'He doesn't like it but he can usually ride with it. He doesn't see much of it anyway. Now, though, he seemed to be getting wound up. *Perhaps it's the drink*, Steve imagined, *or just a "one-off" as he's tired.*

The truth of the matter was, however, that rejection just ate away at him from the inside out. If a girl came to his flat and then suddenly turned "cranky" on him- the way he saw them acting in bars when there was an audience- then he probably would have killed a long time ago.

Two hours later, though, and it didn't mean anything to him anymore. They were both dancing away with two other girls. These girls weren't particularly pretty, they felt, but they were good fun and each had a wicked sense of humour so they were guaranteed a laugh. All this time Steve had not forgotten about Lisa. He talked to one of the girls in order to liberate the other one for Danny to work on but he had no intention of developing anything with her. His mind raced back to thoughts of Lisa and there was absolutely no way any girl could compare. He just wanted to get drunk and have a laugh- and hope that Lisa never saw him- but this girl was very much into him.

For a second or two he became quite forlorn as he wondered what Lisa would be doing at this precise moment and why he hadn't gone out with her. Suddenly, happiness seemed to surge through his body like a balloon filling with air. It felt good. There was no doubt about his feelings. He thought about the future and the way in which Lisa would play a major role in his life.

'I'll be back in a minute. Let me just answer this.' Danny's words snapped him out of it. Danny held his phone out in his left hand. It had been vibrating in his pocket and had interrupted his dancing. 'Hello. What? Hang on!'

Once outside he could hear more clearly. 'Who is it?' The voice on the other end of the phone sounded exhausted.

'Danny, it's Dave. How are you?' Danny never replied, he just listened. 'Sorry to bother you mate. I was just wondering if you could borrow a company van this weekend and give me a hand. I need to take some documents to the incinerator.'

Dave had his own business- a bookmaker's- and every once in a while he would require Danny's services. All the bets that were taken were photographed for evidence of their existence and the time and date was recorded on each in order to prevent fraudulent claims after a race had finished. All the old bets, along with their copies, would need to be bagged and destroyed every six months so Dave would call

Danny. Danny would borrow a transit van from work and they would take the slips to the incinerator for incineration.

'Yeah, no problem. I'll sort it tomorrow and we can go up on Saturday afternoon or something.'

'Cheers mate. You're a star!'

As Danny hung up he noticed a girl coming out of the bar. She walked to the side of the building, as he had done, to receive a phone call. She almost walked into him but didn't register his presence. Danny stared at her intently. It was the "sunbed-obsessed, blonde bimbo" who had been so smug earlier and embarrassed him.

He never took his eyes off her for a second as he walked towards her. As he came to her side, almost face-to-face, he stopped. Noticing somebody by her side, the girl stepped back slightly and turned. She froze in mid conversation as she became confronted with Danny's features: that insane look on his face; his large, athletic frame towering over her; his eyes searing into her flesh. There was a sudden flash and then her concentration was gone. From Danny's point of view, he heard a crack and watched as she dropped to the floor like a rag doll. He had caught her square on the jaw with a right hook and she dropped beautifully, he thought.

Her phone had flown out of her hand and landed about six feet away. In one swift movement he slid over to where it fell and stomped heavily on its face until it was smashed in bits. He then returned to the bar and fortunately, although he did check, nobody had seen what had occurred.

Back in the bar the conversation seemed to be flowing like a river. Steve no longer felt guilty as he had no intention of doing anything sexual with either of these girls and he hardly felt intimidated by their overwhelming good looks as there weren't any in his eyes. They were like a couple of friends. This helped him to lighten up considerably.

The two girls were called Anne and Liz. Anne was very fond of Danny. Liz too but she hadn't been as quick as Anne so had to settle for what she saw as second-best: Steve. He was all right, though, she thought. Anne was 26 and Liz was 29. Anne worked as a manageress in a women's clothes shop and earned a decent wage. She had worked there since she was 16 and was more successful than some of her friends who had chosen an academic route before starting work. Anne remembers one girl who attended the same school as her had completed a BSc, an MSc and a PhD in Virology or something, and she was earning 28K a year. Not bad? Not good! Anne only had three

GCSEs and she was on 35K a year. She had also been earning money since she was 16 so had lots of savings whereas her friend had a £25,000 debt from her student loans, her bank loans and her overdraft facility. All that education didn't seem to be paying off.

Liz worked in a clothes shop too but only as a sales assistant. She was yet to work her way up. They both worked together; Anne was Liz's boss. This sometimes became awkward as Anne was younger than Liz. She was very mature, though.

The end of the night saw them all back at Danny's flat. He had scrubbed the floors several times and Michelle's body was hidden at the bottom of the freezer so he felt that all would be well. Besides, he was drunk and didn't really care. Had he been sober he probably would have thought twice about bringing anyone back with Michelle's corpse itching to give him away.

It usually only took one mistake for criminals to be found out but most seemed to make that one. This was their downfall in committing the perfect crime. Tonight, however, drink-fuelled-Danny was confident that nobody would know. *People won't be interested in delving into the bottom of the freezer. That's cheeky!* He would have to be careful how he handled it as girls had been known to snoop around.

Steve felt that having made it to Danny's flat he was at liberty to leave them to it the moment that Danny would get a piece of "quality time" with Anne. Once Danny had established his feet "under the table" as he saw it, this seemed a good time for Steve to make a sharp exit. He was no longer needed to act as stooge for Liz until Danny 'scored' and this cheered him up.

For the next hour Danny stayed awake with the two girls. He chatted to both now as he had already done his ground work with Anne. He was grateful to Steve for distracting Liz long enough for him to work on Anne. Now he could "steam in there" as he used to say.

Another hour went by and Danny was in bed with Anne; Liz was asleep on the couch in the living room. How he would love for her to get involved as well. Leaning over Anne's body he pumped frantically into her loins. His mind wandered to images of Liz joining in. *If only she was here now; watching, participating.*

The pumping grew more and more frantic as he increased the speed and intensity. His fingers curled around Anne's hair and he gripped tightly. Anne winced in pain but he didn't let go.

'Ow!' she moaned. 'That hurts.' Still he persisted. She flinched again with the pain but was starting to come round to his way of thinking. Up until now she had avoided pain during sex yet here she was getting a kick out of it. Danny's right hand yanked hard at her hair whilst his left hand gripped itself around her throat. Like a piston in an engine he held a regular rhythm until, it seemed, somebody turned the speed up. Faster now but still that regular movement that you could attach a beat to. His thumbs found her trachea and began to press themselves deep into it, suppressing the oxygen to her brain. She panicked and her nails went for his face in self-defence.

With blood dripping down his cheek he portrayed four red lines from his eye to his jawline like two railway tracks running side by side. The coveted result was achieved: he had stopped. Only temporarily, though.

'Fuckin' bitch!' he shouted, and his well-practised right hook came colliding heavily into her left temple. She was out cold. His hand found its way to the affected area of his face and soaked up some of the blood.

'Slag!' he exclaimed and suddenly he heard a creaking sound from the living room. *Liz must be up. She must've heard. Shit! But it's okay. Things just got a bit out of hand, that's all. Liz will understand. She'll have to.*

The blood on his hand went instinctively to his mouth via his fingers. He licked hard and seemed to enjoy it. *I never used to be into blood. So often it is with humans that when we cut ourselves we put the affected area into our mouths. It's natural, apparently. But is it? Perhaps there is some morbid fascination with drinking blood. How can I even think of it?*

An apprehensive tapping sound could be heard on the bedroom door then Liz spoke. 'Are you ok, Anne?' There was a pause. Danny froze over Anne's naked body. She was still breathing so there was no problem there. She would have a headache, though.

The guilt seemed to rise uncontrollably within Danny's body and his muscles tightened so much that he was rigid to the touch. Rooted to the spot, his brain said get up and reassure her; his body disagreed.

The bedroom door creaked slowly as Liz nervously pushed it ajar. 'Anne! Anne! I'm going now. Are you staying?' She poked her head around the door; her heart was pumping. Something was wrong. As the room came within her vision she sized up its contents- wall, picture, wardrobe, bed... It was dark and she couldn't make out if anyone was on the bed. She pushed the door a touch more to allow extra light from the hall to penetrate the bedroom and as she did so Danny came from behind the door and startled her. 'Hi!' he said.

'Oh my god!' she screamed. 'You frightened the life out of me.'

'Ssh!' Danny put a finger to his lips. 'Anne's asleep.'

He nodded to the living room and closed the bedroom door. Liz followed him. 'Do you want a drink, Liz?'

'Erm, yeah, okay. Thanks.' She was still unaware of what was occurring as Danny's calm nature reassured her that her thoughts that something was amiss were exaggerated. After all, she had never even met these lads before tonight and even though Danny was a nice guy he did have an unusual stare at times. Taking a glass of wine and sipping she began to relax more, seeing Danny as less and less of a threat. 'What's up with Anne?' she inquired.

'She's sleeping,' Danny replied. 'Probably drunk.'

'Yeah, she has had a few. So have I, come to that. We came out at 7 o'clock. She took the knock, then?' Danny's brain flashed back to their sex session and he saw himself punching her clean on the temple. 'Yeah, you could say that,' he sighed.

They chatted for a couple of minutes before Danny became bored. He decided to make a move on Liz as Anne was out cold and there was nobody else. She responded negatively at first, thinking about her friend, but eventually began to loosen up. Danny merely filled her head with what she wanted to hear: 'I thought you liked Steve, you see. That's why I spoke to Anne. Steve knew I liked you but he said that you were into him.

Liz was smiling. She was genuinely flattered by all this and she had fancied Danny all night. Apart from his looks there was his great personality and overwhelming confidence that effected a certain trust in him from the people around. He also had a fantastic sense of humour- particularly important for these girls. There was just more and more to like about him, she felt, after talking to him.

Anne had drifted into a deep sleep. The strike to the side of the head knocked her out but the bonus of the alcohol levels in her blood aided in hypnotising her into slumber. Without her interference it appeared that a path was being paved out for Danny and Liz. Danny smooched his way in and Liz yielded to his seduction. Before long they were sprawled over the couch, snogging. Danny tolerated this for a few minutes before he moved into undoing her blouse and caressing her breasts. He was able to focus on this and it became his excuse for not snogging for a long period.

What a fast mover he was. He knew all the moves and had such a good touch that few said "no". He usually had his way with a woman. Not because he was slimy or sleazy, or just a charmer, but because he gave a woman exactly what she wanted, albeit sometimes too early. He said the right things; he performed the right actions. It was not often a girl met a lad like this (how he purported to be) so when they did they felt that they needed to hold on to them. They were happy with Danny- after all, he was a catch- and as he feigned disinterest after his initial spark of enthusiasm it had the effect of them "giving out", as Danny put it, a bit earlier.

Danny rolled off Liz and puffed frantically in an attempt to regain his composure. He and Liz had had sex. Less than an hour ago he had been screwing Anne and now here he lay after screwing Liz too. He wondered whether Anne was okay as she seemed to have been sleeping for quite a while. Luckily for him she was only sleeping and woke about 4am, her head pounding on the inside, her throat dry and sore.

Coming into the living room she saw Danny and Liz on the couch but gave them the benefit of the doubt as to whether they had been up to anything. Danny awoke as she came in. He was desperate for her to join them for a threesome but he never said anything for fear of spoiling a good night. *I'd better behave. I've fucked the two so I should be grateful for that. Better just keep them happy. I'll probably fuck them again. Perhaps both at the same time and get them to perform a little scene too. Better keep them apart now. Don't want them talking.*

'Do you mind if I call a taxi?' asked Anne, feeling a little awkward. 'I don't feel well.'

'Of course not. I'll do it for you.' Danny showed great concern on the outside. Inside, however, he just wanted to get rid of her for the rest of the evening. *She doesn't seem to remember anything. Unless she's frightened.*

'Sorry I can't stay,' continued Anne. 'I shouldn't have drunk so much. I've got to get up early and I need my own bed. And, I've got a really bad headache.'

She doesn't remember. 'That's all right. I understand.' And he did too, more than she knew.

By the time the taxi arrived Liz was awake too so the girls decided to go together.

'We'll share it,' said Anne. Danny had to suppress his sniggering. He couldn't help seeing this as a metaphor for himself. Feeling all pleased with himself he saw both girls to the door and said goodbye. He didn't know which one to kiss first, if indeed he should kiss either of them, so he merely shouted: 'I'll call you' and closed the door before any of them had a chance to question him.

How effective. Both girls threw a leg each into the taxi and both girls imagined that he had intended that for them. Unfortunately for them, though, it was not meant for either as neither Liz nor Anne would receive a phone call after tonight.

Danny looked at his watch- it was 4.30am and he had to be up for 7. Exhaustion hit him all of a sudden as if somebody had just informed him that he was tired because he had forgotten. He fell into the bedroom and crashed on the bed, face down. His arm slid under the pillow. It felt nice. He closed his eyes and, like a television getting switched off, his brain seemed to cease its activity. A thousand images fused themselves together, swirled around and shrunk to a small circle of action. The blackness around it closed in on it until it was all black...and he was asleep.

6

Steve never informed Danny that he was taking the day off as he was avoiding the whole "Lisa" difficulty. He was really keen on her and actually wanted to have a relationship with her but this would have met with great disapproval from Danny. He told Danny that he had a dentist's appointment in the morning and asked if he could make his own way in. He never mentioned the rest of the day though.

Lisa had also taken the day off and she and Steve had planned to go to Blackpool for a break. They even contemplated staying over but decided to make that decision by the end of the day.

Danny had had little time for spending with women in the past as it was but he seemed to be getting worse, Steve felt. This, combined with Lisa being on the scene now was carving a rift between the two. It wasn't a major problem, and neither one had acknowledged it as of yet, but they could both sense that something was wrong. The first time that Steve showed interest in Lisa that didn't amount to just sleeping with her, Danny piped up: 'They're all slags, mate. You might as well go and get a prostitute.'

Steve always took heed where Danny was concerned. He was his idol when it came to pulling girls, a diva at it, he used to think. He even listened when he lectured him over Lisa but this bit would not sink in. She's different, he felt. She's not like that.

'You see, whatever way you look at it...' Danny was on a roll, '...you're paying for it. "Buy me a drink", the slag says. So you buy her a drink. Okay, I'll buy anyone a drink...but then she expects to be taken out – wined and dined. That costs you money. So what are you paying for?'

'They're not all like that,' Steve interrupted, but this was ignored.

'Now I'm not tight, as you know, but when a girl EXPECTS you to pay for her...what's she selling?' Steve shrugged. 'She's selling her body mate: prostitution! She's saying: "If you take me out and spend lots of money on me, I'll sleep with you." A bit like an escort. So she's selling *herself*! In return for your spending you get sex. "And if you keep me for the rest of you life; you know, marriage, then I'm yours for whenever you want.'"

He's really off on one now, Steve thought. He was even adopting a high-pitched voice for the fictitious girl in his argument.

"'I'll cook for you, clean for you and bend over for you. You just keep paying for me.'"

Steve laughed. It sounded like a Monty Python sketch.

'I'm serious mate; prostitutes the lot of them. I met a girl once and she was a bit older than me at the time.'

'She probably still is,' Steve said sarcastically. Danny was unfazed,

'She had a good job and I was a student. But she didn't like this. She pestered me to get a job and me, being the young fool I was at 19, found myself looking in the local papers for jobs. But then I thought, fuck off! It's my life and I want to continue studying. If she'd known I was only two months away from finishing my apprenticeship she might have had a different attitude.

'But you see, if I was the one in the well-paid job and she was a student, or even on the dole, then I'd be expected to take her on. It wouldn't matter for her. She'd just find a rich bloke earning enough to look after her.' Steve nodded. When he spoke about topics such as this with Lisa and they touched on feminism he began to see Danny as a little warped yet when it was just him with Danny he could see his point of view so clearly. Perhaps he just has a great way of presenting his views, Steve thought.

'What bugs me,' Danny continued, 'is that girls won't settle for less but we're expected to. If a girl- like this fucking whore I went out with- is in a good job, is career-minded, then they expect to meet someone who is earning even more than they are. Even a bloke in a normal job, earning an average wage would not be good enough for them. Why is it that rich women are not out to look after guys?

'You sound jealous,' Steve scoffed.

'Well, it'd be nice wouldn't it? Rich women want equally rich men. They're greedy. The average bloke spends between two and six grand dating in the first six months of a relationship. Now that could be six grand he'd be better off with. She takes him for a ride whilst she's earning a decent wage and her money goes into savings. At the end of it the stupid bloke's got no savings but she's loaded. She's had the time of her life for six months – all free – she's got a brand new car and doesn't use much petrol 'cos "Muggins" does all the driving. He's "the man," you see and when she's bled him dry, and he can no longer afford to keep her in the luxury that he's so stupidly set himself up for, she fucks him off and finds another mug.

'He then gets depressed, is on the rebound, and can't even afford to date another girl. He's got nothing to offer a girl, financially, so he gets nowhere. Nobody's interested.'

Steve pondered this for a while before stating: 'Yeah.....you're right 'cos before I learnt to drive I remember some girl dumping me because some other lad she knew had a car. Slag!' He felt himself adopting Danny's attitude.

'That's it.' How many times have you seen girls in the city centre getting into cars on a Saturday night or at least just hovering around them? Remember when I had that convertible BMW for a while, and we went into town?' Steve nodded. 'And that girl came up to us with her mate, done up to the nines, and she said "Ooh! Is this your car?" Fucking slag!'

'But you banged her, remember?'

'Well, exactly! That's my point. She thought I was loaded.'

'That's because you told her you were,' Steve interjected.

'Yeah! Well it worked didn't it? Give them what they want and they'll give *you* what you want. She sold herself for a potentially good time. She gave me sex 'cos she thought I was gonna take her out for weeks and spend loads on her. Hah! Fat chance!'

'Maybe she just wanted sex as well. Women do like it you know!'
Danny frowned. Nobody had ever complained with him. Despite his views on women's actions he did know how to satisfy a girl in bed but he didn't see it that way. He felt they were just happy to be with *him*, not because they particularly enjoyed the sex.

'If she just wanted to get laid then why didn't she pull someone in the club? No, she was outside at 2.15am and saw us in our convertible. There were probably lads buying her drinks inside all night but if they didn't have the tell-tale signs – 22-carat gold rings, chunky, gold bracelets hanging off their wrists, expensive clothing, and champagne on the bar, then they wouldn't be interested.'

'Hmm! I can't say I agree with all that, mate,' Steve replied. 'I mean, you don't know *what* they were doing inside. They might've been really decent women.' Danny frowned.

It was 11.30 on Friday morning and Steve and Lisa were already on the outskirts of Blackpool.

'We'll be there by 12,' noted Steve.

59

'Where to first, then?' asked Lisa

'Well, let's park up and go for a walk along the prom and then we can get some fish and chips, go up the tower and.....who knows?'

Lisa smiled. She loved being with him, they got on so well and he was just her type. For the first time in her life she was really happy. Steve smiled too. He leaned over and gave her a quick kiss on the side of her head. They were sat at the traffic lights on red and as they weren't changing he thought he would use this as an opportunity for another one. Lisa sensed this too and met his lips with hers. They closed their eyes and focused on each other's sensitivity.

Sensations heightened and their kiss became deeper and deeper. Steve held her tightly, his strong arms protecting her, and with his vice-like grip he curled his fingers around her arms. Lisa felt safe and warm. She hadn't a care in the world at this moment.

Steve was getting carried away too. His mind wandered to a faraway forest. Somewhere he could take her and protect her. His instinct was kicking in and right at this instant he had the potential to kill anybody that threatened to come between them.

BEEP! BEEP! The cars behind them were sounding their horns aggressively as the drivers were beginning to get frustrated. The driver behind had not noticed that the lights had changed at first as he was staring out of the passenger window. It was only when a girl three cars back decided she had had enough after waiting a whole ten seconds with the lights on green, and had triggered off the horns, that the guy behind Steve then joined in. And then, like sheep, they all joined in and there was a tail of about 15 cars behind them. Some had even managed to pull out and drive around the lovers, cursing abuse to no avail.

Steve panicked. He threw the gear stick into first and let up the clutch. The car struggled to move. It seemed to rise off the floor an inch and then drop. The handbrake was on. By now all the cars that were left behind were sounding their horns frantically. Steve released the handbrake and stalled.

'Shit!' He panicked more. Turning the engine over, he wheelspun the car away as the lights were changing back to red and the car behind was forced to stop. There was no way the driver would risk it with that camera there.

The sweat was dripping down Steve's nose, causing it to itch. He rubbed it and turned to Lisa with a worried look on his face. She was beginning to snigger so he smiled back. Suddenly, her shoulders began racking up and down and she burst out laughing. Being as infectious as it was Steve could not help but to join in. Seconds later they were both convulsed with laughter as they attempted to control their nerves.

At lunchtime Danny tried Steve's mobile; it was off.
Where the hell is he? he thought. *Would they keep him in at the dentist? No. They don't do things like that. He must have had a tooth out and he's gone home in pain to sleep. I'll call round there after work.* Danny looked at his phone. Nothing. No text messages, no missed calls. He decided to go for a quick pint before his lunch finished. It was twenty-five-to-two in the afternoon and he was due back at two. Fortunately, the pub was just across the road. There were two pubs: The Moose's Head and The Anchor. Danny chose The Anchor.

The Moose's Head was the place to be at lunchtime but he needed a bit of peace so he opted for what Steve called 'the Old Man's pub.' It was too, for when he got in there, there were three people there and the barmaid. One old guy sat in the corner, with his head down and a half pint of mild in front of him. He looked like he was asleep, or dead.

Maybe that's why he only drinks halves, Danny wondered, *in case he doesn't make it through a full pint. Waste of money dying and leaving your beer.*

There was also a man and woman in their late forties/early fifties chatting across a table. Danny propped himself up at the bar and noticed the barmaid had a square badge above her left breast that read 'The Anchor. Kate'

'Orange juice, please Kate.' She smiled. She wasn't going to ask how he knew her name or whether he knew her from somewhere as everyone seemed to use the same chat-up line and Kate was used to it now, having been caught out the first time she wore the badge.

'One-eighty-two, please.'

'Cheers!' He handed her a five-pound note. 'And one for yourself. Is it always like this?' he enquired as she gave him his change.

'Yeah,' she replied, 'It used to be busy in here, but the Moose's Head changed its image and started to go all trendy so all the nerds go there now.'

Danny chuckled, slightly. *This girl is nice,* he thought. He had had no intention whatsoever of looking for a girl at that particular moment in time but Kate was pleasant to talk to and had a sense of humour, as well as good looks. And Danny, being ever-the-optimist: 'I suppose you get bored, then?' Now he was interested and by the look in her eye, so was she.

'It's not too bad. It's just when the bosses come in I have to look busy.'

'You know, I've never understood that.' Danny threw a saddle over his high horse. 'How can you 'look busy?' You either are or you aren't. If I was your boss I wouldn't expect you to faff about doing something when there's nothing to do. Once you've cleaned everywhere and the customers are happy, they're getting served, then what's the problem? It wouldn't bother me if you were stood around.' He seemed to be toying with the roles in his head in order to establish a power system before they'd even gone out together. 'So long as the customers got what they wanted.'

She smiled and her thoughts wandered: *Why couldn't you be my boss?* But Danny was in another type of employer/employee relationship. He had visions of "employing" her for sex and he would be in control. Danny was not so much a control freak, as they say, but he had to have the upper hand. He had to remain in control but still be seen to give a girl a free reign. *Formula for success*, he thought, girls *like to be dominated.*

They got chatting and time got the better of them. The man and woman had left and the old guy in the corner looked as though he wasn't going to make it through his half, let alone a pint. It was five to two, time to go.

'It's been good talking to you, Kate. It's nice to have an intelligent conversation; all I get in the factory is: "Did you get pissed last night? Did you pull?"'

'I've enjoyed it,' was Kate's reply.

'Well ......maybe......no.'

'What?' Kate demanded.

'I was just wondering. I like talking to you and I love listening to what you've got to say (*underlying compliments – good technique – won't go unnoticed*), so do you fancy going out for a drink one night somewhere? You know, just for a drink and a chat?'

'Yeah that'd be great.'

And that's all there was to it. *If only everything in life was that straightforward,* thought Danny, *it would be a pleasure to exist.*

Steve and Lisa were in the amusement arcades. 'There you go, Lisa. Bingo!'

'Shut up, will you! How old do you think I am?'

Steve smiled. 'I like older women,' he joked.

'You cheeky git!' Come here!' Lisa chased him towards the exit.

'Wait!' she cried. 'See if you can win a teddy for me.' She pointed to the glass case with the small crane in that moves backwards then left and right and tries to pick up teddy bears or wallets with £20 notes sticking out of them.

'No chance! That thing will never pick one of those teddies up. It's got a grip like a nancy boy.' He was persistent though, and after putting in about £4.80, he managed to knock a teddy bear towards the hole. 'One more should do it.' And it did.

The crane picked up the teddy bear several times, but each time it could not hold it – it must have been too tired – or when it finally did grip the bear it would recoil its cable in and pull the crane to the top of the case. Banging into this – a deliberate strategic manoeuvre on the manufacturers behalf – it would almost definitely drop its cargo.

Steve's last attempt, though, knocked the teddy bear into the hole. He could have bought one of those bears for less than the fiver he put in for it but he'd had fun getting it. And Lisa loved it. More so that he had won it. Like Sir Galahad fighting for Maid Marianne and winning a trophy for her. He had fought for his life to acquire the coveted chalice or sword or necklace for her. Either way, he was a hero in her book.

Danny finished work about four o'clock and headed straight round to Steve's flat. He called him on the mobile, too, on his way. It was still off. When he arrived there was no answer, much to his dismay. 'Where can he possibly be?' Danny asked himself. He stared at the front door and began to daydream. He envisaged a scene where Steve had killed Lisa and was refusing to answer the door. He was sitting in an armchair asleep whilst Lisa's body lay motionless on the floor. *When I eventually get in there*, he thought to himself, *over the next few days, I'll see if he's ordered a chest freezer. Or perhaps he's in there now cutting the body up into tiny pieces or soaking it in the bath in acid?*

All these suggestions raced through his mind to reassure him of his sanity until suddenly he felt cheated. Steve was stealing his thunder.

63

He no longer felt guilty for what he had done. These moods didn't normally last and he'd go back to feeling guilty again later.

Whilst he experienced these feelings, however, the sudden urge to kill again struck him. Surely it had to be a mistake. No. His blood began to rise in temperature and surge through his veins. He looked down at his forearms and they looked like an A to Z, vascular and taut, each vein represented an A or a B road. There was even a huge thick one that curled from his thumb and ran up towards the bend in his arm. This was the motorway. He wondered whether the string of veins could represent journeys that he would travel in his future. Like lines on a hand they could denote movements in his life. 'Where does that main road lead to?' *Is it the M1 or is it the M6? Would there be people out there who could read forearms? People who could explain what each vein signified?*

Looking up at the door again he thought of breaking it down. He was convincing himself that Steve was hiding inside, covering up as best he could the corpse of his girlfriend Lisa.

'Break in!' a voice told him. 'Break in! Steve will understand. You can help him. He can help you.'

His blood raged through his veins now and it seemed to be rising to his head. His face flushed with redness and his anger and frustration grew. Something inside was aiming to restrain him but it was getting too powerful for him. He raised his hands to crash the door and suddenly....the lights went out. Blackness came and his body fell limply to the floor. It was too much for him, he'd fainted.

Steve and Lisa were in a restaurant about to dine.

'I can't be bothered going back tonight, can you?' asked Lisa.

'No,' came Steve's reply, happy that she was thinking that same way that he was.

'We'll leave the car where it is then. You fancy a bottle of wine?' She smiled.

'Why not?

They ordered a bottle of the house white from the menu. They had never heard of it before, but they thought that at £5.85 a bottle it couldn't be all bad, and the conversation moved on to Steve and his relationship with Danny. 'So, do you always go out with Danny then?'

'Yeah, most of the time.'

'Has he got a girlfriend?' Lisa was inquisitive.

'Well, not quite. He's never committed himself since he split up with his ex.'

'Aw! That's sweet.'

'He probably just hasn't met the right girl yet.'

'Or he's still in love with his ex? suggested Lisa. Steve pondered this for a second.

'No. I don't think he really cares,' he answered.

'Was he really in love with her?'

'I think so.'

'Yeah, it's difficult, isn't it? Relationships can have profound effects on you for years. Some people never get over them. A friend of mine left a guy and he couldn't handle it; threatened to kill himself if she didn't come back to him.'

'What happened?' Steve was intrigued.

'He hung himself,' Lisa remarked and Steve nearly spat his wine out.

'Seriously?' he asked.

'Yeah, his mother came back one afternoon and found him. I think he was a bit unstable to begin with, but…ooh…I shudder to think.'

The thought of this young man hanging himself, and his poor distraught mother being the first one to find him, sent a shiver up his spine. He contemplated the whole scenario for about a minute before stating: 'No, not Danny. He's too strong. He doesn't care about women that much. He's only interested in whether they've got a decent pair of boobs.'

'Melon, sir?' Steve was startled by the waiter. 'Madam…melon?' He had arrived with their starters.

As Danny came to, he struggled to take in his surroundings. As he fell, he had cracked his head and caused a small lump to appear at the top, near the back. He was feeling groggy and imagined at first that he was nursing a hangover. He struggled to his feet and made his way into the street. Images slowly filtered back into his mind until it all came back to him. He decided not to bother with Steve for this evening and instead got back inside the transit van that he had borrowed from work.

As he drove, his head spun and he struggled to restrain the van. It meandered all over the road and the other drivers were forced to keep their distance and showed their contempt with heir horns. Danny felt pissed, and he had all the symptoms. If he was to be stopped by the police they would breathalyse him. They may not find anything although he would have difficulty explaining the drink on at lunchtime. He felt, however, that they could easily settle for dangerous driving or at least driving with undue care and attention.

Undue care and attention, he thought, *I don't care and I can't concentrate anymore.*

It was hurting his head to think. He felt as if a constant ringtone was playing inside it and it seemed to take all his energy to remain focused on his driving.

Pulling up outside his flat, he left the van with one wheel on the kerb and three off. He wasn't sure if he he'd even locked it but he didn't care. Bursting through the front door he fell into the bathroom and not a moment too soon, as his throat opened to its full extent and he vomited freely.

Feeling slightly better, he washed his face, took two tablets of ibuprofen from the kitchen and collapsed in the bedroom, face down on the bed.

'Here's to us,' said Steve, raising his glass.

'Cheers, hun,' toasted Lisa. They were both a little tipsy now and feeling rather close. Since they had met they could talk about anything. Lisa's parents were into property so this often came up in the conversation. Even though neither of them was assuming anything from the other, they discussed various living arrangements and possibilities for the future. They hadn't been together long but they both knew when it was right and neither felt threatened by the other.

After their meal they made their way towards the promenade again and enquired about Bed and Breakfasts to stay in. Luckily, it didn't take long to find one even though it was peak season. There were big events in Liverpool and Southport that weekend and they'd drawn on some of the usual Blackpool crowds.

Everything was sorted. They had checked in and gone back to the car for their luggage – two bags of emergency changes of clothes in case they stayed for the evening. They literally dropped their bags and dashed back towards the bars to avoid wasting "valuable drinking time," as Steve suggested. And what a fantastic night it was. They visited about eight bars where they danced, chatted to locals, watched two girls fighting over a spilt drink (on the girls dress though!) and then by half ten they were back in the amusement arcades.

Feeling giddy and quite drunk they giggled for about ten minutes solid. Throughout this period Steve had tried, desperately, to put a ten-pence coin in the machine with the moving shelves that pushes coins out for collection. Every time he tried, the fits of laughter took control and he couldn't do that single task. Moreover, looking at Lisa's face as she was bent double with uncontrollable giggling discarded any little chance whatsoever that Steve may have had for seriousness.

When they eventually regained control of their senses they suddenly did turn serious on each other. Lisa looked into his eyes and she liked what she saw reflected back. The chemistry was blooming and her feelings were requited. They kissed heavily and passionately for a while before Steve suggested, 'Shall we go back?' Lisa nodded.

They strolled back to their B&B stopping every few minutes to merge their lips together intimately. Once they got back to the B&B, they wasted little time. They kissed again in the privacy of their room – the door locked – and slowly started to undress each other. Both felt nervous as if it was their first time ever they had come into contact so closely with someone of the opposite sex. Steve kissed her neck rapidly and with intensity. His warm breath sent a shiver down her spine and the goose bumps began to rise along the full length of her arms. Her whole body trembled in sensitivity and as he ran his fingers through her hair, it drove her wild. She was still nervous and shy though and proceeded to allow Steve to take complete control. He did this, perfectly in her eyes.

Steve laid her on the bed and kissed her whole body as if he savoured every inch. It was all good. It was all part of her and he loved it. They made love that evening on and off for hours before falling into a sate of heavenly bliss. Both bodies lay still, their hearts still beating powerfully, sleeping contently like babies. Neither had a care in the world.

Danny woke after two hours and he was feeling much better. The ibuprofen had kicked in and he was thinking straight again. He needed a shot of whisky though, he felt. *A large one should do it*. That was the bonus of drinking at home – the measures were always good. He contemplated ringing Kate but thought that it might be a little too soon. Even though a lot had happened to him and talking to Kate seemed an age ago, it was only earlier on that day. He decided he would call her tomorrow.

Danny had forgotten all about Steve. He didn't think for one minute that he would be dining with some young lady up in Blackpool. His mind kept reverting back to the corpse in the freezer.

What? he thought. *What is it? Why do you keep thinking about her? She's gone, she's dead.* And then it came to him. 'I'll have to cut her up,' he mumbled, as if saying his thoughts out loud would somehow mitigate the severity of them and make them normal and easy to deal with.

In the cupboard under the stairs he found a Stanley knife. 'That's no good, you need a saw.' Perhaps telling himself what to do and how to do it could relieve him from the onus and guilt of performing his next task. 'Here we are!' He found the saw and took it to the bathroom. He looked around at the familiar surroundings and somehow they took on a whole new façade. 'This is my operating theatre,' he said, distancing himself from the horrendous job that lay ahead.

Racing back to the kitchen, he threw open the lid of the chest freezer. He was excited about what he was about to do and how he was to dispose of the body. He raked through the ice cubes and threw the bags of frozen food from the right hand side to the left. Delving deep he felt the body. This was no good, he would never lift it. He would have to empty it a bit.

'Inspiration!' he bawled, and shot over to the stereo in the living room. It was Friday night and his neighbours, being young and single, would probably be out so he decided to pump out the sound. Where was his mixed classical album that he had recorded for himself? He found it and threw it in the CD carelessly. Seconds after he pressed PLAY, Wagner's Ride of the Valkyries began to boom out of the speakers. He opened a bin bag and tossed in as many frozen foods packets and ice cubes as he could. 'This should be enough.'

Reaching deep into the freezer he could feel the shoulders of his victim. He went under the arms and lifted as hard as he could. It was a good job that he was strong as the body nearly pulled him back in. Fortunately, the power of Wagner effected greater strength in him and he heaved the body out of the freezer slightly. The ice cubes around it began to sink back into the bottom, falling below the body. He heaved again and more ice cubes showered down the body like a waterfall. Taking a deep breath, he heaved for the final time and the body pulled free of the freezer. It was heavy though and got the better of him.

He tumbled backwards and what was once Michelle, fell on top of him, headless and stiff. Her breasts were in his face but they no longer

68

felt warm and soft. They were solid and the cold bit into his nose. He threw the dead weight off himself, jumped to his feet and spat. There was a horrible taste in his mouth. Recovering temporarily, he dragged her to the bathroom and hauled her up half over the bath. She was solid so he pushed her fully into the bath and viciously ripped away her outer layers of sellotape and bin liners like an excited kid at Christmas. The music could still be heard throughout the flat and, probably, next door too.

Once all the wrappings were removed, Danny raised the right leg as much as he could – it was solid. He picked up the saw and positioned it just above the knee. Dragging the saw backwards, he began to create a groove. The flesh split and the saw began to rip as he sustained a rhythmic cutting action. The Ride of the Valkyries came to an end and Danny paused, waiting for the next track. He had listened to this CD a thousand times and loved it. It was his own recording, his own choice of mix and he was proud.

The opening bars of Beethoven's Moonlight Sonata created a chill to the atmosphere. Danny focused on the leg deeply and continued sawing. His concentration was intense. Beads of sweat began to form on his forehead and one trickled onto his nose. He ignored it and drove the blade of the saw in deeper. This was hard work. It took him forty minutes to finish sawing the body into the number of parts he wanted.

He picked up the hand towel and dried the sweat from his face. He needed a drink!

A shot of whisky and a two-minute rest and Danny was ready to continue with his work. He counted the parts– there were seven. There should have been eight, he thought, but then remembered that the head was still in the freezer in the 'Bag for Life'.

Danny had cut the body up in the same manner that a Samurai warrior would with a sword– the classic eight cuts, clearly utilised from his martial arts days. Counting the parts again he went through the identity of each segment to ensure nothing was missing. Left lower leg, right lower leg. Left thigh, right thigh. Left arm, right arm. Torso. *Excellent*! There would be a bin bag for each.

He tied each one and put any fragments of bone or flesh left over in with the last one. He then rinsed the bath out and, after putting the bags carefully back into the freezer, sat down for a well-earned rest. He refilled his whisky glass and raised it in front of him.

'At last,' he said. 'To the disposal of Michelle and my fantastic idea.'

7

Danny rose Saturday morning just after six, feeling nervous and excited. He decided he just couldn't stay in bed any longer so he visited the local newsagents for the early-morning papers. *About 6 should do it.*

Back at the flat he scrunched up each individual sheet from all six newspapers. He untied the bin bags containing the sawn-up segments of body and filled them with newspapers before tying them again, and putting them back in the freezer when he finished. He still had hours to kill.

After a slow breakfast and a couple of hours in front of the TV, Danny thought he would call his friend Dave.

'Is it still on today, Dave?' he inquired after all the pleasantries were over.

'If you don't mind mate, can you get over here for eleven?'

Fantastic! thought Danny. The earlier the better for him and 10.40, precisely, saw him loading the van up with the bags from the freezer. He pushed them up the top and placed a blanket over them so as to make the van seem empty of anything important.

At Dave's house they loaded the bags of slips in together and Dave never seemed to notice if there was anything in the van beforehand. Danny's talking throughout had distracted him. Dave had asked Danny to bring an empty van as they were charged with weight at the incinerator.

'Drive onto the scales,' ordered the security guard at the gate. As they did so Danny could hear the back door of the van clicking. The guy was trying to open it.

Banging on the side of the van with his hand he shouted, 'Can you open the back, please squire?'

'Squire?' He hadn't been called that for a few years. Danny stepped out of the van.

'Of course.' His heart was in his mouth. *This could be it now. It might all be over in a second or two. If he finds that body...*

Once unlocked, the security guy reached up to the handle in what seemed like slow motion. He pulled, hesitantly, on the door… It opened. Danny scrunched up his eyes and braced himself as if he was about to receive an electric shock, he couldn't watch. The uniformed figure moved into the inside of the van and his head turned from left to right as he scanned the contents. 'Okay,' he said, 'drive on.'

Phew! If that wasn't close he didn't know what would be.

They drove further on to where there were several skips. Danny sprang out of the van and opened the back doors wide. Dave began to take out the slips from the back whilst Danny sneaked the bags of flesh out from the front. They were just behind the seats. He tried to drop them into the skip slowly so as not to burst the bags. Unfortunately, the last one he threw down burst open and a foot stuck out. 'Shit!' he mumbled to himself. 'Shit! Shit!'

He raced round to the back of the van and grabbed hold of two bags then threw them down over his bag, but the foot could still be seen. 'Oh fuck!' Moving even faster he tossed as many bin bags as he could on top of this one bag, until they covered the foot. Another close one but luck still appeared to be with him.

The sense of urgency on Danny's face, along with his erratic behaviour with the bags, caused suspicion to rise in Dave. 'What's up with you? You in a rush?' he asked.

'Oh, I just want to get back, that's all.' Danny was good at acting nonchalant when it called.

As they reversed to leave the incinerator, Dave spotted something peculiar. 'Aye aye!' he said, picking up the 'Bag for Life' that still held the head in. Danny had missed it. 'What's this?'

The instant he went to open it Danny snatched it from his hands. 'Shit, yes. That's got stale food in it. I'll throw it in with your bags.'

'It's heavy isn't it?' inquired Dave.

'Yeah!' replied Danny with a dismissive laugh, 'a few chicken bones and that. Dave seemed to buy this.

Chucking the bagged head into the skip was a pleasure, although he would have liked to have buried it with the other bags. Too late!

Danny took a sudden interest in the whole burning process when he returned to the van. 'When does that skip go in?' he asked.

'That'll go soon. It's full.'

'Shall we wait for it then?'

'What for?' Dave didn't wait for an answer, but provided it himself. 'Mind you, I would like to know that those slips have been destroyed. Wouldn't do any harm then, I suppose.'

'I was just wondering what happened to them.'

'They burn,' Dave added, sarcastically.

They only had to wait for about 5 minutes before the skip was lifted by a crane. Inside, there were windows where you could see the fires in motion, but there was not much to see. *One thousand degrees centigrade and 24-hour burning. Brilliant! Anything would burn at that temperature. And as they keep it burning 24/7 it could be months before they allow it to burn down and cool off. Then there won't be a single trace of her left.*

They were informed that their skip had gone in as there were not many people around. It was all over, he hoped and now he needed a well-earned drink. He was nervous, but something within his body generated excitement and he thought about killing again. Would he get away with it next time? Has, indeed, he even gotten away with it this time? Danny didn't see himself as a killer, but he felt a huge surge of adrenalin buzz through his veins. As they drove off he was grinning to himself.

Steve was also grinning to himself that morning, along with Lisa. They had bonded intimately and become extremely close to each other. They knew how they felt; everything seemed perfect. They were both lying in bed together, silent. Steve turned to face her and her big blue eyes lit up. He smiled, she smiled. They kissed. 'What do you want to do today, babe?' he asked.

'I don't know. Anything.'

'How about....' he paused, '...a big breakfast, then a walk along the prom. Then we can go up in the tower?'

'Sounds good.' At this precise moment, anything would have been good for her so long as she spent her time with Steve.

After breakfast they found their walk refreshing. Both Lisa and Steve breathed deeply as the fresh, sea air was coming to an end and they had to get all they could. Steve was smiling. 'This is nice, just relaxing....away from work. No cares.' Lisa was in total agreement. 'Yeah, this is what life's about. Not running around in an office all day and then rushing home to see the soaps and sort out the bills.'

'I know. Modern life is too stressful'.

Regurgitation was the key here. Danny's theories on life had regularly been passed on to Steve and he lapped them up like a hungry cat as he adopted them for himself. He listened, he agreed, and then he absorbed that particular theory into his mind. It was now part of his own thinking, or so he thought.

Leaping on the opportunity for one such theory, Steve displayed his (Danny's) views on the rat race. 'You see, what they should do- I mean these big offices with hundreds of staff- they should all have their own gyms. An office is like a hamster's cage. It is the worker's home for the day. They work within the confines of an enclosed space and there's no room for individuality. No freedom of speech, no isolation – apart from the toilets.

'You spend eight hours a day in an office and it stresses you out, just like a hamster cooped up in a cage. But the hamster…well…it gets a wheel to relieve the tension. A physical outlet. Office workers…they get the door of the cage opened every night. Why? Because they're intelligent. That is, they know how to come back the next day and they feel obliged. Brainwashed by an oppressive society.

'There should be a treadmill smack bang in the middle of the office floor. Then, when workers need to stretch their legs, or relieve the boredom, they can run on it- like the hamster on its wheel- anytime they want. That way you could keep them there for longer. Perhaps every day. Ignorance is bliss! If they don't know there's an outside, how can they miss it? Think of the productivity.' He was touching on sarcasm now.

'So let me get this straight,' said Lisa. If they give the office workers a treadmill they won't have to let them out at night. Is that good?'

'No of course not,' Steve reassured. 'But that's what society's like. We're all far more oppressed than we think. "Free country," I hear people say. What's free? We work for a living. We pay tax and NI for hospitals, schools and libraries. We pay council tax to have our streets clean and bins emptied. We pay for our water, food, place to live. We're taxed on our wages then we go and pay more tax on goods we buy. We are constantly told what to do- "Slow down!" "Drive at 30," "No entry"- then the government rips us off.

'We pay car tax to use a car on the road. We pay extra to use tunnels and bridges that have paid for themselves 50 times over- they're only roads after all. Road tax should cover them. Then there are toll roads, congestion charges and even pay and display. You pay to put your car on the road but if you don't keep it moving, if you want to stop it, you're charged. And the pay and display machines don't give change – what a con!

'How many cars in how many streets in how many towns do people overpay? If it's £1.40 and they haven't got change, they pay £2. In 60 spaces in one street, cars coming and going all day, hundreds of streets in one city, thousands upon thousands of streets in the UK... Billions of pounds a year in money that's not even theirs. That's on top of the profit, all tax free.'

He hit a crescendo and his blood was surging through his veins, enraging him. Lisa sensed this and immediately soothed him. 'Ssh...I agree with you baby. But this is neither the time nor the place. Relax. Don't worry about it. There's nothing you can do. We're supposed to be enjoying ourselves remember?' He nodded.

'You're right. I'm sorry. Let's go up the tower.' Steve reached for her hand. It was small and soft to hold. She clasped tightly. He couldn't resist kissing her and she responded affectionately. They embraced then meandered off towards the tower.

Kate's phone was vibrating on top of the coffee table in her living room and Michael Jackson's Don't Stop 'Til You Get Enough was booming out of its speaker. She had been finishing her hair in the bathroom. It was just coming up to five o'clock in the evening. She ran in and answered the call, 'Hello'. It was Danny. She'd hoped he would call as she had nothing arranged for the weekend. He was very pleasant on the phone. 'Hiya, Kate. It's Danny. How are you?'

'Okay, thanks. I'm not working tonight as I've been doing days this week.' She thought she would slip that important point in.

'Well, that's a stroke of luck. You got anything planned for tonight?'

'Er, no not yet. I mean.... I'm waiting for a friend to call me back.' She didn't want to come across in a way that made her seem unpopular or lacking in invitations.

'Oh, right. Well, I was just gonna see if you fancied a drink. Not a problem. Another time, maybe?'

'Oh, no. I've not made any plans yet so if you want to do something then great.'

'Ok, I'll meet you in Ronnie's in town at about half eight.' He could be quite abrupt at times and assuming, but it worked for him. She had hardly had time to agree before the line went dead.

Danny was a master at understanding the psychology behind relationships. He knew exactly how to keep the upper hand. He had a way of making a girl feel special but also a method for sustaining interest. Kate now felt obliged to go to Ronnie's Bar, even if it was just to explain her situation. She wouldn't though. She wanted to go there to see Danny, not play games. He had intrigued her enough not to be able to turn down his offer.

8.30 came and Kate had just made it. Unfortunately, she never went in a pub on her own so she had to hang around outside. It also meant that she would miss out on the pre-Danny entertainment: Johnny Bravo swishing around the bar as if he was wearing ice skates.

It was 8.45 before Danny turned up and Kate had spent 15 minutes stood outside on her own and had to persevere with irritating drunks and just general nutters pestering her.

'Hiya,' he said without apologising. They walked in and up to the bar. Danny turned to Kate. 'What do you want to drink?'

'Vodka and tonic' came her reply. Pablo was working on the bar again. He sidled over to Danny to serve him. 'Yes sir?'

'Pint of lager, please.'

'And for the beautiful lady?'

'That is for her. Only joking. A vodka and tonic, please.' Pablo spun round to the fridge, like Torvill turning to Dean, and produced a bottle of tonic water. Drawing the bottle opener from his back pocket in true Clint Eastwood-style, he flicked the top off it with great dexterity of his wrist. The top bounced across the bar and he spun once again to face the vodka optic.

'I only come here for the entertainment,' Danny remarked sarcastically. Kate laughed. There was a great affinity between them already. Danny wondered if he could become more like Steve, rather than the opposite way, and settle for one woman for a while.

Until Steve had met Lisa, he emulated Danny and admired him completely. He still did but now he was torn between the two lifestyles. He had to locate his position in society. He had wanted to be just like Danny but the thought of settling down and loving the one woman was becoming more and more attractive.

Danny was reminiscing back to the days with Jessica and their house they had bought together. It angered him and brought home the reality of exactly how it was going to be with Kate– *as it was with them all*. He would have his way, do what he wanted and then move on if necessary. His barriers raised themselves up and he glared at Kate like she was a piece of meat.

'Are you okay?' she enquired, wondering why the sudden change in him.

'Yeah, fine. Just thought of something that's all.'

'What?'

'Nothing! It doesn't matter.'

'Four-pounds-eighty, please sir' interrupted Pablo, eyeing Danny intently.

Danny and Kate got on really well after Danny's brief bout of concern. They revelled in mocking Pablo for his cartoon-like antics and this brought them closer to each other. Danny had dropped his guard. He felt there was no point being horrible, he just wouldn't get emotionally attached to her.

As he often theorised to Steve: 'Just a slag for a shag,' so it was the case here. The only problem was that they never slept together at the end of the night. They stood on the road edge of Bagel Street at 2.31am. Kate looked into his eyes and said, 'I've had a fantastic night, Danny. Thanks.'

'So have I.' He looked into her eyes. Somehow, it didn't matter that he was going home alone. He didn't mind. There would be other times. Normally he wouldn't think that way. There was never a thought for "other times." If they occurred then it was a bonus. And now, he actually *wanted* to see her again. 'Call me,' she said, stepping into a taxi.

'I will,' he replied and he meant it.

They had had a great evening. From Ronnie's Bar they had moved further in to town and visited several bars. Danny was even dancing at one point which was unusual of him when he was on a date. He had let himself go completely and was enjoying every minute of it. He hadn't had such a good time with a girl since Jessica, his ex. He enjoyed dating girls, and sleeping with them, but he hadn't got affectionately intimate with a girl for a long time. The most intimate he got was sex, but after that the connection broke. He rarely hung around for chats.

The thought of the night with Kate released pleasurable hormones but contrary to this, he felt an urge. Should he be experiencing pleasure, other than sexual, where women were concerned, he wondered. He decided to walk home and think about it. It would only take him an hour and he could clear his head.

Forty-five minutes later though, his head wasn't clear, it was worse. Images of Kate dancing and laughing flashed through his mind. They were nice images but he fought against them.

'She's just a bird,' he muttered to himself. 'A slag, just like the rest of them.' *But why?* She hadn't put one foot wrong that night, and he knew it.

When he finally reached his flat his feet were aching and he was exhausted. It was times like this that he was grateful for his ground-floor flat, as the prospect of facing any stairs was, at this moment considerable to climbing up the north face of the Eiger with no ropes.

The digital clock in his bedroom displayed 04:09 as he collapsed on the bed. For some reason it had taken him much longer to walk home than he had anticipated. Without even enough energy to kick off his shoes, let alone brush his teeth, he snapped, almost instantly, into a deep sleep.

Kate was only just getting to bed, too. She got home around 3am and decided to watch TV with a cup of tea. She was far too excited to go to bed. Her thoughts were, primarily, of Danny. She couldn't stop thinking about how nice the evening had been and how impeccable Danny had seemed. Her eyes saw good looks, great personality, charm, and good career prospects. He had it all. What more could a girl ask for, she wondered, unbeknown to her that there was a lot more to Danny.

Lying in bed at 4.09am, she switched off the light. Content as a baby she sank into a heavy slumber with Danny prominent in her mind. Her last thoughts were that things would turn out right. Everything was perfect!

II

Danny woke at 7.18am, his feet throbbing for release. They had swollen in his shoes and were now sore and sensitive to the touch. He hadn't the energy, or the inclination, to undo his shoelaces so he rolled on his back and pushed each shoe off with the other foot and flicked them onto the floor. Luckily enough he didn't appear to have a hangover, although he imagined it was possible that he was still drunk, and being a Sunday he could remain in bed for the duration of the day if necessary. He snuggled himself up to his duvet for comfort and slept on his right-hand side with his right arm beneath the pillow. There he would stay until at least midday.

The weeks rolled by and September came around quick. Danny had enrolled on an evening course at the local college. He was registered for GCSE French for two reasons. The first was his long-awaited desire to speak another language and he always fancied French over Spanish, Italian or German. Outside of this he didn't see the point in other languages as he had no intention of living in any other countries. He enjoyed travelling but was not prepared to go to any lengths to blend in with other cultures. France, however, he always had a soft spot for. It probably stemmed from his schooldays when he had a crush on his French teacher. Unfortunately, she left 3 months before he took his exam and he let his studying go downhill. His other subjects were fine, seeing him excel in English, Math and Electronics but he got a G for his French efforts.

The second reason was that Danny believed that enrolling on a course such as this would be an ideal opportunity to meet girls. He was confident that the proportion of girls to blokes would be good and decided it was worth the £150 course fee. Kate was still on the scene though, so he had to be careful. Danny was falling for Kate despite the vast amounts of barriers he tried to put in their way. He also did his best not to be faithful. It wasn't that he had to have lots of girlfriends; it was just easier to move from one to the other to avoid any emotional ties.

One form of barrier Danny used to distance himself from Kate was his aim to sleep with other women. He fought hard to categorise her into the same league as every girl he chatted to down the pub and it very often got the better of him as deep down Danny felt that Kate was special.

Ever since he had split up with Jessica he had used and abused (and now even killed) girls. He vowed never to be faithful again after catching Jessica in bed with his (ex) friend John. He was devastated that night:

Returning to the house unexpectedly after a weekend contract in Bulgaria – as a sideline to his job – was cancelled; Danny's aim was to creep up the stairs to surprise his beloved. However, he was confronted with an ugly scene.

Things couldn't have been better for him back then, or at least that's how he felt, and he was so in love with Jessica that he never even looked at other girls. He was even quite rude to them at times if he thought they were chatting him up. How different he thought then to his present thinking.

'Don't put all your eggs in the one basket,' he would now remark to Steve. And once, when he was drunk, he was even reported to have said, 'Don't put all your semen in the one basket of eggs,' which raised a laugh down the pub.

As Danny entered the house he held the latch to close the door without a sound. Slipping his shoes off quietly, he crept up the stairs, avoiding contact between the heel of his foot and each individual stair. He knew the ninth stair creaked near the middle so he surpassed this in one swift movement from the eighth to the tenth. The bedroom door was slightly ajar and emanating from the vicinity of the bed was the sound of heavy breathing. Jessica was fast asleep.

As Danny tiptoed into the bedroom he could feel the laminate wooden floor through his socks and he had to be careful not to slip. He never left the landing light on either as it had been a strong phobia of his since childhood.

…As a seven-year-old lying in bed, his mum used to leave it on for him but he hated it. He couldn't sleep so would normally sneak out and switch it off. One of the reasons was his love of the dark. He would lay for hours in the dark thinking about strange happenings and forming strange shapes from the bundles of clothes hunched up on his chest of drawers. Or the teddies at the bottom of his bed would come alive and they would all go on an adventure- a secret world that only he knew of and one that he could only enter in the dark.

There was another reason for his dislike of the lighting on the landing and this affected the phobia more than anything. He had overheard a joke at school and he took it literally, unaware of its frivolous intention. It was something to do with a plane crashing into a house, he always remembered, and it was because of the landing light having been left on. It was petty but for a strongly imaginative seven-year-old it meant a lot.

Very often his mother would wake him in the middle of the night as she visited the bathroom. Returning to her room she would leave the light on on the landing. Young Danny would sense this and usually wake up soon after, sweating profusely. Nervously, he would slip out of his bedroom, half-expecting to find a huge cockpit facing him on an angle on the landing. The pilot half-through the glass at the front with his arms flailed on the metal nose of the plane. He would flick the switch and once again return to the security of his world...

So the landing light on this particular night was securely off and Danny was about to endow his dream girlfriend with a little pleasure. It was his intention to raise the duvet, pop his head under, perform oral sex on Jessica until she awoke with amorous sensations and then they would make passionate love. "Sleepy sex" was always so much better she used to remark, and he couldn't agree more. Very often, ensuing from an erotic dream, one of the two would awaken the other with sensitive caressing of the erogenous zones. Tonight, however, was different.

In the darkness, Danny's hands slid under the duvet to locate Jessica's legs. Confused, he stretched the span from one to the next. They were more than three feet apart and one was thick and hairy whereas the other was its usual slender, smooth, shapely self. The reality of the situation hit him immediately like a jagged blade in the stomach turning on its way in. Danny's body rattled in mixed emotions. His first reaction was sickness and a twisted feeling deep in his gut. The second was pure unadulterated rage.

Whipping the duvet off with one swift heave and turn of the wrists, and banging the bedroom light on with the bottom of his fist, Danny's bellowing voice startled them both and they snapped into a state of wide-awakeness.

'What the fuck is going on?' he yelled but didn't stop to listen to reason, or any – what he felt would be paltry- excuses and commenced beating John senseless about the head with his fists.

Cries from Jessica: 'Danny, please...wait...you don't understand...We haven't done anything...Just talk to me for a second...Danny, please...Danny ...Listen...Danny....No, please ...You'll kill him,' were to no avail. Her one and only physical attempt to stop him resulted in her receiving the back of Danny's left elbow to her chin sending her flying across the bed and onto the floor.

Danny continued beating John about the head and body. The vicious assault had moved off the bed and onto the floor. John was curled up in the corner by a wardrobe. He flailed his arms and legs in retaliation but it was futile. His level of anger was nowhere near that of Danny's and sheer testosterone would control this battle.

John was out cold when Danny finished his outburst with several stamps directly onto his face, crunching his head into the cherry-coloured surface beneath. Jessica looked on in horror, screaming throughout. She was far too afraid to attempt to stop him as she could see the madness in his eyes. These very eyes that had burned into *him* now turned on *her*. She knew she should have to run but she couldn't. She was mesmerised by his stare.

He flew at her like a wolf pouncing on a sheep and his hands gripped her throat.

'Fucking slag!' he screamed. 'Fucking slag!' He hit her head into the wall and she sank to the floor, dazed. Her hands guided themselves to the affected area and her arms shielded any further attack. Danny glared at her for an instant and then lashed out again, his knuckles catching her on the left ear. He stood back and kicked her in the ribs twice and if the sound of the first crack wasn't enough to soften the hardest of bastards, the second should have. Danny was relentless, though. Jessica fell to her left side, writhing in agony and screaming for mercy. He stamped his foot down heavily on her lower leg causing a clean break and stormed off down the stairs as she slipped into unconsciousness. Both Jessica and John were almost dead from shock.

Danny's mind raced with thoughts of Jessica. He would have taken a knife from the kitchen and finished John if he'd known he was lying there still breathing – *cheeky bastard*. His focus was on Jessica, though, and it was only his powerful love for her that stopped him from running up the stairs and burying that knife deep within her cranium. If he did it, he thought, he would have to do himself too.

He ran to the kitchen, located the knife that played on his mind, and shot into the street. He hurled it over the neighbour's garden to avoid temptation and jumped into his car, a black BMW he had at the time.

Racing down the streets, his mind was flitting through several images like a film projector screen counting down before a film. He swerved all over the road and was totally oblivious to anybody else. As he approached Sexton Park he skidded into it and slammed on in a dark secluded part. He stared intently out of the windscreen. Composing himself and his thoughts he remained still for what seemed like hours but was actually seconds.

It all came flooding into his head in one great surge and he couldn't handle it. He burst into tears and his head sagged to rest on the steering wheel. For ten whole minutes he sobbed bitterly before feeling drowsy and rocking his head back to fall softly on the head rest. He fell into a shallow snooze.

Fortunately for Danny, neither Jessica nor John was keen on pressing charges. Apart from the thought that they were in the wrong and Danny was well within his rights, they were also frightened of repercussions. They were unsure how Danny would react to court proceedings and were not willing to find out in case he killed them the next time. How right they would be. Danny never feared consequences and 18 months of traipsing through court hearings would almost certainly have driven him over the edge.

Jessica had three broken ribs, a fractured jaw, severe concussion and a broken lower leg. John had to have steel pins inserted in his face to hold it together as they reformed it to its natural shape, as well as extreme bruising and one broken rib. His face would never look the same again – only similar. Despite these injuries however, they were both adamant to let sleeping dogs lie.

Since Jessica, Danny had never looked at a girl in the same way, yet here was Kate worming her way in, as he saw it, to his affections. *She's all right,* he thought to himself, *I'll just play along with it until I get bored. I'll enjoy it while it lasts.*

If Steve and Lisa thought their relationship couldn't get any better, they would have been wrong. As every day passed they grew closer and a week seemed such a long time. In conversation they would reflect on events the previous week, but would be astounded as to their close proximity in time.

'Was that last week?' Lisa asked one day, when discussing a film they had seen at the cinema. 'It feels like months ago.' And this is how it was. Things were moving so fast, it seemed, neither they nor time could keep up and Steve and Danny had seen very little of each other. They had been out only once in four weeks. Steve felt to blame so he walked on tenterhooks when the subject was raised. He didn't want to go out pulling girls anymore; he was happy with Lisa. He did miss it though, just the thrill of the chase. And probably even stronger than that he missed his relationship with Danny.

Danny, too, felt partly to blame. He had the impression that Steve was disappointed with him for his time with Kate. But Steve was happy for him and he couldn't see it. Part of Danny disliked himself for putting so much into one girl when there was a chance he would get hurt and the other part portrayed happiness and contentment.

The issue of going out was raised by Danny. He felt that as he was the instigator in such matters he would have to make more of an effort.

'Why don't we *all* go out?' suggested Steve, hesitantly. Danny looked at him quizzically, but then piped up. 'Yeah, all right!' They were standing on the factory floor and things seemed a little awkward so Steve explained: 'I've got something to tell you anyway. And I don't want to do it here.' He gestured to the surroundings. 'You know what I mean?'

8

'So what is it that you've got to tell me, then?' asked Danny, aiming his question at Steve. They were sat by the fire in The Anchor accompanied by Lisa and Kate.

'Well, it's not just something *I've* got to tell you. It's more something that *we've* got to tell you.' Steve put his arm around Lisa. 'We're engaged.'

Danny's eyes opened up to the widest that they could possibly go. He was somewhat taken aback. Kate congratulated them; Danny just stared until Kate, noticing this, nudged him with her elbow.

'Oh, congratulations,' said Danny, snapping out of his short trance. He kissed Lisa, and then shook Steve by the hand. The handshake was sustained for some time whilst Danny's piercing eyes burrowed into Steve although he was smiling. Steve felt slightly uncomfortable but couldn't put his finger on the reason why.

'What are you having?' said Danny, returning to normal and motioning to the bar.

After he purchased a round of drinks, several toasts were made to "Steve and Lisa." On the outside Danny appeared happy for the couple, whilst on the inside, things were far from normal. He was angry for the way Steve had betrayed him, but just as angry at himself for being in a similar situation with Kate. He ogled the contents of his half-empty lager bottle, as if searching for the answers to life in the dregs. His brain contemplated the whole scenario and he couldn't handle it. *I've got to get out of here*, he thought to himself.

He swung his legs round the stool to free himself then stood up from his stool. 'I'm just going the toilet,' he said. 'I don't feel too good.'

'Is everything ok?' asked Kate, caring as ever, which was another reason why he needed to get away. The whole business of having relationships with girls didn't fall into his plan. If he had the opportunity of mapping out his love life for the next 5 years, similar to a business plan, then settling down and being faithful would not be on the agenda. He liked short-term girlfriends. Often he would say to

Steve: 'You get the fun, the sex, the excitement and the novelty of it, but without the hassle – without the nagging. And if they cheat on you, it doesn't matter 'cos they mean nothing anyway.' Always on the defensive, Danny could remain in control. Now, this control was diminishing and he found himself yielding to the relationship.

Inside the toilet, he sat on the seat fully-dressed and commenced muttering to himself: 'What am I doing? I'm young, I'm single.' He pulled his mobile phone out from his pocket and scanned through the phone book: Alice, Andy, Barry, Baz, Ben......he scrolled faster before slowing down on the "Ds" – Dennis, Dominique, Dr James, Denzel.

He stopped, scrolled back. 'Dominique! Ring her, see what she's doing.'

Dominique was a girl he had pulled months previously and had slept with 3 or 4 times. She was good, though, and he'd enjoyed it. *Would she find it cheeky*, he thought, *if I rang out of the blue?* He had kept in touch with her, but not much.

'Hello, Dominique.'

'Hiya, Danny. How are you?'

Great! She'd kept his number and knew it was him. That was a good sign. 'Just wondering what you're up to,' he said, as coolly as he possibly could.

'Nothing! I was just gonna stay in tonight for a change. Where are you?'

'I'm in a pub. Just having a couple of beers with Steve.' He decided to go straight for the kill. 'You fancy meeting up later?'

'Yeah,' she replied, as keen as ever, 'could do.'

'It's Friday night, you can't stay in on your own. Let's see…it's 8 o'clock now… Can you be at mine for 9?'

'Yeah, don't see why not. I'll just get a quick shower then I'll walk round. It's not far.'

'All right, I'll see you in a bit then.' *Now, to explain to the others.*

Upon returning to the table by the fire, there were more drinks as Lisa had been to the bar. 'I'm gonna go, babe' said Danny to Kate.

'Why? What's up?' she asked before Steve cut in with: 'Everything all right, Danny?'

'Yeah, yeah. I'm just not well that's all. I need sleep.'

'Oh well,' said Steve. 'Let's all drink up, then.'

'No!' interjected Danny. 'There's no need for you to come. Don't ruin your night. I just need to rest and possibly sleep. I've got a migraine, I'll see you later.'

He kissed Kate and Lisa then shook Steve's hand. Steve felt that all was not right as Danny left rather abruptly. Kate, feeling like a gooseberry, looked on incredulous as Danny left The Anchor.

'Do you want me to come with you, babe?' she asked.

'No, honestly. I need to go to bed to sleep it off. See you tomorrow.'

They were all dumbfounded as to why Danny should leave so suddenly. Kate aimed her lack of understanding of the situation at Steve in the hope that he could shed a little light on it. 'Do you think I should go with him, to see if he's all right?'

Steve thought for a second before answering: 'No, I think he needs to be alone. I don't know why, but he just does. Maybe he's been overdoing it a bit lately. We'll call him in a couple of hours, see if he's okay.'

Kate, stressing now over intruding on the couple, said, 'I think I'd better be going as well.'

Lisa reassured her: 'No, you don't have to go. Stay out with us. You don't mind, do you Steve?'

'Of course not. You can't go home now. Stay out.'

'Well...I could stay out for a bit I suppose.'

'Brilliant! Right, what are we having? Same again?' They nodded.

As Steve approached the bar, the confusion over Danny distracted him. Why would he suddenly go for no apparent reason? Maybe he really was ill. The thought that Danny was off to see another girl never entered Steve's head. He knew what he was like but somehow thought that he had changed since meeting Kate. He had, of course, but Danny wasn't happy that something could take control of him and alter his whole outlook. Desperately, he had fought against it.

'I'll ring him later,' Steve muttered to himself.

8.15pm and Danny was fiddling with his key to the front door of his flat. Closing it behind him he sensed that Steve, Lisa and Kate would probably call on him. And, if not them, then maybe another girlfriend and he didn't want to be disturbed. Any friends, relatives, or people he wanted to see were told to ring the bell with two short presses, a pause, then two more. This way he could avoid the 'constant harassment', as he used to explain to Steve, of 'Jehovah's witnesses, charities, market research, and gas and electricity companies vying for custom, depending on who you used.' All this, he felt, he could do without, so he never opened the door to anyone who was not affiliated into the secret Bell Depressing Society. Tonight, however, he only wanted to see Dominique so he called her again. 'Hiya. You ok?'

'Yeah,' she replied. 'I've just got out of the shower.' Sensing he was about to cancel the date, she abruptly came to the point: 'What's up?'

'Nothing. I just wanted to say when you come, can you ring the bell *three* times, pause a second, then three more?'

'Why? Who are you trying to avoid!' Dominique was no idiot.

'Nobody. I've just changed it, that's all. I got caught out by the Jehovah's Witnesses the other day so I changed it.'

'Oh, all right then. See you in a bit. Bye.' The line went dead.

'Excellent,' he mumbled to himself. 'That's sorted that one out.'

Entering his living room he switched a lamp on. The curtains were already drawn as he had been expecting to be out late anyway. He made his way into the kitchen and looked in the fridge. Scanning its contents, he saw 12 cans of lager and three bottles of wine. He always kept a good stock in.

'Be prepared!' he used to advise Steve when teaching him the methods of dating women. They would often adopt the role of lecturer/student, as Steve admired Danny substantially and his "track record" spoke for itself.

'Alcohol in the fridge and condoms in the bedroom. The rest requires spontaneity.' As a result, Steve's fridge was also well-stocked with alcoholic beverages and his bedroom lucratively furnished with rubber protection.

Danny withdrew a can of lager at first but then changed his mind. *Might as well open the wine*, he thought.

Turning to the chest freezer he took out a bag of ice cubes and ripped it open. Instantly, his mind dug up old images of Michelle's body and suddenly he really did feel sick. The sickness, however, seemed to pass straight through him. It was as if the imaginary superbug that lay in his stomach, stabbing at him, suddenly vacated through one of his deep exhalations as he panicked and gasped for breath.

Seconds later he had returned to normal and his heart rate dropped to a low beat as though he had never even thought about a corpse in his kitchen, let alone possess one. He plopped two ice cubes into a glass and placed the opened bag back on top of a packet of petits pois.

He gave himself a large measure of white wine and returned to the living room where he settled himself into his favourite armchair in front of the TV. *Fantastic!* Open All Hours was on. That would kill the time 'til 9 o'clock.

Buzz, buzz. Pause. Buzz, buzz. Danny looked at the digital clock on the wall: 8:55. He muttered to himself: 'I wonder if the stupid bitch has forgotten already.' He sat still, staring at the wall, his ear pointed in the direction of the front door. Buzz, buzz. Pause. Buzz, buzz. He wondered whether he should check to see who it was. Perhaps he could do that clever trick with the letterbox. *No. Ignore it.*

He imagined the scene on the step. *If she can't get in then she'll call. I can let her in then, but I'm not opening the door. Supposing it's some bird I don't want to see and Dominique comes walking up. She'll be here any minute. Sod's Law it'll go pear-shaped.*

Whoever it was they didn't hang about. Open All Hours finished and Danny got restless.

'Where is the stupid slag?' he said aloud, and returned to the kitchen for more wine.

Back in the armchair there was nothing but adverts on 'til he flicked to Channel 3. It was a drama about a serial killer and it had been on since 8 o'clock, so it was at the point of gathering interest. He watched as the officer in charge revealed the details of the last killing. It sustained Danny's interest well and he never noticed the clock moving swiftly on to 9:22. It was only when it hit 9:23 that his concentration broke for the doorbell buzzed three times, fell silent and then buzzed three more. He jumped up quickly but reluctantly. It was his intention to get Dominique into the flat as quickly as possible in case Kate should call round.

Dominique entered with an air of haste about her. 'Hiya, sorry I'm a bit late, but I wanted to look presentable.' And she did, Danny thought. Standing in the hallway with her beautiful golden hair trailing down past her shoulders, it was exceptionally straight, he felt. He eyed her up and down. She was tall and slender with oversized breasts for her frame. Her face was thin and featured and as his eyes met hers, it broke into a smile that lit up the hallway. Dominique was shy and softly spoken. She hadn't dated anyone since she'd met Danny six months ago, and waited on his beck and call. She thought he was great and was flattered to be invited out again, even if it was only to the flat to watch a DVD.

'You look gorgeous,' he remarked, Dominique reddened.

Danny poured a large glass of wine in the kitchen whilst Dominique sat on the couch in the living room.

'Make yourself at home,' he shouted in. 'Take your shoes off.' She did so and curled her legs up onto the couch. 'There you go,' he said, meandering towards her with two glasses of wine.

They sat and chatted for a while, but Danny's full attention was not on the conversation. He was distracted by the intricate details of the killer's methods being played out on the TV.

Dominique aimed at regaining his attention. 'I don't like all that stuff about bodies and killing. It's morbid!' Danny never answered her. Instead he stared intently at the TV. 'Ugh!' she concluded, but Danny was not disgusted or sick; he was fascinated.

It was 9.55 before Danny's full attention came to focus on Dominique. She had been a little impatient but felt that he was entitled to watch the end of the drama as he had probably been watching it since it started and she had been late.

From thereon, things went well between them. They watched a film on DVD and chatted freely before snuggling up together on the couch for the film's climax. After kissing and caressing each other for a long half hour, the next step was the bedroom. This was inevitable as they had already slept together in the past and the wine was now doing its job perfectly– it brought them closer and relaxed them entirely.

'Are you ready for bed?' asked Danny, presumptuous as ever. Dominique's reply was good: 'Yeah.'

He led her to the bedroom and then said: 'I won't be a minute. I just need some water,' before slipping to the front door and putting the latch lock on. He then proceeded to the living room to deactivate the buzzer so as not to be disturbed. The box that buzzed loudly when the doorbell was depressed contained four batteries. He pulled two out, put them on the table, then switched out the light and headed straight for the bedroom.

Dominique was already in bed in her underwear. Danny would soon have them off. He got undressed in the dark and climbed in to bed.

'Night then,' she said, turning her back on him. 'That's not even funny,' he retorted and pulled her back to face him. She laughed and turned around so that her nose was pressed against his, then she kissed him. Their passions soon returned to the levels that they had attained previously on the couch and it was not long before they were making love.

'I'm gonna go then,' said Kate. She'd been saying all night that she probably wouldn't stay out late and it was now 12.23am. 'Are you sure you'll be okay?' asked Steve.

'Yeah, fine.' She gestured towards to the black vehicle with an orange light above its windscreen. 'I'll get this taxi.' They said their goodbyes and it wasn't long before Kate was on her way to Danny's flat.

The taxi pulled up outside and Kate paid the driver. She would've gone home but felt that it was her duty to see that Danny was well. If he needed sleep, she could sleep with him and be there for him in the morning in case he needed anything. She buzzed the bell twice, paused, then twice again. She was one of those "in the know" when it came to the secrets surrounding Danny's doorbell and accessing his flat. She tried this combination several times, to no avail. She wondered, then, whether she should bang on the window but thought against it. *If he's in bed fast asleep and he can't hear the doorbell, then he must need it. He would he best left alone. But what if something's happened to him?* She felt she would have to be patient and return the next day. Although something was not right, she made no more of it and decided to head for home.

Inside, Danny and Dominique were in the throes of passion. She lay beneath him, writhing in pleasure, whilst he sustained a fast and hard, but regular, rhythm. He forced himself in deeper and deeper and she whimpered slightly as all her internal organs felt dislodged. She loved it, though.

The intensity in Danny's face grew and an uncontrollable urge rose within him. He slapped Dominique hard across the face. This startled her and she wasn't sure if she liked it or not. She had never associated pain with sexual pleasure, but she had faith in Danny due to his maturity and expertise, so she exhaled a sound of pleasure. He hit her again.....and again. It was getting a bit too much but she was nearing another orgasm so she took it. Their breathing became deeper and deeper and the sweat was streaming down Danny's face and back whilst the first few drops had just started to form on Dominique's face.

The intensity of the rhythm grew in line, with their heart rates and Danny's slaps turned to punches. Dominique couldn't handle it. She had never experienced anything like it. She screamed but this just excited him more and his fists rained down heavily on her head. She

91

was out cold and still he beat her as he tried to climax himself. It wasn't enough. He rolled off her and ran to the kitchen as fast as he could trying not to kill the moment. He took a large kitchen knife from the stainless steel magnetic strip on the wall and dashed back to the bedroom.

Climbing back over Dominique's pulsating body he entered her again and resumed the pelvic rhythm as before. His left hand made its way to her neck and his fingers curled around her windpipe loosely. His weight was all on this arm and he could feel himself approaching an orgasm as he held the handle of the kitchen knife high in his right hand. The excitement was too much and as he came close to climax, he drove the knife into the side of Dominique's body with frantic outbursts.

As he reached orgasm, the knife also entered her chest and pierced her lungs. Dominique's body shuddered and went into a spasm as her unconscious state reacted to the pain. Danny's erratic stabbing motion slowed as his heart began to decrease its wild pumping and the final two punctures of the blade were slow and went in with less ease due to the lack of force. Dominique spluttered her last breath. Danny licked his lips and could taste her blood. His face had been spattered in the process.

He ran his tongue along the back of the blade to clean it. Her blood tasted good, he thought. He then took his left hand from around her throat and curled his whole arm around her waist. Resting his head on her breasts with his right arm alongside her body he fell soundly into a deep sleep, content as a baby. The knife remained in his hand throughout, although his grip slackened.

Kate lay in her bed, concerned over Danny's welfare and unable to sleep. She had been looking forward to going out as two couples but the night had been ruined. She didn't blame Danny, though; she was merely worried. *Why didn't he answer the doorbell? Was he sound asleep? He may be lying there now, unable to move, calling out for help, and here I am, in bed. What shall I do? Perhaps Steve will know better.* All these thoughts shuffled around in her mind.

She picked up her mobile phone from down the side of the bed. It was normally switched off when she went to bed, but tonight she wouldn't dare for fear that Danny would need her. She scrolled through the address book at 'S' and when she arrived at "Steve" she paused a second. *Is it too late? No. This is important.* She pressed the green button to dial the number and held the phone to her ear. After a second or two, it rang….and rang…..and rang.

The phone at the side of the bed flashed with Kate's number but no sound was heard: it was on silent. Steve and Lisa were getting intimate and had muted their phones for peace. They left them on, however, to catch up with any missed calls.

After several rings, Kate hung up and tried Lisa's phone.

The second of the two phones lit up and flashed repeatedly whilst the name "Kate" displayed itself on the screen.

Again, no answer. *Well*, she thought, *I've tried.* She put her own phone on silent and rolled over in an attempt to sleep.

2.51 am. Steve was lying by the side of Lisa; they chatted.
Lisa inquired after Danny: 'D'ye think he'll be all right?'
    'Danny? Yeah! He'll be fine. He's big enough to look after himself.'
    'No. I mean, do you think he's ill or something?' Steve pondered this for a second.
    'We'll go and see him in the morning. What time do we need to set the alarm?'
    'No time! Turn your phone off and let's wake up naturally. No disturbances!' She brought her lips close to his as she spoke and their noses met. Steve smiled, kissed her and passed her phone to her as he switched his off. They were so engrossed with each other that neither of them seemed to notice the missed calls, or if they did, it didn't register.

4.57 am. Something awoke in Danny and alerted his brain. He peeled his head off Dominique's breasts which was stuck slightly with dried blood. The reality of the situation hit him like a sledgehammer and he didn't like it.
    'Shi-i-i-t!' he cried. 'Oh fuck!' The sight of the knife in his hand startled him and his grip released it as he drew back quickly. As it flew onto the floor he jumped up and surveyed the scene. Dominique lay on her back, motionless. There were red marks at the sides of her face and head that would've become bruises if there had been any life left in

her. Her left eye was cut from Danny's knuckle and there were.....one, two, three... Danny counted 14 knife wounds to the left side of her body although he imagined there may have been more, when the blood was washed off.

The blood had streamed out of the wounds and left a small pool at the side of the body that had slowly soaked into the sheets.

What a mess! Danny thought. His stomach imitated the action of turning itself inside out and he suddenly felt the urge to spew.

Almost colliding into every door frame, he made it to the bathroom successfully and hung his face over the bowl. He retched but nothing came up. The sight of the body, though, was not what gave him the urge to vomit. He felt sick at the prospect of killing someone and having to clean up the body and the murderous mess.

Strange thoughts crawled through his mind for a matter of minutes. *No*, he decided. *Just get on with it*. He was no longer alien to dead bodies by now but knew he was no expert on the other hand. This time he knew what to do and how to dispose of the body. Dominique was only light when she was alive and Danny could lift her up during sex, yet she seemed a lot heavier as a corpse. He hauled her body to the bathroom and laid it out in the bath. It was too early in the morning to be sawing as it could draw attention to him. Most of his neighbours would still be in bed.

Danny lay the body on its back with its head towards the plughole. *Now to find that knife*. It was standing upright out of the floor from when he had thrown it in shock. The blade had pierced the carpet and stuck itself into the wooden floorboards beneath. As Danny's hand grasped its handle, there were flashbacks occurring in his mind. He relived the killing of Dominique but instead of being repulsed by his actions, he revelled in the details of, what he saw as, his work. He smiled as the temporary dream came to an end and he returned to the bathroom.

The skin across Dominique's throat cut easily with such a sharp knife and the blood began to drain down the plughole of the bath. He rinsed the knife and made his way into the bedroom as Dominique's very life blood drained from her. What a mess the bed was.

Stripping the sheets off the bed was one thing, but the blood had soaked through to the mattress. The sheets went in the wash and the floor would need to be shampooed too before anybody could use the bedroom again. The mattress was left to dry. Later the mattress would be turned upside down until he came to a decision on what to do with it or how to clean it. He could always just destroy it and buy a new one.

5.59 am. Danny had spent over an hour cleaning. He felt it was worth it as he could not see a trace of blood anywhere and the bedroom looked no more like a murder scene than any bedroom. Emptying it of any necessary items and clothes, he locked the door and decided to use the second bedroom as his place of rest. He now needed sleep before the day that lay ahead of him. His work would continue when he rose.

Stretching out on the spare bed in the second bedroom, he couldn't get comfortable. The bed was not particularly uncomfortable; it was more that his mind was overactive. All the events of the day swooshed around in his head causing him great stress. Eventually, however, he drifted into a sleep and the swirling around altered its appearance into dreams. In his dream, all his concerns masqueraded themselves as threats or worries and they seemed to overcome him. He would not win his battle in the dream until he had dealt with the stress in real life. It was a very restless and disturbed sleep, yet it did suffice in regaining Danny's strength and eagerness. He was a fighter.

11.43am and he could now find the saw and get to work at reducing the corpse into disposable sections. He entered the bathroom with the saw in his hand and he caught his reflection in the mirror, purely by accident. His face was spattered with red and he had forgotten. The obsession to clean the floor, the bed, the bed sheet etc., had overridden the necessity for him to wash his face. Danny was initially disgusted when he saw his image looking back at him. Suddenly, though, morbid fascination came over him and he smiled. The dried blood around his face cracked and he scratched away at it eagerly until it was all off. He then filled the sink with warm water, cupped his hands underneath the water and lifted them to raise the water to his face. It felt good: warm and refreshing.

Danny performed the exact operation on Dominique as he did on Michelle– eight cuts. He also put each segment in a bin bag and squashed them all into the chest freezer. Later he would add to the bin bags scrunched up newspaper to pack them out, but this would not be until he was due for another visit to the incinerator.

Although not superstitious, Danny felt that it would be lucky to put the head into a "Bag for Life" carrier bag from the supermarket as the disposal of the corpse of Michelle had gone fairly smoothly and he wanted nothing to go wrong. It was now just after one o'clock and

Danny was exhausted. He would retire to bed for more sleep, but first he would turn his phone on to check for missed calls.

The grey/blue light of the mobile flashed on and the digital lettering stated "searching." After a second or two, the network was found and each number in the phone registered a name to it. Seconds later there were text messages in abundance. Several "this person called but left no message" ones appeared and the missed calls section of the phone revealed 18 missed calls. There were 11 texts unread that came through one after the other and the small spool shaped symbol at the top of the screen denoted a voicemail.

He called it out of curiosity and there were 14 voice messages to listen to. As tiredness got the better of him, he hung up. He had heard as much as he needed to and realised that Kate and Steve had rung and were worried. He sent a text to both that said:

> "Hi. I'm ok. Migraine gone but still need sleep.
> Ring u later, Dan"

And then, after turning his phone ringer to silent, he snapped asleep.

9

It was 4 o'clock in the afternoon before Danny woke up. He must have needed the sleep. The stress had worn him out, for when he attempted to open his eyes they stung and felt heavy. With the features of a new-born guinea pig, he raised both fists to his eyes and rubbed at his pupils using the top sections of two bent index fingers like an innocent child. Memories of the previous night came flooding back but he dismissed them as dreams. Only a few hours ago he had been sawing human flesh and bone into smaller segments and now he had to return to normal, whatever that was.

The early hours of the morning felt like such a long time ago that it couldn't possibly be real. It was, though, and as he got up to use the toilet he passed the locked bedroom door. It signified another world. A world that he had tried to shut away. He couldn't hide, however, for if the smell in the bathroom didn't evoke enough emotional memory then the sight of the several carcass-filled bin bags in the chest freezer would.

Once again he felt nauseous and insecure in how, if ever, he would dispose of this body. The first he may have been fortunate with but what if he didn't get that lucky again? He wondered why he hadn't just retired after the hassle of disposing of Michelle, why he should make more work for himself and create more chances for capture. What was happening to him? Why did he feel the urge to kill again?

In his eyes, he wasn't a killer. Something had given him a sense of power though. He saw women as a great gift to man yet he now held an underlying fear of them, and strong contempt had built itself into his psyche. Something inside him hated women; hated what they stood for.

How they use and abuse men. Flutter their eyelids when they want something (which usually cost money) or cry when they need attention. Men are used as women will sleep with somebody else behind your back. Danny's thoughts grew deeper.

I've done the right thing, he thought, and his mind replayed a memory of a conversation with Steve 18 months ago: 'I had a friend and he went out with this girl for two years. Paid for her everywhere and she had a good job. One day they were in the cinema, no word of a lie...' Danny rubbed the sweat from his forehead as the excitement of his lecture caused him to perspire. '...and he never had much money left. He'd paid her in and bought drinks and sweets for them both. She said she wanted another drink and he confessed to not having enough money left.

'After a moment or two she sighed and got up to get a drink. She only bought herself a drink and didn't even offer to get him one. He was parched, he said, so he asked for some. Do you know what she said?' Steve shook his head waiting for the answer. He was engrossed in the conversation. 'She said: "No, get your own" and he thought: "Right! Fuck you!" and never saw her again after that.

'The point I'm making is, he spent money on her for two years while she saved up for holidays with her friends and had a nice car– better than his! She probably had about ten grand in the bank while he had next to nothing and once she'd sponged him dry she'd move on to the next mug. He, on the other hand, was left skint so therefore had nothing to go into his next relationship with. He struggled to find a girl for months 'cos every time he met someone they expected to be taken out and he couldn't afford it so they dropped him like a sack of potatoes. It took him months and months to eventually meet a girl who didn't prostitute herself and bleed him dry. By which time he was on his guard and couldn't get close to her anyway. I'll always remember him saying "Never again, Danny, never again."

'You can't sum all women up like that,' Steve commented. At the end of the day we're all the same. If anybody cheats then that's individual. If anybody uses or abuses another then that's individual too. Men do it all the time. And if this guy did meet a decent girl in the end then doesn't that blow the theory out of the water?'

Danny wouldn't be caught on his back foot like a boxer in distress. He surged forward, continuing his pontificating. 'Yeah, mate, but it's very, very rare to find one. And even then they'll probably try and take you for *something*. Put it this way, all the women I've been with, and you've seen me with a few over the years, and I've never met ONE who didn't try and take me for a ride– some did, in fact. I learnt though, and now I use it to my advantage. They're all slags! And then you've got marriage– the ultimate security for a prostitute!' Danny fell silent. Steve was speechless but deep in thought. He respected Danny but knew it was pointless trying to change him.

'Yes,' voiced Danny, returning to the present, 'I've done the right thing.' He looked at his mobile and there were a few missed calls from "no number" and two from a girl called Elizabeth who was down on his phone as 'Liz Wanderer'.

Danny had met her several months ago and slept with her a dozen or so times. Every once in a while, usually two or three weeks, she would text or call and they would meet up, have sex, and say 'Keep in touch.' It had been nearly 3 months though and he had forgotten about her– until now. He contemplated the reasoning behind her calls as he had felt sure that the last time he saw her would be the actual last time he would see her ever. There were also 3 texts to be read.

Steve enquired after Danny and requested that he ring as soon as he was awake. Kate said pretty much the same, only she called him 'hun' and left a kiss (x). The third was off Liz Wanderer. It read:

> "Hi Dan, hope your well, soz not
> bn in touch, busy. Things ain't gr8,
> need help. Hope you don't mind.
> Missed u lots. Liz xxx"

Would she have got in touch if she wasn't in trouble? he mused. *What could be the problem?* He gave her the benefit of the doubt as he had a soft spot for her. Any girl that he slept with on a regular basis, he had a soft spot for. It countered his hard-hearted attitude towards women but he often yielded to these feelings. Danny could be deeply compassionate at times– rather a contrast from his lectures to Steve. Deep inside him he acknowledged that he loved women but he couldn't help feeling resentment and bitterness.

He decided he would call her shortly but then a frightening reality hit him. He suddenly thought she may be pregnant and all sense of compassion was gone. Unsure where the idea came from, he panicked and switched his phone off immediately.

'Soft bitch!' he stated. 'I'll smash her fuckin' head in if she is.'

Steve and Lisa were out for the day in Southport. They had great fun on the fairground rides and apart from a couple of texts in the morning to see how he was, they had completely forgotten about Danny. They sat in a café chatting. For the first time in the day they were starting to relax. When they arrived, Steve had an argument with a traffic warden over his blatant refusal to allow him to park in a space because it meant the car came slightly out of the bay and onto a yellow line.

'You can't park here, sir. I've told you. If you do, you'll get a ticket.' said the warden.

'But it's in the bay!' retorted Steve. 'I've paid into the stupid machine! You can't do me. I've got a ticket– pay and display.' He waved the ticket in his face.

'You're out of the bay and this is a single yellow line.'

'But I'm not even half out. Just give me half a ticket then!' he added sarcastically. He didn't like traffic wardens– Danny had turned him against them– and it showed whenever one was around.

'What about me getting my money back then? You have to do that at least.'

'I can't issue that here, Sir.' There was something affected about the way he said "sir", as if "sir" was a synonym for "a bit of dog turd on a shoe." 'You'll have to write in to Head Office.'

'Sod off. I can't be arsed. Keep your fuckin' three quid. I'll park somewhere else. Get out of my way!' He barged past him and, stepping into the car, wheel-spun off before apologising to Lisa for having to witness his behaviour, even though he thought he was in the right.

After this, they went on just about every ride in the fair so only now had they stopped rushing around frantically. Over their Café Lattes the conversation turned to Danny.

'Has he ever done that before?' asked Lisa.

'No.'

'Strange. He must've been really ill 'cos surely he'd have stayed out for a bit. It was all so sudden him rushing off like that.'

'I know. I suppose he couldn't help it though.' Steve knew Danny extremely well, better than any other human on the planet, yet even he did not suspect there was any foul play involved. How naïve he was. He totally believed that Danny had changed. *He's got a good woman now,* he thought, *to sort him out.*

'Ring him again,' suggested Lisa, and when he did he heard the busy tone.

Danny had turned his phone back on, realising it was futile to avoid a girl. He would merely tell her the situation and put her straight. His phone would be on silent.

'He's on the phone,' said Steve. 'It's engaged. I'll get through in a bit.' But Danny wasn't on the phone. Kate was calling his phone at the same time as Steve and it was her that engaged the line.

'Oh well,' said Steve giving up easily 'at least we know he is okay if he is on the phone.' And after that, Danny was not mentioned again for hours. Kate was not so easily pleased, though. She wanted answers. Danny's actions the previous evening were inexcusable in her eyes, even if he was really ill.

Why couldn't he explain what was going on and why couldn't I go with him? I would be there for him in the middle of the night, if he needed me, and in the morning too. All yesterday evening and now most of today. That was it; she would have to pay him a visit.

She hailed the first taxi that she saw and ordered the driver to Danny's flat just off Lank Lane. As they pulled up she paid him and gave him a pound coin tip. It was quiet where he lived. No kids seemed to play nearby and most of the residents kept themselves to themselves, just the way Danny liked it. She buzzed the doorbell twice, waited a beat, and then buzzed twice more. There was no answer, so she tried again. Again, nothing.

After her third attempt, she began to knock furiously on the front door and banged a couple of times on a window. There was no chance of Danny hearing the bell as he had incapacitated it, yet he heard Kate's frantic knocking on the window. He tried to ignore her, but then, a female voice shouting: 'Danny…..Danny….open the door,' came through the letterbox. He would have to answer. She was not taking no for an answer and insisted on reaching him.

He decided, at last, to open the front door, as it would be better *her* sniffing round the house than the police. Who knows what they'll uncover, even accidentally.

'Are you all right?' asked Kate as the front door opened slightly and a rather weather-beaten Danny appeared.

'Yeah, well…no. I'm knackered. I haven't slept very well.'

'How's the migraine?'

'Oh, better. The pressure seems to have lessened a lot. I took some Ibuprofen. Sorry about last night.

'Oh, that's okay. Don't apologise. If you're not well, then you're not well. I wouldn't want to keep you out against your will.' Kate smiled. 'Well, are you gonna invite me in or not?'

'Yeah, sorry. Come in.'

'What have you done today?' she inquired as she entered, but she was not listening as she was surveying the house closely. Something was different and she could sense there had been wrongdoing in the flat. She would have to do her utmost to avoid delving any deeper as nosiness very often got the better of her. Suddenly, she noticed two batteries on the coffee table and the box lid of the doorbell buzzer. 'What happened there?' she asked innocently.

'Oh, I took them out 'cos I needed sleep with that migraine.'

That's plausible, she thought and sat down on the couch in the living room.

'D'ye want a cup of tea?'

'Ooh, yes please,' she answered.

She followed him into the kitchen as he popped the lid of the kettle up with a gentle squeeze of the buttons by its handle, and began to fill it from the tap. Still she sensed something was wrong but couldn't quite put her finger on it. She asked: 'So, have you slept all this time then?'

'Pretty much, yes. Well, I've had broken sleep really. I couldn't sleep this morning. I was gonna ring you but my head was still throbbing from the migraine so I just stayed in the dark.'

'Do you suffer from them much?'

'No, not often.' He sensed she was fishing for information and he became slightly paranoid although he tried to reassure himself that she was just concerned. He defended his actions. 'This is the second time I've had one this bad. That's why I knew that the only answer was to go home and sleep in the dark. I didn't want you ruining your night, that's why I left alone.'

Softening, she said: 'That's okay. I understand.' She kissed him and then they hugged each other. 'I was worried about you.' Her tone was more affectionate now as her head nestled up beneath his chin. 'I'm okay,' he said and kissed the top of her head.

The steam from the electric kettle hit the bottom of the wall unit for a few seconds before it clicked itself off. Kate released her grip and Danny proceeded to make the tea. 'So will you be fit for work on Monday?' she inquired, all the while scrutinising his tea-making action.

'Oh, yeah, I'll be fine by then.'

'Good. Perhaps we can …don't make mine too strong please…perhaps we can go out for the day, tomorrow?'

'Yeah. Don't see why not. We'll go to Llandudno or somewhere.'

'Cool!' she replied and Danny couldn't help feeling that she sounded good when she said that. *How could she make a word such as that sound so....well, cool? It's a bit dudeish*, he thought. He sensed his fondness for her growing and this irked him. If she would have said "plop" at that moment, he would still have thought that she was with it; she was "cool."

At times he enjoyed the intimacy with Kate and even revelled in the prospect that he might be in love with her, and this was such a time. The hatred, or bitterness, whatever it may have been, remained within him, but controlled. He wondered why he felt so drawn to Kate. Perhaps it was his way of relieving the guilt of having killed two women. His contempt for them was contrasted with his love for Kate. That was, he wondered, if he could love at all. He was confused.

'You okay?' Kate asked, breaking his thoughts.

'Yes, I'm okay; just thinking. A bit disorientated. You know, like jetlag. I'm still in Friday night mode.' *What a thing to say.*

All the events of Friday night came flooding back to him and he felt his stomach twitch. *Change the subject! Change the subject!* 'Shall we go in there?' he said, picking up his cup of tea and doing his utmost to shut out the image of Dominique's blood-stained corpse.

As Kate picked up the cup of tea, it spilled over the edge slightly. 'Ow!' she bawled, 'you've overfilled it.' The drips rolled down the side of her cup and dropped to the floor, bouncing ever so slightly before spreading on the tiles.

'Don't worry about it Kate.'

'No, it's all right.'

She put her cup down on top of the chest freezer and Danny's stomach twisted again as his heart sank. She reeled off three pieces of kitchen towel and dropped to the floor to soak up the tea. As she did so, she noticed something. 'What's that?'

There were two small red spots of liquid on the tile next to the spilt tea and two more further along.

'What?' Danny hesitantly asked.

'There..' she said, pointing. This was it. He would have to kill her too.

'Oh, I had a nosebleed this morning.' He had found his way out.

Lightening the mood, Kate commented: 'Well, don't you clear your mess up after you, scruffy arse?' He laughed, more out of nervousness though.

'I must've missed it. I did mop up, honestly.' And he wasn't lying. He had scrubbed the floor. How had he missed those spots? He was tired. He should have checked over it when his eyes were fresh.

Kate mopped the spots of blood up along with the tea and put the dirty towels in the bin. She drank from her tea and put the cup back down on the chest freezer, Danny was still slightly in shock. Any minute now she would discover what had occurred and he would have to smash her face in with the frying pan. His eyes rolled across his head until his peripheral vision ended and he was forced to move his head too. They met with the rack on the wall; five pans were hanging from it.

Speedily, his brain enacted the scenario of him hitting her clean in the nose with each pan. The frying pan was the best, he thought. In his enactment, it was the one that knocked her clean out.

Kate drank from her tea and placed the cup on the wooden worktop before finding the lid of the chest freezer with her hand.

Don't open that lid whatever you do.

Her thumb curled under the lip whilst her fingers remained on top. She was about to open the freezer. Danny leapt across the floor and unhooked the frying pan.

Bitch! he thought. He raised the pan in his right hand and turned towards Kate.

10

Kate's weight shifted onto her right leg and she fiddled with the strap of her left shoe. She was leaning on the chest freezer for support.

'It keeps coming off,' she said, as she dropped her foot to the floor. She looked at Danny quizzically, the pan raised in his hand.

Realising his mistake he gestured the pan up in the air and brought it down smoothly onto the gas ring of the oven in one ostentatious manoeuvre.

'Would madam care for food?' he asked in his best French accent. She laughed. 'What are you having?'

'I dunno,' he said, returning to normal. 'Beef Stew?'

'Hmm! That would be nice. Is the beef in here?'

Kate had focussed her attention back onto the chest freezer and this time she was about to open it.

'No!' he yelled. 'No, sorry. I didn't mean to shout. It's err...in the fridge.'

He placed his arm on top of the lid to prevent her from lifting it and put his other arm around her to avoid suspicion then kissed her, distracting her attention away from the freezer. 'Why don't you go and wait in the living room and watch TV. Relax! I'll do this.'

'Well, if you're sure. I'll cook for you next time.' They kissed again and she left the kitchen. Danny let out a huge sigh of relief.

'Fuck! That was close,' he mumbled to himself as he reached for some kitchen towel. This time it was to mop up the sweat on his brow.

The beef was in the pan cooking slowly. Danny heard Kate's phone ringing. It played out to a cheesy 90s tune that he recognised but he couldn't remember the name.

'God, that's old,' he remarked to himself and laughed at his own comment. *It'll keep her busy for a while, anyway,* he thought but she never answered it. It rang and rang.

'Why the fuck doesn't she...' his voiced raised: 'Kate, where are you?'

'In the living room,' she replied. 'Why? Do you need something?'

She got up, made her way into the kitchen and said: 'Your phone's ringing, you know?'

'Mine?' But he never had that ringtone. He did once try to get it for Dominique as she said it was her favourite song.

Shit! Dominique! The sound was coming from the bedroom. 'Will you watch that beef for a second?'

He dashed to the bedroom, frantic with panic but it was too late. The ringing had stopped.

Danny swore under his breath as he searched for the phone. After a few seconds it began to ring again. He searched through Dominique's clothes; they were strewn all over the bedroom. *I'd better get rid of these soon.* The ringing grew louder as he unzipped her tiny handbag.

Drawing the phone out of the bag he saw the caller's name on display: "Mum." It sickened him. He was disgusted at his own actions and wished he could repent. Too late, though. He switched the phone off, took out the battery and sim card and threw the contents onto the bed. He wondered if he should have answered it. *No, leave it.*

After he locked the door he returned to the kitchen.

'Everything all right?' asked Kate. His confidence grew and he felt he could pull it off. The reality of it was, he had to.

'I forgot that I changed my ringtone. I thought it was your phone.' He laughed whilst she shook her head.

'What are you like?' she commented.

'How's the beef doing?'

'Fine. Was it Steve on the phone?'

'Err...I don't know. I never got to it in time and it was withheld.' Danny felt that he was getting to be really good at lying.

After their meal they decided that they should go out to make up for the previous evening.

'If you're up to it, that is,' stated Kate.

'Yeah!'

'I'll be off, then. I'd better start getting ready.'

'Okay then, babe. I'll call you about half-eight, see how you're doing. We can arrange a time to meet then.'

'Right! See you later.'

She left and Danny walked back into the living room before sinking into his favourite armchair. He tried to switch off his overactive brain, as if it was a computer, and then breathed a sigh of relief. Unfortunately though, it was not over yet.

Panic found its way back into his system. *That was Dominique's mum on the phone. She'll be wondering where she is. She might even get worried and phone the police. And what was the last contact she had with Dominique?* Danny's mind played out a scenario that frightened him:

'Bye, mum. I'll see you tomorrow. If you want me I'll be at Danny's flat. You remember him don't you? You remember him don't you...don't you...don't you...?'

The words echoed in his head. *The police could be here any second. Think!*

He rushed to the bedroom and unlocked it. Once inside he pictured the scene of the crime. In his mind a strange *mise en scène* formed. Half of his brain relived the killing whilst the other pictured the room cordoned off with police tape, characters in white suits studying the forensics. The montage swirled around as each image united. There was a fat lieutenant stood in the doorway stopping the press from coming too close. Danny appeared in the scene too. He was a criminal psychologist.

When he was younger he had yearned to do this. He had a secret fascination for crime and murder but he never dreamt for one minute that he would be on the other side of the fight.

Am I a killer? Or have I just released my frustration and satisfied my urge to be involved in murder cases? I shouldn't be killing, I should be capturing. Like my games as a child. I was always CHASING the 'bad guys'. Despite this, his senses re-enacted the feeling of power and well-being that he got after stabbing Dominique. A feeling of power more so than when he had choked and killed Michelle.

'I was in control,' he said aloud before drifting back to reality. Perhaps this was not reality, though. In his head he merely went through the motions whilst only sometimes did they make sense. Very often they were disjointed.

'Fuck me, I think I'm losing my mind,' voiced Danny. 'Just get on with it.'

He gathered up the bits of phone and began to reassemble them. Turning the phone on caused the missed calls to display themselves as text messages. He deleted them then scrolled through to the "Create" in the SMS category. His thumb moved rapidly over the buttons and the letters formed on the screen:

107

> "Hi mum. Have gone to Wales for
> the day with a friend but battery
> flat. Will call you later, love
> Dominique."

Before he sent it he thought it best to go through her Outbox to ascertain the style of writing that she would normally use. From her Sent Messages he discovered that, amongst other things, she favoured '2' for 'to', 'u' for 'you', called herself 'Dom' and always left two kisses- 'x x'.

The new text read:

> "Hi mum. Hav gon to Wales 4 day
> with friend. Batt flat so will call u
> later, luv Dom. x x"

This was now more credible in Danny's eyes so he scrolled through the address book to find "Mum" and then sent it.

He noticed from the messages that there was no mention of him so he hoped that she had not spoken of him lately, either. He also discovered that she had been sending text messages to a lad called Alex, although there was no mention of anything intimate between them.

'Slag!' he remarked. 'I'll bet she was with him when I was sleeping with her.'

If Danny had more faith he would have realised that Dominique never slept with more than one lad at a time and she had held out for him. She was crazy about him but confused and this caused her to allow herself not to have given in and called earlier.

Danny's number was stored in her phone and there were recorded calls to his mobile. He deleted his own number from her phone and any record of her having dialled him then paused for a minute or two to think. In retrospect, he decided to delete all the dialled and received calls as they would show up on the bill and it would look strange if only his was missing from the phone. After making a few calls to random numbers he switched the phone off once more and dropped it on the bed.

'You need to get yourself a holiday, mate,' he said to it, 'to Wales. Just as soon as I've rubbed my fingerprints off you.'

Dominique's mother read the text and it reassured her, although she would have preferred to have spoken to Dominique herself. She was a sweet, middle-aged lady who retained her looks and charm. Although 48 she could easily have passed for 35 and Danny had often ogled her when he thought she was unaware. The odd glance down her blouse or up her skirt occasionally would excite him considerably. He often wished for a threesome with Dominique and Sandy, her mother. Sandy had similar golden hair to Dominique only hers was darker and curled naturally.

Everybody commented that she was in fantastic shape for her age; she had looked after herself since her early twenties. She had also encouraged Dominique to do the same, advising her on her diet and training regimen for the local fitness centre. She was brought up to the best of Sandy's ability: well-mannered, educated, modest and caring. She really was a catch for Danny but he never appreciated her.

Sandy had no husband. He had died three years previously of cancer and this brought her and Dominique closer together. She was Sandy's only daughter and they were like sisters. Dominique's brother Lenny had taken on the role of man of the house after his father's death. Sandy and Dominique relied heavily on each other for different things and supported each other entirely.

Feeling temporarily reassured, Sandy made herself a cup of tea. She would only feel completely secure when she had seen Dominique and spoken to her face-to-face.

'Shall we call round to see Danny, then?' asked Steve.
Lisa looked at him and smiled. 'Yeah, see if he's any better.' They were an hour away from Danny's flat but they were not in a rush.

Back at their car Steve started the engine whilst Lisa fiddled with the CD player.

'What disc number is that love compilation on?'
Steve had the CD in his car for when he was "entertaining", although every now and again he would listen to it himself. He considered himself a bit of a romantic at heart and sometimes didn't suit the high-life with Danny: pulling girls, drinking heavily and smashing anybody up who got in their way. That is not to say that Steve was soft. He had a vicious temper when provoked but it would usually take a lot to provoke him. Some things rode over his back whilst others- seemingly petty- would fire him off like a bullet leaving a rifle. Road rage was

one such trigger that ate away at him until somebody gave him the cue to explode.

Coming back from Southport, they found themselves on Lipton Road in Creasby. A car-full of young lads cut them up and caused them to hit the kerb. Steve beeped the horn frantically and cursed them.

The car stopped a little ahead and five lads emerged from all four doors. They were all aged 17-19 years old. Seizing the moment for an aggressive release, and not wanting to be trapped in the car feeling defenceless, Steve leapt out to face them. The showdown began with some verbal exchanges but they didn't last long as the fight soon kicked off.

Steve kicked the first lad that came towards him with his left foot- a "stopper kick"- and then punched him to the ground. He side-stepped the second one and swept his foot from under him. The third, however, punched him clean on the cheek and he staggered backwards as two more punches from the other two connected with his head. The smallest of the group looked the shiftiest. He had a haggard face that resembled scurvy sailors of days gone by. He wore a Chocolate-Brown tracksuit that even the other scallies saw as hideous.

He picked his moment to hit Steve; only when he was sure there would be no comeback. Steve fought back well and realised what his game was. Forgetting the other two he went for "Mr Shifty" as he saw him. His head landed rapidly on his nose, dropping him to the floor. This angered him but he didn't have it in him to retaliate with his fists. He was not a fighter. A bully, yes, but a fighter, no. Queensbury Rules certainly didn't enter his head. He dashed back to the car as Steve fought the two lads that had laid punches on him and the two from the floor as they gathered themselves for a second bout. Recovering enough to pick themselves up they pounced on him.

Mr Shifty, in the brown tracksuit, returned from the car with a baseball bat. It came crashing down on Steve's back and he repeated the attack several times even hitting his friends in the process. There were too many bodies for a clear shot.

One final swing of the bat along with a careful aim. It hit Steve cleanly and squarely on the cranium and he was out before he hit the floor. All five lads now proceeded to kick him where he lay; disregarding any particular target. Steve's face, ribs and general upper body were all pinpointed and one lad even stamped on his head. As he was already out cold they were encroaching on "attempted murder" territory but they didn't care. There were no rules anymore. Every generation seemed to produce people who would stoop to lower levels than previously known. It wasn't the first time that they had beaten somebody up, although they usually picked on lads a lot weaker than Steve so they had had a run for their money.

By this time Lisa was out of the car, too. She screamed at them to stop and even tried to intervene until she, too, was knocked out with a punch. She fell to her right-hand side and her tooth rolled out of her mouth. There were also other cars stopped, the drivers watching, so the five lads decided enough was enough and ran as quick as they could back to their car. They pulled off so fast that the wheels spun; a smell of burning rubber filled the air. None of the other drivers had intervened. Some of them wanted to help but were too frightened. Others just watched for entertainment.

The lads escaped leaving Steve and Lisa to be in severe pain when they awoke. Steve rolled around on the floor when he came to, his body aching all over.

'Bastards!' he spluttered, along with a mouthful of blood and spit. As the liquid dribbled from his mouth so too did his next word: 'B-b-b-as-s-s-tards!'

Lisa came round at this point and, forgetting about her own injuries, ran to Steve's aid. By this time the passers-by had stopped to congregate at the scene and a motorist who had witnessed everything made an appearance; feeling, now, much braver that the lads were not around. He passed on the registration of the vehicle to Lisa but never left his own details as he didn't want to get involved. As Lisa hugged Steve she cried and cursed the lads. Steve, despite his bruises, broken ribs and distorted facial features, was reassuring her that he was all right.

It was about ten minutes later when the ambulance arrived. The paramedics took Steve away to treat him for concussion. His only concern, however, was for Lisa. His distress at seeing her with a tooth missing was too much for him. *She was so gorgeous,* he thought, *her teeth were so perfect.* 'Bastards!' he cried a final time before blacking out.

Later that evening, Danny and Kate were having a quiet drink by the bar in The Anchor. They sat on high stools.

'It's quiet but at least we can get served,' said Kate, feeling the urge to defend the pub she worked in.

'I like it,' Danny replied. He looked into her eyes and thought about the first day that they had met. A warm sensation reeled throughout his body and encouraged him to kiss her. Kate responded with the same enthusiasm. As she looked into his eyes she could almost feel the love growing inside her. They embraced and the kissing became more inflamed as they caressed each other. Kate ran her fingernails softly up his back. He groaned. This drove him wild and she knew it.

Moments later they were getting carried away with their actions before the barmaid, Sue, coughed and walked the length of the bar. She did not want to interrupt but was considering the other customers. She felt that the excitement may be too much for their weak hearts and they may not make it to the exit alive.

Kate's eyes opened then rolled until they met Sue's. Sue's nod of concern spoke volumes. Her head aimed towards an old man sat in the corner, watching intently. Kate immediately recognised the gesture as it was an ongoing joke in the pub.

'Careful! There are a few dodgy tickers about,' Sue smiled. Danny opened his eyes and exhaled deeply. He felt stoned. A small smile found its way to his face.

'Get a room,' Sue added in a joking manner. They both blushed and sipped their drinks.

Danny's phone began to vibrate in his pocket and he almost fell off the high bar stool as he mistakenly attempted to place his drink on the bar with one hand whilst simultaneously reaching for his phone with the other.

'Whoa!' he yelled, then saw fit to complete each action in turn. He did not even need to look at his phone as he had guessed it would be 'Liz Wanderer' but he did anyway. He rejected the call and put it back in his pocket. Kate looked on with suspicion.

'Can't have anybody disturbing our night, can we?' he smiled. Kate returned the smile but it dropped suddenly: Danny's phone was ringing again. He retrieved it from his pocket once again with the intention of rejecting the call and switching the phone to silent mode. It just so happened, though, that he noticed the caller display; it was Lisa. It was safe to answer.

'Hello!'

'Danny!' Lisa's voice had a sense of urgency in it. 'Steve's been taken to hospital, he was attacked.'

'What?'

'We were driving back from Southport and…' She narrated a brief outline of the events to Danny who was riled with anger.

'I'll come and see him.'

'Not now, he needs rest. They said to leave him alone.'

'We'll come and see you, then. Where are you?'

'My house. I've just got in. Give me half an hour to sort myself out.'

'Okay. See you in a bit.'

He hung up and turned to Kate.

'What's up?' she demanded. 'Something's wrong.'

After explaining the events to her Danny suggested having another drink but Kate was concerned for Lisa and tried to convince him otherwise.

'But she asked us to leave it a while so she could get cleaned up,' Danny explained.

'All right! But just *one* more drink.'

Sue served them eagerly. The look in her eyes implied a sense of chemistry between her and Danny and a feeling of jealousy towards Kate. Kate was her friend so she would have to restrain herself, at least for now.

At Lisa's house Danny got the whole story along with the car's registration number. He had a friend in the police who could give him an address to match the plate.

'Fuckers won't get away with this.'

'Did you phone the police?' enquired Kate.

'Yeah. They took details and that but there were no witnesses.'

'No witnesses? What about the guy who gave you the registration number?'

'He won't come forward. Nobody will. None of them would even help us. There were a few cars with people in, just sat there watching and the usual rubberneckers driving by. Nobody helped.'

Kate was disgusted but Danny knew the reality. He had worked in the city centre as a doorman and had seen lots of action on the streets. There was never help when people needed it and when anybody did intervene the people would turn on them.

'They don't help because they usually end in shit themselves,' Danny informed them. 'Remember that time when I stopped that lad from smacking his girlfriend then she hit me on the back of the head with a stiletto?'

'It's not right, though,' uttered Kate.

As Kate and Lisa chatted away, Danny drifted off into his own little dream world. ...He thought back to the days when he worked as a doorman. He knew from experience that the majority of the public hated doormen. They were seen as a "necessary evil." Whenever he had to throw anybody out there were always comments from people around: 'Leave him alone, you bully. Look at you, you think you're hard.' They never stopped to ask why they were being thrown out. This was one of the reasons that Danny had given up the job.

'The managers hate you, the police hate you, the public hate you...' he would say, 'and for what? Doing your job. I don't throw people out for nothing.'

As a doorman Danny was fair, sometimes *too* lenient. He kept his professionalism up at all times. He always talked somebody out of a fight wherever possible. As a member of the public, however, he could be a vicious bastard when provoked. He took grief off nobody...

Lisa looked to Kate for reassurance. 'Could I stay with you tonight?'

'Of course you can.' They made the arrangements and when Danny snapped out of his dream he made his excuses and left.

Back at The Anchor, Sue was loading the fridge with bottles. Danny entered and ogled her thong as her trousers drooped due to her stooping.

'While you're down there, whey hey!' he shouted. She turned, startled and blushed.

'Oh, hiya! Where's Kate?'

'She's looking after a friend.' He eyed her seductively and she sensed the chemistry.

While the cat is away, she thought, *the mice will play.* 'Would you like a drink?'

'Please. Lager. Are you having one?' He threw a twenty-pound-note on the bar.

'I'm okay, thanks.'

'Go on, have a drink.' She paused for a second. 'Oh, okay. I'll have a brandy and coke.'

Danny perched himself on the exact bar stool that he had sat on earlier and shuffled up to the bar, making himself comfortable.

'How often do you work here then, Sue?'

'Usually about four nights. It depends, though.'

'Do you do anything else?'

114

'I'm at Uni.' She ran her fingers through her long brown hair and adjusted her name badge.

'What do you do at Uni?'

'I'm doing medicine, in my third year.'

'Brilliant! Any cheap drugs on the black market, then?' He laughed at his own comment and she smiled to show acknowledgment of his frivolity.

They chatted and drank for about two hours, interspersed only by the odd serving of a customer or two. Without realising it Sue was slowly getting drunk. She wasn't supposed to drink in work but the manager was not around as Sue had proved herself to be responsible in the past. The bar was quiet, too, so she could afford to take a relaxed attitude to the job.

After last orders, Sue was required to clean up. Danny collected the glasses for her and she loaded the washer. The manager had returned twenty minutes previously and never seemed to mind her chatting. He had gone through the back to his office. Danny saw his opportunity after a while and decided to chance his luck. 'What are you up to when you finish?'

'Nothing.' She shrugged her shoulders.

'Do you fancy coming back to mine for a few drinks?' He thought he would come to the point immediately as he had already sensed that she was interested. She had to put on a front though and claim disinterest so as not to appear easy.

'I don't know. What about Kate?'

'She's busy. She won't want to come,' he joked.

'No. You know what I mean. What's happening with you two? She's my friend, you know?' Guilt kicked in and it showed on her face.

'We're just good friends. It's casual.' On his side it was. 'We can watch a film, or something.'

'Well...just for one, maybe.' That was it; she had yielded.

No sooner were they back at Danny's flat they were in bed together; their hands all over each other. It was good at the time, they both felt, but afterwards the guilt penetrated Sue deeply.

'We shouldn't have done that, you know.'

'Yeah but we did so get over it.' Danny's tone was colder now. Apart from the fact that he no longer saw the need to play up to her, as he had had what he wanted, he was also annoyed that a girl could do such a thing as this to her friend and then expect to be forgiven.

115

'I feel really bad. I don't know what I was thinking of.'

'There's no point moaning about it now,' Danny commented, as diplomatic as ever. 'You made your decision so get on with it. There's nothing you can do.'

'You're really into Danny, aren't you?' Lisa delved, aiming her comment at Kate.

'He's lovely. He's perfect. I knew the moment I met him he was different. He's caring and sensitive. I think he's definitely the one for me. How about you and Steve? You make a lovely couple.'

'Yeah, he's fantastic.' Her mind wandered to thoughts of him lying in a hospital bed. 'I hope he'll be okay. Is Danny gonna just go home, then?'

'Yeah. I said I'd ring him later, make sure he's not lonely. It's nice to meet someone who is sensitive to your needs. A man with compassion. That's hard to find.

'You've changed your tune,' said Sue. 'What's happened to whispering sweet nothings in my ear? Why are you so cold now?'

'I'm not cold I'm just straight,' Danny replied. 'You're as guilty as I am and if you say you're not then you're a fucking liar.'

She looked him in the eye but his intense stare disturbed her. 'I...I didn't mean it like that. I just meant... what about Kate? She *is* my friend.'

'So, she's your friend. Her bloke was lonely and needed entertaining and you sorted it. That's what friends are for. What's the problem?'

'I just don't think it's right, that's all.'

'Well it's too late, now. Don't start getting all self-righteous on me. I'm going to sleep. Do you want me to call you a taxi before I do?'

'Can't I stay here?'

'I thought guilt was getting the better of you?' he added, sarcastically.

'Yeah, well. I'm here now.'

'Don't disturb me then.'

He flicked the bedside lamp off and turned his back on her. Feeling lonely she cuddled him from behind but got no reaction. She sighed and did her best to fall asleep.

Danny's phone lit up with a text message but he ignored it, choosing sleep over everything. Five minutes previous to this Kate was switching off her bedside lamp. Lisa was beside her, resting.

'Goodnight,' she said and Lisa replied with the same. 'I'll just text Danny and wish him goodnight, too. I forgot to ring him and I'm sure he's missing me,' she added, half joking, half confident. Her text read:

> Hi babe. Hope ur ok. Just in bed
> thinking of u. Goodnight. x x x

She told herself she wouldn't rely on a reply but she couldn't sleep for over an hour and a half as her mind demanded vast amounts of attention to be paid to thoughts of Danny. Eventually she drifted off, clutching her phone.

Danny awoke in the middle of the night as he needed the toilet. On his way back his mind raced with the dream that he had had: images of corpses intermingled with images of himself in company, socialising. He knew it was all a front and he wondered exactly how long it would be before he would have to give himself up or at least explain the scenario. Why should he give himself up, though? he thought. Nobody knew anything. In his eyes he had committed the perfect crime, or crimes, and there was no recognition.

How can I get the credit I'm due if nobody knows? But then, if somebody knew it wouldn't be the perfect crime; that would be a weak link. A possibility for failure. No! Nobody must know.

Images of Michelle's killing intertwined with those of Dominique's flitted through his mind. They made him feel good. He wondered if this was his way of getting back at the female population. He loved women, generally, but he couldn't control the urge, rising within him, that despised them, and looked for their weaknesses. Now he was really confused.

As he opened the bedroom door, slightly, the light cascaded over the bed. Sue was sleeping heavily.

Perhaps I should have sex with her again? What would she be like dead? In his long-term memory he held his saying for future reference: "She was a good shag!" This he would use in conversation whenever prompted but for now he was not sure how to act towards her. A sudden urge came back to him from his recent encounters with women: the urge to kill. Did he have it in him to commit another act of indecency, he wondered, or even kill again?

Opening the door further reminded him of twisting the shaft of his torch. The beam of light grew in width as the outside light penetrated the bedroom. Sue slept soundly. Danny stared at her pulsating body for three solid minutes. Her chest rose and lowered in synchronisation with her breathing and this excited him. He acted as a spider might in trapping its prey, preferring live pickings. Just as a spider would not entertain a dead insect (Danny had discovered as a child) so too would he show disinterest in a dead body, unless *he* killed it.

Throughout his childhood he watched for hours as a spider would trap its prey. He would even capture flies and feed them to it. He found that they kill their prey fresh and then wrap it. They never understood when he threw dead flies into their webs. Danny portrayed these features. He wanted to kill his own way and remain in control, yet he wished he did not have this urge.

He surveyed Sue's body with a sense of urgency.

Should I fuck her? Should I climb into bed and cuddle her or...should I...? Towering over her sleeping body he watched her rhythmic breathing. He loved it and he wanted to control it. He felt the warmth of her arm as he stroked her. *It's my body. It belongs to me. Drastic issues require drastic measures.*

He walked softly to the kitchen to arm himself and returned, blade in hand. Sue was defenceless in her sleep.

'I'm here for you baby,' he whispered.

Danny scanned the body to see if it was worth continuing with his- as he saw it- work. It was. A rapid surge of adrenalin flowed freely through his body as he raised the kitchen knife up high. It was his intention to drive the blade into her side but childhood morals came flooding back and this stopped him temporarily.

Urges grew, however, and his morals were becoming usurped by an uncontrollable need to stab the knife into something. He felt he was at the peak of his killing. He held his psychotic stance, the blade raised high above his head, his large, athletic frame shadowing its victim from the light.

Images of Sue with her family flashed through Danny's head and as his compassion rose he paused; torn between emotions, his hormones running wild. A tear rolled down his cheek as he felt deep sympathy for this girl; sleeping, defenceless; at peace; harming nobody; the quintessence of sweetness. Compassion effected in him the questioning of his actions and he almost stopped at the stage he was at. The powerful urge to kill was too much, though.

11

'I can't do it,' he whispered to himself. 'I can't do it.' He rested his head on her chest and snivelled himself to sleep like a baby in desperate need of attention.

They woke around nine the next morning; first Sue, then Danny. She struggled to heave him off her.

'Morning!' she said, and smiled as he raised his heavy eyelids. He yawned and replied half-way through it.

'Uuh, moor-nin'! Did you sleep well?'

'Yeah.' She smiled again but her smile quickly left her face when she noticed the sharp blade that he was clutching in his right hand. 'What's that for?'

'What?' He noticed the knife in his hand and it appeared as though he was viewing his hand for the very first time. Nervously he attempted to mitigate his actions: 'It's err...err...' *Quick, Danny, think.* 'I heard a noise in the middle of the night; I thought it was burglars. I went to check then brought the knife back with me to keep it handy. I must've fallen asleep with it and forgotten to put it on the floor.'

'When I woke up you were holding me close. You must have been protecting me throughout the night. That's sweet!'

How fortunate could he be? He fabricated a reason for holding a knife in bed and not only does she buy it but she strengthens his argument for him. His brain swirled all the information about and attempted to make sense of the vast amounts of stimuli bombarding it like an overactive web page. As always from his experience on the Internet, a pop-up window revealed the real reason for him holding the knife and it sickened him.

'You'll have to go soon, you know,' he told her. 'I'm not being rude. I'll make you a coffee and that before you go. It's just that I've got to go and see my mate Steve; he's in hospital.'

'Yeah, no problem.' She kissed him on the head. 'It was nice last night. I promise I won't mention anything.' He half-smiled, accepting her statement.

Steve lay in the hospital bed, his face pinned together like scaffolding around a house. He attempted to open one eye as Danny's voice registered in his head. 'How are you, mate?' Steve raised an eyebrow and even this was an effort. 'Do you know who they were?'

He struggled with the usually-simple function of shaking his head. 'Just blink once for "no" and twice for "yes".'

He blinked once.

'Hmm!' Danny deliberated before continuing. 'Do you need anything?' Steve's one blink told him he didn't. 'Okay, no worries. You take it easy, you need to rest. I'm gonna go, mate. We've got a registration number and the police are involved. They won't get away with it, you know that don't you mate? You know I won't let you down?'

Steve blinked twice. He was confident that Danny would not rest until there had been repercussions to the lads. Danny's gritty determination in achieving something was ruthless. When he got his teeth into a task he was relentless, especially if his pride was at stake.

Outside, he turned his mobile back on. He always turned it off inside a hospital out of respect for the rules. He scrolled through the address book until he came to "Kate" and dialled.

'Hiya, babe,' said Kate, keen to hear his voice.

'Hi. How is everything?'

'Fine. Lisa's still in a bit of pain but she's coping.' Her voice softened. 'I've missed you.'

'I've missed you too.'

'What did you do last night?'

Your mate, he thought, feeling cheeky. 'Nothing! Just had a few cans in the flat and watched the telly. Went to bed early. Can you ask Lisa for the registration number of that car for me?'

'The one with the lads in?'

'Yeah.'

Her curiosity rose. 'Why do YOU want it? The police have already got it.'

'No, it's just...if we can get hold of the lads they may cough up a bit of money. You know, with the thought that they could go down for this. Should be good for a few grand for Steve.'

She was not totally convinced but she did agree to do as he asked: 'I'll text it to you.'

Anthony Jackson was a sergeant in the local police. He was a tall, thin, fair-haired young man who wore glasses; intelligent and extremely capable. He was good at his job because he could "mix it" with anyone. He could mingle with the thieves on the street that would trade in their own grandmothers for fifty quid, and still manage to blend in with his fellow officers- knocking back the sherry at official police outings.

He sat in his flat, watching a film on television. It was two o'clock in the afternoon and he had not long been out of bed due to shift work. His phone rang out to the tune of *Gangstaz* Paradise. He looked at the display on the phone; it read "Danny Gym". Simple, really. It was a lad called Danny whom he had known for the last five years after meeting in a gym one day. Anthony held the phone to his right ear. 'Hello Danny. What you up to?'

'I need a favour, mate: an address. I've got a car reg.'

'Ooh!' replied Anthony with great reluctance as he did not like risking his career, even for a friend. 'Okay. What's it for?'

Danny explained as Anthony listened intently- an occupational hazard for he always sought to obtain as much detail as possible. Not a bad thing, though. When Danny finished telling him he asked: 'Why don't you just let our lads deal with it?'

''Cos you know what it's like, mate. You traipse through courts for months and months and what happens? They get off on a technicality. Plus, there weren't any witnesses. And even if they *were* found guilty- a slap on the wrists and a heavy telling off. That's no good to me mate. And it's no good to Steve either. Steve's lying there with his face held together with pins. He can't sleep and he probably won't eat for a couple of weeks. And when they finally put his face back to so-called normal...what then? He's gotta live like that. They're rats mate.'

'I know.' He agreed one hundred percent.

'The system is just too unfair. It's all in favour of the criminal. You know that, you work with them.'

'I'm just worried about you,' Anthony said, caringly. 'I don't want you to get into trouble when they're not worth it.'

'Look, if Steve goes to court he puts himself on offer, and that's not fair on Lisa. If they decide to slice her face one day, how do you think he will feel? And how could I ever hold *my* head up after not doing anything. You know how it is.'

There was a pause.

'I'll see what I can do mate. Leave it with me.'

Danny hung up and thought for a moment before saying to himself: "Here we go you bastards. Payback time!' The ring on his phone broke his concentration. The caller display read "Don't Answer".

'"Don't Answer!" Why "Don't Answer?"' He was curious so he answered it.

'Hello Danny. It's Liz. You all right?' It was "Liz Wanderer." He suddenly remembered changing her name in his phone book to "Don't Answer" so as not to speak to her but he had forgotten this.

Well that didn't work. I had to answer it to find out who it was.

'Danny, are you there?'

'Hello.'

'I've been trying to get hold of you.'

'What's the matter?' he asked, hesitantly and immediately regretted it.

'I need to speak to you, personally.'

It was not looking good so Danny tried to dissuade her. 'Look, is it important because I'm really busy over the next few days. He threw his brain into overdrive in an attempt to devise an excuse for not seeing her. I'm going away for a few days, with my job.' *Good one. But that's only temporary.* 'And I may not be coming back.' He cringed at his own excuse.

'What! My sister's been beaten up, Danny.'

This took Danny by surprise as he was expecting Liz to claim that she was pregnant. He was pleasantly pleased. 'Is that why you wanted to see me?'

'Well...yeah. I'm sorry if it seems like I'm using you but...'

'No. It's all right. Look, I'll come and meet you. Now, if you want. I'm off work 'cos my mate's in hospital.'

'Me too, only it's my sister.'

'Can you be at Café Café coffee shop on Boal Street in about an hour?' He always met his girls in there. The girl behind the counter had grown to know him really well as he was in there quite regularly with different girls, particularly as his shift work allowed for plenty of daytimes free. He got to know her so well that he slept with her and that had been his biggest challenge yet. He did all the ground work on her for six months before asking her out. This was mainly because he was taking other girls in there in the meantime. He waited because it had to be right and he couldn't face rejection so he had to find a way of explaining four or five different girls each week.

'I run a modelling agency,' he told her once. 'I like to conduct my interviews in familiar and informal surroundings. I always get a feel for the girl's personality when she's in company and this helps me to see if she would be confident in front of the camera. It's all about confidence, deportment and how she comes across socially. Not just looks.

'Having a coffee with a client allows them to feel at ease and open up with me. I can then see if they have charm and charisma because, believe it or not, this shows on film. That's why many film stars have presence. And you see, not every good-looking girl has the potential to be a model.' Seconds later he had moved in for the kill like a ferocious animal stalking its prey. 'I like talking to you. There's something about you. Have you ever thought about modelling?'

He pulled it off well, corny as it was, without sounding the least bit sycophantic and this is why he was able to take different girls every week to Café Café and still sleep with the girl behind the counter every now and again...

'No problem,' said Liz and within the hour she was there. The girl behind the counter was working, fortunately for Danny as it meant his usual free Latte. He didn't even remember her name- if he ever knew it in the first place. She scowled, slightly, as Liz sat down.

'How can she be a model?' she asked strong bitchiness present in her voice.

'I've told you: personality. And anyway, she's a hand model,' he said covering up.

'I'll only use her hands.'

'I've got my test shots back. When are you gonna interview ME?'

'Err...I'll do that next week if you like. Ring me tomorrow and I'll check my diary.' This was enough to dissuade her for now.

As he sat down to Liz with two coffees he showed great concern for her plight.

'So what happened, then? Who was it?'

'Her   ex.'

'I'm not getting involved in a domestic. She'll be back with him next week.'

'She won't. She can't. Not after that.'

'Yeah!' he put in, sarcastically. 'They all say that. If I do anything then she'll hate me next week as well, and you. What's the point? You never get involved in a domestic.'

'Honestly, it's over. They've been finished for over two months and she's met someone else. That's why he beat her up. He dragged her up and down the street and nobody lifted a finger to help.'

'Well maybe he didn't need help,' he added, jokingly before realising the poor taste of his remark, evident in Liz's face. 'Sorry!'
She moved on with the explanation. 'He was calling her a slag but she's done nothing. They finished and she met someone else.'

'So what about this *someone else*? Why doesn't he do something?'

'He's more frightened than her. He's only weedy. He's useless. He was gonna leave her because of it- bastard! I can't stand him.'

'What do girls see in lads like that? What's happened to the days when girls were attracted to blokes who could protect them?'
Liz agreed. 'I know. I don't see anything in them myself. That's why I like you.'
Danny failed to register the last bit in his mind. He shook his head out of frustration.
Don't worry, Danny. It'll all swing back round again and all the girly boys will go back out of fashion. Then all the girls will want you.
The thought of this took him aback slightly. He did not do too badly as it was so it excited him to think he could become even more successful.

Perhaps there aren't as many girly/boy followers as I imagined.
'All right then. What's his name, where do I find him? What's your sister's name? And they'd better be finished 'cos if they get back together I'll fuckin' do her as well.'
Liz's face straightened. She paused before speaking and swallowed hard. 'His name's Joey Wallace and he lives on Cradlebourne Avenue. I'll go down with you and show you his house and where he goes out drinking. My sister's called Cathy. Cathy Smith, in case you need our surname.

'I'm not a bleedin' private detective. I just wanna know what he's done and where I can find him. What does he do for a living, by the way?'

'He's a taxi driver, on the private hires. He's only been on them about six months.'
She took a breath and her eyes filled with tears. Danny stared at her. He felt that a downpour was inevitable.

'I just don't want him touching her again. Please, Danny. Make him stop. It's not the first time, you see.'

'Oh, right. Like that is it? Little shitbag! Finish your coffee we'll go to his house now.'

Outside the house, Liz was wiping away the last of her tears. She sat with Danny in his car- on surveillance. Danny reassured her.

'Don't worry, babe. I'll sort it. Everything will be fine.' She thanked him and burst into tears again. 'Are you okay?'

'Yeah,' she snivelled. 'I'm just thinking about lots of things.'
He looked at her quizzically then, confused, he put her actions down to hormones.

'Right. We don't have to stay now. I just wanted to see where he lived.' He started the engine and Liz grabbed his arm aggressively.

'Wait! That's him now, coming out of the house. Get a good look at his face.'

'I'll do better than that,' he said, getting out of the car.

'What are you gonna do? Don't cause a scene,' she cried after him but to no avail.

'Danny! I'm frightened!'

Danny took lengthy strides towards Joey and shouted to attract his attention. 'Oi, shitbag!' Joey looked round but never stopped walking. 'Yeah, you. Arsehole!'
This time he did stop.

'What?'

'You know why lads hit girls?'

'What?' he repeated but half knew what he was aiming at.

'Because they can't hit *lads*. Bullies. They haven't got it in them for a real fight so they make it up by hitting people weaker than themselves.'

Joey thought, suddenly, that if he put on a brave show and confront Danny then he might think twice about pursuing this altercation. He could not have been further from the truth as Danny loved the retaliation. It urged him on further as he disliked easy targets in confrontation.

'Who the fuck are you?' Joey sputtered, as arrogantly as he could.

'Your fuckin' worst nightmare, mate.'
CRACK!

Danny's fist met up perfectly with Joey's jawline and Joey found it had a knock-on effect to his legs; the pavement seemed to rise to meet him. Half conscious, he struggled to sit himself up, slightly, holding his jaw. Standing was out of the question, for the next minute at least. A blurred image of Danny's character animated itself in his vision before a flash of light resulted in darkness. That was the extent to which his brain could process the information.

Danny's boot connected with the temple at the side of Joey's head. His head rocked and his body slumped. Normally this would be enough for anyone else and they would leave it at that. Danny was only warming up though. He took two steps back like a footballer taking a penalty shot. He then did just that with Joey's head. Liz, frantic upon viewing this level of violence, leapt from the car and began to scream.

'No, Danny, no! You'll kill him.' She ran to him and clung to him, still screaming. Danny was about to take his third kick when Liz intervened. He cast her aside, viciously and then kicked again at Joey's ribs. They cracked under the pressure and the sound echoed inside Liz's ears. She pleaded with Danny to stop.

'I thought you wanted me to do him,' he shouted back.

'No!' she cried. 'That's too much.'

Realising he had thrown her to the floor he reached out his hand to meet hers and he helped her up. 'You all right?' he asked, calming somewhat. She nodded her head, continuing to sob.

Danny gave her a hug and they returned to the car. They left Joey lying on the pavement out cold: the blood trailing from his head, along the kerb and into the gutter. Danny turned to view the trail of blood then looked to the sky. 'We need a good downpour.'

As they drove away Liz continued to sob. The shock was too much for her. She cried...stopped for a brief moment...cried some more...stopped again. Danny could not handle the emotions. Sometimes he could show compassion whilst other times he would be unbelievably cold, as if the devil had taken his soul.

'It's over now, you know. I don't mean to be harsh but why are you still crying?'

'His face...'

'Yeah. And what?'

'There's something else,' she muttered through her tears.

'What?'

'Oh, Danny!' She erupted into heavy crying. Danny grew impatient. 'What?'

'I don't know how to tell you.'

He slammed the brakes on and pulled the car in to the side of the road. 'For fuck's sake! WHAT IS IT?' he demanded.

'I'm pregnant.'

'What!' *Fuckin' bitch! She's trapped me. She's used me to break this to me in this fuckin' sly manner.* He pulled off and looked in his rear-view mirror at the cars nearing him from behind. It seemed like all the cars were coming for him and he felt hugely trapped by the whole ordeal. *There's no way out.*

He thought about throwing her from the car whilst it was moving and switching his phone off. *She won't die but she'll hopefully lose the baby. She might have a miscarriage. How? Punch her in the stomach. No! She might still have the kid and it'll come out ugly. Abortion? Would she agree though?* He was confused except for one thing- the only clear thought he had in his head at this precise moment. It was pointless in his eyes. He did not love this girl. The only true feeling that he had was that he did not want this child, or any other for that matter.

Still in his rear-view mirror he stared for a long time as his thoughts drifted. His jaw dropped slightly, leaving his mouth open. His eyes reverted to the road and he began to dream, only subconsciously viewing the way ahead...

...Back in his school, he was fourteen years old. Walking along the playground with his friend Tommy Pankhurst he saw Julie McFadden, a girl he had been dating for two months. He was in love and, as far as he could tell, so was she. Life seemed great then. He saw himself as married at twenty-five with four kids and a house, possibly a dog. He liked dogs. His future wife? That would be Julie of course.

He spoke to Tommy: 'I saw her again last night, you know.'

'Yeah? Did you get anywhere?'

'I certainly did,' he said, pressing his middle finger up to Tommy's nose so he could sniff it.

'Ugh! That's disgusting! Haven't you washed your hands?'

'Yeah. I'm only joking. She's lovely though, isn't she?'

'She's all right. What about her mate? What's happening with her?'

'I'll sort it for you. Calm down, hot pants!'

Tommy added in a slightly jealous tone: 'Lisa Jones likes you, you know.'

'Not interested, mate.'

'What! She's gorgeous. Everyone in the school's after her.'

'So! I've got Julie, mate. What would I want with her?'

Steven Moorly was older. He was sixteen and reputed to be the hardest lad in the school. He linked Julie's arm and she smiled. She never saw Danny. Danny saw this and grew angry. He walked towards them.

'What's going on?'

Julie seemed nervous. She liked Danny and didn't want to see him hurt.

'Danny, this is Steven. I'm going out with him now.'

'Is that right?' he asked, growing angrier each second. Steven piped up at this point.

'Yeah it's fuckin' right so fuck off you tit.'

Danny's blood boiled in his veins but on the surface he maintained composure. Staring at Steven, deep into his eyes, he asked: 'Who the fuck do you think you are? You think you're hard? You're nobody.'

Steven, better known by his surname, Moorly, feared nobody in this school until now. For some reason there was doubt in his mind. Danny's stare was intense and vacant. He was a difficult enemy to sum up and this created nervousness in Moorly. He did not fear Danny but was definitely ill at ease with him and felt insecure about what was about to happen. Danny's confidence also spoke for itself. It had the effect of Moorly wondering about some secret weapon. He was so confident he must have a good reason, he thought.

Danny's stare disturbed Moorly. It burned into his flesh and seemed almost inhuman. Nervously, but feigning confidence, Moorly said: 'You'd better fuck off, kid, before you get hurt.' Danny weighed him up well.

'You don't believe in your own words,' he said, sensing the hesitation in his voice. There was a pause- five seconds on Danny's body clock and five hours on Moorly's. The first move was made by Danny. He had to. There was two years difference between them. He shot towards Moorly's knees and pulled both legs out from under him, shouldering him over at the same time. Moorly cracked his head on the floor and they began to battle.

Danny assailed the punches and Moorly retaliated as much as he could. They then progressed to scuffling. Later on Tommy would comment on this fight to his friend and refer to it as a 'great scrap' but for now he felt uneasy as this was his best friend. He felt sorry for him, sure he would lose. He didn't though. It was all over when Moorly scrambled out from beneath him and scurried off. Danny had as many injuries as he but what mattered was that he had won as Moorly had fled.

The best fighter in the school at fourteen, this earned him tonnes of respect. The next two years would all be downhill from here. He turned to Julie and she asked: 'Are you okay?' She was willing to go back out with him now. She must have liked the excitement and Danny had proved himself. She was all his but he didn't want her now. Hatred welled up inside him.

'I'm fine,' he replied and punched her on her left cheekbone. She stumbled, fell, then scrambled back to her feet again. Her left hand covered a red mark. Danny had not hit her as hard as he could. Nevertheless, she screamed. Danny kicked her up the arse and she ran off.

'Slag!' he shouted across the yard. She broke his heart but he was a fighter. He always fought back through difficult situations. The hurt penetrated deeply and hardened him up for years.

After this he would usually always be the one to end relationships but even if he was not it never really meant anything to him. He would not find true love- that is, he would not let his guard down as he saw it- until Jessica...

...Back in the car he realised the way in which his dreams had been shattered. If he was to ever have children then *he* would have to choose the time as well as the mother. She would require vigorous training to mother his children. Now, it had all come along at once and he didn't like it. *Where will they live? Does she expect to move into the flat with me? What am I thinking? I don't even want to be with this girl.*

His teeth sank into his lower lip and one word could not help but fall, noiselessly from his mouth: 'FUCK!'

130

12

'So why Wales all of a sudden?' enquired Kate, reclining in the passenger seat of Danny's car. They had just driven on to the M53.

'Because it's nice, it's relaxing. I need to unwind and I'm sure you do too,' replied Danny.

'Where about, then?'

'It's a surprise.' It was also a surprise to him as he was playing it by ear. He hadn't a clue as to where he was headed- just Wales.

Thinking about it he suddenly came up with a suggestion. 'What about Llandudno? We did mention it.'

'Yeah. Sounds good.'

Danny's mind was fixed on Dominique and the way in which he would hide the evidence that linked her to him. He couldn't afford to hang about in Wales as her body was in his flat. There was nothing he could do, though. Even if he got back early there was no way he could dispose of the body before the police had made a search of his flat. Deciding that there was no point in rushing back he relaxed at the wheel and his speed dropped from 98mph to 72; he cruised. Bored of his own thoughts, Danny made idle chatter. 'I used to go to Wales every year, you know. As kids we stayed in the Robin Hood camp.

'Didn't you ever go abroad?'

'No. Couldn't afford it. It was Wales or Scotland. We enjoyed it though.'

Silence fell after a few seconds so Danny turned the volume up on the radio. Talking Heads' Road to Nowhere was playing. How apt, he thought.

Dominique's mother, Sandy, was worried now. She addressed her son Lenny. 'Should we call the police do you think?'

'Let's try her phone again.' He dialled and waited...it was still off. In his head he knew it never looked good but then a typical "things-like-that-don't-happen-to-people-like-us attitude" reassured him. 'She'll be okay. Let's leave it a few more hours. See if she gets to a phone. She's probably enjoying herself.' Sandy smiled. She wished her feelings on the inside could match her enthusiasm on the outside.

Lisa stooped over Steve's bed and kissed him on the head. A tear trickled down her face. Here was the man she loved, normally strong and capable, reduced to this. The nurse put her arm around her and reassuring her said: 'He'll be okay. He just needs rest. His face is mending nicely.' Lisa nodded and thanked the nurse as she moved to another bed.

Sitting by the side of the bed observing him carefully, Lisa held Steve's hand and felt her mind wonder. ...The house was a spacious property of six bedrooms. In the dining room, Steve, Lisa and two children, a boy and a girl, were about to sit and have a meal. The snow was falling outside and it left a white rim around the window.

A huge Christmas tree stood in the corner with about fifteen presents beneath. A real fire was blazing in the fireplace.

'Could I have a drink, please?' the little girl asked.

'Of course you can, darling.' The children were so beautiful and polite that it was unreal. The whole scene seemed straight out of a Frank Capra movie. Steve was laughing at something that had just been said. It was infectious, the children joined in. Steve's smiling face, content and confident held strongly in Lisa's mind like Van Gogh's or Da Vinci's greatest work for a moment, then it faded...

...The smile left his face and steel pins formed themselves around it. His head rested comfortably on the pillow, his breathing rate had dropped.

Arriving in Llandudno Kate noticed that there seemed to be houses in the middle of the hills. 'I've never been here before,' she said, looking bright-eyed like an excited child. 'It's re-a-a-ly nice. It looks a bit like a toy town.'

'Toy town?' Danny questioned.

'Yeah. I mean that in a good way. It's lovely!'

Danny stopped the car and got out. 'I won't be a minute.'

Why was he stopping here? she wondered. *What's he doing*? Danny ran to the nearest public telephone and began to dial.

'I hope they're out,' he mumbled to himself but it did not matter. He only allowed it to ring once then hung up. Paranoid of any repercussions he wiped the receiver and any buttons that he had touched for fear of leaving any fingerprints.

Sandy stood up immediately from her armchair, even though her mobile was in reaching distance of her sitting. She searched for the missed call and was confused when she saw the number. It was not registered in her phone and it was not a local call. Normally she would have ignored it and put it down to a wrong number. Today, however, she saw differently. It could mean a link to the whereabouts of Dominique. She raced to fetch her son Lenny. 'Lenny, come and ring this number.'

There was something about this type of person when they got old. They could never do anything for themselves. They either doubted their own ability or were just plain lazy.

'What is it, mum?'

'I've just had a missed call. Where's this number from? I don't recognise the code.'

He memorised the number then reached for the yellow pages. He identified it as Llandudno then thoughts of Dominique prompted him to return the call. As they had wasted nearly five minutes identifying the code and deciding what to do, Danny and Kate were far away from the telephone. A passer by picked it up.

'Hello.'

'Hello,' shouted Lenny. 'Who is this?'

'What do you mean "who is this?" *You* called *here*. What do you want? This is a public phone box.'

'Sorry. I'm looking for my sister. She's gone missing and we've just had a call from this number. Is there a girl there: about five foot nine with golden red hair?'

The passer by searched around himself. 'No. Wait. There's a lady with a dog, I'll ask her.'

'No...don't...' Seconds later he returned. 'She said 'no'.'

'Where are you?'

'Edinburgh Street...Llandudno.'

'Is there anybody else there? Someone who may have seen...'

'Look, I've got to be somewhere.'

'No...wait...please.'

The line went dead. He rang again several times but there was no answer for about two minutes until a child answered, swearing down the phone. Lenny hung up and turned to his mum.

'I think we'll have to call the police.'

Kate's curiosity got the better of her. 'What were you doing then?'

'Oh, nothing.'

'What do you mean? Nothing!'

She was not going to let it drop and avoiding the issue only made it look more suspicious. 'A friend asked me to do him a favour and I couldn't but I don't think he believed me. I felt bad because I owe him loads. He's done all kinds for me. I said I was going out for the day but I don't think he bought it. I just thought...if I give him a call and ask him if he'd like anything bringing back from Llandudno he'd see by the telephone number that I was really here. Then he'd know I wasn't lying.'

'Oh, right,' she replied, disappointedly. 'Is that it?'

An hour later they were on the cable cars. Kate loved every minute of it.

'I can see now why you used to come here as a kid. It's great!'

Danny smiled. As they passed over a ravine they could see that they were few hundred feet up in the air. They could see the tops of trees beneath them. Danny wondered if he should drop the mobile phone now. He contemplated the consequences as Kate took in the breathtaking scenery. *If I drop it here the chances are that nobody will find it. And if somebody did happen to find it they would think that she had fallen. Wait! That's no good. There's no body. Fuck it! Just get rid of it.*

'That's fantastic that,' he said, pointing to the view of the seemingly-clear blue water in an attempt to distract Kate. She turned and he went to drop the phone over the side before changing his mind. *It would be better found. On the beach! To make it look as if she had drowned.*

'Thank you for bringing me here,' said Kate as she kissed him. They kissed again once or twice before embracing each other passionately and kissing intently. They missed the rest of the scenery as they were too engrossed in each other.

Hours later they were in the pub having some food and Danny was trying to convince Kate to stay. 'We can phone in sick or take a day's holiday. Come on, it'll be good. You said yourself you liked it here, so let's stay the night.' She was reluctant at first as she had not planned it and she was worried about her work commitments. She was also no good with spontaneity. The complete opposite of Danny, whose quick thinking enabled him, not only to be spontaneous but also, to extricate himself from tricky situations.

134

'Okay, then,' agreed Kate, finally.

Danny was happy. He was treating this as a holiday as he envisioned his next holiday being spent behind bars. He imagined that he would return to his flat and it would be swarming with police, tape cordoning off the outside. One tiny piece of evidence to connect him with Dominique and the police would almost certainly look into it. If they searched his flat...

Why didn't he clear up his evidence? Perhaps deep down he wanted to get caught. His thoughts always reverted back to this. An artist needs an audience to appreciate their work.

'Two coffees, please.' Kate was ordering drinks for after the meal. They already had alcoholic beverages but fancied coffees to go with their dessert.

After excusing himself Danny sat in the toilet, fiddling with Dominique's phone. He stored the number for the Gramba Hotel, Llandudno into it, along with some others he had acquired throughout the day. He then dialled the hotel and hung up shortly after it was answered. There seemed just one more act of diverting attention off himself to perform. He texted Dominique's friend, Jenny, whom she had regular contact with. It read:

"How r u? Did I tell u about
James? Hes gr8. Took me away
with him to Wales. Hope ur ok. X"

He sent it then turned off the phone. Later, at some point, he would have to wipe off his fingerprints from the phone and try to avoid any traces of DNA.

He put the phone back in his pocket and then returned to the bar to find Kate, two coffees and two pieces of chocolate fudge. 'What's it like?' he inquired, noticing Kate eating voraciously.

'Scrumdiddlyumptious!' she replied, chocolate all round her mouth.

'Bring some back to the hotel room,' Danny said, his eyes wide and sexually suggestive. Kate blushed but never stopped eating.

They got drunk together, danced together, had a fantastic time and made love for hours in their room at the B&B. Without realising it, Danny had grown so intimate with Kate that it was difficult to see things any other way. His old lifestyle of being single and pulling in bars was leaving him rapidly and he was not aware of it. He still pulled girls at most opportunities but the hunger was wearing thin. Luckily, his relationship with Kate was still fresh.

The next day Danny left his phone off. He had convinced himself now that his flat was overrun with police and if he was to turn it on then there would be a call from them asking him to come home and himself in.

Down at the beach Danny had an idea. *What the hell!* he thought. *It's worth a try,* and put Dominique's phone near some sunbathers. He was careful not to be seen by anybody. Kate was skimming pebbles off the surface of the water. An obese man and an almost-obese woman lay side by side sunbathing.

'I'd hate to go shopping with you two,' he mumbled to himself before placing the phone next to their cooler bag, crammed full of sandwiches, biscuits, coke and lager. He circled round a bit to avoid suspicion then went to Kate. 'Let's move further down the beach, babe.'

'Why?'

'Well, for a walk. It's good for you.'

'Why don't you just say 'let's go for a walk?''

'Okay,' he said, realising he should have thought up his reason before approaching her. 'Let's go for a walk.'

As they wondered off, Kate gestured towards the two fat sunbathers. Danny's heart sank. He was certain she knew something. 'Look at the size of those two,' she remarked.

'I know.' He breathed a sigh of relief. 'The things you see when you don't have your harpoon.' They laughed together and continued walking.

For some reason Sandy and her son had not called the police. Ever-the-optimists, they waited for her to get in touch, shutting out thoughts of her being in trouble or in need of help. Sandy had called Dominique's friends and not one of them could help her. The last they saw of her was when they left her alone in the house watching TV. It was Friday night; she had made no plans and chose to stay in. Sandy looked at her son Lenny, her eyes filled with tears.

'Pass me the phone,' she said. This time she would make the call herself. She related the incident briefly over the phone and gave a short description of Dominique before a voice informed her: 'We'll send a couple of officers round to you shortly.'

'Thank you.' She put the phone down and sobbed heavily, realising that she may never see her daughter again. Lenny comforted her. His eyes also began to leak as he tried desperately to swallow the imaginary golf ball that had appeared in his throat.

The happy couple drove home before it got too late and darkness made the journey less enjoyable. Danny looked at the digital clock on the dashboard: 17:33. Kate was smiling. Although it was less than two days they had done so much together that they felt as though they had been away for a week.

She put her hand on his thigh and looked at him through glazed eyes. She had fallen for him in a big way. He returned the smile but remained focussed on the road. His thoughts now were of walking into a trap. He wondered exactly how close he would get to his flat before they pounced on the vehicle and armed officers dragged him out, a gun to his head. *I might as well put up a fight. There's no way I'm going to prison. Better to die along the way than die in prison.*

The thought of spending time closed up without the company of women was too much to handle. He hated women at times but he knew he could not live without them. There was no way he would ever incline himself towards homosexual activity, and prison, in his eyes, would drag him kicking and screaming down that path. He thought so much that his head hurt.

I'll take some of them with me. It's a fucked-up system with fucked-up women. The WPCs would be the first target. *Those bitches in men's jobs; putting men out of work. They get the job but they can't do it. How many of them is it going to take to pin me down? Twice as many of them as men. They'd better spray me with gas 'cos I'm gonna spit in their faces. Slags!* 'Fuck the lot of them,' he said, accidentally out loud. Kate was baffled.

'Eh? What did you say?'

'Hmm!' Danny snapped out of it and glanced at Kate before returning his eyes to the road. He was unsure how much she had heard. He wondered whether he had thought all those words that traversed through his mind or whether they were voiced. The voices seemed so loud in his head she must have heard them. Kate frowned before asking:

'What's the matter?'

'Uh? Nothing! I was just thinking about a few things and got a bit pissed off. Sometimes your so-called friends just get to you.'

Even though he was extremely vague she would not delve any further. Instead she pressed 3 on the CD changer to change the disc. A brief pause of five seconds as the CD player did its job and then Coldplay boomed out of the speakers. They both stared ahead at the road as the music entertained them.

Lenny came in from the garden, put the kettle on and addressed Sandy. 'Any news?'
She looked sad as she stared at the floor, his voice only briefly registering. It took all her strength to muster up a reply: 'No.'
There was silence for a moment. Sandy's mouth fell slightly open. The look of hunger for life had vacated her eyes since the reality of her daughter's situation had established itself in her head. Deep down she feared she would never see Dominique again but she clung to every last hope. Deep and pensive she came to a decision. 'I'm gonna go there, ask around. Someone must have seen her. There must be hundreds of witnesses; people who saw her; people who served her in shops. Somebody asking her the time- somebody telling her the time- anything.'
She resumed her staring. Life seemed pointless now. Her only daughter was missing and the chances were that she would never again see her alive. Slowly she uttered her next words. 'The police will do all that. There's nothing we can do...nothing.' She rocked her head, slowly and deliberately, forwards and backwards. The pressure appeared to be getting to her.
Lenny was in two minds about what he should do. Should he go and look for clues as to Dominique's disappearance, see if he could shed some light on where she was staying, or should he stay and console his mother who was obviously distraught? What a dilemma! He was keen to find out something about his sister yet he couldn't leave his mother in that state. She was unstable and needed a little tender, loving care. It was situations such as this that brought families closer together. Tragedies brought on more love. Such was the case here.
Lenny decided to stay. There was nothing that he could do in Wales that the police could not do and about three times as effective too.

Taking her eyes off the road Kate turned to Danny. 'Are you sure you don't want me to come and stay with you?'
'No, honestly. I need an early night and I wouldn't mind a bit of time on my own. Kate was slowly coming to terms with what she

thought was Danny's solitary cravings. She could sense that he needed space so she would give him it. She loved him a lot so would never dream of smothering him. She was sensible enough to allow somebody time to handle their own affairs and when it came to relationships she had quite a healthy approach, often advocating: "don't live in each other's pockets, 24/7" to her friends.

Perhaps this was why they worked so well together. Danny needed space. He was a lonely animal in a hostile world and his defensive barriers were up, often self-incarcerating to the point of almost becoming a hermit. Kate felt she understood although her knowledge in relation to him was comparable to a 19th century expert in psychology in a 21st century world. She was extremely intelligent but Danny was deep and didn't give much away on the surface.

As it was, she would have to let him go for the evening- like an uncontrollable animal being released back into the wild. It needs to go where it belongs and live the way it knows.

'Okay then. I'll see you soon, hopefully,' she sighed. A tear welled up in her eye. It was a tear of frustrated joy. She was happy but wanted more.

'Thanks for the mini break, babe. I really enjoyed it. Llandudno is great! Plus, I got to spend it with a wonderful guy.'

She kissed him and he returned the affection. Pressing their lips up against each other's, their tongues intermingled. Their hearts raced for over two minutes before dropping their pace again.

'See you soon, babe,' said Danny. 'I'll ring you.'

Kate smiled and merely said: 'Bye.' They parted on good terms. Kate vacated his car and then Danny retreated into his thoughts:

Well that's it. There'll be hundreds of them surrounding my flat. No doubt they'll have been in and rummaged round- god knows what they've found. Oh, and Dominique's body. Ah, well!

He breathed a sigh of frustration. He had it planned in his head: the way in which it would go. They would surround the car and scream at him. Rifles and handguns aimed at the windscreen and side windows. They may even use one of their vehicles as a blockade in case he was armed. Then they would yell at him: 'Put your hands in the air where we can see them. Step out of the car. Lie down on the floor. Keep your hands where we can see them. Spread you legs. Put your hands behind your back.' *I reach for one of their legs and they stumble backwards, dropping a rifle. I get the rifle and open fire on all of them.*

A slow-moving image of himself taking a bullet and staggering around, before falling to the floor, formed in his head. It disturbed him somewhat but at the same time it took away the pressure. Perhaps he should not go back at all. No. Curiosity told him he should at least go and see if there was anyone there. *The criminal always returns to the scene of the crime, apparently.* Where had he heard this? He did not believe it when he first heard it.

Why would a criminal revisit the scene where he had been and risk leaving evidence?

How could you be so stupid as to put yourself on offer? Yet, here *he* was returning to the flat that both murders had been committed in. *But I live there. That gives me a valid reason. Plus, I have to go back. I don't have anywhere else.*

He turned the corner into Lank Lane and expected to re-live the scene previously imagined. There was not a soul about though. Where was everyone? He paused for a second. *Of course, it's an ambush. As soon as I try to gain entry to my flat they're gonna pounce on me.*

Realising that he did not have a gun the "fight-it-out-with-them" scenario went out of the window and he decided to give himself up. He parked up outside his flat then feigned opening the door with his key, half expecting the door to open and five or six men to pounce on him. Nobody came and he had to open the door himself. 'What are you waiting for?' he asked the walls of the flat. 'Here I am. Come and take me.'

Nothing!

He entered the flat and was, even now, still anticipating to be arrested by undercover officers. He walked into the kitchen and opened the chest freezer. Nothing had been touched. He dug beneath the ice cubes and could feel one of the bin bags containing a body part. Realising now that the police had not been he thought it would be in his best interests to clean up any evidence that could link him to either Michelle or Dominique. He remembered Kate finding the spots of blood and the seriousness of the whole situation dawned on him. Contemplating the whole affair, it did not seem clear as to why the police had not discovered the connection. They probably would sooner or later, he felt. Perhaps they were following the "Wales" lead. *Surely this could soon be traced, though. If they got in touch with the phone company they would discover that I had been in contact with her on Saturday night. I could just switch my phone off to avoid them calling.*

He thought about the practicality of it. *That's no good. My phone is registered to this flat, on contract. They'll be round here like a shot.*

It was clear that the young girl was missing, she had not been in contact with her mother or anybody, but there were not strong links to connect Danny, apart from the phone calls. He could talk his way out of these providing that the flat was clear of evidence. *If the plod come sniffing round here and get the slightest whiff of any connection with her they'll ransack the place. They'll have forensics here and then I'm fucked.* He wondered if they would look into the calls to and from his mobile then it clicked in his head. He was as sure as anything that he would be getting a visit.

Inside the bedroom Danny put all of Dominique's clothes into a bin bag and cleaned up as best he could. He spent hours but it was worth it, he felt, as it looked much better. It would be best to check it again the next morning as there were bound to be items that he had overlooked, such as the blood spots that Kate saw.

'I'd better get shut of that body as soon as I can,' he said. How soon would it be before Dave would visit the incinerator again? He picked up his phone and began to call him. *What can I say?* he thought. Dave answered almost immediately.

'Hello Danny. How are you doing?'

'I'm okay, thanks. You well?'

After the pleasantries and the usual catch-up gossip, Danny got straight to the point. 'When are you due to go to the incinerator again?'

'Err...I'm not sure. Maybe a few weeks. Why?'

'Oh...er...no reason. Welll...I suppose there is *one*. I met this bird the other night and she works in the offices at the incinerator but...the trouble is...I lost her number.'

'Well just go down and see her.'

'It's not that easy, mate. She was gorgeous and well up for it but I can't even remember her name. I can't just go steaming in there asking for what's-her-name, can I?'

'Hmm! I see your point. Well there's always stuff to shift so you could take a half-load I suppose but it'll have to be next week. Unless you want to go on your own.'

Dave exploited the situation. He decided he could use Danny to take up a half-load with him and he would not need to be there himself. He could stay with his business and have a free removal of waste slips. Dave was tight with his money, which was why he was in business in the first place. He had saved hard and every penny was accounted for.

He knew that Danny would provide the van but Dave usually saw to it that the petrol was already paid for. After all, it was only fair. He was getting the van and Danny for free.

He would even get out of paying the petrol on this occasion by making out that it was a favour for Danny. This was perfect for Danny, though and he wasn't bothered about a bit of petrol. He preferred to be on his own then Dave would not realise what he was up to. Also, he would not have to worry about being nervous; there was nobody to play up to. All he would have to do was act normal in front of the incinerator staff and this would be easy. They were strangers and meant nothing to him. Danny had a talent for role-playing and he could lie to anyone with no remorse whatsoever.

'I'll leave you my card,' said Dave, 'but don't let me down. I have a good relationship with them and I don't want to lose it.'

Dave didn't possess any fears that Danny would let him down but seeing as he was doing this "wonderful favour" for him then he would not even mention the petrol. Danny did not care in the least. His one thought was of destroying the evidence surrounding Dominique and disposing of her body. He agreed to Dave's terms and they made arrangements.

Danny would drive to his head office the next day, about 11am, and load up. Then, unbeknown to Dave, he would return to his flat for Dominique's remains. One last look around the flat. It was clear. Dominique's clothes would go to the incinerator too. But that was all tomorrow. For now he needed to relax.

In the kitchen Danny found some whisky. He had developed quite a taste for it now. Settling into his favourite armchair, he flicked the TV channel onto G.O.L.D. Red Dwarf was on. Great! He watched four episodes back-to-back and slowly worked his way through three quarters of the bottle of whisky. When he got up to visit the toilet his legs almost gave way and he staggered across the room. He hadn't felt drunk sitting down but now it suddenly kicked in. He laughed to himself. When he was drunk he could find even the smallest things amusing.

Danny fell through the doorway managing to scrape both sides on his way through. On his way back from the toilet he did the same, bouncing off each wall like a pinball. He was really pissed and hadn't realised it. The effect of not having eaten for over six hours and the drop in blood sugar levels from his heavy cleaning session resulted in the drunken stupor he now portrayed. The whisky had gone straight to his head.

He opened the chest freezer and dug beneath the ice cubes, lots of them falling on the tiled kitchen floor. He eventually found what he was looking for- the supermarket "Bag for Life" and carried it into the living room. He sat down, poured more whisky, and lifted the head out of the bag. It was frozen solid. He played with her nose as if she was alive and stroked the hair as best he could; it was rigid. Drops of water began to trickle down her face as his warm hands thawed the surface.

'Don't cry, babe,' he said as a droplet of water appeared to roll from her eye. Danny's head tilted slightly as he stared at the head before him, resting on his lap. It was hard to imagine that this head was once moving, speaking, even thinking. Yet, he could see it. To him, at this very moment, she was sleeping. He wondered if *he* was sleeping.

Perhaps I'll wake up and it'll all have been a dream. I'll wake up next to Dominique and then we can go to the park.

A droplet of water rolled down his own eye- a real tear. He clutched the head into his chest and closed his eyes. The cold never seemed to bother him.

It was forty-five minutes later when he awoke and there was a game show on the TV. He noticed the time-12.48 am- before noticing the wet patch on his lap, then the cold set in. He lifted the head by its half-defrosted hair and stood up. 'What the fuck!' he exclaimed, looking at, and feeling from beneath his trousers, the cold and wet area above his knees.

He looked at Dominique's face; it sagged. He dropped it with the shock and ran to the bedroom to change into a pair of tracksuit bottoms, comfortable for him to sit around in although he also thought that soon it would be time to retire to bed. The tops of his thighs had numbed with the cold but the short nap had helped to clear his head. He was still drunk but thinking clearly now.

The head went back in the bag and back in the freezer and he would be in and out of the shower, and in bed, by half one- 1.28 to be precise. He crawled under the duvet after setting his alarm for 9.30 the next morning. The night was silent, peaceful. He soon drifted off to sleep.

Kate had had a relaxing evening. After Danny dropped her off she soaked in a hot bath for nearly an hour and then slipped into her pyjamas. Her mum quizzed her over the phone about her and Danny. 'When am I gonna meet him?'

'Oh soon enough, mum. I'll bring him round for dinner if that's okay with you.'

'Of course it is.'

She didn't mind the idea of cooking for Danny as her curiosity was running wild. Her only daughter was content at last and she wanted a part of that.

'I'm happy for you, dear.'

'I know you are, mum. How's dad?'

'He's fine. He's watching the telly. Do you wanna speak to him?'

Kate chatted for about fifteen minutes to her mum and about two to her dad. Dads never had much to say, thought Kate, other than 'How are you? Do you need anything? Have you got enough money?' It was the same with all her friends' dads. She loved him, though. Who cares if he didn't want to chat all night; he was always there for her.

After that Kate watched TV herself before going to bed early. At first she couldn't sleep. Danny was the foremost in her mind and she missed him. He had left her less than five hours ago yet she was missing him already. She couldn't help feeling that their trip to Llandudno was the way it should be forever: spending lots of time together, being there for each other in the middle of the night for a cuddle and reassurance.

For the first time since before she met Danny she felt lonely. She had got used to being on her own, and even preferred it at times, but now she had found somebody that she could let into her life; somebody that she wanted to share a space with. And when he wasn't there, there seemed to be a huge gap. Perhaps he would move in with her or he would let her move in with him. It was exciting to think about the future; just like Christmas. She closed her eyes and fell into thought.

The digital alarm clock in Danny's bedroom turned from 09:29 to 09:30 and the radio came on almost immediately. Fat Boy Slim's Praise You was playing. It was old but he liked it. It would help him get out of bed.

He stretched and then threw his legs off the bed before following them with his upper body. As fast as the snapping of fingers he changed from feeling on top of the world to a groggy, head-hurting, lethargic sloth. Unmotivated and tired. He had remembered drinking the whisky and the hangover kicked in. It was almost as if he prompted it and if he had not reminded himself of his drinking then he would

144

have been all right. He would have to fight through this one. His head throbbed as if his heart was inside, pumping away. *Turn the bass down*, he thought as the pressure beat at his temples. *Ibuprofen, quick!*

An hour later he had been showered, the Ibuprofen had controlled his headache, and he was just finishing the last of his bacon toastie as he pulled up outside the head office of Dave's business. It only took twenty minutes to load up. Dave gave him the card and said 'See you later.' Still no sign of petrol money.

Loading the bags from the freezer to the van might have been a problem due to the particularly nosey neighbours but Danny thought that it would be best if he acted quite blatantly about his activities. If he tried to hide anything he would almost certainly be seen and suspicions would be aroused.

Stepping into the kitchen he felt the squelch of wet surface beneath his feet. The ice cubes that fell onto the floor the night before had melted and were now forming a small layer of water over the surface of the tiles. He mopped this up, annoyed with himself for getting drunk. He remembered falling asleep with the head on his lap and it sickened him. *Another reason*, he thought, *not to get drunk.*

As he walked to and from the van with a bag in each hand he whistled. He was probably a bit overconfident at this stage but not for long. His third journey from the kitchen to the van caused him great distress. As he walked to the back of the van there were two kids looking inside, fiddling with the bin bags. He had left the doors open for ease as he did not want to stop at any moment in case one of the bags ripped. His heart sank as his eyes met the back of two twelve-year-old brats opening the bags.

'Oi!' he screamed. 'Sod off!'

Luckily they ran off as usually the kids around that area would stay and fight. They all seemed to have attitude problems and feared no adult whatsoever. They were clever and knew the law. These two must have realised that there was nothing in the van worth arguing over, and causing a scene for, so fled. They were after better pickings. Nevertheless, Danny panicked. What did they see? They only had to see one bit of flesh to become suspicious and tell someone. *Maybe that's why they left so willingly. The sight of flesh in a bag might have frightened them away.*

He locked the van each time he left it from now on and loaded up as fast as he could. As least if they did tell anybody he might have time to dispose of the body and could fight his case against children with overactive imaginations. Without a body he felt there was not much to pin on him. Perhaps blood and DNA but that is not to say that she is dead. He raced off down the street once all the eight bags of body parts and the bag of clothes were in the back.

This particular set of traffic lights on King's Drive was a pain in the neck. It was always congested; traffic crossing always backed up and blocked the road. The lights took ages to change and he waited twice as there was nowhere to go when they were on green. Eventually, some considerate driver had stopped on green at the other set of traffic lights, knowing that they wouldn't make it through, so when the lights changed in front of Danny he had a clear run.

'Thank fuck for that,' he said, the sweat dripping off his nose. His heart raced and he floored the accelerator, almost as if he was trying to catch it up. Suddenly, a man ran out in front of him, misjudging Danny's speed and he had to make an emergency stop. He was not far off hitting the guy. Both cursed each other. Danny screamed aggressively out of the window: 'You fuckin' idiot! What're you doing?' The man replied, equally as vicious: 'what are you driving like a maniac for, you wanker?'

'What!' Danny was in no mood for being called anything by anyone. He leapt out of the van with pure road rage inside him waiting to explode on his victim. The man stood back, unsure what to do. He did not want to fight but would if he felt he had no option.

Suddenly, realisation hit Danny smack in the face and it was much more painful than this man could punch: he was standing on the grass verge in the middle of a dual carriageway with his van stopped in the outside lane, blocking the traffic. On top of this there was a dead body in the back of his van, carved up and bagged into eight handy segments. He had one chance to get rid of it and he was increasing his opportunities for capture, rapidly. Deciding it was not worth it he spat at the man and got back in the van.

There were cars beeping their horns behind and within seconds there seemed to be mayhem. As he drove off the guy kicked the van but Danny didn't care. Luckily, the man had not thought to take note of his registration plate. This luck could not last forever, though, and stupid stunts like fighting on the grass verge at eleven thirty in the morning with your vehicle causing a backlog of traffic would take a great deal of luck to pull off. He even decided not to speed as speeding could result in him being stopped and as well as getting a fine Dominique's body could also be discovered. Was it too late, though? A police car was behind him. How long had it been there? How could he shake it off?

He drove as normal as he possibly could but it was not going well. The sweat covered his face and as he wiped it he swerved ever so slightly and cranked the gears mid-change. It was not a drastic swerve but it felt to Danny that he had shot across three lanes. Even though it was not a major thing he knew it only took one reason for them to spark off an investigation. *Shit! What if they pull me over for a random check? They couldn't hit a better target.*

He turned a corner and they followed. He did not even want to go that way. He took a right to take him back towards the motorway to where he was headed. The police car also turned right. *They won't want to go down here,* he imagined, and turned left. But they did. They wanted to go everywhere he went. They were obviously interested and to prove it they gave him a sign. On the top of their vehicle a blue light flitted from left to right and back to left, constantly. It was accompanied by a short-lived siren. *Now what,* he wondered. *If I stop I'll go down- simple as that. If I speed off I'll never outrun them but perhaps I can get to somewhere then get away on foot.*

He pushed hard on the accelerator and the siren blew again. The two officers inside prepared for the chase. 'If I go now,' deliberated Danny, 'I'll be on the run. The van is registered to the company; they know I've taken it. They know where I live. If I did get away I couldn't go back to the flat?' The siren resumed and this time remained on. 'But I've got a dead body in the back. Shit! Fuck off! Leave me alone.'

Memories of himself playing as a child drifted into his head. How he felt back then. How great his life was going to be. He left school with good qualifications and had so much potential. He was going to work all over the world, have his own business by twenty-five. A thick cloud of smoke in his head engulfed the memory and stole it from him. When it was gone all he was left with was reality.

'Oh, well,' he murmured, 'perhaps I could plead insanity.'

He pulled the van in to the gutter as close to the kerb as he could and switched off the engine. A uniformed woman got out of the driver's side and a uniformed man vacated the passenger seat. The woman shouted instructions, slowly and clearly in a loud voice. 'Throw the keys out of the window.'

Strange, he thought, *like some police drama. She can't know what I've got in here.*

147

'Put your hands where we can see them.'

He rested his hands on the wheel as the female officer came to the side of the van. She was aiming a gun straight at his head.

'Shit!' he cried. 'That's a bit strong!'

'Keep quiet,' she ordered. 'Now get out of the vehicle, slowly. I wanna see your hands all the time.'

She opened the door for him with her left hand, her right hand aiming the gun between his eyes. He stepped out of the van like a toddler taking its first steps.

'DOWN ON THE FLOOR.' He lowered himself down. 'FACE DOWN...ARMS OUT.' He complied.

'Let's open the back, then,' said the male officer. Danny turned his head on the floor to face him. *Shit!* he thought, *it's all over.*

13

Lisa was collecting Steve from the hospital. His jaw was still held together by pins and a metal casing. He walked slowly down the stairs. Every tiny jolt hurt so much.

'I can't believe they let you out so quickly,' Lisa said. 'I thought they'd have kept you in to monitor your progress.'

Steve raised an eyebrow and dropped his mouth. Lisa read this as: 'They don't care, do they? They just want to get rid of you so they can get someone else in.'

'I know...' she added, '...shortage of beds.' She was right. Steve nodded.

Outside she waved her arm to a black vehicle. 'Let's get this taxi. They said you can come back in a couple of days to remove the pins.' The taxi driver seemed to find every bump and every pothole in the road. Steve's jaw shook with every judder of the vehicle's motion. By the time they got to his flat he was incredibly grumpy.

'I'll make a nice cup of tea,' offered Kate, forgetting that he had to drink it through a straw which meant leaving it to go lukewarm. He shook his head, gently. If only he could tell her that tepid tea was disgusting. He settled for water.

Steve lay down on the couch and Lisa sat by him, stroking his forehead. His grumpiness began to disperse and he was happy to have her there, looking after him. This was one thing you did not get when you went out pulling different girls all the time- somebody to tend to you when you needed a little care. He interlocked the fingers of his right hand with hers and gripped tightly; his small way of saying "thank you."

'Danny! Danny! I thought that was you,' said the male officer who had rode in the passenger side of the police car. It was sergeant Anthony Jackson, his friend.

Danny went to get up but then stopped and looked at the female officer. *She could at least lower her gun.*

'Come on, get up,' shouted Anthony to Danny then addressed the WPC. 'It's all right, Debbie, I know this guy. He's a friend of mine. Blow through to HQ would you. Tell them it's all right. The suspect is clean.'

'Okay, sarge.' Anthony turned back to Danny. 'So where are you off?'

'Er...just dropping some things off for a friend. I didn't know you were in the Armed Response,' he added, quickly changing the subject.

Yeah. I'm just working with them this month. You know I teach self-defence?' Danny nodded. 'Well, we've got special weapon training coming up and I'm getting involved. It's great 'cos they let me go out on the road as well.'

'Oh, right. So why are the Armed Response stopping drivers for spot-checks with big, fuck-off, Dirty Harry guns?'

'We're not. We're just following up an armed robbery that involved a white van like this but nobody got the registration. There were three lads in the front and three in the back and they've all got shotguns or handguns. A man was shot in the process and he may die. He's in a critical condition. This could become a murder inquiry. All he did was stand in the way and try to reason with one of them. Instead of saying "move", which you can when you've got a gun in your hand, he just shot him in cold blood. They're vicious little bastards!'

Danny nodded throughout. He was too nervous to say anything in case he dropped himself in it. Anthony continued. 'So we saw you and you weren't driving too good- what were you doing? Were you on your phone?- and we tailed you. We couldn't see who was in the front. After you did a few unusual turns we stopped you. Why did you turn left, then right and then do that left again? It was obvious you didn't have a clear route in mind.'

'Well, to be honest...I've got a dead body in the back and I didn't want you to see it.'

Anthony laughed and added: 'It wouldn't surprise me mate. I've seen it all in this game.' Sometimes Danny's humour could be quite inappropriate. 'No, I've just been arguing with my girlfriend. I was gonna pull in and ring her back. I turned a few times, looking for somewhere.'

'But you passed a lay-by and then turned again.'

Danny's brain clunked up a gear. *Fuck! He's on the ball.* 'I know. When I saw you I thought the last thing that I want is to get questioned when my frame of mind is not too good. I was pissed off and thought,

150

if somebody annoys me now I'll probably tell them to fuck off and that wouldn't look good, would it?'

'No. It wouldn't.'

'I thought you'd drive on and I could sit and get my head together; gather my thoughts then call her back.' Anthony viewed him with suspicion.

'It's not like you to have a girlfriend. Well, at least a girl that you call your girlfriend.'

'I know but...I met this bird and she's great- at least she is most of the time- and I thought "what the hell!" I'm nearly 29, not far off 30. Possibly time to settle down, I don't know.'

Anthony laughed and accepted this. Well it's probably about time, mate.' The other officer reached her head out of the car and interrupted. 'Sarge! We've got a sighting.'

The sergeant nodded an acknowledgement and spoke quickly to Danny: 'I'll have to go mate. I got that reg for you, by the way. I'll come and meet you, discuss it, make sure you're not gonna do anything silly.' He dashed to the car and shouted: 'I'll ring you.'

They sped off, lights flashing but no siren. Danny looked up to the sky. The gods were looking over him. He splayed his arms out wide and mimed "thank you" to the clouds. He then breathed a huge sigh of relief. A breath that suggested it had been in his lungs for months and had been building up every day.

He fell onto the van using his back to break the tiny fall and tilted his head back to rest on its metal side. His mind wiped itself clear and two clouds passing over each other became the most important thing in his life for the next three minutes...

Snapping out of it he realised he had work to do. Three minutes was not enough for anyone to escape the pressure and stress of modern life but it would have to do; he needed to move. His confidence grew.

Back in the van and on the road- now he could drive normally. It was unlikely that he would get stopped again but he must get his story right, anyway. Fortunately, he was good at fabricating stories ad hoc as was the case with sergeant Anthony Jackson. Anthony nearly guessed that something was amiss but his friendship for Danny glazed over the suspicion. One thing was for sure, Danny never wanted to go through that ordeal again of being held at gunpoint and ordered to lie on the floor like a dog. Worse than the humiliation, though, was the fear. *What if that gun went off? Trained officers or not, you see horror stories every day in the paper- HE REACHED FOR THE DOOR AND*

151

SHE SHOT HIM. SHE THOUGHT HE WAS REACHING FOR A GUN. That would be why she opened the door for me, he thought, *one hand on the gun, the gun trained at my head.* He shivered. 'Frightening!' A police car overtook him with its siren wailing and blue light flashing. How many times could his heart sink to his stomach?

Once he got on the motorway he stayed in the inside lane and stuck rigidly to 68mph. He would not dare risk going above 70 but he also could not drop speed too much as driving slow also attracted attention. He wanted to blend in with the traffic, go unnoticed. Luckily, he did.

He arrived at the gates to the incinerator and showed his pass. Everything was good so far. He drove onto the scales to be weighed and then was stopped again further down.

'Open your back doors please Squire.'

He panicked. *Shit! Probably they know Dave and don't see the need to check up on him. They don't know me.*

He jumped out of the van and dashed round to the back doors. 'Bit stiff,' he said, nervously, fiddling with the lock. The van doors became open and the guy inspecting browsed through some of the bags. 'Are they all betting slips?' he asked.

'Oh, yeah. Nothing else!'

'You a big gambler, then?' the guy asked, attempting humour.

Not as a rule but I'm hedging my bets now. 'No, not at all. It's a business...'

The guy nodded and winked before adding, 'I know.' He didn't seem satisfied, though.

'So what's the nightlife like round here, then?' inquired Danny, desperately trying to divert his attention. This was the wrong guy to ask this type of question. He had not been to a nightclub for about fifteen years.

'Eh! Nightlife is it? We used to go to Morranto's. I don't know if it's still there though.' He fumbled through the bags and came close to the bin bags of hacked of limbs. Danny's nerves were on edge. He tried to distract him. 'Morranto's eh? That the place to be at the weekend, then?'

The inspector ceased searching and instead looked into the air to search for thoughts. 'Let's see. The Red Devil. That's were all young uns go.' His attention came back to the bags. 'That's too young for me, though. I don't go to nightclubs now.' He had just commenced opening one of the bin bags. It must have slid down to the back of the van with the momentum of the vehicle in motion. Panic set in Danny's head.

Where's nice to go?'

Just in time. Another five seconds and this guy would have been lifting out Dominique's left calf, complete with foot. He paused to think.

'Food! Food! Let's see. Yeah. I've got it. Sissy George's on the High Street. They do a lovely steak. And the chicken curry is nice too.'

He went into intricate detail about the food and the service in this bar and it bored Danny near to tears. He feigned interest, though, as it meant he was distracted from opening that bag.

Phew! It worked. The guy got so engrossed in talking that he was fairly lackadaisical when it came to paying attention to the bags. He forgot he was about to open one of them and even closed the doors of the van for Danny.

'Take it easy now, Squire,' he said, 'don't you take your good lady anywhere else. Sissy George's, it's lovely. You'll impress her.'

Impress who? he thought. Danny had not even mentioned taking a female out. *Mad codger! Jumping to conclusions.*

The good thing was was that he was back in the van and free to drive to a skip and unload. Normally Danny would not have patience with people like that but he persevered with him as he held, potentially, Danny's liberty at stake.

Finding a skip that was fairly full he reached behind the seats and commenced throwing the bags of Dominique's segments into it. He then hurled the bags of slips on top. Unloading a van such as this would be tiring, normally but Danny found inner strength. He knew that this was the last part of the whole killing process and he was glad for it to be complete. He just wished that he could see this skip emptied into the fire, just like the last one. It could be hours, though, or even days and he couldn't afford to hang around. He was not safe yet.

As he drove away from the incinerator he felt as though a load had been lifted from his shoulders. In a way, it had. In a short while, he hoped, there would be nothing left to trace him to Dominique just as there was with Michelle and he would be free. The feeling of freedom was great but it took away his sense of fulfilment and he felt that he had no objectives to achieve any longer. The urge to kill grew once again. It was as though Danny had found his forte in life.

Sometimes he saw his killings, even though only two, as a work of art. This was his skill. Finding a victim, selecting her method of death then lying to all around to cover up whilst he disposed of her. His secret. It was an art form, he thought. Skilful in his work, every item had to be meticulously seen to. Strategic planning! There wasn't though. He had relied on spontaneity and luck at the time. That was how it was but that was not how it would be remembered.

Memories can be different from the real event as our brains shut out certain objects or actions. He thought to himself for a short while before coming up with the thought that he would have to retire from killing. He could not rely on luck forever. Soon it would run out.

And then what? Quit while you're ahead!

He viewed his killing days as over but the urge to kill again was strong. Danny had nothing to work towards, he felt. He would have to suppress his urge. Hopefully it would remain latent.

Four weeks had passed and Steve was talking to Lisa over the telephone. 'What are you up to later, then?' he asked her.

'I don't know yet. I haven't got plans. Why? Did you want something?'

'Yeah, we can go out for a drink.' They had not been out for a while as not only was Steve busy with work but Danny saw to it that their single life should be reborn too. They had gone out a lot lately and each time Danny had either pulled a girl or at least attempted to. Steve was coerced into speaking to their friends but he never did anything. They even went back to parties with girls and Steve would have to lie to Danny about what he had been up to. As Danny had slept with a lot of girls, Steve had always remained faithful. He pretended to Danny that things were as they were, in the past, because he was a friend and he admired him so much. The truth was, however, he had moved on since then. He loved Lisa and that was enough for him.

Kate's position meant that she had to take a back step; she had no choice. She still loved Danny but felt he needed a lot of space. She never knew he was unfaithful to her as he was clever and manipulative. He would also lie very easily and very well. Most of all, however, she wanted to believe him. This meant that any lies from Danny would be accepted and any actions that could not be explained, or seemed a little suspicious, were discarded. She shut them out of her mind as if they were never there.

Sitting in The Anchor on Friday evening Danny and Steve supped their drinks. Sue was working behind the bar. She asked: 'How's

Kate?' Danny looked across towards the fridge that she was standing in front of. He eyed her legs then moved up over her crotch and breasts before eventually finding her face. 'I was gonna ask you the same thing,' he joked.

'I haven't seen her in nearly a week,' Sue added. 'I don't know what shifts she's been doing. I wouldn't be surprised if she wasn't working here anymore. Nobody tells me anything.'

'It's probably nearly a week since I've seen her. I spoke to her on the phone yesterday, though. She's okay.'

Danny's eyes reverted back to Sue's breasts as their eye contact broke. He had forgotten that he had slept with her. She was all right too, he thought. He leaned in to Steve and whispered: 'Do you know what, mate? I might dabble in that again.'

'Might as well; she's nice. She's got...' Steve stopped suddenly realising what he had said 'What! Have you shagged her?'

'Ssh! Yeah. Didn't you know?'

'No. What about Kate? That's her mate. Doesn't she know? She'll probably tell her.'

'What, and make herself look bad. No!' He took a mouthful of his drink. 'Fuck her, anyway! I couldn't give a shit!'

Danny started to think about Kate. He really missed her but he would never admit it, not even to himself. He pushed her image out of his head and pictured Sue naked. For the first time ever Steve was beginning to lose respect for Danny. He felt that sleeping around was bad enough but sleeping with her friend, the girl she works with, was low down.

'I reckon it's about time we go and see those lads who did your face,' Danny said, changing the subject. Steve reached his hand towards his face and pulled gently at the loose skin around his cheeks. He agreed. 'Well I'm game if you are. It's been weeks and the police are just sitting on their arses. They know who it is but they haven't even arranged a court date yet.'

'Don't rely on them, mate. We'll go and fuck them over and you can still carry on with the case. Let it go on for ages, let the little bastards sweat. Then near the end, when it looks like they're gonna reach a verdict, we'll get a wedge off them and you can drop it.'

'Then we can fuck them over again,' added Steve, bitterly.

He remembered the day clearly up until the point he was knocked out. There were quite a few faces he would recall when necessary. He was always good with faces. He raised his right eyebrow as he thought for a second then glanced upwards as if searching for inspiration before returning his concentration to Danny. His manner was inquisitive. 'So what do you think we should do then?'

'Well...we've got an address so we sit off outside it.'

'Then what? They won't all live in the one house. There were four or five lads in that car and I don't know if I'd remember all of them.'

'Hmm!'

Danny thought for a moment. His brain was fast, it would not take long for him to reach a decision. 'I've got it!' he snapped. 'We take it in turns to follow them around- see where they hang out, who they hang out with, then when we've got a rough idea who's involved- we do them. One by one.'

'It could take weeks.

'What's the rush? And it won't take weeks because rats like this usually only move around in packs, little firms, 'cos they know they'll get turned over by "rival rats." They won't be too far from each other. If they "deal" then they'll stick close and stay in certain little factions. In the meantime they sweat it out waiting for their court appearance.'

'Not "they." It's only the driver that they've got, because of the car. All the rest won't hand themselves in, will they?'

'Relax! We'll sort it. If they're all willing to jump in with each other and use baseball bats then they'll all be close mates. I've told you.'

All right, then. There was one thing I was gonna ask you, though.' Danny's chin jutted out and his head jerked back slightly as he appeared to give Steve consent to speak.

'Why did your mate, the copper, take so long in getting back to us?'

'Because not long after I asked him he was going away and I said that there was no rush. When he got back I never saw much of him and I never mentioned it. I thought I'd just leave it 'til he was ready. Then I saw him when that bitch had me pinned to the floor. Remember me telling you?' He bit his lip whilst Steve laughed. He had heard the story of what had happened to Danny although Danny omitted the gory details of the contents of the van so the edge had been taken off it.

'Fair enough!' Steve sighed.

The first address was 28 Maple Avenue. Danny sat in his car with Steve in the passenger seat, over the road from the house. This was the address to which the car was registered. They waited patiently but an hour later there was still no sign of anybody. Danny sighed. 'This surveillance malarkey is boring,' he commented. You don't realise how long it takes and how slow it goes. We've only been sat here an hour. Now I know how those coppers feel when they sit off somewhere for about eleven hours. I expected us to have a few addresses by now but there's been no movement.'

'They could be out all day,' Steve said cheerily, then added: 'All night! They might have even gone away on holiday.'

'Don't say that.'

Four hours went by and apart from two young lads playing football outside, who looked into the window, knocked, and then ran off, there was nobody about. Another two hours passed and Danny gave up. He started the car.

'Wait!' shouted Steve, 'If you drive off now they're bound to come.'

'I don't care. I can't hang around forever. Like you said- they might've gone away. We'll come back tomorrow. And the next and the next...and even the next if necessary. We'll catch him.'

'I suppose you're right.'

The next day the same thing happened. Seven hours went by and still nothing. Why didn't they come, especially the weekend? A thought suddenly occurred to Danny. 'This is an empty house- just an address. Nobody lives here.'

'Shit! They've moved. So how are we gonna catch them?'

'No. You don't understand. They haven't really moved. At least I don't think so. I think they use it for deliveries, a drop-off point. They're probably signing on from this address and at the same time there's probably loads of "Brown" or "Coke" in there. There might even be guns in there. You don't know what they're up to. Sooner or later, though, they'll have to pick up the post. Then, we'll pounce.'

Just as he said this a BMW X5 pulled up outside the house. The windows of the vehicle had been blacked out. The passenger window zoomed down halfway and a breath of nicotine smoke emanated from within. This was quickly followed by a cigarette stub. It flew into the middle of the road. The window zipped up seemingly quicker than it lowered and the back door opened. A lad of about twenty-five/six-years-old got out. He was dressed in a full Lacoste tracksuit and wore a heavy, gold bracelet on his left wrist. His hair had been shaved to a really short length.

Walking up to the front door of the house he took a key from his pocket and entered. Two minutes later he returned and Danny could just make out that it was money he was putting in his pocket, a huge wad of it. He then took a box from out of the back of the X5 and took it into the house.

'Bingo!' said Danny. 'It's a drop. That money must've been left in there 'cos nobody's gone in or out while we've been here. If that's what I think it is in that box then our little rat friends won't take long to show their faces. I think we should try and watch this 24/7.'

Steve nodded but he was worried inside about having time away from work. An electrician had been called in to cover his absence whilst he was in hospital and the electrician was still used as a back up to allow flexibility for Danny and Steve to take holidays or for future illnesses.

Two hours later a blue Vectra pulled up to the house. Steve got excited. 'That's the car, that's it!'

'Wait!' said Danny, domineering the action. 'Let's see who it is and watch what they do.'

There were three lads in the car; all three had been involved in the incident with Steve. Steve half-recognised them but knew from instinct that it was them. He made to get out of the car suggesting: 'Let's fuck them now!' before Danny stopped him.

'Don't be silly. We wanna get them all, don't we? I'll tell you what; they didn't waste time in getting here, did they? They must've had a phone call to say that the stuff had been dropped'

As one of the lads got out to enter the house Danny crouched lower in his seat.

'Get down!' Steve crouched before asking why. 'They're looking over.' The lad who entered the house was just coming out the front door when the driver beeped the horn and he went back inside and closed the door. He returned empty handed and approached the Vectra. 'What's up?' he asked.

The driver sounded concerned as he answered. 'That car over there, with the two lads in. They could be coppers. Let's get off.'

'Okay then. Take the reg. We'll come back later.'

Danny was aware of what was happening. It was obvious to him that the lad had gone in to collect the box but the sound of the car's horn was a warning to leave it. He drove off as the driver of the blue Vectra reached for a pen. He was too slow to read the registration and none of the others caught it either. They all blamed each other before the passenger outside the car said: 'They're not coppers. They would've hung about. They can't know we're on to them. He jumped in the back seat and they drove off.

158

The passengers in the car were Max, who was in the front in the passenger side, and George in the back. Max was nineteen and had never worked since leaving school- at least not officially. The closest resemblance he had had to a job was two days and one morning in an amusement arcade in Waketon. He had always done a bit of "wheeling and dealing" and had been connected with drugs of some sort since he was twelve. Johnny was the driver. At twenty-three years-old he was the oldest member of the group. His hair was just long enough to be brushed back. Dark in colour, it flowed across the top of his head smoothly.

'Are you gonna go back?' asked Max, scratching his skin head. Johnny turned his head quickly to Max and then back again, as if he was throwing the answer at him. 'Yeah! We'll drive round for a bit and then go back. I think it's all clear.'

Danny and Steve had driven around their estate and were just nearing Maple Avenue once more. Danny pulled the car in and bumped onto the kerb. Steve was incredulous.

'What are you doing?'

'We're getting out,' replied Danny. 'We'll walk round from here. Can't risk being seen again. They turned the corner then ducked backed quickly into the bushes of somebody's garden.

'What's up?' Steve asked. 'Why did you come this way?'

'Look! The blue Vectra.' Max and Johnny were outside the house once again. They looked extremely nervous and acted highly suspicious despite all the efforts to look otherwise. Once their confidence grew they entered the house once more. Steve's patience ran out. 'Let's go through the front door, take them in there.' He motioned forwards with a considerable amount of energy but Danny caught him in time and restrained him. 'Wait!' he said. 'Don't be so hasty.'

'But they'll go.'

'They won't. And so what if they do anyway. If they're doing it once they'll do it again. They probably always use this address and as long as they don't know we're onto them they'll carry on.'

'But what if they get suspicious 'cos they saw us drive off before?'

'No. They won't. They'll think nothing of it. If they were suspicious then they wouldn't be here now. They've obviously got faith in what they're doing. They don't know who we are but nothing happened anyway so they'll forget about us. There must be loads of lads driving around with their mates. Don't worry about it. Yeah we looked a bit suspicious and we drove off. What of it?'

Steve shrugged. Danny added: 'Let's build up a little portfolio of the bastards so if any give us the slip we know their movements. Plus, we can also try and figure out who is involved.'

Steve nodded at this point. In his mind he felt that Danny was right. Once again his respect for Danny grew and apart from his ideas towards women, because of his treatment of Kate, he agreed with him totally.

The lads left the house and piled into the Vectra; the box was deposited in the boot. As it accelerated away Danny and Steve dashed towards their car. Danny fumbled in his pocket for the keys whilst still running. His running slowed as he searched vigorously and Steve reached the car before him. He patted the roof with his hands, impatiently. Danny managed to retrieve the keys and open the car with the remote control, ten clear yards to go. As Steve leapt into the car Danny threw open the driver's door and bounced inside in true Starsky-and-Hutch style, they thought. The wheels spun and the vehicle jolted forwards.

Skidding left around the corner they could just make out the Vectra in the distance. Danny floored the accelerator in an attempt to catch it but as they caught up with it they had to slow down in order to avoid getting too close. They left as much of a distance as they possibly could to continue to tail and avoid losing them.

The Vectra pulled into an estate and Danny and Steve dropped back considerably. If they were to drive through the estate too it would become obvious that they were pursuing them.

'Get out and follow them,' shouted Danny. 'Call me and I'll be right behind you in the car.'

Steve got out and ran in the direction that the Vectra had travelled. He then got on the phone. Danny followed in the distance but allowed the Vectra to be lost from his sight, relying on Steve for further information. He looked down to see where the additional music was coming from. It did not synchronise with the car CD that was playing so attracted Danny's attention. It was his phone, vibrating by the gear stick.

'Hello!'

'Hello mate,' came Steve's voice on the other end. 'Turn left into Saxon Road and then right onto Beach Lane.' Danny did so as further instructions came through: 'Do another right into Moorcroft Avenue.'

As he turned he saw Steve on the phone. He had been running and was now out of breath. Danny pulled up beside him and opened the passenger door. 'Get in,' he shouted, but never completely stopped. Steve threw his right leg in then dropped himself onto the seat of the passenger side. His left leg remained outside and Danny raced off; seemingly just in time. Steve managed to get his leg in as they skidded left and the momentum forced him towards Danny.

Moorcroft Avenue was long so it gave them the opportunity to catch up with the Vectra that was now driving slowly; about to make a stop. They followed it as it turned left into Craig Street. Danny stopped so Steve got out.

'I can't get any closer,' Danny explained, 'They'll get onto me.'

Steve approached the house that the Vectra had stopped at. From the other side of the road he could just make out the numbers. There was no number on the house but, fortunately, there was on each of the houses beside it- 130 and 134.

'One-three-two,' he said to Danny as they drove off.

'What happened?' Danny asked.

'They took the box inside and all three stayed in there.'

'All right! Let's go back and sit off outside for a bit and see what happens. They turned back and pulled in outside number 159 so as to direct suspicion away from them. Danny switched the engine off and turned the radio down so it could just be heard in the background. Reclining in his seat he said: 'Here we go again!'

They waited an hour before anything materialised. Max and Johnny left the house and got back in the Vectra. They drove off slowly and cautiously, Danny and Steve tailed at a distance. Twenty minutes later they were in Old Haverton Street, Danny knew it well. Johnny stopped the car and Max vacated it. He had an apartment in the building above some shops. As he entered Steve followed; Danny waited patiently. It was Steve's intention to acquire as much information as possible without being seen. He imagined himself as a detective from a film and this helped control his nerves slightly.

Max waited for the lift whilst Steve ducked behind a wall with a huge plant standing upright in front of it. Steve looked at the plant and it seemed to inspire him. He dashed through a set of double doors and raced up the stairs, stopping on the first floor. He then pressed for the lift, pulled his baseball cap down slightly to cover his eyes and turned his collar up. He had seen it in a film and he liked it. He knew that Max would be in the lift but he felt that he held less suspicion getting

161

in on the first floor. If he happened to get out on the first floor then Steve would have to hang around and pretend to be doing something.

Hopefully he'll be going up a few floors, he thought, *and I can join him. He won't know I'm following him if, in his eyes, I'm already in the building.* His only fear was of being recognised.

PING! The lift doors opened and Steve's heart sank. Fortunately, there were three people inside: Max, an elderly lady with a small dog in her arms and another lady of about twenty-five. Steve stepped in in trepidation. Max never paid him much attention. The old lady got out on the third floor and the rest vacated on the fifth.

Which way now? he wondered.

Max turned left and made his way to room 507. Entry for him would be easy as he had a key but Steve knew that once he closed the door behind him that that was the closest he would get to him so decided to return to Danny in the car.

'Room five-o-seven,' he informed him. 'What's the other one doing?'

'He's just waiting. I presume the lad you followed will come back out.'

As he said this Max walked out the front door and hurried his pace up to reach the car. He was carrying a red, A5-sized book. Danny tailed them again as they drove back to 132 Craig Street, managing to stop at two separate phone booths to make calls.

Danny recapped out loud: 'So they don't use their mobiles all the time, they make phone calls from public phone boxes, they get deliveries to an empty address...and that book...what do you reckon?'

Steve shook his head. 'Well it's not their accounts. That must contain phone numbers and addresses, although why they didn't have it with them I don't know.'

Danny made a clicking noise with his mouth whilst he contemplated the whole affair.

Suddenly his eyes lit up. 'You know what?' Steve's ears pricked up and he turned his attention to Danny, silent but observing. 'Why don't we call the plod in? Now I'm not a grass as you know...but...it would make it easier for us. Then we can knock shit out of them and drop the case at a later stage and they'll get done for dealing. We won't be seen as snitches 'cos we'll have dropped our case. They'll still go down for that and they'll still have to traipse through court for months. Danny went quiet and stared at the house. Steve mulled it over in his mind for about a minute and a half before replying with: 'Fuck it! I'm not a grass either and at first I thought: "No, I couldn't do that" but, you know, it's what the little rats deserve. So when do we strike?'

'All in good time, matey. All in good time.' They headed towards The Anchor, phoning Kate and Lisa along the way.

14

Danny took a large mouthful of beer and swallowed hard. He turned to Steve and asked: 'Where are they meeting us?' Steve seemed confused.

'In here. That was the plan wasn't it?'

'What! Don't bring them here. I'm gonna nail that barmaid again and you're bringing the girls here?'

'Yeah! She knows about Kate anyway. For fuck's sake. She works with her.'

'Yeah!' he came back, mimicking Steve. 'But she doesn't want it shoved under her nose, does she? I haven't told her what's going on so she won't know if I'm still...' He looked round nervously as though he had just become aware of his surroundings. '...shagging Kate. Rule number one, mate. You don't burn your bridges. You don't piss in the drinking water 'cos there might be a drought.' He pointed his finger at Steve, an action that resembled a teacher scolding a child. Steve remained taciturn. 'Get on the phone and change the meet. Pick another pub and I'll do some groundwork here. He indicated in Sue's direction.

Steve was not entirely happy but he obeyed nevertheless and arranged for them to meet Lisa and Kate in Finney's wine bar in the city centre. Secretly he wished that Danny could be found out to put a stop to his shenanigans.

After making the phone call he returned to the bar to find Sue blushing. He had never seen her blush before and, therefore, admired Danny's tactics even more. Sue trotted off to serve another customer.

'How are you getting on?' asked Steve. He was interested in Danny's approach due to his track record with women yet he was still disgusted inside at the way he treated Kate. Steve liked Kate and enjoyed meeting up in a foursome. For him, it was good fun and better than the hassle of "pulling" every night. He had changed and now he wished Danny would too. Unfortunately, however, Danny never seemed to have Steve's image of happy families in his head. Even for

Steve this image was slowly deteriorating and he was beginning to see Danny as an out-and-out bastard.

'I'm gonna meet her tomorrow after work,' Danny informed Steve. 'I'll come here for one 'cos she's on an early shift and then when she finishes we'll go straight out. One or two beers and then straight back to mine for some good lurrr...ving!' Steve smiled. Even in his disgust he admired him.

Finney's wine bar had been impressively restored and refurbished after the fire. Six months ago somebody had thrown a petrol bomb through the window in retaliation to the gang warfare at the time. Paddy Finney who owned the bar had had some dealings with a guy who owned four sunbed salons. They were both involved heavily in distributing heroin, cocaine and, to a lesser extent, ecstasy tablets. The owner of the sunbed salons, Max Wall, had ripped Finney off for fifteen thousand pounds and Finney saw fit to pay for all four salons to be sprayed with a hail of bullets. Hence, the petrol-bomb, return. But where would they stop?

It seemed that each person attempted to go that much bigger and better each time and these "wars" were rife in the city. By the end of them most had gone way beyond control and the police appeared to be fighting a losing battle with the weak judicial system in effect. After the fire the fighting ceased for a while. It would come again though. It always did. The pandemonium came in waves; uncontrollably at times and frighteningly quiet at others.

Lisa and Kate were early. They shared a bottle of wine and chatted. Fortunately they had a lot to chat about and the time went by quickly before Danny and Steve arrived. It had been quite some time since they had all been out together. Kate was excited at the prospect of reviving the social circle that the four shared. After the pleasantries were over she addressed Lisa in a familiar manner: 'How's work, Lise?'

'Not too bad,' she replied. 'Keeps me active. How are you and Danny now?'

'I dunno! It's hard to say. We started off really well and we got close quite soon but then it all seemed to come to an end. It was as though he became frightened and put his barrier up. I tried not to come on too strong, and I hope I haven't scared him off 'cos it'd destroy me not to see him again. I know it sounds dramatic but I don't think I could go on if he wasn't a part of my life in some way.'

Lisa nodded and as if on cue Danny and Steve arrived and approached the table that the girls were sat at.

'All right, girls!' said Danny, breaking their concentration from each other. 'Anyone fancy a drink?' They both smiled simultaneously. Danny looked at the bottle of wine and made his way to the bar. Steve sat with the two girls and broke the silence. 'Hiya! You two on the wine, then?'

Lisa looked towards him then asked: 'How are you babe?'

'Okay!' he replied. The barrier of coldness started to break as all three fell into friendly chat.

Throughout the evening the two couples had visited several more bars and were rather worse for wear. The relationship had resumed to the level that it was prior to Danny "going off the rails" as they saw it, and "guiding Steve away from Lisa and back to single life."

At the end of the night Steve took Lisa back to his flat and Danny took Kate to his. Steve had only just taken the key from the lock, after opening the front door, and Lisa pounced on him. They kissed heavily before undressing each other on the way to the bedroom. They left a trail of clothes all the way back to the front door before leaping into bed naked. Their bodies entwined and their lips pressed hard against each other's. It was the best sex yet for both of them. Perhaps it was because they had moved a little apart, doing more things on their own, and they were experiencing the effects of first-time excitement once again.

After "the best sex session yet", as Lisa called it, they slept like babies in total peace and calm. Everything appeared stress-free. It was as though they had been really close for years and nothing had ever come in between them.

Danny put the key in the lock and fiddled aggressively. He may have been drunk but he remained focused. Kate was unaware of his mood and was merely enjoying herself. Danny grabbed her by the arm and shook her.

'Get in the bedroom,' he demanded, strongly.

Kate didn't know what to do. Reluctant as she was she obeyed. Danny followed her into the bedroom and began to tear at her clothes.

'Careful!' she said, but he was far from it. He pulled her dress down over her shoulders ripping it in the process. Kate was startled but went along with his ways as she felt the animalistic passion rise within her. Danny pushed her onto the bed and began to bite her neck as he wrestled with the belt on his jeans. Kate's breathing increased rapidly and she grew short of breath.

Once inside her, Danny fucked her hard. The more he excited himself the more aggressive and rough he became with her. Kate began to feel uncomfortable. Beads of sweat trickled down her face, her eyes were closed. No sooner had she opened them there was a flash of light and they seemed to close of their own accord and pain impulses raced to her brain. Danny had slapped her hard across the face. Before she could complain she was hit again. She yelped in pain and let out a cry of resistance but Danny ignored it. In fact, he got off on it. His fingers curled themselves around her hair and he pulled at it hard. She screamed:

'Ow, Danny! You're hurting me.' But still he persisted.

Through half-glazed eyes she surveyed the ravenous beast above her. Its eyes were ablaze and frighteningly intense. In her head this was no longer Danny, but a stranger; a psychopath with a fetish for sadism. Throughout all the time she had known him she had never seen this particular facial expression. This was the first time she had been with him that she feared him. From feeling safe and protected to this was too much for her to handle. She attempted to wriggle free but the slaps became more frequent until they turned to punches. Her heart pounded; this time from fear not sexual excitement. She screamed for him to stop. Still, he ignored her.

'Danny...please...stop...let me go.'

Her feeble attempts at pushing him off only aided in exciting him further. He held her arms and began to bite her neck but the biting crossed the line of fun: it pierced the skin. Danny raised his head to look at her again. The intense, vacant stare; the psychotic look, effected one last, long and extremely loud scream from Kate. Surely the neighbours would hear her, she thought.

In the morning Steve had dropped Lisa off and headed to work. Lisa had forgotten to turn her phone on until her first break in work. As she did so she noticed lots of missed calls from Kate from the early hours of the morning. There were also several text messages. Through these messages and one voicemail the events of the previous evening were related. Lisa was shocked. She could not believe what she was reading. The voicemail corroborated the story further and the anxiety in Kate's voice was evident. Lisa dialled her number. The voice on the end of the line was croaky and hesitant.

'Hello!'

'Kate! You okay?'

'Yeah! Just a bit shook up. Danny went mad on me last night. I can't go into work today my face is all bruised.'

'What happened?'

'He just went wild. I couldn't control him. I think he must've been on drugs or something. We were making love and he started to hit me; just like I said in the texts. At first I thought he was just getting a little excited and it was good but when he changed and began to get really rough it scared me. I'm frightened, Lisa. Last night he was insane. I thought he was gonna kill me.'

Lisa laughed. 'Danny! He wouldn't do that.'

'It's not funny. You weren't there. He was psychotic.'

'I'm sorry. I didn't mean to laugh. I just find it incredible. I mean...Danny's so...protective towards you.'

'I know. That's what I don't understand. I can only put it down to drugs, although I didn't think he took any. Someone must've spiked his drink. It's just not like him.'

'Have you spoken to him today?'

Kate panicked: 'No! I'm too frightened. Do you think you can speak to Steve and see if he knows anything? Don't tell him you know what happened; just say you think we've had an argument or something. Honestly, Lisa, those eyes! He was like a madman staring down at me. It wasn't the Danny that I know.'

Lisa agreed to phone Steve on her lunch and the conversation came to an end as she had to get back to her work.

In the living room, Danny scrutinised his reflection in the mirror on the wall. He needed a shave. Events from the previous evening came flooding into his mind. He remembered Kate screaming and running out of the room when he had released her. She left the flat half-dressed. Her bra and knickers were still on the floor by the bed whilst her blouse and shoes were by the door. She had put on her torn dress and grabbed her bag before running out into the night in fear of her life.

Funny how they never forget their bags.

It was now 11.30am and Danny had not turned in to work. He looked at his phone that had been left on the couch. There were fourteen missed calls.

'Fuck it!' he voiced, before switching it off.

169

After showering, he made himself two bacon toasties for breakfast and sat down to watch TV. Daytime TV reminded him of one of the reasons that he worked for a living.

'I can't watch this drivel,' he muttered to himself and pressed the red button on the remote that left the television set on stand by. Gathering up fifty pounds from his jar on one of the shelves of his bookcase, he made his way to the front door. 'Go and get some more shopping!' His thoughts were becoming more and more voiced and he wondered if he was going mad by talking to himself. Somebody had said, once, he recalled, that 'if you think you are going mad then the chances are you're actually quite sane.'

'That'll do for me,' he uttered.

As he was closing the front door he could hear the phone in the flat ringing in the distance. He pulled the door hard. 'Fuck it!'

'Steve! Can I have a word?' Steve's boss was confused over Danny's absence.

'Yeah, sure.'

'As you know, Steve, Danny hasn't turned in but I haven't heard from him. Now, I know if you knew anything you'd have told me, but I was just wondering if you could shed any light on the matter.'

'Erm...well, I don't know what he does these days. I don't pick him up anymore 'cos we sort of got out of the habit. You know, we used to take it in turns. I haven't seen him, sorry.'

He felt it was best not to mention the fact that they had been out the night before.

'Well...if you hear anything let me know.'

Steve took an early lunch and drove to Danny's flat. When he got there it was quiet. He rang the bell in the manner that would inform Danny that it was a friend. There was no answer. He banged on the windows and tried to call from his mobile. Danny's mobile was off and his landline rang out; Steve could just make it out from outside the front door. Still no answer.

He scribbled a short note from a scrap of paper in his car and posted it through Danny's letterbox. He then gave up and went for his lunch.

The wide aisles in the supermarket were perfectly designed to stroll, seemingly aimlessly, whilst one gathered one's thoughts. Danny was relaxed and his mind had only one clear objective in sight- to acquire the items of shopping on the list in his head. At least, he thought he had a comprehensive list in his head but it got longer and longer as he stumbled across items that he felt could be of interest or useful to him.

As he came to the dairy section he picked up a two-litre, plastic bottle of milk with a green top. It wasn't exactly heavy but somehow it dropped out of his hands. What had caused this sudden slip was shock. Danny was startled to the point of relaxing his grasp on the bottle- for on the side of it was an information sticker for missing persons and... Dominique's picture was on it.

Danny dropped to his knees in an attempt to cover up the action but it was too late. The bottle had burst open on impact and over half of its content had now spilled onto the floor. He knelt in the milk before realising the consequences of his movement. An assistant rushed to his aid.

'Can I help you sir? Can I help you sir?'
The words echoed in his head in a dream-like manner. His vision became distorted and he struggled to differentiate between thoughts and reality. It appeared that everyone in the store was watching him now, all eyes focused on his actions. The voices were indistinct, muffled. The faces became a blur, too.

His eyes left the milk on the floor and found themselves rising until they reached the shelf full of milk. There were over fifty Dominiques staring at him. They all suggested to him that they knew what was going on and they were about to talk.

'Are you okay?' came the voice of a supermarket employee.
Danny could not even discern if it was male or female.

'Excuse me, sir.'
The eyes on the milk bottles followed him and it reminded him of the Mona Lisa painting he had seen as a child.

'They know!' he screamed. 'They know! Tell them to leave me alone.' He fainted and fell to the floor. Several customers had begun to crowd round.

There was darkness, a pause, then light. In the light faces began to emerge. All eyes were focused on him.

'What's going on?' he asked.

A man in a white suit was leaning over him. 'It's okay sir, you fainted.' He gave him a glass of water. 'How are you feeling?'

'I'm all right.' Danny stood up and brushed the flecks of milk from his jeans with his hands.

'Would you like to take a seat, sir?'

Danny walked off in a hurry. 'I'm all right, honestly.' His pace quickened and he made his way out to his car. The man in the suit addressed the crowd:

'Ladies and gents, if you could please carry on with your shopping. Thank you.' Turning to his assistant, he ordered: 'Johnny, clean that up.'

The crowd dispersed. Outside, Danny fumbled with the keys in the ignition. The sweat was streaming down his face and his heart beat viciously. The drive home was automatic. Even though his eyes were looking through the windscreen he was not paying attention to the road. Images of Dominique on the side of the milk bottles sent a shiver through his body. She had come back to haunt him, he thought.

The thought of her dead body lying on his bed did not seem real anymore. Neither did the image of her frozen in the chest freezer; packets of frozen peas covering her face.

Swerving around the corner he entered his road and manoeuvred the car onto the kerb in one go. It was far from straight or well-parked but he didn't care at this point. He closed the front door behind him before running to the bedroom and diving on the bed face down. He pulled the pillow over his head and wept.

Steve left work around four o'clock and called Lisa on his mobile. As he spoke he got in his car and drove to Danny's flat. Lisa was excited and eager to speak to him. She felt there had been a fresh impetus imported into their relationship. She answered her phone immediately. 'Hello, babe! How are you?'

'I'm okay,' came Steve's reply. 'What are you up to tonight? Do you fancy coming over to watch a film?'

'Yeah, definitely. What time?'

'Oh, I don't know. Any time after seven, I suppose. Don't have any dinner I'll get a couple of pizzas in.'

'Okay, great! You heard from Danny?'

'No, I'm just on my way there now. So what happened, again? They had an argument, you say?'

'Yeah. I don't know the full details but there was something about him going a bit mad. Kate said he wasn't himself. She thinks he may have had his drink spiked so, obviously, she's worried.'

'Oh, right. Well I'm nearly there now so I'd better get going. I'll see you later then babe.'

'Okay, hun. MWAH!' She blew him a kiss and then hung up.

Moments later Steve was outside Danny's flat. He locked the car and walked up the path. The bell was depressed twice, there was a pause and then a further two pushes were executed. Steve expected no reply so was quite startled when the door opened.

'Danny, you all right? Where've you been? Why didn't you show up for work?'

'Hiya Ste. Come in.'

As they walked in Steve surveyed the hallway. His brain was working overtime in an attempt to find out what Danny had been doing.

'Do you want a cup of tea?' Danny asked, closing the door behind him.

'Er, yeah. Please, mate.' Danny put the kettle on and Steve followed him into the kitchen, firing questions at him without giving him the opportunity to answer.

'Why didn't you answer your phone? Why is your mobile off? Where were you today? I called round.'

There was a pause as Danny looked at him. He was calm and collective.

'Finished? Now which one do you want me to answer first?'
Steve composed himself then asked, 'What happened last night?'

'What do you mean? We went out didn't we?' Danny seemed confused. Steve read this as avoiding the question.

'Well...it's none of my business but...are you and Kate all right?'

'Yeah! Why shouldn't we be?'

'Well it's just that...well...like I said, it's none of my business but she seemed a little upset today. I just wondered if things were going well. And of course you never turned in to work.' He raised his eyebrows as if to prompt Danny for an answer. Danny shrugged.

'I wasn't well today,' he said, coldly.

'So, last night?' Steve pushed.

'Last night? I don't remember much. I must've fallen asleep 'cos Kate was with me I'm sure but when I woke up she was gone. She probably left early in the morning. Why? What's she said?'

'She hasn't said anything. She just seemed a little upset, that's all.'

'She must've said something if you're snooping around.'

'Relax, mate. She hasn't said anything. I'm just concerned, as a friend. You don't seem yourself and she was quiet. That's all!'

'Okay. Sorry. Thanks for trying to help, anyway.'

'No problem! I can't hang about, mate. Lisa's coming over for tea and I've still got a few things to do.'

Steve eyed Danny and attempted to read his body language in order to ascertain more meaning. Nothing was clear, though. It seemed that there was a huge piece of the jigsaw missing so he persisted further: 'Perhaps you and Kate would like to come over?'

'Oh, no. Not tonight. Thanks but I'm going round to see Sue.'
This was certainly not what Steve wanted to hear. All he could think of was the foursome that they made up when they went out in couples.

They said their goodbyes and Steve left. Danny returned to the living room and called Sue from his mobile. They made arrangements for Sue to visit him at his flat at about eight-thirty then Danny called Kate. She answered, the hesitation and nervousness evident in her voice: 'Hello,' she said softly.

'Hiya, Kate! How are you?' He acted as if nothing had happened.

'Okay! And you?'

'Yeah, fine. Steve told me you're a bit upset. What's the matter?'

'I...er...' She struggled to answer. After a short pause she added: 'Do you remember what you did last night?' He thought for a moment.

'I'm not sure. What exactly are you getting at?'

'You beat me, Danny.'

'What! *I* beat you! What in, chess?'

'No! I mean BEAT. You hit me.'

There was silence for about ten seconds as he contemplated her statement. He was incredulous: 'I BEAT YOU?'

'Yeah, when we made love...' She related the events to him and he seemed genuinely shocked at what he saw as disturbing actions. He apologised profusely.

'Honestly, babe, I don't remember a thing. I didn't even know we made love. I thought I took the knock.' Kate lowered the phone from her ear and began to sob. 'Kate! Kate! Are you okay...are you there?'

'I'm here,' she said, through tearful eyes, attempting to compose herself.

They spoke for a while as Danny did his best to console her. He even offered to see her that evening but she declined, suggesting that it was too soon and that she would need time to think.

'I understand,' he told her. 'I'll come and see you tomorrow.'
Everything he said about not remembering she believed, or rather she wanted to believe. Half the battle was over for him. She did not want to leave him.

'I think they're sorted now,' Steve informed Lisa. 'I spoke to him about twenty minutes ago and he said that they were meeting up in town tomorrow. I don't know what went on last night but he doesn't remember a thing. Maybe he *was* spiked.'

'It certainly sounds like it,' Lisa added. They were both in the kitchen of Steve's flat, Steve was cooking. 'Smells nice!' complimented Lisa, indicating the large wok on the stove.

'Sweet and Sour Chicken.'

When they sat down to eat Lisa quizzed him over the events of the beating that he had had in the road-rage incident. After discussing it briefly Steve concluded with: 'We've got quite a few addresses now, well three, and we're gonna pay them a little visit soon.'

'When's the next court appearance?'

'A week on Tuesday, one o'clock. It'll get adjourned, though. They always do.'

'Be careful because you might find yourself roped in on an assault charge.'

'No. It won't be like that. They're just gonna get what they deserve. And they're dealing drugs so if there's something we can do to spoil that too...'

'Make sure there are no repercussions. I couldn't bear to lose you.' She leaned over and kissed him on the forehead. They stared into each other's eyes, both silent.

'I love you,' Steve uttered, breaking the silence. Lisa blushed. The excitement grew within her; she was almost speechless. She just about managed to voice 'I love you' back to him.

They kissed deeply and held their lips together as their tongues explored each other's mouths. After a few minutes of passionate kissing Steve stood up and held her hand. He then led her into the bedroom.

Danny's doorbell chimed the correct number of times. He raced to the door knowing it was Sue. His hands were sweaty and he struggled to turn the latch. 'Won't be a minute,' he shouted through the door. He dried the latch with his shirt and then tried again, this time opening the door. Sue stood there smiling; Danny greeted her: 'Hello!'

'Hiya!'

'Come in.' He took her coat. 'Go in the living room.' She made her way in and sat facing the TV. 'What would you like to drink?'

'Oh, I don't know. Anything, tea.'

'Tea? Have something a bit stronger than that. How about a glass of wine?'

'Yeah, great!'

Danny entered the room with two large glasses of wine and sat next to her on the couch. 'To us,' he toasted, and they drank.

'So what's happening with Kate, then?' Sue asked out of the blue.

'What do you mean?'

'Well, are you still with her?'

'Would it bother you if I was?' Sue shrugged, Danny smiled. 'Why are you here if you think I'm still with her?'

'I dunno. I like you, I guess. Maybe I think that you like me and you won't stay with Kate. Maybe I just ignore the fact that you're with her or even think that you're not. I'm not sure what I think.' She needed reassurance, he thought, and the best way of providing this was to lie.

'I'm not with her. We weren't really going out anyway. We were more friends than anything else. I like her as a person but that's as far as it goes. Now, you! When I saw you that was instant attraction.' Sue's face reddened as she responded positively to the flattery.

'You're just saying that,' she said, pushing for more compliments.

'No, honestly! I wasn't out to get a girlfriend as such. I'm not normally good at relationships. I say the wrong things, or act in the wrong way, and I don't mean to. Girls don't understand me.' This was all good stuff. It won him several sympathy votes and Sue saw it as her duty to make more of an effort. This made it easier for Danny. He knew exactly what he was doing. He continued: 'I would like a regular girlfriend but I don't think that's what girls want these days so I just go with the flow.'

'Oh, you'd be surprised! Girls need security now as much as they ever have done. And I'm sure men do, too. It's just that people cheat on each other so much it's difficult to hold down a steady relationship.'

'I know, it happened to me.'

'Oh you poor thing.' She kissed him softly on the lips. He could have kissed her again but felt the urge to add a few more items to his persona to get closer to her. 'I can't be bothered with all that "copping off" business. I want somebody I can grow to love. Somebody I can get to know really well- better each day. Somebody who understands me.'

That was enough music to Sue's ears. She pressed her lips up hard against his and proceeded to "snog his face off" as she used to say to her friends. This led to some amorous caressing and petting before Danny suggested going to the bedroom. Sue concurred and before they knew it they were making love intensely.

In the throes of passion Danny became excited and slapped her hard across the face. She seemed to enjoy this and asked for another. Danny was taken aback. He was used to girls resisting and cowering as he raised his hand. This was what endowed him with his power. Here, however, his authority was questioned. She was asking for it and this lessened Danny's control. He slapped her again and she exhaled a breath of excitement. He thrust in hard at her then punched her in the side of her head. She seemed to like this also; now Danny was confused. *Crazy bitch!*

Suddenly, she caught him by surprise and off his guard. She slapped him hard, without warning, and this interrupted his pace. He punched her a second time, and a third; she lashed out in return causing him to lose his patience. He gripped her hair tightly and shook her head vigorously.

'Uh, yeah!' she shouted, and hit him in the chin with the palm of her hand. Danny's head rocked backwards before he regained his balance. He punched her again, this time catching her on her cheekbone and piercing the skin. She reached up with her nails and scratched viciously at his eyes. He was temporarily blind and rolled off her, his hands protecting his face. Sue ran her fingernails across his neck, leaving four red trails. She then punched away at his head. Danny clutched his face, protecting his eyes. He still could not see.

'DO YOU LIKE IT ROUGH?' she shouted, beating her fists upon his head. Danny took the punches well. They never really hurt him at first as he was a tough lad and had had many punches in his time. The more he rubbed his eyes the less he could see. All of a sudden the pain became too much for him and he blacked out. Sue had struck him with the bedside lamp, cleanly on the crown of his head.

When he came to he had a severe headache and Sue was nowhere to be seen. Running into the living room to gather himself, he discovered a note. It read:

"You're obviously a wuss and can't handle it so have gone home.

177

Ring me when you've toughened
up."

'Fuck me!' he cried, clutching his head. 'What a crank!' but he
could not help feeling he had met his match.

II

The next day Danny showed up for work early. He made his apologies for the day before because he had fabricated some story about hurting his back and not being able to get to the phone. He was scolded for it but as it was feasible it had to be accepted. Moreover, up until the last few months Danny had never taken time off work for illness and was always on time.

'What's happened to you, Danny?' his boss asked him, shaking his head and walking off before he had a chance to answer. Danny shrugged it off and went to find Steve. Steve was in good spirits: 'Hello mate. You turned up, then?' He was sat in the canteen having a coffee. Danny greeted him and sat down before informing him of his previous evening's entertainment: 'That fuckin' bird is a crank.'

'Which one?'

'What's 'er name? Sue! She's lost the plot, mate.'

'Why?' Steve laughed.

Danny pulled the collar down of his shirt to reveal four red trails of scratches. They were still tender.

'Ooh, that must've hurt. Is that where those marks on your face are from as well?'

'She started scratching me and lashing out as I was shagging her.'

'Hmm, kinky!'

'It's not funny, mate. She nearly had my eyes out.'

'They do look red. So what do you reckon, then? "Call out?"' Steve joked.

'Shut up you tit.' Danny changed the subject. 'So what's happening with these lads, then? Do you wanna pay them a little visit or what? Fuck knows I'm up for it at the moment.' He touched his face, gently. 'Bitch!'

'I thought we were gonna wait a while.'

'Fuck that! Strike while the iron's hot- I'll stick a hot iron on their fuckin' faces- and anyway, these little gangs are always falling out with each other. They get greedy, you see. They earn a bit of money selling drugs and think they're gangsters. Then they start playing with guns like they're toys and start competing for the position of "top dog". Before you know it somebody gets hurt. They shit themselves and realise it's not a game anymore.'

'I'm game whenever you are. I can't wait to get at the little bastards. Time goes by and it sort of mitigates it but I won't forget. I remember what we went through at the time: what they did to Lisa and humiliating me in front of her.'

The blood began to surge through his body and his veins were standing on show.

'Relax,' Danny soothed. 'You'll burst a blood vessel. You did your best. There was a car-load of them and you were on your own. You weren't humiliated, you stood your ground. Right! Tonight we'll meet at mine...No, I'll pick you up. There's no way you can drive in that state. You'll only wind yourself up all day. Try not to let it get to you.'

A siren sounded in the factory which was the signal for them to start work. 'I'll be down about seven,' Danny added. 'We'll discuss it at lunchtime anyway. Come on, before I get into more trouble.'

After they finished work Danny popped round to see Kate. Several knocks later she opened the door wide but on seeing Danny she immediately half-closed it, peeping her head round from within. There were bruises around her cheekbones and her ear was scabbed over where it had obviously been cut. She was nervous and tense. Danny spoke first:

'You okay, babe?' She nodded. 'Did I do that?' he asked, gesturing to her bruised face. She nodded again. There was an uncomfortable pause for a moment, neither one knowing what to say, before Danny broke the silence. 'I'm sorry, babe. I don't remember.'

A tear was forming in his eye. Kate swung the door open and gave him a big hug. He squeezed her tightly and apologised again. Tears were now streaming down Kate's face as she exploded inside with confused emotions.

'Come in,' she said, after a minute.

Danny stayed for over an hour. They chatted and sorted things out and he was even sensitive to know not to try it on with her in her vulnerable state. Deep down he loved her but he hated himself for it. He despised the lack of control that he held over his emotions and he could never see himself telling her that he loved her.

It was now past five o'clock and Danny was due to pick Steve up at seven. He rushed home, grabbing a sandwich on the way- he went to a different supermarket as he was still embarrassed over the milk incident. Once home he searched for weapons. He brought a baseball bat, a heavy metal torch- 22 inches in length, and a small blade of about four inches. He also saw fit to pack a large machete in case things got out of hand and he was outnumbered. When he arrived at Steve's flat Steve had only thought about bringing a cosh.

'You might need something else, you know,' informed Danny, 'in case you drop it. You should at least have a blade of some sort. Always have something in reserve 'cos you never know when these things are gonna go tits-up.' He was thinking of the machete at the time. 'There you go,' he suggested, 'what about that bread knife?'
Steve's eyes widened considerably. 'What! I'm not gonna kill them. No, no blades. That's nasty.'

'We're not going on a fuckin' picnic, you know.'
Steve shook his head. 'This will do,' he said, picking up a set of Tonfas from his martial arts days.

'What, both of them?' Danny interjected, sarcastically.

'No! Just one. Hey! I've got a pair of nunchakus upstairs.'

'Oh yeah, great. What are we gonna do- perform a kata in front of them and hope they shit themselves?'

'All right! It was only a suggestion.'

'Yeah, a shit one. You need to think practical, mate. We're gonna go in, do some damage, then get out as fast as possible.' Realising he was wasting his time he added: 'Just bring the tonfa and the cosh. Come on.'

They pulled up a little down from the first address, 132 Craig Street. Danny reached into the glove compartment and took out two balaclavas. Steve was startled.

'What are they for?'

'For fuck's sake! You haven't done this before, have you? In case we have to go through the front door. You don't wanna be recognised do you?'

'No, but I'm not a bleedin' bank robber.'

'Just put it on in a minute. It's a good idea to wear it anyway.'
Steve's heart sank to his stomach. He suddenly realised the gravity of the situation. Danny was aware of his nervous state. 'Relax! I know you're tense. So am I. Control it!' He wished he could.
How can Danny remain so calm? he wondered. *He's like a robot!*

'Right!' voiced Danny. 'There's that blue Vectra. There's somebody in there. Let's go and have some fun. He got out of the car and made his way to the boot. As he opened it Steve caught sight of the baseball bat lying inside. He suddenly felt excited as if he was a bit of a gangster himself and this helped his confidence. Danny took out the bat and fed it up the sleeve of his coat. He then pushed the torch deep into his back pocket. Steve reached for his cosh for confirmation that it was still sitting in the side pocket of his jacket. Danny drew back a towel and the machete became visible, partly gleaming, underneath. Steve swallowed hard and suddenly he had second thoughts.

'What the fuck?'

'I told you it might get a bit nasty.' He reached in and withdrew it by the handle. Steve's mouth fell open in shock.

15

'No, wait,' Steve urged, placing his hands on Danny's arm. Let's not go over the top. Not the machete! Fuckin' hell! That's attempted murder. Maybe we should just call it off.'

Danny turned and grinned. 'Lost your bottle? No, we're not calling it off now. I'll tell you what, I'll leave the machete but it better be okay in there. I don't wanna get hurt just because you're shitting it. Don't forget, these are rats. If it gets out of hand just reach round for anything you can find 'cos believe me, they will.'

He put the machete back in the boot and closed it. As they walked up the path Steve urged Danny to change his mind and go back home. Danny was annoyed. 'Shut the fuck up, will you. We're here now so it's game on.'

He knocked. The front door had a square window at eye line so they could just make out movement inside. Danny looked to Steve who was sweating profusely and whose legs were shaking. 'Follow my lead,' he said. 'Don't do anything until I do.'

'We've left the balaclavas in the car.'

'Don't worry about them. It's too late now.'

As the door opened they were confronted by a young lad with a skinhead; it was Max. He said nothing, he merely gestured his head to them to ask what they wanted.

'Hello, mate.' Danny began. 'We're just in the area replacing old damp proof courses and we wondered if you wanted that removing.' His left hand pointed to the bottom of the bay window as his right relaxed and allowed the bat to slip down from his sleeve, unbeknown to Max.

'Remove what?' Max asked and turned his head to look at the bottom of the bay. Danny saw his opportunity and swung the bat up in the air above Max's head. It came crashing down on his skull and knocked him clean out. Steve raced into the house after Danny and they burst in the front room. Five lads were sat around smoking joints of marijuana. All five were startled as they entered. Three stood up to confront them whilst the two on the couch cowered in their seated positions. Danny swung the bat round and it connected with the face of one of them. Steve smashed another on the head with his cosh but then got into a scuffle with him and another whilst Danny swirled the bat about, hitting everyone in turn. He was fast but eventually three of them overpowered him. Steve was still scuffling with his two.

Danny sunk his teeth into the face of Johnny and bit a chunk from his cheek. He screamed and fainted. One lad ran out the back way in fear of his life as Max came back in from the front. By now one of the two scuffling with Steve had managed to obtain the cosh and was using it on Steve.

Danny pulled the blade out from his pocket, it was ready to use. He then repeatedly stabbed into as many of them as he could until two of them backed off, holding their wounds. They did not know they were being stabbed at first as the strikes felt like punches due to the amount of adrenalin flowing. Once they saw the blood they panicked and suddenly felt weak.

Max fell to the floor with several stab wounds but he was determined to fight on. Too late for him, though, as he was down and it would prove extremely difficult to get back to his feet. Danny stomped on his head, crushing his skull and face. The two who had backed off were up against a wall, half-frightened to death.

'FUCK OFF!' shouted Danny, and indicated to the door. They saw their opportunity and fled into the street. Danny then turned to the two fighting with Steve. He stabbed viciously into their bodies until they stopped. One escaped and ran off into the street whilst Danny swept the last one to the floor and held him there by his throat. 'Want some more, do ye? Do ye want some more?' he said through clenched teeth, holding the blade to his temple. The lad froze but inside he wanted to move. His brain told him to wriggle and fight but his body resisted. Danny rolled the blade down his face, just piercing the skin.

'No,' shouted Steve, but it was too late. In one swift movement he left him with a scar for life. The blade of the knife cut into his temple, down past his eye and over his cheekbone before finishing with a large gash in his cheek. The lad screamed and Steve panicked. 'Shit!'

'Come on,' ordered Danny, let's get the fuck out of here. They ran into the street, the blood dripping from them. Steve was in tears as they leapt in the car and sped off. Danny drove as fast as he could, skidding round every corner and almost losing control. He screeched into a nearby park then slowed considerably before bringing the car to a halt in a secluded spot.

Danny had previously used this place for his "relations with girls" as he termed it, before he moved out of his parents' house.

'I used to come here when I was young,' he said. 'You never see anyone.' Steve was still crying and Danny was annoyed at this. 'What the fuck's wrong with you? You've lost it. You're turning into a bird. You used to be streetwise. You're softening as you get older.'

'What the fuck have we done? We'll go down for this.'

'Stop whingeing! They're only rats. They won't do anything; they won't go to the plod.'

'What if the neighbours saw us, they'll have your reg.'

'No they won't. Look at this.' He got out of the car and walked to the back. Steve followed and Danny pointed to the registration plate. The numbers and letters had been altered using black insulation tape.

'I went over the whole of each letter and each number so you can't tell where the tape ends and the real figure begins. It's good, isn't it?' He began to peel it off. 'Of course, up close you can tell it's tape but if you were to clock it from afar, a window for instance, you'd read it wrongly. And even if you could tell it was tape you still can't read the real reg.'

Steve was beginning to compose himself. 'Have you done the same on the front?'

'Of course. You take that off while I'm doing this.' He looked at his blood-stained hands. 'We'll have to get cleaned up as well.'

The following night Kate was working with Sue in The Anchor. Sue quizzed her over the marks on her face that were just fading. 'DANNY did that to you? I thought you were going out together.'

'We were. I think it was just a one-off. He was not himself. I think he may have been spiked or something. He's usually so protective over me, you see.'

'Oh!' Sue nodded. 'So you're still seeing him then?'

'Yeah, well...sort of...why?'

'Oh, nothing. It's just that you haven't mentioned him for a while so I thought you'd moved on.' Sue was loading bottles of beer into a fridge as she spoke. Kate was supposed to be helping but she functioned in a lackadaisical manner.

'No. We haven't stopped seeing each other at all. We did go through a patch where we never saw much of each other but we never finished.'

185

Sue's eyebrows raised and she gestured her head as though she had just been enlightened. 'Well, it's none of my business but you can't have a guy hitting you like that. How would he like it?' She half-smiled on the surface whilst inside her a huge smile was beaming through her body as she became aware of the irony of it.

'He didn't mean it,' Kate defended. 'He's not into that sort of thing. He's protective towards girls. He'd never hurt a fly. It's just that he got spiked and who knows what was going on in his mind. He probably felt threatened and saw me as an enemy or whatever. When you've been spiked you don't act rationally.'

'Well, as long as you're sure,' Sue replied, closing the door of the fridge as it was full. 'It wouldn't be nice if he did it again, would it?'

'He won't, I know he won't. I know Danny; he's not into violence!'

Danny and Sue were walking towards The Anchor. They had around a hundred yards to go.

'So let me get this straight in my head,' said Steve, 'because it's ludicrous. The girl you've fucked TWICE works in this pub?'

'Yeah!'

'And your present girlfriend...'

'Fuck-buddy!' Danny interjected.

'Sorry, your present "fuck-buddy" is working in here too.'

'That's right.'

'So what if Kate turns up...or even worse, if she's working...what are you gonna do?'

'Nothing, mate. I'm going in there to get pissed and get pissed I will. That Sue's a crank anyway. If she says anything I'll smash her fuckin' head in.'

'Ever the diplomat, eh?'

The conversation ended with over fifty yards to go and it never resumed until they were inside The Anchor.

'What do you want?' Danny asked.

'I'll have a pint of lager please, mate.'

Sue was the first to see them. She shook Kate by the arm and suggested that *she* might want to serve them.

'Oh, no. You please,' begged Kate. 'I'm still a bit apprehensive.'

'All right then.' Her voice rose to a shout and she headed down the bar towards Danny and Sue.

'What'll it be boys?'

'Two pints of lager.' Danny said, drily. He too was a bit apprehensive about talking to Sue. He had to come and confront it though in case she thought he had lost his nerve since she hit him over the head.

Sue pulled the pints whilst Danny smiled towards Kate. 'How are you?' he asked.

Kate reddened slightly. 'I'm okay, thanks. You been working?'

'Yeah!' The silence was awkward but Sue broke it: 'Four pounds, ten please, Danny.

He handed her a ten-pound note and moved further down the bar to be closer to Kate so he could address her personally. 'Can we talk?'

Kate shrugged. 'I suppose so.'

'Come over here, babe,' he said, indicating a table in the corner. She came out from behind the bar and made her way over. Before she sat down Danny hugged her. 'I'm sorry, babe. I'm so sorry. I don't remember anything.'

The tears welled up in her eyes. 'It's okay, you were spiked. It's not your fault. You don't have to apologise again. I forgive you. Let's put it behind us.'

Sue came back from the till and saw what was happening. She turned to Steve, her manner, aggressive: 'Here! His change!' Danny and Kate came back to the bar.

'Why don't I cook dinner for us all on Friday night?' Danny suggested. Steve and Kate nodded. 'Do you think you'll be able to get Lisa to come, Steve?'

'Yeah, don't see why not.'

'Brilliant! Kate, I'm just gonna talk to Steve for a while. You don't mind do you, babe?'

'Of course not. I'm working anyway. Is everything all right?'

'Yeah, yeah! We just need to sort out a few things. We need to discuss his court case.' Kate looked into his eyes. She was madly in love with him and there was nothing she could do. It saddened her to think that he might be in some kind of trouble. 'Be careful, hun!'

He winked. 'No worries.'

'What's this about the court case?' Steve asked when they sat down away from the bar.

'I just said that to her. I'm talking about those lads from last night. I just wanna make sure you don't blab to anyone. Now I know you're getting quite close to Lisa but just remember- she's a bird and you can't trust her. In fact, don't trust anyone. Don't mention what happened to anyone.'

'I won't.'

'I mean it, Steve. If you think it's all exciting and gangster-like then think again. There could be serious repercussions if it gets out. The less people that know the better. It's possible those little rats might remember you from the road-rage incident but I reckon the chances are they don't. Which means we're home and dry. But they might so we have to take that chance and be on our toes. It's probably best if we just keep our heads down.'

'I agree. I couldn't do that again, Danny.'

'Relax! You won't have to. We got lucky. We might not have got them all but there were faces there you recognise weren't there.' Steve nodded. 'Well then, that should do it for now.'

'For now?' asked Steve, bewildered. 'If I recognise them then they'll recognise me.'

'It doesn't work like that. You would have taken more of a mental note because you feared for your life. They were just bullying you. They probably do it all the time, the little shits. Let's see what happens. The main thing is...are you satisfied?'

'Yeah, I suppose so. We got them, didn't we? Yeah, I'm satisfied.'

'Good!' Danny looked at his glass, it was nearly empty. 'It's your round.'

Steve stood up and made his way to the bar. He turned halfway. 'So the court case is off then?'

'No, not exactly. Get the drinks and I'll explain.'

Back at 132 Craig Street, a young lad called Eddie, whose name was on the tenancy agreement, was chatting to his friend Tommy. Tommy was the lad who had fled when Danny and Steve had gone bursting in to the front room. Eddie was getting annoyed.

'So come on, what happened?' he asked.

'They burst in with bats and blades. All the lads needed stitches and Max is still in intensive care. Jimmy's got a scar down his face, or at least he will have when the stitches come out.'

'So how come you're so fuckin' intact?'

'Well...er...I never got stabbed.' Eddie sensed the hesitation in his voice. 'I was fighting...I punched the crazy one quite a few times. He was a nutter, Eddie, a fucking psycho!' Eddie did not look convinced and Tommy knew this. Tommy's hands became sweaty and he felt he needed to do something to convince him.

After wiping the sweat from his hands on his trousers Tommy, in a quivering voice, added: 'I don't remember much...it all happened so fast.'

'I'll fuckin' bet you a fuckin' grand you don't remember much...' Tommy looked startled. His heart raced. '...because your story doesn't add up.'

'I did my best, Eddie. Honestly!'

'That's not what I heard. No, if you did your best the chances are you'd be scarred up like the rest of them. I heard you bottled it. I heard that your arse went and you legged it.'

'What! No, Eddie, I didn't. I tried to stop him but he was a maniac. I nearly got stabbed.'

'What kind of a blade did he have?'

'Er...it was a big thing...like a kitchen knife.'

'YOU FUCKIN' LIAR,' he shouted, and slapped him across the face. 'I've seen some of the wounds; I've spoken to some of the nurses in the hospital. The blade was a small thing, almost like a penknife. A bit like this.'

He produced a small flick-knife from his pocket and pressed a tiny button on its handle causing the blade to spring out.

'Like I said, it all happened so quickly. I can't be sure.'

'You know, you were the only one that never got hurt that day. But you should've done. By rights, you should be in hospital now. It's not fair that you're not so I think that somebody should even the score.'

Eddie stabbed the knife into Tommy's right side and retracted it quickly. Tommy let out a loud shriek, more through fear than pain, and Eddie repeated the action a further two times. Tommy held his side; the blood poured through his fingers. He backed off, staggering and stooping.

'Eddie! No! Please!'

Eddie wiped the blade on a handkerchief that he had had in his pocket and drew out his mobile phone.

'There, that wasn't so bad was it? You should've joined in, lad.' He dialled 999 on his mobile phone. 'I'll get you an ambulance now, get that sorted. Hello...ambulance please...'

He covered the phone with his hand and addressed Tommy: 'And no fuckin' mention of me or I'll finish the job, all right? You've just been mugged and come running to me.'

Tommy held his side to comfort himself and ease the pain. All he could do was to nod his head.

'...Hello! I want to report a stabbing. That's right, yes, a stabbing.'

'So why isn't it off, then?' asked Steve.

'Because, numbskull, they may press charges against you if they recognise us. And if they don't recognise us then they'll guess it was us when we drop the charges. No, if we carry on we've got the upper hand and we can still make a few quid on it.'

'I don't like it, though. I just want to wash my hands of the whole affair.'

'A couple of months, mate.'

Steve's phone was ringing. 'Hello! Hi Lise. Yeah...it was about Friday. Danny has invited us over for dinner.'

Kate came over to sit with them. 'So what are you cooking on Friday, then?' she asked.

'Well, it's a surprise.'

'Ha! You mean you don't know yourself yet?'

'No! It's a surprise.' He smiled and Kate returned the gesture.

Friday evening came around quick. Danny was in the kitchen of his flat cooking chicken in Cantonese sauce when the doorbell chimed. He ignored it. Outside Steve, Kate and Lisa were stood facing the front door. 'He won't answer,' Steve said to Lisa. 'You only pressed it once. Look!' He pressed the button twice, paused a second then pressed it twice again. Seconds later Danny was at the door.

'All right guys! Come in.'

As they entered Danny relieved the girls of their coats. 'Go into the front room,' he suggested. Steve followed him into the kitchen.

'Hmm! Smells nice, mate.'

'I hope so. Do you want a drink? There's wine in the fridge. Pour the girls a glass too.'

'We've been looking forward to this night all week you know Danny?'

'Yeah? Good!'

'Yeah, nice relaxing night. I've brought a few films with me as well.' He indicated a small selection of DVDs in a carrier bag. 'And Lisa's brought some games.'

'The food won't be long,' said Danny.

Kate walked into the kitchen and noticed the aroma of Cantonese sauce. 'Hmm! Smells good! Do you need a hand with anything? What about the washing up?' She turned to the worktop and lifted up a large, sharp knife that Danny had used to chop up an onion earlier. Danny's eyes widened and he dropped the spatula from his hand and into the wok of Cantonese sauce. 'NO!' he shouted. The sight of Kate stood there with a knife in her hand was too much for him to handle. He had not slept well for the past few nights as memories of his killings were playing on his mind. But he was torn between his two feelings. The images of the two girls' bodies mutilated, sickened him on the one hand and exhausted his thoughts so much so that he couldn't sleep. On the other hand his urge to kill again was growing and he realised that suppressing it would only be temporary. Sooner or later this vicious streak within him would unleash itself and now he was frightened that it would take control.

There was a long pause as Danny's eyes burned into Kate's. Steve looked on. Kate held her stance, frozen and too afraid to move. She sensed that something was not right and she was still not a hundred per cent comfortable with Danny since his wild attack on her when they had made love.

Danny lost control of his thoughts and...suddenly saw himself snatching the knife from Kate's hand and running the blade across her throat. He turned to Steve, stabbed him directly into the heart and finally plunged the whole length of the sharpened steel into his own stomach. A sickly feeling welled up inside him and he snapped out of his thoughts and returned to reality. 'It's all right,' he said to Kate as he took the knife out of her hand softly, you're a guest. And anyway, all the dishes can be washed up together after we have eaten.'

He kissed her on the head and immediately she forgot about his loud exclamation and trance-like action. Steve hadn't, though. 'Are you feeling all right, Danny?'

'Hmm? Yeah, yeah. Fine! Right! That rice should be done now.'

They sat down to dinner and had wine with the meal. Afterwards they watched a DVD, played a few board games and then it was time for music.

'What are we having then? Wagner?' Danny joked. 'Chopin, Beethoven?'

Lisa never saw the joke: 'What? Haven't you got anything...well...modern?'

'Stevie Wonder's greatest hits?'

191

'Yeah that'll do. Stick that on.'

They continued drinking and Danny spoke to Lisa whilst Steve spoke to Kate. It was a refreshing change. At about half eleven they were all feeling a bit tipsy and the conversation they were having never made much sense or fell into any relevant context. However, to them it meant a lot. Lisa got up to use the toilet whilst Danny made his way into the kitchen for more wine.

On seeing Lisa enter the toilet he rushed towards it and followed her in. She was slightly startled at this. Danny put his finger to his lips as if asking for silence in a primary school.

'Ssh! It's okay!' He closed the door behind him and locked it. 'I just wanted to speak to you.'

'What about?'

'Well...me and Kate don't seem to be close anymore and I was wondering if she'd said anything to you.'

'Danny, she loves you. She worships the ground you walk on. And you're both so suited. What are you worrying for?'
He sighed. 'I don't know.'
Lisa felt strong affection for him. They were all good friends and got on well. The combination of her trust in him and the effect of the wine compelled her to embrace him.

'You two were made for each other,' she said and squeezed him tightly as he kissed the top of her head.

'Why can't she be more like you?' Lisa smiled. 'I've been noticing you a lot, lately, Lise. Your personality is great. I love talking to you.'

'That's why we're all such good mates, she interrupted.

'You're good looking...'

'So is Kate.'

'I dunno. There's just something about you.' He brushed the hair from her face with his hand and kissed her forehead.

'I need a wee,' she said.

'Sorry! Go on.'

He released her and she hesitated as first but being quite drunk at this stage, and feeling comfortable with her boyfriend she raised her skirt, took her underwear down to her ankles, sat on the toilet and began to urinate. Danny saw his opportunity and straddled her where she sat. He kissed her face and she responded positively. They then kissed on the lips for a short period and Danny began to fondle her breasts. Suddenly, the reality of the situation hit her and she panicked.

'Stop! No! What are we doing? We shouldn't be doing this.'

'It's okay.'

'It's not okay. Get off.'

'What's the matter?'

'What the hell are you doing?'

'What the hell am *I* doing?'

'All right! Partly my fault. What are *we* doing? I'm with Steve, I love him to bits, and you've got Kate. This is silly! I really like you Danny but we're mates and that's as far as it goes.' She looked down at herself sitting on the toilet with Danny astride her. She felt embarrassed. 'Come on, get off!'

He stood off her and she tidied herself up before hitting the flush. 'Let's get out of here. How would we ever explain this?' Danny, like a scolded child, unlocked the door and left. Lisa followed soon after.

Steve and Kate were getting on brilliantly although not as intimately as Danny and Lisa and they had not even noticed that the pair were absent at the same time. Danny returned with wine and nobody questioned it.

Detective inspector Jenkins was questioning Dominique's friend Jenny: 'So, do you know of any places that she would ever go to on her own? Perhaps some secret location that she used to get away to when the stress became too much or she preferred her own company.'

'Not really, no. Dominique was a lively, social person. It was very rare for her to be on her own.'

'Okay!' He noted everything down. 'And were there any friends, boyfriends for instance, that she might go away with or stay with?'

'Err...she did have a couple of boyfriends, or male friends, over the last two months but I don't think they were serious or anything. She was always focused on her own life and friends. She never had a lot of time for boys.' The Inspector nodded. 'There was a lad called Bobby that she went out with for a while.'

'Would you happen to have his address or know how I could get hold of him?'

'Yeah, it's on King's Drive. I don't know the number but I know the house because we went to a barbecue there. And there was Alby; he's a friend of my brother. I'll get his address for you.'

'Thank you.'

Seconds later she returned holding an address book. 'That was it really. Oh...there was a guy called...Dave. No, Danny. Yeah, that's right, Danny. I don't know much about him though. It was a few months ago, now, so I don't think she could have seen much of him recently. I don't know where he lives and I never saw him. Don't think there's anything there. That's all I can think of for now.'

'That's okay, you've been a great help,' the inspector replied, copying down the address. 'I'll come back another time to see you about that house on King's Drive. If you think of anything else don't hesitate to call me. Even if you think it's only trivial. Sometimes so-called trivial information turns out to be the key in solving a case.'

'Yes, of course. You will find Dominique, won't you?' She swallowed hard.

'We'll do our best Miss Jones...we'll do our best.' Jenny put her head down and nodded slowly.

The local radio station boomed out as Danny's digital, radio alarm clock turned to 09:30. He groaned a bit and rubbed his eyes. Kate awoke too; she was lying next to him.

'Uh! Why so early?' she asked, looking at the alarm clock on the bedside table.

'Don't you remember? We said we would all go out for the day.'

'Oh, yeah. Vaguely! Where are Steve and Lisa?'

'They're in one of the spare rooms. I still feel drunk.'

'You probably are, Danny. We didn't go to bed 'til about half four.'

'Do you want a coffee? I'm gonna jump in the shower.'

By half ten they were well on their way to Southport and by half eleven they had parked up and were strolling down the beach. Danny waited for an opportunity to speak to Lisa alone but it seemed as though it would never come.

After about three quarters of an hour on the beach, however, Kate was on her way to purchase ice-creams from a van about two hundred yards away and Steve was skimming stones off the surface of the water. Danny and Lisa were temporarily alone.

'Lisa! About last night!'

'Yeah?'

'Well...I may have been a bit out of order.'

'Oh don't worry about it, we were all drunk.'

'You do know what I'm referring to, don't you?' She nodded. 'Well I don't want to embarrass you but I'm sober now so it should mean more...I can't stop thinking about you. It wasn't the drink talking last night. I really do like you.'

'What! Don't be silly!'

'I'm serious. I think we get on really well and I'm sure we're suited.'

Lisa grew nervous. She looked round to see who was about. Steve was quite far away and not paying any attention to them. Kate was nowhere to be seen.

Danny continued: 'I know you're with Steve now, but that won't last. Steve's not one for commitment. Don't get me wrong, I really like Steve; he's my best mate. The thing is, though, I don't like to see a nice girl like you just plodding on in life when there's so much out there. I wouldn't like to see you get hurt.'

Sue's eyes widened. She was speechless. Her mouth dropped open a little as if words were about to emanate from it, but none came out.

'We can go away if you like, just the two of us.'

'I can't,' she rejected, I love Steve. He's your best mate as well. You shouldn't be doing this.'

'Last night, when you went the toilet in front of me, really brought home the chemistry between us. I feel as though I could do anything in front of you, or tell you anything. I'd share my darkest secrets with you and hopefully vice versa. I feel really comfortable around you. There's no need for any pretentious behaviour.'

'Look, Danny! This is stupid...I...'

'There's more to me than you know. I'm deep.'

'I'm sure you are. Most people are when you scratch away the surface.' He took offence to this as if she was mitigating his experiences.

'No, you don't understand. I've done things, bad things.'

'I don't want to know who you've killed,' she said jokingly. Danny could not have been more serious though.

'Come and meet me some time.'

'It's not gonna happen, Danny.'

'Please, at least to just talk.'

Kate suddenly came into Danny's vision. She was walking towards Lisa with four ice-cream cones.

'You need some help, Danny. You need to re-focus your attention on Kate. I'd tell her what you've just said if I thought it wouldn't hurt her. You're probably just a bit confused, though. Yes, let's put it down to that. I like you Danny and I know this isn't you. You love Kate; show it. Here she comes. Give her a kiss and I don't want to hear any more about it.'

Danny tried to talk to Lisa again later that afternoon but she rejected his advances. Later still, they were all out drinking and he flirted with her and made another pass at her. Once again she refused his attention.

Sunday afternoon, 4pm. Lisa answered her mobile phone.

'Lisa! Hi! It's Danny...'

'Danny! What do you want?'

'I'm sorry to bother you babe but I need to talk to you.'

'Not again, no. Get to the point and make it quick because I'm gonna hang up.'

'No, please! Don't hang up. Just hear me out. You can at least do that.'

'Okay but if this is one of your stupid little ploys to...'

'It isn't,' he interrupted.

'Go on then.'

'I didn't mean to come on to you yesterday, you know. Kate and me...we haven't been getting on too well lately.'

'She never mentioned it to me.'

'That's probably because there's nothing anyone can do. We probably just need to talk. You see, I don't want anybody else but I'm confused. I came on to you but it wasn't because I was gonna cheat on Kate. If you would have said to me: "Come on, let's go to bed" I would have said "yes" at first but I wouldn't have gone through with it. I would have realised after a bit. I couldn't be unfaithful to Kate. I couldn't bear to lose her. I think I just needed somebody to talk to; a shoulder to cry on.

'Steve doesn't understand. You're a girl, you probably know how she thinks. I just wanted to find out a little bit more about how she is feeling, what her expectations are and why she acts in certain ways.'

'Hmm! Yeah...sure. Ask away then.' Lisa was beginning to open up to him now. He asked her several questions before suggesting that she came over to the flat. She declined and threatened to hang up, claiming it was a ploy.

'Wait! Lisa! Okay, there's no need for you to come over to the flat but please don't hang up. I've got nobody else to turn to.'

There was a short pause. Lisa spoke first. 'I'm sorry. I'm just a bit defensive. Go on.'

'If you feel that I'm trying it on with you then just revert the conversation back to Kate and I'll back off. I'm just a bit confused, that's all. I can see that now but then I get lonely. I wasn't asking you to come over and sleep with me. I just wanted some company. But anyway, we can talk over the phone.'

'Exactly!' added Lisa. 'So what's the problem, then? In what way is the relationship failing?'

'That's just it, I'm not sure. I think she loves me but then she starts acting strangely.'

'In what way? How do you mean, strangely?'

'She says things like: "I don't wanna get close because I'll get hurt. Let's just be friends", but then she says: "Don't ever leave me babe", and it's so confusing! I was just wondering if she'd said anything to you.'

'Err...no. Nothing that I can think of off-hand. You see, what you're saying doesn't add up. She never once said to me that she doubted you or your relationship. Everything she said was positive. She said you were perfect. So I can't see why she would act in any other way. The only thing that *I* can think of is when you had your drink spiked...but that wasn't your fault. She couldn't fall out with you for that. She knows it was only a one-off and that you've never done it before. Drugs have profound effects on the mind. She knows that, she's not stupid. She loves you Danny.'

'Then why do I feel so lonely? Sometimes I feel like I can't carry on any longer. How silly is that? I don't want to die, I certainly don't want to kill myself but sometimes...it seems there's no alternative.'

'You shouldn't talk like that, Danny. It's silly! You're not gonna do anything like that are you? People who take their own lives are usually a bit mentally unstable- even if it's only temporary. It's not a permanent feeling, remember that.'

'I know but when you're depressed you don't think rationally. Up to about three months ago in my life I always thought that suicide was a coward's way out. I also thought that you'd have to have nothing else in your life. Now I feel different. I never thought, until three months ago, that I would ever, not only contemplate suicide, but understand how a person feels when they're at such a low ebb that death seems the only way out. It's horrible. You can't see the light at the end of the tunnel. You live for the here-and-now and you can't see outside of the parameters of your blinkered vision. I see that now but sometimes I slip into that rut and suicide has become apparent to me on a number of occasions.

'And you don't have to have nothing in your life. Sometimes you could have everything but it feels like you've got nothing. There's nothing worse. Can I rely on you to talk when I'm at a low ebb? I promise I won't come on to you. I need somebody who is close, somebody who understands.'

'That's what Kate is for. You should speak to her.'

'The problem is, I'm too close to Kate. I need an outsider who can sympathise with the situation, possibly even empathise, and give their neutral viewpoint. And how can I talk about Kate- to Kate?'

'Of course, I'll be here for you.'

'Thank you. I think last night I was psychologically testing the strength of our friendship, trying to get closer. I feel better already but need to talk a while longer.'

Lisa yielded, and conceded to his wishes: 'Look, I can spare you an hour, if that's okay. But no longer.'

'Fantastic! You're a star! You're helping me loads. And if you ever need to turn to anyone for support or advice- about Steve, for instance- then don't hesitate to call.'

'I'll be over in about three quarters of an hour.'

'Are you sure? I don't want to put you out.'

'No problem!'

Danny hung up and made his way to the bedroom. He stretched the quilt tightly over the bed and fluffed up the pillows. He then went to the kitchen and counted the knives on the rack. 'All there!' he exclaimed, then retrieved the tap from the inside of a fresh box of wine and poured himself a glass before returning to the living room. He sat down and fantasised over Lisa.

16

Before he knew it the front doorbell chimed twice and, after the usual pause, twice again. Danny sprang to his feet from his favourite chair and ran to the door. He hadn't moved from that spot for over an hour. Lisa was a little longer than expected but the time had gone quickly. She smiled when he opened the door.

'Thanks for coming,' he said. 'You don't know what this means to me.'

They went inside and Danny put the kettle on. 'Coffee?'

'Er...yes please.'

'So you say Kate really loves me, then?'

'Yeah.'

'So why the mind games?'

'I don't know, exactly. What sort of mind games?'

'The usual sort. What does it matter?'

'It's just that Kate is quite straightforward and not one for mind games, usually. Was there anything in particular that she did that was so unusual?'

'All that blowing hot and cold shit. I can't be dealing with that.'

'You need to give her a bit of time, and probably a bit of space.'

'Whoa! Wait a minute. I don't smother her, you know.'

'Yeah I know. But you have to realise that she has had some, shall we say, dysfunctional relationships and they've probably had their effect on her.'

'That explains a lot.'

This was all hypothetical as there was no major problem with Danny and Kate's relationship. Danny used this tactic to become close to Lisa. He continued and this time his soapbox came out. 'The thing is, you see, people put their barriers up to avoid being hurt; it only takes one to create a vicious circle, and when they do it is usually to the wrong people. We defend ourselves when we are not being attacked, our guard goes up and this does not allow us to become close to a person. We move on and then that person puts their barrier up to someone else because they've been hurt etc etc. When we do finally

199

let our barriers down, again, it's to the wrong people and they get hurt again.

'We seem to crave attention from people who can potentially threaten us and we still go back for more. We chase lost causes. That's how we get hurt.'

'Phew!' said Lisa. 'That's some speech. I think you're right, though. We do allow ourselves to be hurt by trusting the wrong people. And that's probably what Kate's doing. It's not that she doesn't love you because she does. It's just that the guy before you, or guys, probably conditioned her way of thinking.'

Danny swallowed hard. The thought of Kate with another man, even before he knew her, was unbearable. He stared long and intently at Lisa. She suddenly became frightened. *Those eyes!* she thought. *Lifeless! No soul!* She was beginning to regret coming over. 'I think I'd better be going,' she said.

'But you promised me an hour. Surely you can give me just that,' pleaded Danny.

'Seriously Danny, I don't know what to do for the best. I want to help you but...'

'But what?'

'Well...don't take this the wrong way but...you frighten me.'

Danny softened immediately, realising that his whole approach was not working. 'Come here, silly,' he said and embraced her. She also softened somewhat. 'Would you like a *proper* drink?'

'Yes, please. I could do with one.' He exited towards the kitchen and returned in less than a minute with two large glasses of wine.

'That was quick.'

'Well I've only got an hour, haven't I? Let's go in here.' Danny gestured with his wine glass to the living room. It seemed so empty, Lisa felt, without Kate and Steve. She sat on one side of the couch and Danny sat on the other, kicked off his shoes and tucked his legs up into himself. 'Take your shoes off, put your feet up, make yourself at home. Whatever you feel comfortable with.'

'I'm okay, thanks.

They chatted for about half an hour and Danny refilled his glass up twice and Lisa's once. She was starting to relax more and without realising it two hours went by. She was fascinated with Danny's quips on life and the strange way he viewed everything. By this time she had had four large glasses of wine and was feeling tipsy. Danny had had seven.

'You know, Danny,' Lisa started, 'I've never really seen this side of you. You've really opened up and I'm beginning to understand you. You love Kate, don't you? But you're quite insecure deep down and you hide it well on the surface. I think that you're afraid that Kate will leave you or somehow you'll get hurt.' Danny's head drooped slightly and he stared into his wine glass. It appeared as though he wasn't listening yet he could hear every word. The look of forlorn on his face caused her to move closer to him. He had earned her sympathy and now he could sit back and let her do the work.

By feigning closure he allowed Lisa to open up to him and attempt to get close. Not just physically, in her eyes, but psychologically. She felt at this moment that she really knew him. He was a lost little boy who needed help. How little she knew. She was only scratching the surface and accessing one facet of his complex mind. She summed him up and, desperate to comfort him, permitted her sympathy to overwhelm her other urges.

She put her hand on his leg as she asked him if he was all right. He nodded. Putting her arms around his shoulders she pulled his head into her breasts and a tear trickled down from his left eye. He lay there like a baby. Another tear rolled down his face as the realisation of what he might do to this sweet and innocent girl almost choked him.

Lisa's voice soothed him:

'Don't worry, babe. I think it's great. We're all really close. I wish Kate and Steve were here. Let's call them, bring them round.'

She made to get up but Danny pressed his weight into her hard.

'No!' he said. 'Not yet. In a minute. Just give me a moment. I'm not sure I'm ready to see Kate.'

Once again Danny was torn between two heavily contrasting emotions. He was enjoying the attention from Lisa and agreed with her that it was fantastic that the two couples were also great friends. Friends who could share strong emotions and understand each other, he informed her, regardless of which two were together. They were all close and feeling this it would not have been a problem to envisage Steve in a similar position with Kate. However, opposing this was a huge urge to grope Lisa, to abuse the proximity of their friendship. And this urge was rising.

As Kate answered her mobile Steve's voice immediately came through. 'Hi, Kate. You okay?'

'Yes, thanks.'

'I was just wondering if you had seen Lisa. I've phoned her a few times and left a few text messages but she hasn't got back to me yet.'

'She's probably in the shower or something.'

'Well I thought that at first but it's been a couple of hours now and I was supposed to meet her.'

'She must have left her phone somewhere. I haven't seen her, sorry. If I do, though, I'll get her to call you.'

'Thanks. What are you up to tonight?'

'Not sure yet.'

'I've been trying to get hold of Danny, too, but his phone is off. I thought that the four of us could do something; I dunno, see a film or whatever.'

'Yeah, that would be good. Let me know what you decide. I'll send Danny a *text*. He can reply whenever, then. Maybe his phone has just got no signal.'

'It's okay,' suggested Steve. 'I'm gonna go round there in a bit. I've got a feeling he's sleeping, the lazy git!'

Danny snuggled his head between Lisa's breasts and put his arm around her waist.

'Can we call Steve, now?' she asked.

'I'll call him for you in a moment. I don't want to move because you're so comfortable.' She smiled and stroked his head then added: 'I really like Steve. He's great and his mates are great.' Danny's eyes were closed but that didn't stop him from smiling. 'Steve talks about you a lot you know, Danny. He's always saying how good you are to him. He looks up to you.'

The guilt welled in Danny's stomach. 'Forget him,' he said and raised his head to kiss her.

'I can't, Danny. We can't do this. Don't spoil it.'

'Come on you said you liked me.'

'I do! We're mates.'

'Fuck, mates. I want more.'

'I'm gonna go now, Danny,' she stated, nervously, attempting to push him off. He resisted, though and threw his lips on hers.

'Danny, get off. I wanna go.'

'Don't give me that shit. You know you wanna be here just as much as me.'

He grabbed both her arms and pinioned her against the back of the couch, kissing her. She turned her head away from him and cried for release. It was no good; he was too strong. He kissed her face, her neck. His eyes then travelled down towards her breasts. He kissed them also.

'Danny! This is not funny. Please!' Her left arm escaped his clutch and her nails clawed at his face, scratching it across his eye. The wound bled immediately.

'Ah, bitch!' he said, backing off and holding his eye with an open palm. She then lashed out with her foot, after wriggling it free, and her heel connected clearly on Danny's stomach. It took the wind out of him for a second. Lisa seized this opportunity and leapt off the couch and ran towards the door. Danny was quicker, however. He caught her left arm and pulled her back. As she attempted to pull away, he spun her round and punched her in the face. She fell to the floor but was still conscious.

'Want to play games do you, you fucking slag?'

Lisa was crying out for him to stop but could not find it in herself to scream. As she came onto her knees in an attempt to stand he slapped her hard on the head. She fell, lying and covering her face.

'Stay down, slut!' He stood over her.

'Danny...why?' She was crying hard.

'Tell me you want me, bitch! Tell me you want me to fuck your brains out.'

'No, I don't want you. Leave me alone,' she cried.

'I don't handle rejection very well, you know.' He yanked at her hair causing her to fall prostrate once more.

'Danny, please let me go. Please, you're hurting me.' Her voice was barely audible through the stream of tears. He kicked her in the stomach causing her to cough repeatedly. 'You're not going anywhere, slag!'

A mixture of heavy sobbing with her fit of coughing stressed her to the point that she began to choke. Danny watched over her as she struggled for breath. After a few seconds she controlled the coughing but continued to cry although softer at this point. Danny knelt over her. 'I'm sorry, babe. I'm sorry. I don't know what came over me. I'm sorry. He held his hand out and immediately upon it resting on her shoulder she wriggled around, got herself half-up and scratched along the wooden floor to escape, dragging her legs behind her.

'Get away from me,' she screamed. 'Get away from me. Leave me alone.'

'But babe...'

'Get away. You're a psycho! Get away from me.'

'I'm only trying to help.'

He crossed towards her then stood bent over her. She had scrambled into a corner. A shot of adrenalin surged through her body and a huge explosion of energy enabled her to scurry up his body like a ferret going up a drainpipe. Her nails clawed their way to the top and she took him by surprise, scratching at both eyes and causing further bleeding.

As Danny cried out in pain his hands reached for his face whilst his body was bent-double. From out of nowhere Lisa's knee came up swiftly and connected with his nose. It erupted with blood as he stumbled backwards and fell to the floor. Lisa ran to the door. Surveying it as quickly as possible she ran her hands over every lock. Why were they all fastened? she wondered.

The bolt at the top was released and then the latch unlocked on the Yale, along with the chain. Finally, a bolt below that. She pulled hard at the door: it didn't open.

Danny's slow, clonking footsteps could be heard as he fumbled his way around, temporarily blind. Lisa noticed a bolt at the bottom of the door. She released it and took one last look. Danny was getting close. She turned the latch and pulled hard once again- nothing! 'Oh, shit!' she cried. Danny was almost upon her, sensing his way forward by following the heavy breathing and scratching sounds on the front door. Lisa scanned the door twice, dumbfounded as to what was preventing it from opening. Suddenly, she noticed. There was a mortice lock about halfway down. Where was the key? Too late, Danny was upon her. She turned and lowered herself as she ran past him. He flailed his arms out but to no avail.

Back in the living room she grabbed her bag and searched for her phone. It was not there. She realised then that he had taken it out and that this had all been staged. Would she ever get out of there alive? she wondered.

The cordless house phone was on the table. As she picked it up to dial she realised that it was dead. She could hear something, though: heavy breathing. She spun round fast and saw Danny facing her, his noisy exhalations torturing her ears. Danny's eyes were half-closed and his nose appeared flat against his face. The blood was everywhere; he spat some from his mouth.

Noticing one of her stiletto shoes on the floor by the couch, Lisa made a dash for it. Danny came racing towards her. She was just in time to sweep the heel from the floor and bring it crashing down on the top of his head. As he recoiled in pain she struck him again. Absorbing the pain this time, his body pumped with adrenalin, he reached out his arm and his leg, and in one swift movement he swept her legs from under her. As she fell she landed awkwardly on her left arm. Pain flooded her body but in particular her arm. It was either broken or badly sprained, she was not sure which. Danny towered over her once more, exercising his power. He spat a mouthful of blood over her. 'Slag!'

Clasping both sides of her head he pulled upwards. Lisa complied and scrambled to her feet to avoid her head from being pulled off completely. He threw her onto the couch, his vision restoring itself to about fifty per cent. 'Like it rough, do you?' Danny wiped the blood from his face with his sleeve. 'I'll show you what rough is.'

He leapt onto the couch and punched her hard in the side of her head. She fought against him and they wrestled until he took control. Lisa reached down, searching for one of her stiletto shoes. Unfortunately she could not reach it. Danny pulled her back onto the couch and bear-hugged her. She struggled but he was far too strong. Even her hidden strength, brought about through fear, was no match for the mentally disturbed power that Danny possessed as he knew of no limits. His brain did not seem to be governed by social conditions and he had no idea when to stop. 'You're mine, now,' he said in her ear. 'Mine! You're in my control and I'm gonna do whatever I want to you.'

Steve was getting in his car before he realised that he had left his phone in his flat. He ran back inside to retrieve it and was just in time to find it ringing. It was Kate.

'Hi, Steve. You haven't been to Danny's yet, have you?'

'No, not yet. Why?'

'Well I can't get hold of him. Like you said, his phone's off. I need to know what he's doing about my light in the bedroom.'

'Why, what's wrong with it?'

'I can't use it. He knows because I told him yesterday. It keeps shorting out and blowing the fuse. When it was on it gave off a horrendous smell. Like plastic burning.'

'Leave it off and if you haven't spoken to him by the time I get back I'll come over and have a look at it for you.'

'Thanks, babe. And ask him to phone me anyway so I know he's all right. He usually has his phone on all the time.'

'I will do.' They hung up and Steve headed for the car. He wondered again what Danny could possibly be up to but it never caused him to hasten too much. Steve had plenty of time to cruise over to his flat.

Lisa was crying softly. It seemed that all her energy had been taken from her. She was almost ready to give in. Danny held her tightly and hushed her as he kissed her neck. Too tired to resist she sagged her head forward. 'Oh, baby!' Danny muttered. 'Hmm! That's nice, honey.' He bit gently at her neck then sucked playfully at her flesh. 'You taste good!'

Lisa got her second wind and began to wriggle. She was now on more of a high than Danny who had mellowed extensively. This gave her the upper hand momentarily. She wriggled loose and tried to vacate the couch as he held her by her foot. Realising that he was losing control Danny utilised his inner strength more. He pulled her back. Her wriggling was fuelled, however, and she got away again. Danny jumped up and reached his arms out to restrain her. She turned quickly and caught him off his guard, the palm of her hand smacking him on the nose. Once again it erupted and this drove him wild. It had only just stopped bleeding about a minute before.

Lisa clawed around as before but this time he kept his distance. He parried her arms down and then punched her in the side of the head. She flew back and hit the wall but remained standing. Anger compelled her to run at him. Stepping aside he jabbed her in the ribs and then again in the face. He was playing with her. Determined to fight for her life she retaliated with further clawing. She just managed to catch him before he held both her wrists and head butted her on the nose. He heard the crunch as the cartilage collapsed underneath. Blood streamed down her nostrils and a myriad of pain signals raced to her brain. She reeled as they overtook her senses. She was dazed. Danny slapped her in the direction of the couch and she fell cleanly.

'Now stop fuckin' about, you slag. Don't question my authority. Tell me you love me and you want me to fuck you and I'll think about it.'

As he spoke he leaned over her. Lisa was flopped on the couch, her hand trailing on the floor. It moved slightly across the floor until she felt something touch it. It was one of her shoes.

'I'm waiting!' Danny ordered.

Swinging it up as fast and as hard as she could she smashed the heel into his face, catching him just above the eye. She continued the assail with several more strikes before Danny fell to the floor. Once again she had caught him off his guard as he was not fighting at his best, believing her to be an easy target. The blood pouring from his nose, in conjunction with his eyes watering, gave her a distinct advantage.

She ran through to the kitchen and tried the back door. It was locked. She half-expected it but hoped she might get lucky. She saw the bigger picture now. Danny had lured her there under false pretences. She searched furiously for the keys but they were nowhere to be seen. She kicked at the door in frustration but realised it was futile and only served in wasting the precious little time she had left. Running into the bedroom she tried the windows; they too were locked.

Where would he put the keys? she wondered. *He probably has them on him- in his pocket.*

Lisa convinced herself that this was the only way out. She peered in the living room. Danny lay on the floor, he was out cold. She crept towards him but fear got the better of her and caused her to hurry back to the kitchen.

'There's got to be a way out of here,' she cried to herself.

She opened all the drawers and cupboards but there were no keys anywhere. It was no use; she would have to search him.

Deciding on speed rather than caution she raced to where he lay and fumbled through one of his pockets. His arm moved towards her and she shrieked in fright. He was still unconscious and his arm had fallen naturally through its own weight. Nothing in that pocket. She moved on to the next one, conscious of the little time that she had before he came to. Again, nothing! His pockets were empty except for some ten-pound notes and some loose change. Racing back to the kitchen she realised that her only escape would be to break a window. She scanned the room frantically for something to use; something heavy.

The window in the door contained a steel wiring system that strengthened it. Lisa became aware of this when she struck it with a saucepan. The metal underneath would prevent her escape. She seemed to be clutching at straws and had to compose herself to plan a better escape route.

She smacked at the window above the sink. The saucepan bounced back and the vibrations caused her to drop it. She held it firmly for the second strike and effected a crack then repeated the striking until the glass broke and she had penetrated both panes of the double glazing. Unfortunately, the hole was not big enough to climb through; she could only just get her hand through. She panicked and wondered if she would have time to make the hole bigger.

Stretching herself over the sink she screamed through the hole: 'HELP! HELP!' A smashing noise distracted her and caused her to turn around. A cup had fallen from the worktop- knocked off by Danny.

He stood in the doorway, his seemingly huge frame filling it. He appeared bigger than ever. In his right hand he held a large kitchen knife. He had taken it from the magnetic strip on the wall and knocked the cup off the worktop in the process. Lisa froze, speechless. She was fixated with his eyes. His breathing deep, his walking heavy, he ambled towards her.

'Come on!' shouted Steve to the car in front. 'You've got loads of room.' He was stuck in traffic and getting deeply frustrated. Although only five minutes from Danny's flat it would probably take him about fifteen. Roadworks had brought Smithdon Road to a halt.
'I don't believe this,' he muttered to himself.

Steve was not in the habit of talking to himself, except when driving. He always found that this was acceptable, usually due to the fact that the main part of his conversation was aimed at other road users. They couldn't hear him, of course, but that never stopped him.

He picked up his mobile phone from the dashboard and scrolled through the address book until he found Danny's number. The call went straight to his answer phone. He left a message: 'Hello, Danny! Hiya mate, it's Steve. Give me a call when you get this message 'cos we're all worrying about you. I'm just on my way to your place now so, obviously, if I haven't seen you then get back to me. Kate's worried. She wants to speak to you. See you soon, mate.'

He hung up and resumed his rant at the other drivers on the road. 'Come on!' he shouted at the windscreen. 'This is ridiculous. We're not even moving.' As he said this the car in front crawled forward about ten yards and then stopped.

Danny had ceased moving. He stared at Lisa, deeply. His eyes frightened her. She did not even have the strength, let alone inclination, to scream. Speechless and glued to the spot, it was as if she wanted to die. Her whole life flashed before her and she really believed that this would be the end. It all seemed so good as a child. Life was a big adventure; she could hardly wait to grow up. She wanted to see the world, to explore and experience everything...

No! she thought. *It's too early! I'm too young! I haven't lived.*

Danny took a step forward and Lisa's heart raced even faster even though she did not think it was possible. He relished in the drama and revelled in observing Lisa fear for her life. He knew that at that moment he had drawn out one of the strongest emotions and feelings that this girl would ever experience. He had taken her to the peak of her fear and he savoured the moment.

Lisa wondered why he did not just kill her there and then. She was thoroughly exhausted from fighting, panicking and moving in general. The horror of it all took her breath away when she needed it most. Would she have enough energy for one final bout of resistance? She would have to. In her mind she knew that she had nothing whatsoever to lose and should give it all that she possibly could. The words 'I can rest when I'm dead,' barely voiced themselves from beneath her breath. They were way out of earshot of Danny.

He took another step forward, the knife glistening in his right hand, his eyes burning into her soul. Somehow it no longer felt real for Lisa. Her eyes flicked in all directions as she searched for something for her defence. She noticed the saucepan that she had used to break the window; Danny did, too. She snatched it up in one swift sweep and Danny closed the distance between them. She swung the pan rapidly towards his head but he was too quick and dodged sideways. He slashed across her stomach with his knife, only just drawing blood. Lisa let out a cry of concern. He was playing with her again. Like a child that tortures an insect before killing it, he toyed with her first. Each time she waved the pan around in an attempt to hit him he would slash an arm or a leg, or stab at her gently with the tip of the blade.

By now, she had several wounds and they were all bleeding. Danny lunged forward to stab her in the side and lost control. He slipped on a grease spot on the floor tiles. One small blob of margarine that he had dropped earlier, but forgotten to pick up, now became dangerous. As his foot slipped from under him he went down on his other knee. Lisa saw her opportunity and wasted no time in smashing the pan down on his head. He fell further and she ran past him and out of the kitchen, still holding the pan. Danny winced at the pain streaming through his knee and his head alternately. He staggered to his feet and limped forward.

'Fuckin' slag!' he bawled. 'No more Mr Nice Guy for you.' His voice lowered as he addressed himself. 'I'm gonna finish you off now, bitch.'

Lisa found a pen and paper in the living room. She scrawled as fast as she could but her words were barely legible. The note read: 'Please help me. Madman. Trapped. Danny is going to...' The door burst open and Danny emerged into the room. Lisa dropped the pen and paper on the arm of the couch. It deflected off and fell by the side.

If I'd have finished that I could've tried to get to the front door and slip it through the letterbox, she thought.

Danny was still holding the knife. 'I won't be needing that,' he claimed and threw it to the floor. 'It's more fun without it.'

He clenched his fists but Lisa was not interested in his supposedly-sporting attitude. She retained the pan in her grasp. Danny looked at it. 'I'll give you that. Let's just say it's your handicap.'

'Why are you doing this, Danny?' Lisa asked, changing her approach.

He shrugged. 'I like you, babe. I want you.'

'But what about Kate? She loves you...and you love her. Why would you want me? Let's stop all this now, before it goes too far.'

In her mind it had gone way beyond far already but it seemed like her last chance. 'Just let me go Danny. Please! I won't say anything to anybody. Please, Danny! Look at me, I'm bleeding. You wouldn't want to kill me would you, Danny? Could you really be responsible for killing someone?'

He smiled and stated: 'It's already too late.'

'I can get you help. Get you better. You need to talk to someone. You can't carry on like this.' Inside she was shaking and hurt from her wounds. Slowly they were draining the life from her but she fought on. She felt that she was penetrating what little compassion he had left so she persisted. Danny's head drooped and he allowed his shoulders to sag. 'I...' He swallowed to moisten the back of his mouth. 'I...I've killed two people. Two girls.'

Silence fell for a moment and Lisa's heart began to pick up its pace again. She spoke softly. 'Where's your phone? We need an ambulance. Tell me where the keys are, Danny.' Her main concern was to get out alive and she would try any means that she could.

Danny walked over to a dresser where there were some books on a shelf. He pulled two out and retrieved a phone from behind; it was Lisa's and it was on silent. All the time he moved he retained his stooped posture, mimicking a scolded child. He seemed to be yielding to her requests.

Lisa looked at her phone and saw eleven missed calls. She dialled 999 and raised the handset to her ear. Danny looked up, suddenly. He flailed his arms up in the air until they came down and one came into contact with her arm and sent the telephone flying into the wall and crashing to the floor. It broke into five pieces- the battery, the front and back covers, the rubber keypad and the rest of the phone.

'NO!' Danny yelled. 'You're not getting me put away. Why don't you want me? What's wrong with me?'
Lisa tried to soothe him but it was useless. 'I'm gonna get you help, Danny.'

'Fuck the help! Answer my question. What's wrong with me?'

'Nothing! And that's why Kate loves you.'

'I don't give a fuck about Kate. I want you.'

'Please, Danny! No!'
His voice became slow and deliberate. 'I've told you, I don't respond well to rejection. Fucking slut!' He punched her hard and she fell to the floor.

'Aargh! Please...'
Her body would not stand up to much more of this abuse.

He kicked her while she was down- in the ribs, in the face and finally in her head. Danny did his usual. He stepped back and took aim, imagining himself as a footballer- his target, her head. His right leg swung back before it came forward, connecting on Lisa's chin and driving her head upwards. Her neck snapped like a twig and her lifeless body slumped to the floor.

Seconds later the doorbell chimed its usual two times and two times intermitted with a short pause. Steve hung about outside, eagerly awaiting entry. He tried again. Still no answer. 'Where the bloody hell is he?' he muttered to himself. His actions within the car had rubbed off to the outside and he was frustrated and angry. He rang the bell again.

Inside, Danny was sat quiet on the couch. He saw a spider scurrying across the floor towards Lisa's body but left it. He sat still, waiting for Steve to go. Outside, Steve had scribbled a quick note in the car asking Danny to call him and was just putting it through his letterbox. He rang the bell one last time but returned to his car without waiting for an answer. Danny heard the engine start up. He pulled the letterbox open from the inside with a thin knife, just in time to see Steve driving off. He then returned to Lisa's body and dragged it along the floor and into the bedroom where Dominique had lain. Even though he should've been used to hauling dead weights about by now he still struggled with Lisa's corpse.

He drew back the quilt from the bed and tossed it on the floor before heaving Lisa onto the bed. She had bruising on her face and blood covered a major part of her as she had several wounds across her body. He still found her attractive, though, and kissed her. He moved away as though waiting for a reaction and then kissed her on the lips before snogging her as best he could.

'You see, you do want me. You were just playing hard to get.'

He started to undo what was left of her blouse. It had been torn in the fight. After her blouse he reached around to the back of her, undid her bra and slipped it off. Her breasts fell to the side and he became excited. 'Oh my God!' he exclaimed. 'Yeah!' and kissed them passionately. He spent about twenty minutes doing this, savouring the moment and heightening his anticipation before removing her jeans.

Once she was naked he kissed her from head to toe, particularly her wounds. It was as if he would make her better, bring her back to life. The blood did not seem to bother him. He licked the inside of her thighs and nibbled each one gently. 'You see, you wanted me all the time didn't you baby? Is that nice?' He continued kissing and spoke in between. 'You weren't rejecting me were you, honey? Tell me you want me. Tell me.'

He began to bite her and as he received no reaction bit harder. Lisa remained motionless. Danny sunk his teeth into her until he pierced the flesh. 'You like that, baby? Eh?' He bit again. 'That feels good?' A small chunk of flesh hung between his teeth. He spat it out on the floor and repeated the process. 'How's that, babe? Is it good? You like it rough, don't you? You ready for me now? You want me?'

He raised her leg as high as he could and then bit off another chunk of flesh, this time from her buttock cheek. The leg fell heavily as he dropped it. 'What's that babe? You wanna fuck me? Well...I don't know. You were playing hard to get, remember. What if I play hard to get?' He punched her in the ribs and they cracked. 'Don't ever fuck me about again, you slag.'

212

He pushed her legs open and tore away at his own jeans, pulling them down as much as he could. He couldn't wait any longer. He struggled to get inside her at first but after a little forcing he managed it. He was excited beyond belief. Pounding his way in and out of her corpse he began to lose control. 'I told you I don't like rejection,' he gasped, slightly out of breath. 'Look at you now. You're just the same as the rest. Fucking slags! Prostitutes! You're all the same you're just holding out for a different price. Yeah, I'll take you out. I'll spend money on you...for what? Sex? I'll just get a prostitute. She's cheaper. And she doesn't fuckin' moan.'

He laughed out loud at this, still pounding deep inside her. Another urge hit him and he punched her in the face. 'Yeah! Take it, bitch!' He looked at her wounds and his curiosity grew. Running his finger up to a hole from one of his bites he dipped it inside. It reminded him of his childhood- dipping soldiers of toast into an egg. He bit again, this time at her left breast, then thrust as hard as he could until he came inside her.

He slowed down, his heart rate dropped and he eventually came to a halt. He lay on top of her stroking and tickling her arm. He felt content, as if they were lovers. Closing his eyes his brain took him on a fantastic voyage.

17

Danny walked along the playground on the first day in his secondary school. Charlie Higgins was two years older than him, he was thirteen years old and a bully to anyone he could get away with. He walked in front of Danny and stood in his way.

'Empty your pockets' he demanded.

'What? No!' Danny replied.

'Empty them, I said'

Danny looked at him squarely in the eyes, said: 'Fuck off!' and then walked on. Charlie came behind him and punched him in the side of his head. It was a good punch and Danny's leg reeled.

'Empty your fuckin' pockets, now.' Composing himself after a second or two, he made his way face-to-face with Charlie. His eyes widened like the curtains of a house opening in the morning. The occupants seemed to vacate the place at the same time. Placing both hands in his pockets as though searching for something, he head-butted Charlie as hard as he could, knocking his two front teeth out and leaving two small indentations in his own forehead. Charlie fell to the floor, then sat up and wept. The blood horrified him and made him feel sick. He never bullied anyone again after that.

Danny sat in the class, quiet until the teacher left the room for 5 minutes. He turned to the blonde girl behind him and asked her out.

'No. I don't go out with people like you,' she replied. 'You're too violent. I don't like violence.'

'Me, violent? That wasn't my fault. He hit me first.'

'I don't care. I don't like violence, violence, violence....'
Nineteen-year-old Danny walked up to the bar, proud of his new girlfriend. Two drunken lads were at the bar. One of them addressed the brunette with Danny. 'All right, love? You wanna drink?'

'I'm with him,' she said, indicating to Danny.

'You can do better then him, love. Dump him and come with me.'

'She's with me' interjected Danny. 'Didn't you hear her?' The lad ignored Danny.

'Come on love! Dump the zero; get with a hero, ha ha!'

'I said, she's with me. She's going nowhere.'

'Oh, yeah? What are you gonna do, you tit?'

'What? I'll.....' He looked at his girlfriend. 'Look, lads. We're not out for trouble. Just leave it, eh?'

'No I won't just leave it, you shithouse.' He pushed Danny.

'Come on,' said Danny to his girlfriend 'we're leaving.' He held her arm and walked her out, the lads shouting from behind. 'I'll see you again, pal.' Immediately they were in Mrs Mullins tea rooms. His girlfriend gave him the bad news. 'I don't want to go out with you anymore.'

'Why not?'

'I need a real man, a man who can protect me. What you did the other night in the pub....I was frightened. I don't want to feel like that.'

'Eh? I thought you girls weren't into violence.'

'Well, there's a time and a place, isn't there?' I'm not being funny but you should have protected me. Any real man would have.'

'Any real man would have? The words echoed in his head. '*Real man! Real man!* Aah!' he screamed. Disorientated, he opened his eyes. He had been sweating profusely and he felt a strong sense of frustration and anger. Lisa's body beneath him was cold.

Steve knocked on the door of Lisa's flat but there was no answer. He tried her phone again. It was off and the answer phone kicked in. 'Lisa, it's Steve. Where are you babe? I'm worried about you. Give me a call when you get this message.'

He hung up and looked at his watch. It was five to nine and pretty dark. He noticed the curtains were open. He tried Danny's phone but it was still off so he rang Kate.

'Sorry to bother you again babe.....'

'That's all right. What's up?'

'I still can't get hold of Lisa. I'm outside her flat now and the curtains are still open. It's pitch black, where is she?'

'Have you rung her?'

'Of course I have. Her phone was ringing out earlier but now it's off.' I can't get hold of Danny either. You don't think they've gone somewhere do you?'

'I don't know. I wouldn't have thought so. I mean....where would they go together?

216

'Well, yeah. It doesn't make sense but it's not like her to just disappear and not say anything.

'Disappear? Don't you think you're overreacting a bit?' You haven't seen her for a few hours, she's out late and forgot to take her phone – possibly even lost it – and you jump to conclusions that she's on the missing persons list or something. Calm down. Do you want to come over here? We'll have a drink and then sort something out.

'Okay!' he retorted, feeling quite agitated.

Danny dragged Lisa's lifeless body into the kitchen and hauled her into the chest freezer. He didn't even cover the body this time. The blood was everywhere throughout the flat and several items were smashed and strewn about the place. He turned to locate the draught that was creeping across his neck and noticed the broken window. He wondered if the neighbours had heard anything. Fortunately the kitchen led to the back of the house and there was a considerable distance between that and the other flats so the chances were, nobody had seen. He hoped, anyway. The residents in the other flats were noisy and there were parties every weekend with more than their fair share of screaming. Even on a Sunday afternoon Lisa's screams would have gone unnoticed.

Danny's luck was still holding out, but his chances for capture were growing all the time. How much longer would this luck hold out? He set to work on cleaning the flat but stopped suddenly as he realised that the order of arrangement of covering up his tracks would have to be prioritised. If he could prevent the police from sniffing round his flat that would give him more time. This was essential as Lisa would have to remain in the chest freezer until a suitable time for disposal arose. He located the phone on the living room floor where he had knocked it out of her hand. Piecing it together again he hoped it still worked. As the network was discovered, messages began to come through. Danny read her text messages and listened to Steve's voicemail. Confident that all was not well at this stage he searched through Lisa's handbag for the keys to her flat. Before he left he took two strong painkillers and cleaned himself up quickly. His head ached, his eyes were bloodshot and sore, and he lost track of where exactly in his body the pain signals were coming from.

Outside Lisa's flat, Danny felt secure that nobody had seen him and nobody was around. He had parked a short distance away and walked the rest, his hooded top and baseball cap concealing his features.

Inside Lisa's flat, the curtains were drawn. He un-tidied a few drawers of clothes with his gloved hands and took several items of clothing and everything of value he could find, packing them into her case. As he did this, her phone rang 3 or 4 times. He ignored the first two then rejected any after that before sending Steve a text message:

"Need space. With a friend."

He thought the shorter the better as the longer the text the more chance he had for putting his own signature to it. He turned the phone off, switched out the light and left, taking the phone and case with him. There was still nobody around and it was looking good until he heard a whistle. A man was walking his dog. It was sniffing around Danny. He tried to shake it off without looking suspicious. The man called it and it eventually left him alone.

Danny walked further on watching the dog over his shoulder until....crash. He collided with a girl on her phone. She was distracted with the conversation and hadn't seen him. He was distracted with the dog sniffing the contents of his case.

'I'm really sorry,' he said, helping the girl back to her feet and picking up her phone from the floor.

'It's my fault' she stated, 'I was on the phone.'

He looked into her eyes. She was gorgeous. Her eyes opened further and Danny could read the signals. The chemistry was there, she fancied him. Hating himself for doing it and cursing at fate, he walked on. 'Fucking typical!' he whispered. The girl looked back, smiled then continued on her way. Danny contemplated being adventurous and running back to get her number, but thought the better of it. Time was getting the better of him and he had a whole flat to clean up.

'Look at that!' Steve showed Kate the text off Lisa's phone. 'What's that supposed to mean, "with a friend?" What friend?'

Kate shook her head. 'It is a bit strange. Has she been under a lot of stress lately?'

Steve pondered this. 'Not that I'm aware of. I'm gonna go over and see her.'

'Can't you read, dumb arse? It says "need space" – so give her some.'

'Yeah, but I wanna know *why* she needs space. We haven't been arguing. If she told me she had a problem, I would've helped left her to get on with it, if that's what she needed.'

'Maybe she didn't want to approach you in case you persisted. I know when I need space; I sometimes just get away for a few days.'

'Yeah, but you'd tell someone?'

'Well, I would.....but I wouldn't want to get into a conversation about it.'

'I'm gonna go and see her. She owes me an explanation.'

'You see. That's it. She feels she owes you an explanation and you feel you've got the right to one and you want it....but she doesn't want to give it. Maybe she can't explain herself. When you wanna be left alone you don't wanna be going into intricate detail of why you need to be alone because then you're NOT alone. You know what I mean?' He thought for a moment. 'I'm gonna go and see her.'

'Wait there, then, I'll come with you.' Huh! Men!'

Steve was looking through the letterbox of Lisa's flat. 'She's not in.'
'Well, obviously. She said she needed space. Even if she was in she wouldn't answer the door. And I don't blame her if this is the way you act.'

'Do you think she's got someone else?'

'No! What a horrible thing to say. The poor girl just wants to be left alone and you're accusing her of all kinds.

'I'm not accusing her of anything. I'm just saying it's strange that she's suddenly gone this way. We're really close. We're soul-mates. If she had a problem, she'd tell me. She always does, then we discuss it.'

'She doesn't want to discuss it. That's the problem. You can't solve the problem of needing to be alone by sitting in a group of people and discussing it. I know exactly how she feels. Your best bet is to leave her alone for a few days, maybe not even as long as that, and she'll talk to you when she's ready.'

'The curtains are closed.'

'What?'

'The curtains! Remember I said to you over the phone she's left the curtains open and it's dark?'

'Hmm, yeah.'

'Well there you go, then. They're closed now. Someone's been in.'

'Of course they have. She has. She's been back and closed them then left again or she's in there now.' Her voice softened. 'I think she's in there now. So why don't we just head back to mine, have a drink then see if we can get hold of Danny?'

'Something's not right. It's just not right.'

Danny turned his phone on. He thought he had better keep up to date with happenings and keep in contact with Kate and Steve to avoid arousing suspicion. His messages came through so he called Steve.

Steve sounded anxious. 'Danny, where've you been? Lisa's gone missing.'

Kate's voice could just be heard in the background: 'How many times…? She hasn't gone missing.'

'I was sleeping. I haven't been well,' Danny said in his best sleepy voice. 'What do you mean she's gone missing? Where are you?'

'I'm in Kate's.'

'Yeah I thought I could hear her voice in the background. Hang on, I'll come over.'

He hung up before Steve said goodbye. Half an hour later he was at Kate's flat. He wore his baseball cap to hide the lumps on his head that he felt made his head look twice its size. They couldn't be seen, though; unlike the scratches.

'What happened to you?' Kate yelled and immediately hugged him.

Inside Kate's flat, he explained to Steve and Kate how he had stopped some guy from beating his girlfriend in the supermarket car park and both of them turned on him.

'That's horrible,' cried Kate. 'Oh, baby I wish I'd been with you.'

'It's okay.'

'Never get involved in a domestic, mate,' Steve chipped in. 'I thought you knew that. In fact, I think I remember you saying that to me in the past.'

'I do but this was different,' he said, tersely.

'Your eyes are all red,' Kate added.

'I know. I hope I haven't caught an infection. She attacked me with her nails. I didn't feel too good this afternoon so I had a lie down. So what were you saying about Lisa?'

Steve broke in first. 'She's gone missing.'

'She hasn't gone missing,' interrupted Kate in an attempt to correct him. She sent him a text saying that she was with a friend and needed a bit of space, that's all. Now he's panicking because he can't talk to her.'

'She doesn't go missing like this. She always says where she's going.'

'That's on normal occasions, yes, but she said specifically that she wanted to be left alone so obviously she's under some kind of stress and you should back off and wait for her to contact you.'

Steve twisted his face in disapproval and then looked to Danny.

'I'm afraid I have to agree with Kate, Steve. She's right. You should give her a wide berth until she sorts herself out.'

'I'll put the kettle on,' suggested Kate.

Whilst she was out of the room Danny spoke softly to Steve. 'Don't say anything to Kate, because obviously they're friends, but I heard a little rumour that Lisa has been seen around with some guy.'

'Who?'

'I'm not sure of his name. All I know is he drives a silver Mercedes and his dad owns some building company.'

'Lisa wouldn't do that.'

'Sorry mate. I know you like her, and I don't mean to be blunt, but you're my best mate and I don't wanna see you walked all over by some bird.'

'Lisa's not like that, I know she isn't.'

'They're *all* like that, mate. You can't trust any of them. It happened to me, didn't it? You feel secure one minute- with a house, a job, a lovely girlfriend and you wonder what could ever go wrong. Then the next minute she's out sleeping with all kinds of different men behind your back.' Steve sat and put his head between his hands.

'I can't believe she'd do that to me. I'm sure she's not like that. Who is this guy? I wanna know who he is, I wanna see him'

'What for? If they're interested then they're interested. It's hard, mate, but if she fucks you off then she's not worth fighting over. You know what I'm saying and you know it's true.' There was a pause. 'I don't suppose it makes you feel any better if I say he was ugly.'

'What does she see in him then?'

'He's rich, isn't he? Told you...money...prostitutes. They're all prostitutes it's just that some demand a higher price. If she can get 'customers' who can give her anything- financially- then it's obvious that she will go with the comfortable 'wage rise'.

'I'd appreciate it if you didn't talk of Lisa in that way.'

'Sorry, mate. I didn't mean to be so insensitive. It's just that I need to open your eyes to things sometimes.'

Steve thought for a second. He wondered if Danny could be right. He had always been right in the past and had always been such an admirable figure in Steve's eyes. The first time that he had ever questioned him was when he met Lisa. He felt that Danny had been wrong about women and was changing for the better when he met Kate. Now it had come full circle and Danny's argument was winning him over.

'Happy families don't work, do they?' he said aloud.

Just at that moment Kate returned with three mugs of tea. 'What's up' she asked, sensing the atmosphere.

'Nothing!' said Danny, before Steve's open mouth was allowed to voice its feelings. Danny made eyes at him, too, for him to keep it to himself. 'We're just wondering who that friend can be,' continued Danny, 'because, if anyone, I'd have thought she'd have rung you.'

'Yeah, that's what I found strange,' retorted Kate. We're really close so you'd think she'd ring me.'

'Oh well, maybe it's because of me.'

'Eh!'

Kate and Steve looked confused. Danny enlightened them. 'If she calls you to talk about it then you'd probably be inclined to tell me, at least that she's all right.'

Kate felt attacked. 'I wouldn't if she didn't want me to.'

'Wait! Listen! She doesn't know that for sure. She knows we're close…she knows Steve and me are close…ergo, she needs to keep it to herself.' Danny was looking smug. 'If she didn't then she would have just approached Steve herself.' They both nodded in agreement and sipped their tea. A few seconds passed and nobody spoke. Suddenly Steve suggested: 'What about Sue, behind the bar? Is it possible she could be with her? I mean, they got on well didn't they?'

Danny was caught off his guard, slightly. He had relaxed himself with the thought that he had the upper hand of Steve but now he was becoming inquisitive and the last thing Danny wanted was to be reminded of Sue.

He made his riposte: 'We can't do anything tonight, anyway. Let's just leave it for now; sleep on it and she'll probably be back in the morning. If she hasn't been in touch with you by tomorrow evening we can go over to The Anchor and see if Sue's working. I still think that you need to give her that space though, mate.' He made sure that Kate could not see then winked at Steve. 'She'll never forgive you if you hound her and she needs to sort herself out.' His eyes burned into Steve as he ended on: 'It's all in the text.'

Steve agreed to leave it at that and Danny left to finish cleaning the flat. Kate suggested going with him but he claimed he never felt very well and needed rest after fighting earlier.

He had only just sat in the car when his phone rang. He pulled it out of his pocket and looked at the display as he started the engine. It was Liz, the girl who had said she was pregnant.

'Shit! I forgot about her. Oh, fuck off, leave me alone. He rejected the call but as he pulled off she rang again. She persisted in calling him until he eventually answered it.

'HELLO,' he shouted, angrily.

'Hi, Danny, it's Liz,' came the slur on the other end of the line.

'Are you pissed?'

'I've had a couple. Where are you, babe?'

'I'm just going home. What do you want, it's nearly midnight?'

'I wanna see you, babe. Did I tell you I was pregnant?'

'Yes.' Danny's voice was cold.

'You're gonna be a daddy, baby.'

'That's if it's mine.'

'Of course it's yours. I haven't been with anyone else.'

'Yeah, yeah! Look, what do you want because I'm tired?'

'I'm just having a drink in The Bear and Penguin, hic. Come and get me. We're getting kicked out in a minute.'

'Oh, Liz. I'm going to bed.' He thought for a second, and then as a wave of inspiration flooded over him: 'Who are you with?'

'Just a friend.'

'Okay. You'll have to give me a bit of time. Walk round to the main door for about twenty past and then I'll meet you on the corner of Westwood Avenue.'

'It's dark there, hic. I might get jumped.'

'Don't be silly. There's no-one about this time of night. Just the pissheads and you've been drinking with them all night. Besides, there's nowhere to park.'

She agreed with him and he raced home and changed into black tracksuit bottoms to go with his dark hooded top. He brought a white t-shirt with him and a light blue jacket to change into then dug out his black leather gloves and balaclava. It was ten past when he pulled over in Ryder Street and made his way onto Westwood Avenue. Liz was early. She stood on the corner with a friend.

'Shit!' Danny muttered to himself. 'Who the fuck's that?'

'Go on, you get in this taxi,' said Liz to her friend.

'I'll be okay I'm getting picked up now.'

'Are you sure?' she replied.

'Yeah.' She reeled into the middle of the road and flagged down the hackney cab. As her friend got in she slammed the door, not realising how drunk she was.

'Call me' Liz mimed, holding her little finger to her mouth and her thumb to her ear to denote a phone.

The taxi pulled off and she was stood on her own but right on cue her phone rang; it was Danny.

'Can you walk down Westwood Avenue?'

'I'm by there now. Just turning into it.' As she did so, he put his phone away and put on the gloves and balaclava then put his hood up. He hid in the drive of a house, just behind some hedges. When Liz staggered down, he leapt out and punched her in the stomach. She bent double and reeled backwards, then he punched her in the face and she fell to the floor. He kicked her in the stomach twice and once in the head before relieving her of her handbag. He left her lying unconscious as he ran off up Westwood Avenue. Cutting through the back way into Ryder Street he removed the balaclava and emptied the bag into his carrier bag before tossing it away. He kept the £20 note that she had and her loose change, credit cards and phone and dropped her bus pass further down.

Back at his car, the carrier bag was thrown in the boot and the car was taken to a secluded spot by the side of St Luke's Church. He quickly changed and put the hooded top, gloves and balaclava in the boot. As he drove up Westwood Avenue, two men were standing over Liz. He drove past slowly then reversed back. He got out of the car and spoke to the men.

'Excuse me, fellas. Have you seen a girl…What's happened there?'

'We don't know,' replied the older, fatter guy with a moustache. 'We just found her.' Danny reacted to the girl on the pavement as though he'd just recognised her.

'Liz! LIZ! Oh my god! That's' my girlfriend. I was just coming to pick her up and…'

'It's okay,' said the fat guy 'we've called an ambulance. We didn't know who she was. She's got no bag. We think she may have been robbed. She needs treatment though. Look at the blood.'

'Bastards!' Danny cried. 'Why?'

The fat guy consoled him again. 'Don't worry, mate. We'll stay with you until the ambulance gets here. Do you want me to call the police?'

'There's no point is there, they never catch them.' Danny sighed. 'I was just coming to pick her up as well. It couldn't have happened long ago. I told her I'd get here at twenty past and it's only…' He looked at his watch. '…twenty three minutes past now. I told her not to walk down Westwood Avenue. It's too dangerous this time of night. Danny followed the ambulance to the hospital but after it was agreed that there was nothing more he could do he left for home. He still had lots to do.

The next day, Steve spoke about Lisa on every break. Danny had had enough by the end of the day. 'For fuck's sake, Steve. You've been going on about it all day.'

'Sorry. I'm just worried.'

'I told you what I heard, didn't I?'

'Who told you?'

'I can't tell you that, mate. You don't know her anyway.'

'Her? So it's a girl?'

'Look! It doesn't matter. All I can say is this girl can usually be trusted.'

'I spoke to Kate last night, just after you left.' Danny eyed him suspiciously. 'Oh I didn't stay long…and I never mentioned what you said or anything. I…I just asked her what she thought about the possibility of Lisa seeing someone else.'

'Yeah?'

'She said there was no chance. She said that they're both really close and Lisa never talks of anyone else.'

'Maybe.' Danny walked off and Steve ran to catch him up.

'What do you mean maybe?' He stopped.

'Well…you know I had my phone off all day yesterday?'

'Yeah!'

'There was a reason for that…I needed a bit of space myself …I don't wanna see Kate anymore.'

'Why? Have you been arguing? You both seemed fine. She was worried about you.'

'Yeah, I'm not saying she wasn't, but …you know that girl…the one who told me about Lisa.' Steve nodded, he was transfixed. 'She also told me a few other things.'

'Like what?' Danny took a breath.

'She said that Kate had been spending some time with a guy as well. Just on and off.

'And do you know the worst of it mate?' Steve shook his head. 'They're brothers. The two fellas who've been getting into our birds are brothers. Both girls know what's going on. That's why Kate's so reassuring to you. She's at it herself.'

A small tear beamed in the corner of Steve's eye, more from anger than sorrow though. He didn't believe it at first; he didn't want to believe it. But now it all fell into place. It had to be true. It made sense. He trawled through his memories of their times together. It hurt. As he did so he searched for evidence of her infidelity and it was there. Every cross word, every misconstrued statement, every unusual action all made sense. He fitted the pieces together in his head and formed a different picture. Every time Lisa had been nice to him he saw this now as under-handedness.

How conniving was she? Every time I took her out, every time I did something nice for her – she was laughing at me behind my back.

He slapped his hands to his head and dug his nails into his temples as he let out a cry of frustration. 'Aaah! How fuckin' stupid am I? Bitch! Slag! I'll smash her fuckin' head in.'

'All right, Steve, calm down. Let's go and get a drink.'

'Okay! I'm not going to The Anchor though.'

Inside The Cat and Whistle, Steve knocked the whisky back.

'Take it easy, mate,' advised Danny. 'That stuff's lethal.'

'I don't care. It doesn't matter anymore.'

'You're getting pissed already. Slow down!'

'I wanna get pissed. I want to enjoy myself for a change. Fuck the women.'

'That's it mate. They're not worth it.'

'Why would she do that to me Danny? Why?'

'One of life's great mysteries, mate: the female mind!'

'We got on really well, you know?'

'I know you did.'

Danny didn't want to hear anymore but he tolerated it as it was a way of distancing Steve's affections for Lisa. The sooner he forgot about her the sooner Danny could get on with his life. However, he had, as of yet, to dispose of the body. They both got a bit tipsy, Steve more so than Danny, and it didn't take Danny long to charm his way in to two girls. He chatted away for nearly ten minutes before returning to Steve with the good news. 'They're "certs", mate. We're in there. One's got her own place as well. She said we can go back there.'

'Great! Introduce me.'

Danny brought the girls over to sit at the bar with Steve. He introduced them as Jane and Debbie. Jane had her own place whilst Debbie still lived with her parents.

'I'm staying at Jane's tonight,' she told Danny. 'We might be having a party if you fancy it.'

They stayed in the bar for another hour before they were ready to head off. They were all quite drunk at this stage and they all wanted to go back, although the girls did not want to come across as easy.

Steve worked on his one, Debbie, to encourage her to go back with him. He and Danny wanted to separate the two in order to get to know them individually. The conclusion of the conversation was that Debbie would go back to Steve's flat and Danny would go to Jane's house. He lied about his own living arrangements, saying that he had been staying with his brother and his wife- since selling his own house- and could not take girls back there. Fortunately, Jane bought this. Either that or she didn't care and just wanted to get intimate with Danny.

Debbie was just walking into Steve's flat when she received a text message. She was quite drunk, but seemingly sober enough to respond to Jane. She said that she was just about to go to bed with Steve and that she was fine. The text ended with:

"Don't wait up."

Jane was wild in bed with Danny. He enjoyed it but for the first time he did not go too wild. He had sex with her quite normally. There was no violence, no stabbings. Was this the lull before the storm? Passions rose but Danny remained in control of his actions. Perhaps at the back of his mind he was aware of Lisa's body in the chest freezer in his flat. He had enough on his plate, having her to dispose of, without accumulating more bodies.

Steve and Debbie had a coffee and chatted for a while before retiring to bed. Debbie's drunken state effected great playfulness in her. She was really in the mood for being sexy, and teased Steve for ages. Finally, down to her underwear, she toyed with Steve's emotions further. No longer could he resist, he threw her to the bed and held her down by her arms. She took this in a good manner, resisting slightly but not completely. Steve overpowered her and ripped off her underwear. Half-claiming rape and half-enjoying it she struggled to break free as Steve made love to her quite aggressively. He thrust himself deep inside her and began to bite at her neck. She moaned and groaned at this but it was still not clear how much she liked it and how much she resisted.

The pounding became faster and heavier; he squeezed her wrists tightly. His strong vice-like grip demanded authority and his control over her actions grew.

Something inside Steve compelled him to release a beast-like nature that must have been latent for a number of years. The sex began to border on violence as he pulled at her hair and bit more aggressively.

'Ow! She cried, excited but slightly taken aback. She had never had such a wild sex session in her life.

Steve's crazy actions progressed further: he took to slapping her. Debbie's response said it all. She wasn't used to this kind of sexual fulfilment although it did arouse her. Steve slapped harder as he neared a climax.

'That hurts,' Debbie moaned, but to no avail. Steve was oblivious to her. He punched her in the mouth and made it bleed.

'Wait!' she cried, 'you've gone too far.' He punched her again; she winced. 'I don't like this; it really hurts.

He demanded that she go on by interlocking his fingers around her hair and punching her in the ribs. He felt her wince and this turned him on.

Another punch to the face and Debbie was pleading for him to stop. She could not take much more. Steve persisted like a wild, hungry dog setting its sights on meat.

He bit at her neck until it bled then pulled huge clumps of hair from her head. As she screamed at the pain Steve thrust in harder.

'Oh, yeah baby. Say you want me.'

Debbie was frightened now. Her whole body ached and she had lost chunks of hair in the process. Steve ignored more of her pleas for him to stop until he grew so excited that he couldn't restrain himself. He punched her again and again before the third punch knocked her clean out. At this point his excitement hit its peak and he released his fluids into her body.

After cleaning himself up he attempted to wake Debbie up from her unconscious state. He wondered, now, just exactly how hard he had hit her and what damage he had done. She refused to wake and this angered Steve. Shaking her vigorously, his frustrations got the better of him as he could not wake her. He felt for her pulse but couldn't find anything so proceeded to beat at her chest with his fists.

'Wake up! Wake up!' he shouted. Still, nothing! 'I've killed her,' he cried. Hugging the body, and resting his head on its bosom, he cried himself to sleep.

18

Danny picked up the local newspaper in the newsagents and scanned the headlines:

"Arson Attack Kills Three"
"Taxi Driver Found with Two Kilos of Cocaine"
"Local Girl Missing"

He skimmed his eyes across all three articles but the one that took up most of his attention was "Local Girl Missing" in the bottom left corner of the front page. There was a small photo of Lisa and a write-up, complete with a telephone number for people to ring up should they have any information. Danny bought the paper then dashed home to read it.

Reaching into the cupboard in the kitchen of his flat he poured himself a large whisky. He hadn't touched a drop for nearly a month but now he felt he couldn't restrain himself any longer. Panic embedded itself in his body as his eyes read over the article. It had been over a week since she had gone missing and her body was still in the chest freezer. He imagined that the net would be closing in on him and if he did not dispose of the body soon then he could never hope for anything but capture.

How soon will it be before the police come knocking on my door? Surely their investigations will fall my way.

Danny ran to the freezer and opened the lid then. He was nearly sick but baulked at the last minute; a small amount of vomit making its way up to his mouth. Staggering, slightly, he fell to the sink and spat it out. He then reached over and turned on the cold tap, holding his mouth underneath. The cool water was refreshingly nice, he felt. A vibration emanated from the living room followed by Wagner's Ride of the Valkyries. *How eerie!* he thought, and began to regret downloading it as a ringtone.

'Hello,' he bawled into the phone.

'Hi, Dan. It's Dave.' How coincidental. Danny needed to speak to him about making a trip to the incinerator. It would work out better, though, if it was Dave who rang him.

Dave went through the usual rigmarole of 'How are you?' and so on before making his request. He needed the van to move some furniture.

'Aren't you going to the incinerator?' Danny asked.

'Well I wasn't planning on it. I suppose I could do, though. Let's see... It's Saturday now...Would you be able to get a van for Monday or Tuesday?'

'Yeah, no problem. I'll sort it for Tuesday.'

'Brilliant! Yeah, come to think of it I will shift some slips. They are building up a bit.'

'I'll come with you if you like.'

'Yeah, whatever. You can help me shift the furniture,' he said, finding as always, another way in which he could get something from somebody. 'You just wanna see that bird, don't you?'

Danny had forgotten about his previous excuse for wanting to visit the incinerator.

'Well...' he blushed. The arrangements were sorted and Danny hung up. He looked up at the ceiling and his eyes travelled through it. 'Please don't let them come before Tuesday.'

The doorbell of Danny's flat chimed twice, fell silent then chimed twice again. Steve rushed in as the door opened.

'Have you seen the paper?' he shouted, clutching the local newspaper under his armpit. 'Look at this! Lisa's on the front.'

As he held it out Danny's eyes raced across it then reverted back to Steve. 'It says she's gone missing. Maybe she hasn't run off with that bloke.'

Danny pulled the newspaper down from in front of his face and spoke calmly. 'She has, mate. She's gone with him and fucked everything off.'

'But how come it's hit the papers then? She must've told someone.'

'She probably did but if she wants to make it look like she's gone missing then she's not gonna advertise that she's off gallivanting with some millionaire.'

'Well I think her family should know at least.'

'Maybe they do, mate. Maybe they're just biding their time and they're gonna fuck off too.'

'But why? Why not tell someone?'

'Because when you tell people you've got money you suddenly start inheriting all these friends from out of nowhere. Even your worst enemies find it in their hearts to forgive you. I tell you...people don't wanna be bothered with all that shit. This guy's family have got millions. There's enough for them all to live off. I reckon it's all staged.'

'Hmm! I don't know.'

'Let me tell you something, then. Lisa's mother...' Steve nodded. '...I saw her the other day. She never even looked upset.'

'You saw her? Where?'

'In the supermarket on Carrington Way but that's irrelevant. The point I'm making is...it's all a farce. Her only daughter's gone missing and she's smiling away to herself, picking fruit at her leisure.'

'Are you sure? I've never known her to go there. She always goes to the one on the corner of the High Street because she knows them.'

Danny shrugged. 'Strange fish! Probably doesn't want to be recognised in there enjoying herself when she, apparently, doesn't know the whereabouts of her daughter.'

'The police, then. They've got a right to know.'

'Fuck her, mate. Let her get caught and get into shit for wasting their time. That's not our problem. And you certainly don't OWE her anything. Birds like that...they deserve everything that comes to them. She'll be back if it doesn't work out. You'll see.'

This seemed enough convincing for now. Steve mulled it all over in his head before the sound of his phone broke his concentration. He looked at the display, it read: "Debbie." 'Shit! It's that bird from the other night.'

'Which one?'

'That Debbie one. You know, the one I took back to mine.'

'So what's the problem?' Danny looked puzzled. 'If you don't wanna see her, just tell her. If you wanna blast her again then answer it.'

'No, you remember me telling you about her pissing me off in bed?'

'Yeah.' He rejected the call then continued. 'Well... she didn't exactly piss me off. What happened was...we were having sex and...you know what you were saying about wild sex...about liking it rough?' Danny nodded. 'Well, I went a bit mad on her. I started slapping her around. I didn't tell you about it because I was embarrassed.' Danny smiled. 'Anyway, I punched her a few times and I sort of got off on it. I couldn't make out whether she liked it or not.

233

She seemed to but...I went a bit too far and knocked her out.' Danny laughed loudly. 'All right, all right. It's not funny. I shit myself. I thought I'd killed her.' They both laughed at this point, Steve more so through nerves.

In retrospect Steve could laugh but he still had visions of her taking him to court for rape or assault and even though she had left on good terms he couldn't bring himself to talk to her. He rejected her further calls.

'Seriously, though,' said Steve, after a minute had passed, 'I'm gonna go and talk to Kate. There's still something missing.'
Danny shook his head. 'No, don't do that. She'll deny it. I promised her I wouldn't say anything to you. But how could I carry that pretence on? How could I deceive my best friend into thinking his girlfriend's been murdered or whatever when I know that in reality she's fucked off with some mega-rich twat? And besides, she's up to all kinds as well so I wouldn't believe a word that that slag says.'

Steve's frustrations were beginning to get the better of him. 'They're bitches, aren't they? They're all bitches. Fuckin' slags the lot of them. You meet one bird who you think is decent and what happens? She prostitutes herself for some ugly, fat bastard with a bit of wedge. I'm going, Danny. I can't handle any more.'

'I'll call you later, mate. Don't let it get to you.'

Danny walked back in the flat and had a large mouthful of whisky before cutting out the photo and article from the newspaper. He put it into a drawer in the kitchen and sat in the living room by the TV.

'What are we gonna do, Kate?' he muttered to himself. 'What are we gonna do? Oh, it's a fucked up world.'

Kate couldn't believe her own eyes when she read about Lisa's disappearance.

'I know that girl,' she informed the young lad on the till at her local newsagents. 'She's a friend of mine. She's supposed to have gone off with one of her friends to get a bit of peace.'
The young lad nodded and showed as much concern as he possibly could for a complete stranger. 'I'd better ring Danny and we can go the police.' She slammed down a pound coin on the counter and ran out of the shop clutching her newspaper, not stopping for her change. The young lad shouted after her but it was too late. She dashed back to her flat to use the landline. Danny's mobile was busy.

'Oh why doesn't he have a landline?' She wondered whether she should call the police. She dialled '9', then '9' before hanging up. 'I shouldn't use the emergency number,' she mumbled, confused over the whole event.

Attempting Danny's phone again she found herself through to him in person. He sensed the panic in her voice. 'Calm down and talk to me.'

'Have you seen the papers? Lisa's pictures...'

'I've seen it. What of it?'

'What do you mean: "What of it?" It says she's missing. That means that she's not with a friend. She really has gone missing. You don't think anything's happened to her, do you? I know it's been about a week since I saw her but that's normal. She was busy with work and we haven't all seen a lot of each other, have we?'

'Relax! You're feeling guilty but there's no need. She'll be fine. They'll find her.'

'I'm gonna go to the police, tell them what we know of her. You'll have to tell them about that friend. And Steve as well. He knows her best. We'll all have to be interviewed.'

'Now look, don't be hasty. There's a perfectly logical explanation for it all. We don't want the police sniffing round us every five minutes.'

'Why not? She's our friend. She deserves our help. I'm going even if you won't.'

'All right, listen. I didn't want to tell you this because it's none of our business.' Kate pressed the receiver hard up against her ear for fear of missing anything. 'She spoke to Steve on the phone. She went off with a friend because she wanted space, yeah?'

'Yeah, go on.'

'So, the next thing is she texted him and said she'd met someone.'

'No!' she interjected. 'She wouldn't. She loves him to bits.'

'Listen, it's true. I couldn't believe it, either. Steve's distraught.'

'But how could she just meet someone like that?' Kate enquired, still not satisfied.

'She didn't. She's been seeing this guy for months.'

'She couldn't have...'

'She has, believe me. I saw her out with him, once, and she couldn't explain it. She said it was a one-off and begged me not to tell Steve. For the sake of their strong relationship versus one regrettable fling...I didn't. I should have done but I didn't. I didn't even tell you in case

235

you fell out with her and we all lost our friendship. And I was worried that you'd talk me into telling Steve. I wasn't sure what to do for the best so I said nothing. I honestly thought that there was nothing in it until Steve told me the other night.'

'Aw, poor Steve. I'm gonna ring him.'

'NO! No, don't do that. He's very embarrassed and doesn't want anyone to know. If he knew that I'd told you it would destroy him. Please don't say anything. He'll never trust me again. He just wants to move on and forget about her. That's why we don't want the police sniffing round, putting everyone's noses out of joint.'

'But somebody should tell them.'

'They'll find out soon enough. They won't put too much effort into it. After a week or two they usually declare them dead, even though the case is still open, and they stop looking. They don't tell you that it's just all routine. You see, people just don't go missing for that length of time for no apparent reason. Their whereabouts usually becomes known.'

'I don't get it,' said Kate, baffled at the complexity of a simple matter of cheating. Danny related his tale of her meeting a millionaire and laying low to avoid friends. He told her everything that he had told Steve with the necessary twists to add all credence.

'So what do we do,' she asked.

'Nothing, we do nothing. We just wait for her to surface naturally or wait for the police to get her. Whichever comes sooner.'

Later that evening Kate gave Danny a surprise visit. He expected to find Steve on the doorstep so much so that he opened the front door and walked back into the living room. Kate followed him in.

'Are you not gonna say hello, then?' she asked as she entered the living room.

'Oh, it's you?'

'Well who did you expect it to be?'

'Eh! Nobody. Er...I don't know. I wasn't expecting anybody in particular. I just thought that it would be Steve. No reason, I just did.'

'Is it a nice surprise or what, then?'

'Of course it's nice. It's always nice to see you.' He kissed her on the cheek. 'Would you like a drink? Tea, coffee?'

'Have you got anything stronger?'

'Of course. Lager, wine, spirits?'

'I'll have a wine please, babe.'

He poured her a glass. 'Are you staying for tea?'

'I don't mind. Would you like me to cook it?'

'No, I can manage. Unless you particularly want to cook it.'

'Yeah, why not. It'll give you a break. I don't mind it's my treat. I'll pop over to the supermarket and pick something up.'

'No need. There's a chicken in the fridge, rice in the cupboards and plenty of vegetables. And in the bottom drawer there are loads of different sauces. I like to keep a stock in, you see.' Kate was impressed.

They had a few drinks and chatted for a while. The conversation fell naturally on Lisa. Every discrepancy that Kate had about Lisa's disappearance was raised and every time Danny had a reason for her actions. It all made sense when he explained it. In fact, he presented his case so well that Kate couldn't imagine the situation in any other way.

Everything was going well until she decided to be experimental with her culinary expertise. The fresh vegetables were great but then she remembered that there were no peas.

'Have you got any peas? It doesn't matter, I'll look for myself. Frozen will do.'

She opened the chest freezer and got, probably, the biggest shock of her life. Inside, Lisa's body lay there, her vacant eyes staring upwards. The face, solid, held its expression. The eyes stared blankly through their target. The whole body took on the appearance of a waxwork figure: so lifelike yet lifeless.

Kate's mouth dropped open and for a second or two she was speechless. Struggling to find the breath to scream, her lungs seemed to be exhaling at the very point in which she needed more air. Her eyes were transfixed on Lisa's face as her brain shifted into overdrive in order to process the information. Air eventually rushed into her lungs in one deep gulp before it bellowed back out, vibrating across her vocal chords along the way.

The scream was so loud Danny nearly fell off the chair he was sat on. Realising that he had been careless enough to have let Kate into the house before he had disposed of the body, he raced into the kitchen. By this time Kate had screamed several times, each seemingly louder than the last. It was all too much for her brain to cope with, though.

This visual stimuli swirled around in her mind, along with a myriad of other images, and it attempted to make sense of it all, to desensitise itself for future survival, but failed. Kate took a final gasp of air before she passed out. Danny closed the freezer lid and spun round as the doorbell chimed. He edged his way to the front door wondering if anybody had heard the scream. Voices came from the other side of the door so he opened it about six inches only to be confronted by two men and a girl. One of the lads he recognised from living in a nearby flat.

'Is everything okay?' he asked.

'We heard screams,' added the girl.

'Eh? Oh, yeah. It's my girlfriend, she saw a mouse.'

'A mouse?' questioned the second lad, laughing.

The girl nudged him. 'Oi! Don't laugh. That's happened to me.'

'No, I wasn't.'

Danny intervened. 'She's a bit on edge anyway because she's just lost her job. Thanks for checking on us. I'll have to go back in. Got to console her. You know how it is?'

'Yeah, we understand.'

'And on top of that I've got a bloody mouse to catch.'

They smiled and said their goodbyes. Danny closed the door and sighed as he leaned on it from the inside.

Kate was just regaining consciousness when he returned from the kitchen. He gave her a glass of water. After two sips it all came back to her. She gasped for breath and struggled to move away from him.

'Don't touch me,' she yelled. 'Don't you dare touch me.'

'Wait! Listen! Let me explain. Calm down.'

'HELP!'

He gagged her mouth with his hand. 'Just listen to me for a second, please.' He removed his hand and spoke softly. 'It's not what it looks like, babe. You've gotta believe me. It was an accident.'

Fear held itself strongly inside her but she controlled it for an explanation. Nothing was making sense in her eyes but she temporarily let him take control.

'It was an accident,' he repeated.

'H-how?'

'Steve's been cheating on Lisa; he has been for a while. I've had words with Lisa but she won't listen. Well...I couldn't say anything because obviously you'd tell Lisa; I mean, it's your mate isn't it? I thought if Lisa gets to know it should at least be me who has told her. Or even better: Steve himself. So I was stuck in the middle.'

'You're not making sense. How does all this fit in with...?'

'Let me explain. So, like I said, I was in the middle.' He helped Kate to her feet. 'Let's go in the living room.'

Inside the living room they sat on the couch. Danny held her hand and continued:

'So, do I (a) withhold information from a friend-Lisa- and watch as Steve carries on with this other girl, sneakily behind her back; or do I (b) tell my friend, show her that she's being deceived but then fall out with my other friend, my closer friend, Steve. And the chances are they'd end up sorting it out then they'd both turn against me. It's a domestic, isn't it? You don't get involved. So, anyway. Until I decide to do (b) I'm doing (a) whether I like it or not.'

Kate looked more confused.

'So what happened to Lisa?' she inquired. 'And you said she was cheating with someone, anyway.'

'She was. I told Lisa to leave Steve alone because she was hurting him and she agreed that it wasn't gonna work out. I then happened to mention- just as a stab at her for what she had done- that Steve had somebody else. She didn't like it. Even though she was with this millionaire guy now she didn't like the idea that Steve was cheating on her. She went away with this guy but she was only ever with him for the money. She actually did love Steve, though.

'Unfortunately her love of money was stronger. That takes us up to the time when you last heard of her.' Kate nodded. She found it hard to believe but she was intrigued. After seeing Lisa's body lying in the freezer she felt that nothing would be difficult to be believed anymore.

'Go on,' she prompted.

'So...a couple of days ago Lisa returned unexpectedly. She'd gone off and didn't need to come back. She had all she wanted- money. But she rang me and said that she needed to see me so I invited her round. She also said that it was private and asked me not to tell anyone, although I would have told you afterwards. So when she got here she rambled on about how great that bloke was- Andy I think she called him- but how she missed Steve. I called her a hypocrite and she slapped me. She said everything was fine with this Andy character but I got the impression that he had fucked her off.

'This was the point that I started to realise who my real mates were and I saw then that she was just using whoever she could. She claimed to be missing Steve and wanted to see him again so she didn't like it when I told her that he wasn't interested anymore. Even if she went back with him she would only do it again with the next bloke that came along, driving a Mercedes convertible or whatever. I told her to fuck off and said that she'd made her bed- and had someone else in it- so should lie in it, and she went for me. She tried to punch me and scratch me...' He indicated where the scratches had been.

Kate turned her head, slightly, as she thought about the scratches. She had heard the story of him defending a girl in the supermarket car park and how the girl had turned on him but she never made the connection. She remembered the scratches so this helped to corroborate the story.

'...so I pushed her off. I told her that Steve wasn't interested and to get out but it just made her worse. She went berserk and started screaming and attacking me. I slapped her and restrained her but it was hard because she was so wound up and I was so calm. She even tried to bite me.' He pointed to his upper arm. 'I hit her in the face with the palm of my hand as I pushed her off but she still kept coming at me. She even hit me with a pan. Look!' The lump on his head was, although slight, still visible. 'And then she threw the pan at the window.'

Kate turned to view the crack above the sink. It all made sense. 'And then...when she was getting too much for me...you have to understand it was just an accident...I tried to wrestle her to the floor. Her legs went from beneath her and I lost my grip on her. As she fell backwards her head rocked and smashed into the floor. It was a horrible crack. I'll never forget it. Then the blood...The blood ran away from her head like a stream. I was gonna call an ambulance but I panicked. I lifted her up to see if she was all right but her body was limp. It was at that moment that I realised that I'd killed her...I sobbed for hours.' He paused. 'I wanted to tell you, or anyone. I wanted to get it off my chest. I couldn't believe I'd done it. I left the flat and went for a walk, for fresh air. I had to clear my head. I didn't know what to do, babe. Honestly!'

Tears began to form in his eyes. He was giving a fantastic performance. So good that regret became evident in his face. Kate bought every word, mainly because she wanted to.

'W-w-when I came back she was still there. I guess I expected to come back and find her gone and then get a phone call off her saying: "Danny, you twat! You didn't half hurt my head. I've got a headache now." No, it was real. You see it in films but you never believe it. You read it in newspapers but it's always like it's in another world. You never dream it could happen anywhere that you know. It showed me how vulnerable we are. It puts everything into context: why do I go to work? Why do I struggle paying bills? For what? You see something like this one incident in your life and it changes you forever. I'll never be the same again. I'll go to prison for a long time and why? Because I defended myself.'

'No! It's not your fault. Why should you?'

'Because the system won't see it like that. The system judges, it doesn't see. It doesn't understand.' He cried heavily and Kate hugged him.

'It'll be okay,' she said, and also began to cry.

Steve was pacing about in his flat, restless. He couldn't take his mind off Lisa.

Why has she been so sly, so manipulative?

The ring of his mobile phone broke his concentration. It was Debbie again. This time he answered it.

'Steve, I've been trying to get hold of you for ages.'

'Sorry, I've been busy. How are you?'

'I'm okay. You haven't spoken to me since the night I left your flat.'

'Sorry,' he said again.

'I think we need to discuss a few things.'

He was in no mood for a discussion. 'Like what?'

'Well...the way you acted for a start. You called a taxi for me when I woke up then I left. But I was a bit disorientated. I wasn't sure where I was or exactly what happened.'

'Yeah!'

'I'm not into all that stuff, Steve. I like you but...'

'I know. I'm not into it myself. I don't know what came over me. I've never been like that before. I haven't long split up from my last girlfriend so I think I might've gone a bit mad. I'll make it up to you.'

'Okay, then. I suppose I can forgive you. What are you doing this evening?'

'I'm not sure yet. I haven't made any plans. Any particular reason why?' he asked.

'Yeah. I thought perhaps you could make it up to me this evening.'

He thought for a moment. 'I don't fancy this evening. Tomorrow I will. We can go for a meal.'

'That'd be nice. Anywhere you had in mind?'

'Are you a vegetarian?'

'No.'

'Good!'

They made arrangements to meet in The Leaning Tower of Pizza, a restaurant famous for its hundreds of varieties of pizzas. After the phone call Steve grew angry at himself.

'Why didn't I just tell her to fuck off? I don't need her. Cheeky bitch! Telling me off! If I wanna slap a bird, I'll slap a bird. I don't give a shit what they say.' He wondered if he should call her up and hurl abuse at her down the phone but decided against it. His brain returned to its constant replaying of memories with Lisa. It was beginning to drive him mad.

Looking into a large mirror above his mantelpiece he scrutinised his appearance and spoke aloud. 'Why would she do that? Why? Why do girls act in this way? I don't understand. What's wrong with me? Surely I'm not that repulsive. I don't think I'll ever trust another girl again. I'm certainly not gonna have another relationship. They're just disasters. Girls like this seem to travel around, using and abusing people. I get talking to them and they go all cranky on me.' He pulled a few faces in the mirror as he concentrated on his thoughts.

Danny's voice trailed down Kate's back as he spoke. 'I don't wanna go to prison.'

'I don't see why you should. I don't know what we can do but there must be a way of avoiding it.'

'Well, we could always hide the body.'

'We can't do that? If I get caught I'll be seen as an accessory, accident or no accident.'

'I need a bit of time, Kate. I need a bit of space.'

'Okay, what do you want me to do?' She held his hand. 'Where do you want to go to get away from it all?'

'I've got plenty of holidays left. Let's just go away somewhere in the week.'

'Yeah! Wednesday sounds good to me.'

'We can just get in a car and drive- to the middle of nowhere- then book in a hotel if we like it.'

'What about the body?' Kate frowned.

'Don't worry about that. I've got a way in which we can dispose of it without questions.'

'How?'

'Just trust me on this one. The less you know the less you can tell. After it's done we can go and get pissed and have a laugh, whatever. We can see a bit of the world; different culture, maybe. I don't know. Where do you fancy?' Kate opened her mouth but nothing came out in time. 'Just leave it to me, actually. I'll sort it.'

Steve sat watching the TV, getting pissed. After having one or two shots of whisky round at Danny's flat once, he had now taken to drinking it when he wanted to get drunk quickly. He had been watching TV for over two hours but had not paid any attention to the programmes. Lisa sat heavily on his mind. As much as he wanted to move on he couldn't.

'FUCK!' he shouted. 'Get out of my head.' He was confused as his body displayed signs of mixed emotions. Sometimes he grew angry and hated Lisa but when that passed he began to pine for her, to miss her greatly.

As the whisky took effect he grew more and more suicidal. Rationality vacated his mind and left him with strange views on life. Never had he felt this lonely yet all he had to do was to pick up the phone and call Debbie. And if he needed a friend there was always Danny. Right now he couldn't face up to Danny, though. He felt that in a funny sort of way he had let him down. Steve's admiration for Danny was so high at one time that he envied him so much that he wanted to be him. He wanted all that attention.

Yielding to his urge to ask Debbie round he picked up his mobile and called her. She agreed to come over. Steve, feeling worse from the effects of the alcohol in his system, had decided that he needed company but hated himself for doing it. He thought that a prostitute probably would've been a better option as she could have left straight afterwards but felt he wanted company for the night. Either way he had very little respect for Debbie. His eyes were feeling heavy and beginning to close.

'Danny's right,' he mumbled to himself. 'Slags! They're all fuckin' slags.'

Tuesday evening, 5:30pm. Danny had been out all day. He had helped Dave to move the van-loads of furniture and had disposed of Lisa's body in his usual way. It hadn't gone smoothly, though. He had sweated so profusely when unloading the bags into a skip at the incinerator that Dave had noticed and become suspicious of his actions. He fabricated story after story to get Dave off his back. The last thing that he wanted was added stress. He decided to himself that he just couldn't put himself through such trauma again.

Wishing he would never kill again, hoping to never be in that position again, he knew he could be fighting a losing battle. He was losing control and knew, deep down, that when the urge came there was nothing that he could do. Over the phone he made arrangements with Kate for a short break: three days.

'Once you're packed I'll pick you up and you can stay at mine tonight. Don't tell anyone we're going 'cos I really don't want to be bothered, he stated.'

'You haven't told *me* where we're going, anyway.'

'It's a surprise. Tell everyone not to bother you for three days. Say you can't get a signal on your mobile or something. We'll have a nice break and get a bit of peace. After what's happened I can't talk to anyone. There's only *you* in the whole world that I trust.'

She smiled, but Danny didn't catch it over the phone, then said: 'You can rely on me.'

Steve only spoke to Danny briefly that evening. 'So come on, what's the big secret? Where are you going and who are you going with?' he asked.

'I've got this little bird on the go. I'm gonna take her to Wales for a few days. You know, a mid-week, dirty weekend.'
Steve laughed. 'You dog! I might give that Debbie a ring.'

'Oh, you getting into *her* now?'

'No. She's all right but I get bored. I can't stop thinking about Lisa, you know. She's just...'
Danny stopped him immediately. 'She's not worth it, mate. Fuck her! You can do better than that. Her and Kate...'

'Are you over her yet?' Steve interrupted.

'I was never into her. I liked her, don't get me wrong. But you know me, I can't settle down.'

'Have a good time, anyway; don't go too mad. And stop telling me about your crazy, rough sex sessions. You've got me doing it. I've found myself slapping girls when I'm shagging them.' Danny laughed loudly. 'And some of them like it. It's scary!'

'What have you stumbled on, eh?' asked Danny. 'I'll have to go, I'll see you soon.'

'Okay! Take it easy.'

19

Danny and Kate left just after 5.30am on Wednesday. They wanted to get out early to avoid sitting in traffic. They stopped off for the usual coffee/toilet/food breaks before arriving in Kilthistle in Scotland around 11.30 then it only took them a further ten minutes to find the B&B where Danny had reserved a room.

'Wait here,' he said in the car, 'I'll go and check us in.'

The owner of the B&B was a lady called Mrs McGregor. Danny wasn't sure if her affected Scottish accent was due to her eccentricity or whether it was a gimmick for tourists. She had a long, crooked nose, bucked teeth and a huge mop of curly red hair that Danny was convinced was a wig. To him, she was straight out of a Hollywood comedy.

'One night was it not, Mister?'

'Yes, one night. M.i.s.t.e.r...and...M.i.s.s.u.s...S.m.i.t.h,' he signed. A cat walked across his foot and pawed at his leg. Danny jumped.

'Och! Don't mind old Migsy. She's only a-playin'. I think she likes ye.'

'Forty-eight pounds! Is that right?'

'Aye! Will yer missus be joining ye soon?'

'Yes, she's in the car. What about breakfast?'

'When you get up! Breakfast is a morning meal.'

'Yes, I know, but what time is it?'

'Seven-thirty sharrip!'

'Seven-thirty? 'Til when?'

She half-closed one eye and ogled him with the other. 'Seven-thirty sharrip!'

'Oh, Right!'

As they walked up the stairs Danny asked her questions about the area. 'Is there a local pub nearby?'

'Aye! The Merry Sailor.'

Unusual, he thought. 'Is there a town close by where we can get food?'

'Aye!' Danny waited for the rest but she never continued. 'Here we are Mister. Number four.'

'Oh! Just one more thing. I noticed that there's a bar downstairs. Does it stay open 'til late?'

'Aye!'

He waited again for her to elaborate but when she never he asked: 'How late?'

'LATE!' she spat out, half closing her left eye.

'Is there a TV in the room?'

'Aye! Would you be wantin' an early moornin' alarum call for breakfast?'

'Aye! I mean, yes. Thank you.'

He dashed back out to the car to fetch Kate and the luggage as Mrs McGregor wandered off into the kitchen.

'It's lovely, isn't it?' Kate said as she paced around the room. 'How much was it for three nights?'

'Don't you worry about that. It's my treat.'

She thanked and kissed him as they sat down on the bed together. Her curiosity grew. 'Danny!'

'What?'

'It's about Lisa.'

'I thought we agreed not to talk about it.' She sagged her head forward. 'Okay! One more thing and then we agree not to mention it for the next three days?' Danny requested.

'I was wondering. You know you said she wasn't faithful to Steve...well...there wasn't anything going on, was there? I mean, between you two.'

'Of course not. How can you say such a thing?'

'I'm sorry. I just thought it was weird- her being in your flat.'

'I've already explained this to you. Don't you believe me?'

'Of course. I just thought...Things like this happen and it destroys your faith in everyone. I thought Lisa was great. I thought I could trust her...I think I'm just a bit confused.'

'Aw, babe! I don't want to see you like that.' He kissed her. 'You know how much I like you. I'd never do that to you. If I lost you it would destroy me.'

They kissed again and fell backwards onto the bed, entwining their lips as they did so. It began to get heated as the caressing came into play.

'I've got an idea. Why don't we christen this bed?' suggested Danny. Kate smiled and blushed.

Minutes later they were down to their underwear, stroking and smooching. They played for about ten minutes, enjoying each other's company, before they progressed to consummate their love.

It was only a few minutes into their throes of passion when the door that led to the hallway swung open.

'Yer left yer sootcase ootside,' said Mrs McGregor as she stepped in and placed the case on the floor. She walked back out without saying another word. Danny and Kate stopped. They looked at each other for a second and then burst into laughter.

'Did you see that? She didn't even bat an eye,' observed Kate.

'That was probably deliberate,' added Danny. 'She probably does that with everyone.'

'Dirty old cow!'

'I'll tell you what, though. She's put me right off now.'

'Me, too. Let's go and get a coffee.'

Lisa's mother, Betty, was interviewed by the police in order to build up a profile of her daughter's character and movements. Betty was distraught. She never knew much about Lisa's life as Lisa lived such a private existence. She did know two vital things, though. She knew that she had a friend called Kate and was seeing some guy called Steve.

'That shouldn't be too hard to trace,' said Sergeant Wilson. 'We'll contact the phone company to give us a list of her calls for the last two months.'

'She may have some old bills lying about the house,' Betty said. 'I'll go and have a look for you.'

When she returned she also had with her a photo of Lisa with Steve, Kate and Danny. She identified the people in the photo as best she could. 'That's this Steve guy and that's her friend Kate. I'm not sure who the other guy is though.'

'Never mind! You've been most helpful. That gives us enough to go on for now.'

'Are you sure you wouldn't like a cup of tea?'

'No, thank you. I think we've bothered you enough for today. We'll be in touch. Goodbye!'

'How's your coffee?'

Kate looked down at the frothy top. 'It's fine...Thank you for these three days, Danny. I'm having a good time already. Sometimes it's good to just be with you; for us to spend time together.'

'I know. We haven't done enough of it lately, have we?'

'That's all right. We can make up for it now.'

'I suppose so. Yeah, you're right. Let's make the most of it.'

'Do you mind me asking you something, Danny?'

'Of course not. What is it?'

'I heard the landlady say to you, just as we came out, that we should check out before twelve tomorrow. Well...I was just wondering...'

'You were wondering why we are checking out *tomorrow*?'

'Yeah!'

'I was gonna save it as a surprise for you but...I thought it would be nice if we moved on. I've reserved a room in Glencairn. It's really nice there. I thought we could see a couple of towns while we're here.'

'Brilliant!'

'There's a waterfall and all that. It's lovely. Beats going to work, doesn't it?'

'Yeah, definitely.'

Later that evening they visited the local pub, The Merry Sailor. They got quite drunk within an hour. A remarkable achievement, Danny thought.

'I'm worried, Danny. I'm worried what may happen to you if the police should find out.'

'How are they gonna find out?'

'It's not difficult. They've only got to add up two and two and they'll see that our names keep cropping up.'

'That's nothing. We were her friends. Why should we worry about being questioned? They're never gonna find her body now so...without that what are they gonna accuse us of? Kidnapping and hiding her? No. They'll sniff around for a bit, follow a few leads, and then it'll get stored away with the hundreds of other unsolved cases. They need the corpus delicti.'

Kate thought for a moment before enquiring: 'Where did you dispose of the body? I mean...I don't want to know if it's horrible or anything.'

'Let's just say that it can never be traced now.'

Curiosity got the better of her. 'Where?'

'It's been burnt...in an incinerator. It's so hot everything will burn. Even the bones.'

'That's horrible! Poor Lisa!'

'I know, but she's in peace now. You do realise it was an accident, don't you?'

'Of course. You told me what happened.'

He eyed her for further reactions then reached the conclusion in his head that she was happy with the story.

Changing the mood he asked: 'Would you like another drink?'

Kate nodded. Danny stood up to go to the bar and seemingly out of nowhere an old man, about seventy, in a shabby suit with short, dyed black hair and an abundance of dandruff on his shoulders, addressed Kate: 'Hallo ma dear. Is it oot-of-tooners that ye are?'

Kate was confused. 'Erm, yeah. I think so.'

'Either ye are or ye aren't,' he added pedantically. 'What's the nature of yer business?'

'Er...holiday.'

She grew nervous and looked to catch Danny's eye at the bar but he had his back to her as he was getting served. The old guy continued to question her, his beady little eyes penetrating her bones.

'Holiday, ye say? Are ye sure ye no from the FBI?'

'FBI? That's in America, isn't it?'

'Aye! That's right, dearie. Ye seem to know a lot aboot them.'

A voice came from the bar: 'Ted! Will you stop bothering the strangers?' The man behind the bar walked over to the table that Kate was sat at and led the old man away. 'I'm sorry for him, love. He doesn't mean any harm. We're not all like this in this town, you know.'

'Oh, no. I'm sure you're not.'

The man tapped his finger on his temple. 'Ted's not right in the head.'

'That's okay. We have our fair share of those where we come from too.'

'What's going on?' asked Danny, returning from the bar.

'Just some old guy talking to me. He's a bit mad.'

'I can't leave you alone for five minutes, can I?' Danny laughed.

'I always attract nutters,' added Kate.

Danny sat down and drank a large mouthful of his pint of lager and his paranoia became apparent. 'Don't talk to them. We came here for a bit of peace.'

'It's not my fault. He started chatting to me.'

He shook his head as he spoke. 'Why can't people be normal?'

'You'll have to stop drinking you know, Steve?' Debbie sat opposite him in his flat.

'I know. I just can't help it lately. I'm sorry, babe. You're a decent girl. Why don't you just go?'

'Go? And leave you like this? No chance. Look, I know you said you hadn't long split up from your ex, and I gather you're quite cut up about it...' Steve shrugged his shoulders and gulped a mouthful of lager. '...but you can't go on drinking like this. You're gonna do some damage to yourself. And it's only a false world that you're closing yourself up in. I know you need to escape, we all do sometimes, but you also have to face up to reality. Sometimes you need to take a problem by the scruff of its neck and...just deal with it.'

'I know. You're so right. I just need a little thinking time, that's all.'

'No. That's exactly what you *don't* need.' He listened intently. 'Because a little "thinking time" leads to a little "drinking time". The more you think about it the worse it gets. Believe me, in a situation like this- thinking is destructive. You need to focus your energy on something. Something that takes your mind off your difficulties.'

'How are you such an expert?'

She stood up. 'I'm not an expert. I'm just an outside pair of eyes. If I was sat there moping you would probably be able to advise me.'

'I'm not moping.'

'Sometimes you can't see things 'cos you're too involved. You've heard the expression: "You can't see the wood for the trees" or whatever it is?'

'Yeah!'

'Well that's what it's like here. You feel down and you want to drown your sorrows. Fine! But you seem to be drinking every night. Once you start that you're on a slippery slope and it's hard to fight your way back up. You need to move on and focus your energy elsewhere. Don't think about it it'll drive you up the wall.'

Steve carried on drinking, despite the protests.

Two hours later, Debbie cradled him as he lay on the couch asleep. She spoke softly to him, although he could not hear.

'You're a good guy, Steve. I quite like you. You shouldn't drink though.' She stroked his face in admiration. 'I bet we'd have lovely kids. I want my boys to be just like you. You'd make a great dad.'

She continued stroking him, drifting into her own dreamy little world. 'We could have a big house, six children, a car in the garage...a huge garden....a dog...a cat. My family could come and visit us...my sister would be so jealous.' She stared at the wall for a moment, picturing the idyllic scene of a happy family in her head.

Suddenly, her concentration broke by the sound of Steve snoring.

'Pig!' she exclaimed. 'Drunken pig!' and slapped his leg.

'Normal, you say.' Danny turned to find a huge man at the next table addressing him. 'You don't think we're normal up here, then?'

Danny was beginning to regret choosing a small town and not opting for Edinburgh.

Fuck! Here we go. Fucking local pubs, they're always a recipe for disaster. I should've known. It's the same everywhere, they don't like outsiders. 'I'm sorry, did you say something?' he asked, smiling to avoid conflict.

'I said do ye nae think we're normal up here?'

'Of course! Everyone seems fine.'

'Perhaps you'd like tae step ootside an' we'll discuss it?'

'Why? Is it a secret? If I've got anything to say I'll say it here and if you've got anything...' he gestured to Kate. '...we're good friends. She's okay.'

'Ye dinnae catch ma drift. This pub happens to be owned by a friend o' mine so I don't want any hanky-panky on the premises.'

'Quite right! But I don't want any hanky-panky with you- inside or "oot" 'cos you're not my type.'

The man slammed his drink down on the table and Danny tried to defuse the situation.

'Look! I think you've got the wrong impression. I'm not saying anybody's abnormal...' *Although you clearly are,* he thought. '...People are people, wherever you go. I know that.'

The huge man eyed Danny up and down then persisted: 'I'll ask ye one more time. Do ye nae wanna step ootside so we can talk?'

Danny's hand found a glass ashtray on the table. His fingers fell inside it whilst his thumb cupped its base.

'And I'm telling you one more time. If "stepping ootside" is some crazy metaphor for "let me smash your brains in in the car park" then I'm afraid I'll have to politely decline.' He turned to Kate. 'Let's go! Whatever happens, you head back to the B&B. Don't worry about me.'

The man stood up, his gargantuan frame towering over Danny. Danny's hand gripped the ashtray. 'I don't want any trouble.'

'You've already got some, sonny.'

251

Everyone in the bar had stopped and begun to take note of what was occurring.

'Lenny! Leave it out!' cried the barman. 'Not in here.'

One of the wives of the men at the bar made her way over to the giant of a man. Her 5 feet, 2 inches positioned itself beneath his 6 feet, 7 and voiced its opinion. 'Lenny! What are you doing? These people are tourists in our town. Behave!'

Lenny straightened himself up to his full height, now standing at just over 6 feet, 8 inches. 'He thinks we're all weird,' he bawled. 'Thinks he can cause fights in our little town.'

'No he doesn't. They're just out for a quiet drink. Sit down, Lenny.' Lenny sat. The woman turned to Danny and Kate. 'Sorry about that,' she said.

Danny released the ashtray. 'That's okay. Glad you were here. Could've gone a bit pear-shaped otherwise.'

'Lenny's a nice guy, really. A gentle giant. He's just proud of where he's from.'

'And so he should be. We'd better be going, anyway.'

'No! Don't go because of that.'

'No, really. We need some sleep. Thanks again.'

Back at the hotel room Kate spoke for the first time in over half an hour. Although still drunk, the incident in the pub had cleared her head and now she felt sober.

'Why would anybody act like that? Why can't people be nice to each other?' She made eye contact with Danny. 'There's so much evil in the world. Why?'

'I guess it's just what makes the world go around. It's all a vicious circle. Evil people do evil deeds and others suffer. Then *they* turn evil themselves. When you're nice to someone they take it as a weakness and abuse it, so you harden up. That's life, I suppose.'

'It's wrong, though. It's all wrong. If everybody was nice to each other then there'd be no greed. We could all have a nice big house, eat what we wanted. There'd be no jealousy, no wars.'

'Where do we draw the line, though? Wars are horrific but they bring the population down. Just like diseases and illnesses. They seem to come in waves, too, like they're planned- huge government conspiracies to control humanity. Perhaps there's an alien existence ruling earth. Or what about a god? Some controlling force. It starts wars, creates diseases and keeps us within our limits.'

'You think a god is causing all that?'

'If you believe in a god then that god is certainly allowing it to happen.'

'But surely the notion of a superior force is an excuse to take the onus off humanity?' Kate questioned, 'An excuse to say "why do these things happen?" rather than, "yes, we fucked up. Perhaps we should try a different approach."'

'In a similar way it seems that we need evil to illustrate to us what good is. If there was no evil in the world then we wouldn't know what good was.'

'This is all getting a bit too deep for me at this time of night. I need sleep.' She kissed him. 'Well...' she added, 'not just yet.'

Alcohol levels from their drunken state effected a closeness between them. They touched, caressed and kissed before they enjoyed each other's bodies on a higher level and made love.

Danny paused in the middle. 'Ssh! Can you hear something?'

'No.' There was a faint sound of scratching and fiddling on the door.

'Mrs McGregor!' he whispered, 'She's listening again.' Kate put a hand over her mouth to suppress a laugh. 'She wants a show,' Danny stated, 'let's give her one. Ooh! Baby! Oh, yeah!'

They continued their lovemaking and found it funny to shout out various cries of sexual pleasure and erotic comments including heavy breathing and lots of voiced sighs but after a while they became engrossed with each other and ignored the world around them. They became so involved that they never noticed, until they had finished, that the door had been opened slightly and left ajar. They laughed about it afterwards.

'What time is it?' asked Kate.

'It's nearly one o'clock,' replied Danny, looking at the clock on his mobile phone.

'Are you sure there's no way of tracing Lisa's body if the police start investigating?'

'Are you still thinking about that? Don't worry, she's long gone. By the time they put that fire out, and cooled it, 'cos it's quite deep, there'd be nothing left whatsoever. And that's only if they got a tip off as to the body being taken there.' His eyes opened to their full extent and they seemed to lose their warmth. 'You and me are the only ones in the world who know about her.'

A chill struck itself deep in her spine. 'Let's not talk about it anymore, eh?' she added.

They awoke bright and early the next morning. The excitement of sleeping in a new place and being in a position to see some interesting sights fuelled them with enough energy to make it down the stairs in time for breakfast. They walked into the dining room and Mrs McGregor walked off into the kitchen shouting: 'I shan't be a minute. Two breakfasts coming up. Help yourself to cereal,' over her shoulder. Danny looked at his watch and said aloud: 'Seven-thirty sharrip!'

They sat at a table in the dining room opposite a woman whose eating habits left a lot to be desired, they felt. Kate never considered herself "stuck up" yet she resented poor table manners. She noticed that the woman had short, cropped, blonde hair and wore a shabby cardigan that, despite its appearance, was new. As she crunched and slurped on her cereal it became evident that the fingernails of her left hand had been bitten so far down that her fingers resembled those of a child's. The tops of her fingers were red where the skin was growing over her nails.

As she snorted, Kate turned away in disgust, pushing her own cereal bowl, half-eaten, away from her. 'I don't feel like that,' she said.
Even Danny cringed and he was never put off his food. 'Never mind,' he reassured her, 'there's eggs and bacon on the way.'

A man of about forty came in and sat at a table just to the left of them. He was dressed in a smart suit and drew out a laptop from his bag.
He's starting work early, Danny thought.
The man put some cereal in a bowl, added milk, and proceeded to eat it very slowly whilst fiddling with the buttons of the laptop. When Mrs McGregor came in he refused a cooked breakfast and continued to eat his cereal. He ate so slowly that Danny and Kate had finished their eggs and bacon and had drunken three cups of coffee each before he finished. Danny found it all rather odd but said nothing. He wasn't sure if Kate had noticed that he had taken over half an hour to eat one bowl of cereal. If she had it had not been acknowledged.

Danny stood up, patting his stomach. 'Come on! We'd better get a shower and pack.'
The woman opposite them also stood up and shouted a "thank you" to Mrs McGregor in the kitchen. There was fresh milk spilt down the front of her cardigan along with bits of cereal. As she stood finishing the last of her coffee she brought her sleeve across her mouth to soak up the two dribbles that never quite made it in.

'You'll like Glencairn,' Danny stated as they drove along an old B road. 'I remember visiting it as a child. It was snowing and all the mountains were white. Very picturesque!

'We were even there in the summer, once, and that was good, too. It was hot but up in the hills the breeze was refreshing. There's one mountain there in particular that you can walk up. Well, I suppose it's not a mountain really. Just a very big cliff or hill or something. It takes over an hour but it's well worth it for the view. You don't notice how steep it is until you get to the top and realise how high you are. The back of it is almost a sheer drop; when you look over it's scary. Fantastic, though!'

'Pity we never brought a pair of binoculars.'

He smiled. 'I did. I know what it's like up there. You can see for miles. There's nobody around at all, just the odd house, barely visible in the distance. They're probably farms or something. There's no way I'd come here without binoculars.'

'Where are they? I want a look now. This is quite scenic.'

'It's all scenic here. They're in my bag on the back seat.'

She reached in to get them and felt a sharp nip on the end of her finger. 'OW! What's that?'

As she withdrew the object it became apparent that it was a large Bowie knife.

'What's this for?' she screamed. 'DANNY!' The car skidded, slightly.

'All right, calm down. It's just an outdoor kit,' he said as he pulled the car into the side of the road. 'Look! There's a compass and that in the handle.' Kate looked horrified. 'Don't look at me like that. You know I like the outdoors.' She didn't, though. This was the first time he had ever mentioned it. 'And besides, we're out here alone. We need to protect ourselves.'

'What against? Hungry coyotes? Aggressive hedgehogs?'

'You know, wild animals, mass murderers.'

'Don't talk like that. I don't like it.'

'Shut up about it then. For fuck's sake, it's only a survival kit.'

He drove on and she relaxed a little. 'Put it back and get the binoculars out. See if you can see that house over there.' He pointed across a field to a small cottage in the distance.

'WOW!' Kate sounded, pressing the binoculars up tight to her eyes. 'You can see everything. These are really powerful.'

'What can you see?'

'There's an old woman sitting in a chair- it looks a bit like a rocking chair- reading a newspaper.'

'What, the rocking chair's reading the newspaper?'

'No, silly.'

'Can you see the date?' Danny laughed. 'I can't imagine it's today's. There isn't a shop around for miles.'

Kate sniggered. 'She might buy all the newspapers on a Saturday then read them all week. She's probably way behind in her news.'

'Yeah. No doubt she'll read about Lisa going missing next week.'

Kate ignored this comment. She felt that references towards Lisa were offensive and inappropriate.

'Hang on!' she said, changing the subject. 'There's a guy just outside. He's got a dog with him. It looks like a little cottage.'

'Probably is. Can't see them putting a council house in the middle of a field.'

'It isn't in the middle of a field, smart arse. There's a road running along the front of it.' She gave him a smug grin and he returned the gesture.

'You can get out here if you like,' he joked. Shrugging it off she leaned over to kiss him. 'Decided to stay in, have you?' He kissed her back, alternating his focus from the road to her and back. 'Shall we pull in properly?' he suggested, letting the experience of nature get the better of him.

'What! Out here? You must be mad.'

The idea fixed itself in his head and he pushed on. 'Oh, come on! It'll be good. Exciting! The prospect of getting caught.'

She reflected for a moment. 'I don't know. I suppose the scenery is nice.'

Danny took this as a "yes" and pulled the car over onto the edge of an embankment. Noticing a way into a field he drove in.

'Wait a minute! I just said the scenery was nice, that's all.'

'Shut up!' he played. 'You'll enjoy it.'

'What if somebody's watching?'

'Who? There's nobody around for miles.'

'Binoculars!' she said, raising them towards his face. Somebody else might have a pair. They might see us.'

'What...like some little old lady in her rocking chair? "She reaches in the top drawer for her 50x300 standard, army-issue field glasses and, lo and behold! 'Dost mine eyes deceive me?'" So what if anybody saw us, anyway. If they did they'd only continue watching for voyeurism. They'd be enjoying it. Another couple would see us and they'd probably do the same.' He reached over and put his arm around her. 'You've got nothing to be ashamed of, anyway. You're gorgeous!'

She blushed as he kissed her softly and this led to heavier ones. The caressing grew passionately and before they knew it they were down to their underwear.

'I'm nervous, Danny.'

'It's okay. Relax! We're on holiday, remember.'

Before long they were naked and making love. Kate lost her inhibitions completely and began to revel in the thought of somebody watching. She even fantasised that a young couple were in the cottage watching. The fantasy excited her and she grew extra sensual. Danny picked up on this and he, too, grew more excited.

Kate's feelings grew ever more uncontrollable and a tingling sensation formed in her stomach. Pleasured to near-limit she looked at Danny's face as he lay beneath her. There was not much space but they made do, improvising around the reclining seats. Kate moaned, a shudder sent itself through her spine and she felt that her whole world was shaking. She had heard the expression about the earth moving but never before believed it.

Glancing up she noticed the trees in the distance leaving her. Through the side window she saw the blades of grass pass her by. The combination of the "moving scenery" and her "naughty sex" in the outdoors, as she imagined it, was too much for her to control and it took a second or two for her to realise that they were rolling further into the field. She panicked and yelled:

'DANNY! The handbrake!' frightening him almost out of his mind.

Danny threw his body up and hit the brake pedal with his bare foot. They both sighed with relief as the car came to a halt and Danny pulled the handbrake lever. Their hearts were racing but they need not have panicked as the car would only have travelled about another twenty yards before it stopped naturally at the end of the gradient.

'We're lucky we didn't hit anything,' said Kate.

Danny looked out of each window in turn until his vision had taken in all 360 degrees.

'Like what? A cow? There's nothing around for us to hit,' he retorted.

Kate took a good look too, until she realised that they were in the middle of a field, surrounded by...grass. Their eyes met at the exact

257

time, as if planned, and each one waited for the other to laugh. Danny pulled a face and Kate began. They both fell into raucous laughter, for the most part dispersing their nerves.

Once they started they couldn't stop and they continued for around two minutes- a long time to sustain constant laughter, they knew. It was broken temporarily by child-like attempts to stop that failed miserably.

When they finally controlled themselves Kate hugged Danny. 'I can't carry on,' she said.

'Neither can I.' There was a silent period as they shared a moment with each other and reflected on all that had gone on. Then Danny added: 'Let's get dressed.'

Steve had taken an early lunch from the factory. He sat in The Anchor drinking whisky.

'You okay, there,' asked the barmaid.

'Another large one, please,' he replied, ogling the new member of staff. 'Are you new, er...' He leaned over to read her name badge. '...Julie?'

'I started two days ago.'

'How are you finding it?' he inquired, striking up a conversation.

'It's good. All the other staff are great, the customers are nice...it's such a relaxed atmosphere in here.'

'Did you know Lisa?'

'I met her once.'

He sneered and muttered the word "bitch"under his breath before asking 'Where else have you worked, Julie?'

'Loads of places. I'm a student, I only work part time.'

'Oh, student, eh? Er...'

'English,' she said in answer to the question that she guessed he was about to ask.

'Right! Do you like it?'

'Yeah, it's not bad. Let me just serve this guy.' She flourished along the bar to pull a pint of beer.

When Julie returned Steve ordered another large whisky.

'Day off, today then?' she asked, rather abruptly.

'Not exactly. I'm on my lunch.'

'Your lunch? Are you allowed to drink so much?'

'Probably not. Who cares, though?'

She returned to face him with a double whisky in her hand. 'Is it a woman?' He nodded. 'Well is there anything *I* can do to help?' she asked, rather forward in her manner.

Steve's eyes lit up. It had been a long time since a girl had offered to help him out.

'Like what?' he replied, kicking himself immediately after saying it.

'You're a good-looking guy and you have a nice personality. I mean...I don't know who she is but...I would say she's not worth it.'

I think Danny's right. None of them are worth it.

After listening to Danny's explanation of Lisa's absence and now this pretty, young and intelligent girl confirming his own beliefs he concurred. 'I should get on with my life, shouldn't I?'

Before Steve left, he and Julie exchanged numbers. The fresh air of the outside took him aback and suddenly he felt really drunk. He staggered off in the direction of the factory. He had taken an early lunch by an hour but had spent over three hours in the pub and it was now more than an hour later than he would normally finish. In addition to this he was caught by his boss who walked in behind him.

'What time do you call this?'

Steve swivelled on the spot and nearly lost his balance. His speech was slurred.

'W...what? I've been t' lunsh.'

'I know where you've been,' his boss stated, moving closer towards him. 'And you're drunk! What are you doing coming back into work like that? Go home, you're no good to me. You'll lose a day's pay, too.'

Since Steve and Danny had been quite liberal with their attendances they were both on warnings and the factory had taken on another electrician. The role was very much overdue and had to become a necessity before it was filled.

Dismissed from work for being intoxicated, Steve made his way home before crashing on the bed. He was so drunk that seconds later he was asleep. Afternoon drinking had taken its toll.

'It's just up here, babe. Keep going.' Danny prodded Kate in the back.

'Danny, I'm shattered.'

'Come on, lazy. This'll get you fit.'

It was now close to four o'clock in the afternoon and the sky was heavily overcast. A dark blanket of potential rain had formed itself at the top of the mountain.

'Nearly there.'

'We'd better be.' Kate was exhausted and out of breath.

As they reached the summit Danny looked at his watch- 4.13pm and Kate looked at hers.

'We can't...gasp...we can't stay long, Danny. It's getting dark.'

'I know, I know. Just look at that view.'

Kate had to agree. She thought it was fantastic. Danny embraced her from behind as she stared out, the view travelled for miles. Lights could be seen in the distance, a small Hamlet. The Tip of the river Cairn could just be discerned.

'When I was a child I came here with my parents. We never had much money so holidays usually consisted of resting. My dad worked really hard, labouring ten hours a day. For what? To put bread in our mouths and drive himself into an early grave. I remember when I was eleven. My dad was really ill so we came to this village to rest. It's where his mother was from, you see. I walked up this mountain on my own and stayed here for over two hours.

'There were search parties out and police patrols looking for me. I probably caused my parents more grief than they could handle but I only intended to give them a break. I thought that if I got away for a few hours then my dad could rest and get better.

'He died three weeks later and I don't believe my mother ever forgave me after that. I know she blamed me for adding to his stress. I knew he was dying. You just do, don't you.' Kate clasped his hands tightly. A small tear rolled down her cheek as if it had escaped from her eye and was making a break for it.

'Over two hours I was here,' he repeated. 'I looked out onto the landscape and I planned my life. I was to be married at twenty five with four kids. Obviously with a big house, car and so on. I wanted to make a big impression on the world. Perhaps a famous actor or sport's star. Who knows? I needed my life to have an impact on others.

'When my dad died it nearly destroyed me. I crawled into my own little world and refused to come out. I was walking home from school one night when the anger and frustration grew within me to an unbearable level. I was bitter with the world. Sammy Wilson was the name of the young lad- he went to our rival school...I didn't know it at the time but I heard later on in the school assembly when they appealed for witnesses and saw it in the local newspaper... I ran past him and stabbed him in the neck with a fountain pen. He was with two other lads- I never knew them, they never knew me. Nobody knew who I was and I ran for my life. It felt good, as if I was transferring my own pain onto another. It felt good to have a stab back at life. It wasn't his fault, though. He was just a scapegoat. He was in intensive care for two weeks and nearly died.'

Kate glanced over her shoulder to catch Danny's facial expression. It was blank. His eyes looked like they had been left in the past. Realising he was deeply hypnotised by the view she turned back to join in the vision.

'My dad was the stability in the house. My mum brought me up after that- and I loved her to bits- but she never did a very good job. All my intentions were tossed out of the window. My dream to make it big, and exercise a huge impression on the world, collapsed. Or I should say, shrank? I had smaller impacts that affected individual people rather than the masses. I saved my neighbour's life, one night. He came in, put a pan of chips on and fell asleep. The smoke was killing him. I called the fire brigade, kicked his front door in and dragged him out for the fire officers to give first aid to when they arrived. They said he would have died if he had stayed in there much longer.' He stroked Kate's hair.

'I was a bit of a romantic at heart when I was younger. I had a picture of my ideal woman in my head. She was brunette, tall, thin, and beautiful. When I met my ex, Jessica, I thought I'd found her. Whether she fitted the description perfectly or whether I fitted her into it in my head is another story. The point is, she was perfect. Well, almost. She was the only girl, up to then, that I'd ever truly loved. I would have died for her.

'When you really love someone that much you never get over it. It was as though she was the only woman in the whole world for me and a one-in-a-trillion chance had brought us together. I'm sure everyone has their perfect match out there but whether you have to look worldwide or whether they're on your own doorstep is impossible to say. I don't know, but an ideal match is certainly a possibility. I never put much into girls before that. Or after, for that matter. Obviously I'm not including you. I'd lusted after them, supposedly fell in love with them, but this love was different. Even my first love I could define now as "lust" in comparison, even habit. You become accustomed to someone and to doing certain things and that becomes your way of life. Change upsets!

'That's the way I see most love affairs- temporary habits. You take away the habit and people don't know how to act. They merely need re-adjusting. Everybody feels that when they are in love it is special- and it is- it's just that I compare this with the other times I have been in love and there is a difference.' He paused slightly and took a deep breath. 'Deep down, I still love her. Even though she cheated on me with my best friend.'

Kate was happy for him to be frank and open with her but she did not like hearing about Danny being in love with someone else.

'I believe that inside you you have *the* love, and once it's given away it can never be taken back, despite surface actions. Sometimes- probably in most cases, actually- our real love is contained within us and we never feel strongly enough to release it. It then becomes a suppressed emotion.

'The problem for me came when she cheated on me. All my ex-girlfriends- those I was in love with- effected in me love, initially, but then hatred later on. In many cases the love probably turned to hate. With Jessica it was different. Yes, I hated her for what she did. Yes, I hated her for abusing the greatest feeling in the world- true love. Deep down, though, I always loved her. Even when I caught her red-handed. I could've killed her that night, easily. Then nobody else could touch her.

'Even six months later I loved her. I had met someone else and she was great but I never stopped loving Jessica and that was confusing. Whatever she did to me, hurt me in whatever way, I could hate her but I would always be aware that she was my main love, if you like- *the* love...It fucked me up! I met other girls, fell in love, but nobody ever matched up to her. Nobody else could take my main love. It was gone. I get involved with girls now and then suddenly become aware of this, although up to now I think it's been subconsciously.'

Kate was speechless and deeply hurt but she wanted to hear more. She swallowed hard and remained as quiet as possible.

'Looking out at this landscape today has taken me back. It's helped me to understand. As my main love has gone I don't feel that I have any love left so I distance myself from girls. And I hate them for what they've done to me. It was a girl who took away my main love. That same girl caused me to hate her. In a way, to me, she's a representation of all girls. I'm bitter! I'm frustrated! Why? Because I look around me and see malice, spite, bitchiness. Pretty devils! Sly and manipulative. As men we're stupid. We accept them at face value.'

He fell silent for a minute. Kate began to cry softly. She really felt for him but was also upset with his candid outlook. It was a long minute but, for Danny, it was soothing. The only sound was that of the wind whistling past their ears.

'Lisa's death was not an accident...'

Kate broke away and spun to face him; a look of horror on her face. She remained taciturn and focused. She listened intently, staring into his eyes. She wanted to hear what he had to say.

'...At least not in the way that I described, although I didn't set out to kill her. It all went a bit mad. Lisa's the third girl I've killed.'

Kate struggled to form the words in her mouth into a sentence. 'I-...is this...some kind of joke? If it is it's not funny.'

His facial expression never changed. 'I wish it *was* a joke. I wish it was all a joke. It's a farce but it's not a joke. I don't need to go into intricate details about how I killed them. Let's just say...I got the urge. Something inside me compelled me to do it.'

'What, voices?'

'Ha ha! Voices! No, not voices. What do you think I am some kind of monster? No! Reasoning. I wanted to do it. At the time I wanted to kill each one and, do you know, I don't think I regret it. It's just something that urged me. Perhaps something from my past. I've thought about it a great deal. I want a relationship with someone but I can't have one. You know how I am. I feel trapped and my good nature is abused. I think I'll always distrust women.

'When I met you I started to fall in love with you. I do love you, in fact, but I could never tell you that. If I did I'd quickly regret it. You were starting to interfere with my pattern of life. I was happy being single- no-one to fuck with my head- I'd resigned myself to it. Women whenever I wanted but only when *I* wanted. You came along and confused matters. I wish you could understand me...then you could be with me. I don't think I can keep you any longer, babe.'

The gravity of the whole situation hit home to Kate. She knew now that her life was in danger. She was terrified but something inside her retained a certain logic.

How could I have been stupid? She thought. Her brain kicked into overdrive as she devised a plan of action. *Why didn't I see? There's a dead body in the freezer of his flat and he fills me full of rubbish about some accident. And I believed it. I knew he needed help- at least counselling- to get over Lisa's death but, more so, reassurance. He had been through a lot and I needed to support him. But the deaths were deliberate. Deaths? Who were the other two? The last thing I should've done is go away with him for a break. Especially up in the deep hills of Scotland with nobody around for miles. As well as that, we're on top of a mountain. Perhaps someone will see us. It's doubtful, though. I'd better talk my way down. Reassure him and win his favour again. It's the only way I can guarantee my survival...Too late!*

Danny pounced towards Kate where she stood on the edge. As her body spun she espied the long drop from the top to the floor. A white flash and a thousand memories swirled through her mind almost simultaneously. Each memory represented aspects of her life and her brain made sense of every one.

The floor rose to meet its victim. Seconds later...blackness and no pain.

20

The bright gleam of early-morning daylight shone through the window of Danny's bedroom. The curtains were open and he awoke with the rise of the new day. He had slept well and now craved a hearty breakfast. The time was just after six o'clock. It was always great to get up early on a Saturday morning, he thought, if he wasn't working, as he had the day to himself.

After a coffee and a quick shower he was ready to face the world again. He made his way down Lank Lane until he came to the cafe on the corner.

'Large breakfast, please, and a coffee,' he ordered.

'Anything else?'

'Yeah, two extra toast, please.'

'That's four-eighty, please.' He gave her a five-pound note and she gave him the change before adding: 'Take a seat. I'll bring it over to you.'

'Thanks.' *This has always been a good cafe*, he thought. The guy that owned it cooked all the breakfasts himself and kept the kitchen spotless. Danny had gathered all this information when he slept with Marie a couple of times; a young student who worked there. *Not exactly a "greasy spoon" but the breakfasts are excellent.*

He sat down in the corner after picking up a newspaper to read. His eyes scanned the pages yet his concentration was elsewhere. His mind wandered to the events of the last few days. Had everything with Kate really happened or was it all part of that pleasant sleep that he had had during the night? There seemed to be too much evidence against the suggestion that it was not real. Flashbacks of the night Kate was pushed over the edge of the cliff became prominent in the foremost part of his brain.

...Something had caused him to be really careless that evening and initially he had left Kate's remains at the bottom. Attempting to shut it out of his mind he had driven off but after about twenty minutes the reality of the situation, along with the fear of capture, caused him to turn back. He returned to the scene of the crime and located the spot where the body had landed. He made every effort to ensure that the car was as close as possible to her. He believed in his mind that many psychologists hold the opinion that criminals need an audience, they require acknowledgement and appreciation.

As a result of this, criminals could very often make silly mistakes or leave clues, perhaps subconsciously, because they want to be discovered. Sometimes they just can not go on with what they are doing and want a stop to it. This is the way in which he viewed his initial actions. Leaving a body for the police to find would be a strong link to connect him with her death, and perhaps others. He had decided, though, that he wasn't ready to be caught yet and felt that if he craved recognition he would just have to wait until he had a lot more events to take credit for.

At the mountainside Danny hoisted the body up and hauled it for over five hundred yards before he reached his car. Kate's corpse was deposited in the boot whilst her phone, which he had managed to obtain earlier, was kept in his possession. From it he texted Steve:

> 'Hi Steve. Please tell Danny that I
> really like him but need to move
> on. I couldn't bear to speak to him
> personally as it would hurt me far
> too much. Kate x'

He also texted a couple of her friends from her phone book and explained that she (Kate) may be travelling to California in the near future but that she would stay in touch. He then switched her phone off in case anybody tried to call her.

The drive back was horrendous. Every traffic light appeared to be against him and held him there whilst other motorists pulled up alongside, seemingly staring at him. It was as if they knew. He wondered why they wouldn't know.

Surely my face shows all? Surely it's common knowledge?

Focusing back on the road, he wiped the sweat from his forehead with the sleeve of his jacket. Normally he would find this action repulsive. Tonight, however, he didn't care.

There were more than the average number of police cars patrolling the area, or so he thought. One in particular followed him almost a mile. It finally turned off at a different exit on a roundabout as he headed onto the M6. Never had he performed a bigger sigh. For the second time he wiped his brow. This time the *beads* of perspiration had turned into *pearls* and they were rolling down his nose. He hadn't dared to take his hands off the wheel whilst the police car was tailing him.

The officers in the car had run a check on the car to ensure that it was insured and not reported stolen. Happy with the results they headed back into town leaving Danny clutching the wheel with all his strength and desperately trying to control his rapidly-beating pulse rate. He contemplated pulling in to the hard shoulder of the motorway but knew that this would only be a valid reason for another police car to stop him.

When he finally reached his flat he darted into the kitchen to locate one of the whisky bottles from his stock. He felt he was becoming a real whisky connoisseur. The body was left in his boot whilst he drunk himself to sleep in his favourite armchair...

'...One large breakfast with extra toast and a coffee.'
The words broke his thoughts. The girl in the cafe was walking away from him. Danny looked down to see a large plate full of breakfast items. 'Fantastic!' he muttered to himself and tucked in.

After breakfast he strutted out of the cafe feeling on top of the world.

'A good breakfast always sets you up for the day,' he used to remark to Steve. He thought of Steve as he ran over the line in his head. Reaching for his mobile phone he pressed and held the number 5 button. Steve's number was on his "speed dial." It connected the call.

'Hello.'

'Hi, Steve. It's me.'

'Hello, mate. How are you? I haven't heard from you much these last few days.'

'I'm okay, thanks. Do you fancy going out for a few on Saturday?'

They made arrangements to meet up at Danny's flat at 8pm. Steve was up for a chat but Danny cut it short, suggesting that they needed to talk face-to-face.

As the call was disconnected Danny felt that he needed time to compose himself and reflect on his actions so far. He crossed the road to the small grocery shop and purchased a loaf of bread. He then made his way into Sexton Park, stopping only when he reached the tiny, wooded area where part of the lake could be seen. As he broke up bits of bread and threw them down, the ducks came from every angle, wading through the water and running up the bank.

How relaxing! he thought. *How nice to come here and put your life into some sort of context.*

The ducks gulped at the bread and swallowed it whole. *Why don't they chew it?*

His thoughts now resembled the ripples on the lake; disrupting the surface of the water and travelling out into...nowhere. *Where do they go...? Where is my life going?* His thoughts were slipping away from him and he was losing control.

Kate's body had lain in the boot for two nights after he returned home. He had finally plucked up the courage to drive to Sexton Park late at night and put the body into a sack. He could do this here as it was dark. He knew that the neighbours would see him opening his boot and he could never hide a body unless it was covered. He then took it home and into his flat, depositing it in the chest freezer.

'Well at least I've had my money's worth out of this freezer,' he muttered.

Luckily there was no blood. Kate had probably broken her neck, or something, Danny imagined, but there were no cuts apart from the grazes from the fall.

Sexton Park! Funny! Here I am feeding the ducks and a few nights ago I was feeding a dead body into a sack for disposal. Such a lovely place by day. People feeding the ducks; students lying on the grass to study; couples engaging themselves romantically; runners everywhere, attempting to get fit; families out for the day, at one with nature; kids playing football...then there's me...cutting up dead bodies...driving around with a corpse in my boot...roaming society. They must know about me. I feel that everyone knows. I wanna shout it out to the world.

Steve had had only brief contact with Danny since his return from Scotland. Danny had informed him that he had been to Wales with a girl for a "mid-week, dirty weekend." Steve felt it his duty to break the news to him about Kate: 'I got a text from Kate. She said to tell you something.'

'I can guess, mate. I've got a pretty good idea. I know she's knocking about with that rich guy, her and Lisa, remember me telling you?'

'Yeah, she told me to tell you that it was all over and that she was gonna move on.'

'That doesn't surprise me, mate. They're all the same. I've told you that.'

'I tried phoning her to get some sort of explanation for you but her phone's off. If you ask me she's changed her number.'

Danny nodded his head and showed a look of forlorn on his face. Inside, however, a smile was beaming.

More and more Steve was beginning to believe in Danny again. He thought that Danny had been wrong and that he knew better but everything had come full circle. In Steve's eyes they really were slags and not worth it. Initially they were nice girls and, supposedly, different. *Fuck! How could I have been so naïve.*

'They all show their true colours in the end,' suggested Danny. Steve was angry with himself.

'I don't know why I fell for it. You were right all along. I'm sorry, mate.'

'What for?'

'That time we sort of drifted apart. It was my fault. I thought you were wrong and I think I was choosing Lisa over you. I should never do that, I realise now.'

'Don't worry, mate. They're scheming, manipulative bitches and they get a hold on you. You lose control and it's shit. Some people call that love. But how can you love a slut? How can you love someone who will sell you out to the highest bidder? I had it all when I worked on the door; girls throwing themselves at you to get into a club or a bar. They love you on the way in- and lads fall for it- but, do you know on the way out...they fuckin' hate you. You go back to being a rag-arse doorman. Fuckin' slags!

'All kinds of sexual favours were offered when they were desperate to get in. What's that if it's not prostitution?'

Kate's body had lain in the freezer for a considerable number of days and Danny seemed in no rush to dispose of it. He had spoken to Steve on a number of occasions but had never gone into any great depth to explain his actions. Each conversation was brief, such as the second phone call:

'You never did tell me where you'd been.'

'I did, didn't I? Wales. I took some little slapper with me. I just fancied a bit of a change. It was good. We had a look round the shops and then went for a few drinks in the evening. One night, in the pub I was in, this Welsh geezer was coming onto the bird I was with. We nearly got into a fight but then I thought, fuck it! No! I want a shag. So we got off before we upset the locals too much.'

One of the key features of Danny's lying was to relate events as close to the truth as possible, allowing only marginal room for error. He utilised his experiences of Kilthistle to fabricate his Welsh holiday.

'I thought you got on well with the Welsh,' said Steve.

'I do, normally,' he answered, 'but you can't account for everyone.'

Back in the park a duck had marched up to his feet and was now only inches away.

I could kick it, he thought, *it's that close.*

He visualised himself kicking the duck, lifting it off its feet, but pangs of guilt ate into his insides. Although he wondered what it would be like he could never bring himself to do it.

That's wrong! I could never hurt an animal. Human, yes, 'cos they're innately evil. There are probably loads of sick kids in this park who would find it funny to lash out at these delicate creatures. If I catch them I'll show them what it feels like to get kicked.

Danny felt sorry for the duck, having to scurry around for food but at the same time he envied the simplistic lifestyle. He looked on as it feasted on the bread. It was as if the duck had not eaten in months.

The body of Kate, lying in his freezer, became prominent in his mind and he began to express his thoughts aloud: 'How can I go on living this lie? How can I live a normal life? What is NORMAL? I don't think I could face burning another corpse. What if somebody found out? Maybe I should just bury this one. Why do I get a kick out of killing?'

All these thoughts entered his head and he attempted to discuss them out loud. People began to look, however, as he walked along the lake, seemingly addressing the ducks. He became aware of the people watching and went quiet.

After feeding the ducks, Danny decided that his life was in need of a big change.

'Ordinary sex is crap!' he remarked. 'I think I need a bit of excitement. Perhaps some little slut? No, later. I'll work on that tonight.' In the meantime he thought he could work on his CV. He spent over two hours on this and eventually it was ready. He had a specific reason for updating his CV. There was a job in the newspaper for an electrician in the Leatherwood area, about a hundred miles away. Danny applied for it as, he felt, it could provide that necessary change that he needed. A new life, a new start. *Perhaps I can be normal again.*

Later that evening he surfed the Internet for electrician jobs throughout the country. *Perhaps,* he wondered, *if I went away for a while then all this fuss over Lisa, Kate, Michelle, Dominique and whoever else would sort itself out. When I go away I can start again but I need to go far; the further the better.*

Any jobs that were suitable for him, regardless of where they were in the country, he applied for.

Kate's disappearance hit the headlines with her mother expressing strong concern for her welfare. Danny had read the newspapers but never saw fit to mention it to Steve. Steve, on the other hand, brought it to his attention.

'Don't listen to all that crap,' said Danny as he sipped his bottle of beer in Eric's Bistro. 'You remember with Lisa?' Steve nodded. 'I think it's the same. She was fucking off to see some other fella and her family knew all about it. They played along with all that shit about not knowing where she was but they never convinced me for one minute. I was on to them from the start. Money talks, doesn't it?'

Steve looked deeply as he thought about what Danny said. Danny was usually always convincing but something was lacking now.

It was Friday around 1.30pm and Saturday night was approaching fast. Danny and Steve were having lunch in the local "greasy spoon" about three hundred yards from the factory. Steve was still not over Lisa.

'Women are weird, aren't they?' he stated.

'You only just discovering that?'

'No. I knew a few were odd but...I thought...'

'You thought Lisa was different? That's what they call falling in love, mate,' he added, patronisingly. 'You think a girl is okay. Then you think she's a bit special...before you know it there's an affinity between you that NO-ONE (apparently) can disrupt. She becomes special, she becomes important. All of a sudden she's a one-in-a-million and you feel like you'll never meet anyone like her again. You're wrong!

'There are tonnes of birds out there and they've all got different personalities. There's a shit-load that you'll meet and think...hey! she's special. It happens to everyone, mate. False sense of security. False world in which they live. False identity, even. They're not who you think they are. It's all a con, it's all a front. They're not what they seem. It's not love; it's a habit. You get used to one way of living your life. You get used to certain people and there are certain actions that you do. You get used to certain ways in which you do things and that becomes the norm. Upsetting this norm goes against your mind, which wants to regulate events and maintain stability.

'When you stop having fun with someone the stability goes out of your life. There's no regulation anymore. When you say you love someone, what you're really saying is that you're comfortable with the ways in which that person affects your life and changing it would seem strange. Their personality is appropriate for you. You accept it and adopt it as part of your own. This is why you feel you "love" them. If you take away that person, with their certain personality and their mannerisms, then you lose that security. You lose what you've grown accustomed to and can survive with. I think it's a survival aspect of nature. When we're comfortable with something, and there are no problems, then we cling onto it. Change could represent death, you see.

'When that change finally occurs we become upset. That particular person leaves us and we feel insecure. We have a new way of life to cope with and it's undermining.'

Steve nodded throughout. Deep down he was upset and wanted answers. He was back to believing every word that emanated from Danny's lips.

Danny continued: 'Haven't you ever noticed how we sometimes miss previous jobs, sometimes miss classes that we attended in the past or gyms that we used to go to? I worked up in Southside a few years ago and I had a great social life at the time. I really miss that at times. Sometimes even to the point that it's upsetting. Well, I think that's because I was "in love" with that way of life. The lifestyle that I had at the time was great but now I've moved on. I enjoy my life but really miss those times.

'To me...there's not much difference between that and becoming accustomed to a certain lifestyle, i.e. with a specific girl. It's all love and it's all hormonal dysfunction. In fact, I'm not even sure if it is hormones. It could just be the chemical/electrical activity that occurs in the brain. One thing is for sure- it's a way of thinking. It's a way of reacting to situations in a positive manner. In retrospect, too, all events always seem better when they are in the past. We exaggerate their true significance. All-in-all, I'd say that love is habitual. We love someone because we know them and feel secure with their actions.'

'I understand what you're saying,' replied Steve, 'yet I don't know where that leads us.'

'It doesn't lead us anywhere. We just need to clarify a few points on understanding.'

'My head hurts,' complained Steve.

'It's really easy. You just have to concentrate. I've simplified it for you.'

'Tell me more about these two rich brothers.'

'Well...they've got a few quid but for some reason the girls want to keep a low profile. Probably in case we think they're slags.'

'They're not gonna surprise me anymore. They fucked off with them and that was the last time I saw them. The main thing we know is that these guys have got a bit of cash so we know they're selling themselves out. They've gone for money, the slags. These fellas are obviously happy to release their money in return for sexual favours.' Steve drank from his bottle then added: 'It's nice here, isn't it?' Danny nodded. 'We should come here more often.

'No birds though, mate.'

Steve's head spun round as he surveyed the room then he nodded in approval. 'Still, it's nice for a chat,' he said. 'Do you want another one?'

As Steve made his way to the bar Danny took Kate's phone from his pocket. He turned it on and switched it to silent mode. All the while hiding it under the table. After a minute or two it began to light up and several text messages came through. Danny got up off his stool as Steve returned holding two bottles of lager.

'I'm just gonna nip the toilet. I won't be a minute.'

He locked himself in a cubicle and then proceeded to reply to each text. Each one held pretty much the same content. They were short and to the point. They asked for space on behalf of Kate and ensured each person that she was well. As soon as he texted her mum he switched the phone off again. Kate's mum was expected to believe that Kate was going away, possibly abroad, and would explain all in the near future.

Whether or not she believes it, Danny pondered, *is another matter. The judicial net must be closing in on me.*

Kate's mum was fair-haired and looked well for her age. She could have passed for Kate's sister quite easily. Everybody complimented her on her smile. Now, however, she wasn't sure if she would ever smile again. She sat in a large leather armchair in her living room and addressed the officer in charge.

'Any news?'

'I'm afraid not. We've got a few leads that we're following up but we need more information. Now this Lisa Reynolds girl who was recently in the paper...You say it could possibly be the girl who used to call Kate, a friend of hers?'

'Yes!'

'Well, we think it was. We've traced the number and calls were made from her phone to your daughter's.' Joan, Kate's mum, began to cry softly. 'I'm sorry, Mrs Bedwell. Would you rather I came back at a more convenient time?' he asked, showing as much compassion as he could muster up for this run-of-the-mill exercise.

'No!' replied Joan, sputtering out the words through her tears. 'It's okay. I know you need to do your job.'

'I assure you, Mrs Bedwell, our officers are doing their best. If she's out there we'll find her.' He paused for a moment before continuing. 'Some of the witnesses who came forward to inform us about Lisa's character will be contacted again. Perhaps they can help with this case too. They may be able to help us strengthen the link between Lisa and Kate.'

'There's something else,' added Joan. 'This afternoon...I received a text message from Kate. She said she was fine but needed a bit of time to herself.'

Officer Andrews looked up from his notebook and suddenly took great interest in what Joan had to say. Prior to this it had all been routine for him but now there was a lead.

'Go on,' he urged.

'She said she might be travelling abroad. She didn't say who with.'

Alarm bells rang in the sergeant's head. This disappearance was similar to a couple of others that he was involved in. He was confident that the coincidences were linked.

'Can I see the texts please, Mrs Bedwell?'

'Of course!'

He made a note of the date and time and copied the texts exactly as they were into his notebook.

'Can I ask you not to delete these texts and to inform us if you receive any more?'

'Y-Y-Yeah! Whatever you want.'

'Thank you. Have you tried calling her or texting back?'

'Of course I have. Her phone is off. I called straight away and I haven't had a delivery report for the texts that I've sent her.'

'Right! If there's nothing else I'll head back to the station. I think I may be able to dig up a few more leads.' He put his hand on her shoulder where she sat. 'Don't worry, Mrs Bedwell. Like I said...if she's out there we'll find her.'

Joan's head drooped as she sobbed softly.

Saturday night came round and Danny and Steve were excited about going out. They were drinking a few cans of lager in Danny's flat. Danny flicked through the television channels.

'Saturday night TV is so shit. No wonder people go out for the night.'

Steve agreed. 'It's all game shows isn't it?'

'Yeah! You see, they probably have this hidden agenda when choosing these programmes that says: 'Let's give all the poor people- or the sad bastards who have to sit in on a Saturday night- a hope, a dream. Let's show them how they can get out of this rat race. You can win money, cars, holidays, whatever. The materialistic urges of the working class. It's all designed to keep us going. A bit like the American Dream.'

Steve's eyes almost crossed. 'What's that?'

'Well, it stems back to migrant workers entering the newfound land. A land that had not been discovered so had, therefore, vast amounts of potential. But basically what it is is a carrot-on-a-stick routine. It purports to endow the average person with the ability to make it in life. I mean, there are aspects that are true. Many so-called average people can do well in life if they've got the tenacity to stick it out. We can't all be millionaires, though. Tax sees to that.

'You work all your life and you finally pay for your house. Then you snuff it and pass it on to your children but for some reason they've only got so much percentage of the ownership- sixty, is it? They have to sell in order to pay the Inheritance Tax. And if you *give* it to your children before you die then they pay Gift Tax. Pathetic!'

Steve nodded to show his approval. This was the old Danny that he knew, ranting on about one thing or another. Frustrated with the world and always had a peculiar slant on life.

Danny took a sip of lager then continued. 'Have you ever sat and watched the telly in the daytime? It's terrible. There are loads of adverts aimed at old people reminding them that they are gonna die soon and advising them on what they should do. Preparing for their funerals; that's nice isn't it? And debt management ads. "Consolidate all your debts into one easy, monthly instalment." In other words, don't owe everyone else money; owe it to us. And for this service we expect a huge backhander. You'll still owe your money and extra for our exploitation of your desperate position. You won't see it 'cos we'll just wangle it into the repayments." They must spend a fortune on these adverts. They're on constantly, which means they're obviously making a packet.'

'Yeah,' replied Steve and looked at the clock. 'It's half-eight. What time do you wanna head out?'

Danny looked at his watch and then at his drink. 'Let's just finish these then get going.

The first pub they arrived at was the Blacksmith's Anvil. It didn't take Danny long for him to move in on two girls. He bought them both a drink and then he and Steve joined them at their table.

'This is Steve,' he gestured, with a drink in his hand. 'This is Laura, this is Kelly.'

Laura smiled and Danny honed in on her. Her confidence appealed to him. 'How come you're drinking in here, it's an old-man's-pub?'

'Maybe I wanna find myself a rich old man,' she replied, joking.

The first word that came into Steve's head was "prostitutes" and it angered him. Danny never expressed concern over the problem. He knew it was intended as a joke.

'I *can* tell you girls that, although I'm not old I am rich. And my friend Steve, here...' He gestured towards Steve and all eyes fell on him. '...is loaded beyond belief.'

'I'll have another one of these, then,' suggested Laura, pointing to her glass. The girls giggled.

'All in good time,' added Danny. 'I don't believe in spoiling somebody for the sake of it. No, seriously though, what do you do for a living?'

'We're both social workers,' said Laura.

'So you know all about care in the community?' asked Steve.

'Well, we do our best,' Kelly chipped in.

'I think that's really interesting. So you're good at dealing with people; talking to them and sharing their problems?'

Danny cut in: 'He wants you to look after him, you see.'

The girls laughed. Steve continued. 'No, I think it's good. Do you deal with a lot of personal problems?'

Danny cut in again: 'Oh, no! Not the wart. Don't mention the wart.'

The girls laughed again and Steve grimaced until they stopped.

Sensing the atmosphere, Kelly stood up and said: 'I'm just gonna go to the toilet.'

'Yeah, I'll join you,' added Laura.'

'Can't I join you?' Danny joked.

Whilst they were gone Steve expressed his annoyance: 'Don't make a tit out of me.'

'Listen mate, we're only having a laugh. You can do the same to me. They're not gonna look down on you. Just retaliate with some good one-liners and we'll be in here.'

'I just don't want to be the butt of the joke.'

'You won't be. We're all the butt of the joke. You just have to pass it round. It's all in good fun. And anyway, I only did it to snap you out of the crazy mood you were in. You were gonna scare them off. Don't start all that boring bullshit. We want to keep it light-hearted. If they think we're a good laugh to be with then they'll *want* to be with us. You know what I'm saying? He sipped his drink. 'See the jugs on both of them?'

Steve smiled, 'All right, all right! We'll do it your way.'

Deep down he wanted to go with the flow because he knew Danny always made the right decisions. Even when they were quite bizarre he seemed to know what he was doing. If a girl was for the taking then he was the man to get her.

When the girls returned Steve bought the second round. He and Danny had made a pact that even though Kelly and Laura would not necessarily have to buy them lots of drinks in return, they wouldn't ply with them all night either. Luckily enough Laura was the next to buy the drinks. If she hadn't then she would have got the hint anyway when Danny went to the bar to order just his and Steve's.

'We're not staying long in here,' said Kelly. 'Where are *you* off tonight?'

'Greene's,' jumped in Steve, trying to be involved in the conversation.

'Wherever,' said Danny, keeping his options open. He imagined his vague reply would allow him the opportunity to somehow end up in the same place as these girls in case they didn't pull anybody else. Fortunately for him, however, he didn't need to appear vague. The girls were interested.

'Oh we're going to Greene's,' Laura commented.

'We'll meet you in there,' Danny suggested, wasting little time. Everybody agreed and mobile numbers were exchanged so that they could meet up.

In the next establishment, Mitzy's- a wine bar, Danny tried his hand on a couple of thirty-year-olds at the bar. He thought he was doing okay but it was only a stop-gap to the next bar and he rushed his move on one of them. She blew him out and the anger welled up inside him.

'Fucking lesbians!' he remarked.

It was Steve who came to the rescue by chatting up a girl sat on her own whilst her mate was outside on her phone.

'Danny, this is Emma. Emma, Danny.'

'Your boyfriend in the toilet, is he?' joked Danny. Steve was good with girls when he knew them but it was unlike him to be first in, especially before Danny.

Emma's friend Megan sat down and all four chatted for about half an hour before Emma said that she would have to leave early: 'I'm working in the morning so I can't stay out late.'

'Which phone shop is it that you work in?' asked Steve.

'The one on Church Road in town.'

'I might pop in and see you. So, I suppose you know how to work one of these?' He produced a small flip phone from his pocket.

'Yeah! These are new out, aren't they?' She took it from him. 'What do you want me to do with it?' He looked into her eyes and said: 'Put your number in.'

'Cheeky!' She did so, though, and Danny got Megan's. He would have preferred Emma's but settled for the way the situation had fallen.

That's what happens when you let someone else in, he thought. He imagined, now, how Steve must have felt when *he* was chatting girls up and Steve had no choice but to wait for second prize.

Greene's nightclub was huge. It had three floors and it took Danny and Steve a while to find Laura and Kelly even with the help of text messages. They all got drunk and danced until around 2:30am and then took time out to talk and recuperate. Danny was not into dancing by any means but he gave it a whirl as the rest seemed to be having fun.

'What time does this place close?' asked Kelly.

'Six,' Steve answered. 'Do you think you'll make it?'

She shook her head and then consulted Laura.

'We're gonna go, soon,' said Laura, addressing Danny. 'What are you doing? Do you want to come back with us?'

Danny was taken aback, slightly. This was normally his question and he usually had to work hard to coerce girls back to his flat.

'Where are you going?' he asked.

'I'm staying at my parents' house in Anderton. They're away. Kelly's staying there, too.'

'Yeah, okay.'

In the taxi they all got a bit raunchy and the subject of sex came up. Both Steve and Danny were surprised to see that the girls were open in their speech but they saw it as a positive sign.

Too many strange things occurring tonight, Danny thought and was even more surprised when he heard Kelly say: 'Girls need sex too, you know.'

Inside Laura's parents' house, Laura prepared cheese on toast for everyone. It was Danny's recommendation when Laura suggested that they should eat after a night's drinking. It was washed down with lots of coffee and within an hour or so it was the girls who suggested that they should all go to bed. At first Steve expected to be left on the couch but Kelly led him up the stairs.

His eyes opened wide to take in the surroundings- an average-sized bedroom with a small, but soon to be seen as, comfortable, single bed. Danny joined Laura in the big room with the double bed; obviously her parents'.

Laura stripped herself naked and then set to work on Danny who had been slow undressing due to staring at her. She flicked the light off seductively and pulled him onto the bed.

Girls need sex too, he thought. *I'll have to remember that.*

www.ingramcontent.com/pod-product-compliance
Lightning Source LLC
Chambersburg PA
CBHW020738250626
47155CB00003B/807